The Last
MAGICIAN

The Last

MAGICIAN

A Novel By

Janette Turner Hospital

Henry Holt and Company

New York

Published in Canada by McClelland & Stewart, Inc., Toronto.

Published in Great Britain by Virago Press, 20–23 Mandela Street, Camden Town, London NWI OHQ.

First published in 1992 by University of Queensland Press, Box 42, St. Lucia, Queensland 4067, Australia.

Library of Congress Cataloging-in-Publication Data
Hospital, Janette Turner
The last magician: a novel / by Janette Turner Hospital.—1st American ed.
    p.   cm.
    I. Title.
PR9199.3.H596L37   1992
813'.54—dc20   92-9253
ISBN 0-8050-2097-7   CIP

Henry Holt books are available at special discounts for bulk purchases for sales promotions, premiums, fund-raising, or educational use. Special editions or book excerpts can also be created to specification. For details contact: Special Sales Director, Henry Holt and Company, Inc., 115 West 18th Street, New York, New York 10011.

First American Edition—1992

Designed by Katy Riegel
Printed in the United States of America
Recognizing the importance of preserving the
written word, Henry Holt and Company, Inc.,
by policy, prints all of its first editions
on acid-free paper.∞

10   9   8   7   6   5   4   3   2   1

ACKNOWLEDGMENTS

Quotations from Dante are taken from the translation by John D. Sinclair. The Divine Comedy of Dante Alighieri. *3 Vols. With translation and comment by John D. Sinclair. (New York: Oxford University Press, 1961.)*

Journal entries on female convicts are from Robert Hughes, The Fatal Shore *(New York: Alfred A. Knopf, 1987).*

Quotations from the I Ching *(used entirely for my own imaginative purposes) are from* I Ching: Book of Changes, *translated by James Legge. Edited with Introduction and Study Guide by Ch'en Chai with Winberg Chai. (New York: Bantam, 1969; c. University Books, 1964.)*

Allusions and partial line references from T. S. Eliot are from "The Love Song of J. Alfred Prufrock" in Collected Poems 1909–1935 *(London: Faber & Faber, 1936).*

Finally, I wish to pay tribute to A.A., whose restaurants and wildly imaginative photographs gave me the idea.

For my daughter
Cressida

CONTENTS

Book ONE

Charlie's Inferno

The first message is that there is disorder.
James Gleick

There is no question that there is an unseen world.
The problem is how far is it from midtown and how late is it open?
Woody Allen

ONE

In the middle of the journey, I came to myself in a dark wood where the straight way was lost.

No. That is not the way to put it. In the middle of darkness, I came to the black fact that there *was* no straight way— no way on, no way out. This knowledge engulfed me, a thick sack over the head. Suffocation was the least of it.

Ah, how hard a thing it is to tell of that wood.

Do you see the two boulders where the rapids make a sort of courteous ruffle of detour? That was where the bones were found. They were wedged deep down, *pushed*, prodded under the rocks with the blunt end of something far more complex and disturbing than hate, and they might have been missed for another ten years.

But I mustn't think of that now. I cannot start there.

The wood is dark, and full of the soft rot and manic growth we call rainforest. The rainforest has always spawned secrets. Light itself is clandestine here. Under the matted canopy the sun becomes furtive, it flickers, it advances by stealth, it hides, it is coy, it sneaks down through the tangle of treetops, creepers, leggy bird's-nest ferns, lianas, orchids, battling its way earth-ward through layers of aerial clamor, slithering below ground fungi to breed green yeast. The rainforest smells of seduction and fermentation and death. It smells of Queensland.

Like the dark wood itself, which can burgeon into anyone's

sleep, Queensland is fluid in size and shape, it ebbs and flows and refuses to be anchored in space, it billows out like a net that can settle without warning over its most wayward children and pull them home. There is no escaping it. It is always larger than would appear on the map. At this particular point, however, in the middle of the dark wood, it is known as Cedar Creek Falls and its coordinates are finite and precise: latitude 27 degrees and 19 minutes south; longitude 152 degrees and 46 minutes east of the Greenwich meridian.

Here are directions: from the City Hall and King George Square in the heart of Brisbane (capital of the state of Queensland, Australia; population 1.3 million), follow Ann Street one block to George and turn right, proceed to Roma Street, then continue along the northwest artery toward the State Forest. The artery snakes through lush but well-manicured residential suburbs and mutates through various names: Kelvin Grove Road, Enoggera Road, Samford Road. Depending on traffic, you should reach the suburb of Ferny Grove, end of the railway line, in just under an hour. Somewhere between Ferny Grove and Samford Village, a mere five kilometers further on, you will cross that indistinct and provisional line where the city of Greater Brisbane could perhaps be said to end, and primordial time could be said to begin.

Perhaps the crucial point is where the road surface changes.

Not far beyond Samford, you will cross Cedar Creek, and here, if you wish to locate the falls (which are really many miles of rapids bumping and churning down an escarpment of the D'Aguilar Range from Mt. Glorious), you must turn off the road and follow an unpaved detour until it ends, and then you must leave your car and enter the dark wood and keep going until the straight way is lost.

When I say I came to myself in that black wood, I mean it literally. I mean that without any warning, in a darkened theater on the other side of the world, I stumbled over my own feet as it were, bumped into myself on a cinema screen, sitting on one of the two boulders in the spuming ladder of Cedar Creek Falls. The shock was so great that I blacked out.

This happened in a theater in London, at a little cinematic hole-in-the-wall, and when I came to myself all the rainforest paths and all the best-laid paths in the world led straight to chaos. Dazed, I wandered about, got lost in the underground, surfaced at Tottenham Court Road, and phoned Catherine.

Catherine, I wanted to say, I've just seen both of us in one of Charlie's films. I've seen you, and Charlie himself, and Cat and Gabriel, and His Honor Robinson Gray. The whole bang lot of us, Catherine.

Catherine and I work together, but I'd just got in the day before (I'd been away for several months, New York, Boston, another documentary) and I hadn't managed to make contact yet. For us, this was unusual. I dialed the number of her townhouse in Harrow.

I let the phone ring ten times.

No answer.

There had been no answer the night before either. She had not been at the studios that morning, she was not away on location, where was she? I found myself inside the little pub that was three steps from the telephone booth. I made myself sit over a drink for an hour, refusing to panic.

Catherine, I needed to say. I *miss* them, Catherine. I'm scared.

We baffle people, Catherine and I. She is, I suppose, practically old enough to be my mother, not that I ever think of us in terms of age. But people talk. People find our closeness odd, I don't know why. We work together (well, for the same television company anyway; and frequently on the same projects) and we are often seen together in the evenings as well. People talk. *They do have men from time to time*, people whisper, *so they're not, you know* . . . And no, we're not. But we need each other. The bond between us is intense.

I made myself sit in the pub on Tottenham Court Road for an hour then I phoned again, first the studios (no; no sign of her, no message), then Harrow.

Still no answer.

I panicked. I completely flipped out. Not Catherine too, I thought. I was getting used to people disappearing, I was getting horribly used to it. There are too many missing people and too many damn deaths, I thought. The whole bloody world is crowded with absences.

Much has been fomented by panic: wars, stampedes, stock-market crashes, and worldwide depressions, to name a few. Great accidents and remarkable trains of events from little anxieties grow, and when I found myself staring blankly into a travel agent's window, when temptation presented itself in a poster of the harbor and the bridge and the Opera House, I hesitated only for seconds, yielded, went inside and bought a ticket home. MasterCard, Qantas, London–Singapore–Sydney.

This was extreme. I knew I was being extreme, but something Charlie once said was buzzing inside my mind like a fly in a bottle and it was clear I wouldn't be able to shut the din off till I went back and settled things. In any case, when you travel as much as Catherine and I do, living on the move half the time and treating the world as an office, there is nothing so very unusual about arriving home one day and leaving again a day later. It happens often: we unpack, do the laundry, repack, head for Heathrow and the next assignment. I didn't try to call Catherine again for fear of what I might find out. Once I got to Sydney, I'd decide whether to head up to Brisbane or not. First, I wanted to find out if Sheba, at least, was still around.

She was. She was still in Sydney. She was still barmaid at the very same bar, though its name had changed several times. "Well whad'ya know?" she said. "If it isn't Lady Muck herself swanning back in." But she grinned and tapped off a schooner and stuck it in front of me. "High bloody time," she said. "Whyn't you send a telegram and give me a day to get a party up?"

"Sudden urge, Sheba," I told her. "I saw one of Charlie's films in London. I saw all of us in it. Well, not you, but the rest of us. It's given me the most dreadful ideas, I had nightmares all the way out on the flight. It's Charlie's bloody black magic again."

"Bullshit," she said. "It's jet lag. It's those travel sickness things you take. You mix them with alcohol, watch out!"

"Sheba," I said, "have you seen it?"

"What? Are you kidding? One of Charlie's arty things? Do you think I'm bloody likely to?"

"It's knocked me for six. I feel as though we're all lost in a dark wood, and there's no way on and no way out."

"You mean we're going round in circles?" she said. "You just figured that out? Jesus, Lucy, get a hold of yourself. Brisbane's right where it always was, and so's Sydney, and Catherine's in London (I saw her on TV the other night), and the quarry's spreading, they reckon, but so what? We got beer on tap and the world's still turning."

"And what about Gabriel? What about Charlie and Cat?"

"Oh well," she said, "there's too many missing people, I'll give you that. But there always bloody well has been, hasn't there? You're not gonna make the evening news with that."

"And what about Robinson Gray?"

"He keeps coming around, naturally," she said. "He's got the Order of Australia now, isn't that a blast? He got his picture in the paper for the Queen's Birthday whad'ya-call-'ems. He thinks he's Lord High Mucky-Muck now, if you please, but I still call him Sonny Blue."

"Look," I said. "Charlie's put this thought inside my head, it's buzzing like a bloody mosquito in there and it scares me to death. I think I'm going to ride the ferries for a while."

"Suit yourself," she said. "But don't blame Charlie. We've always known what's what, you and me."

I stared at her.

"We know and we don't know," she shrugged. "And *you* don't *want* to know, Lucy. Look, the problem with people like you and Gabriel, you just won't admit the way the world works. Cat and Charlie, they knew. Catherine knows."

"I'm going to ride the ferries," I said.

"You're not gonna change anything," she said. "You're just gonna make yourself sick for nothing, or get yourself killed."

"I'm going to ride the ferries," I said.

And then at Circular Quay, what did I see but another poster for Charlie's film? Now was that a coincidence or wasn't it? Charlie believed the world was thick with messages, you could hardly move for secret codes in Charlie's world. I found the theater and saw *Charlie's Inferno* again, and I blacked out again—I can't explain that, since I already knew what to expect, although there were certainly a few telling details I'd missed in London on the first time round. Perhaps it was my febrile imagination projecting translations onto the screen. Or perhaps it was something else.

Whatever Sheba says, I believe it was part of Charlie's magic.

And whatever it was, I blacked out.

TWO

Very likely, though I remember nothing, people were solicitous. They probably offered water, air, advice, assistance, and I imagine I said quite polite and rational things. It's nothing, I probably said. Or perhaps, apologetic and dismissive, I murmured that it was just a dizzy spell. (But were they looking at me strangely? Did they recognize me? Did someone say: Excuse me, but aren't you the woman in the film? And if they didn't say it, what would that mean?) Anyway, no doubt the formalities were observed. And after that I must have made my way onto one of the harbor ferries by instinct, because I've always done that when I'm in Sydney and in the grip of an obsession. I can go to Manly and back six times and watch my theories shape and unshape themselves in the water. Leaning over the ferry railing and staring at the sleek green curl-and-spin below, I can see the undersides and loopholes of hare-brained ideas, the way their parapets hide secrets, the way they spiral into minarets of possibility before they disappear with the ferry wake.

Wakes. Now there is a pertinent topic.

No, I do not want to think about wakes.

This is the thing: my instinct is for comedy (Sheba would consider that a great joke; it is nevertheless true), but events keep trying to cast me in a darker role. Forget it. What would I say to a shark, for example, if I swam into its arms off a Queensland beach? Listen, I'd say, you've got yourself in a bit of a bloody mess here, haven't you, mate?

"Have you?" this bloke says, leaning over the railing beside me, nice and friendly, managing to imply that the slow wallow of a dowager ferry is entirely responsible for the pressure of his frontage against my thigh. Some things never change. Your average Sydney male has a limited repertoire of enticement. One thinks of freight trains blundering about in heat.

"What?" I say.

"Got yourself in a bit of a bloody mess?"

"Oh bugger. Was I thinking out loud again?"

" 'Fraid so," he says. "Bad sign, eh?"

"You don't know the half of it," I say. "I've got this friend, Charlie, and I've just seen one of his films."

"And who's your friend Charlie when he's at home?"

"Oh well. Now there's a question. You ever read the Russian novelists? One of the Russians—I think it was Tolstoy speaking of Gogol, but it could have been Gorky on Tolstoy, whichever. Anyway, one of them wrote, 'While that old man is alive, the stars will stay in their proper place.' Or something to that effect, I'm probably not quoting exactly. Anyway, that's how I feel about Charlie."

This guy laughs. I can tell he thinks he's got a nut on his hands, the kind he reckons will be easy game.

"What's your name?" he asks, lunging sideways as a wave almost as big as a bathtub spillover licks the ferry hull, grabbing at the railing on the far side of me with his left hand, surprise surprise, moving in for the kill.

"Lucy."

"Mine's Tony." He maneuvers easily, swiveling around on his plumbing, getting his downspout up. "Rough trip, eh?"

"Oh yeah," I say dryly. "I can feel a bit of a swell."

"You've got a nice little bum, Lucy," he offers.

"And you want to buy me a beer in Manly, right? And after that, if one thing leads to another the way you hope, a quick fuck." I love doing that, taking the wind out of their sails.

"Jeez," he says, affronted, all innocence. He actually licks his index finger and makes an X somewhere left of his sternum. "Cross my heart," he says, as evidence that a carnal thought never entered his head.

"The thing is," I tell him, "I've got another man on my mind. Two, actually. Forget dessert, but if you want to listen to a monologue, you can buy me the beer"—because I need to conjure up Charlie and Gabriel again. I have to. "I just saw them both," I tell him. "I saw them on film, their moving breathing celluloid selves, looking as though they were alive."

Tony lifts one eyebrow. "I think you lost me," he says.

"Sorry. It's a reflex. That was Browning. 'My Last Duchess.' "

"Never seen it," he says. "Any good? Can you get it on video yet?"

I have to laugh, because this does strike me as curiously appropriate. I imagine how Charlie might do it: someone's duchess of the moment sprawled naked across a bed, one arm bent a little awkwardly beneath her perhaps, a bit of blood splashed on the wall (*I call that piece a wonder now*), fully dressed middle-aged man in legal robes, juridical mane falling lavishly about his shoulders, a platinum tendril brushing one cheek, whip in hand, tear in one eye.

> Even had you skill
> In speech—(which I have not)—to make your will
> Quite clear to such an one, and say, "Just this
> Or that in you disgusts me. . . ."

"Not unless Charlie's done it," I say. "You never know. It's exactly the kind of thing that would catch his eye." Yes, the more I think about it . . .

The thing is, I've got into the habit of thinking Charlie's thoughts. You say a word like *duchess*, you push a button, and the retrieval system spills out a whole drawerful of associations and they all cluster around the theme you've already got in your mind. Before you can snap your fingers here you are at Titian's *Venus of Urbino*. Oh, he'd certainly start with that on his video, Charlie would. I've got the hang of it now, I'm inventing for him.

"I'm not sure if it's out on video yet," I tell Tony. "But it's worth waiting for. It's about a painter and a duchess and a prostitute."

"Yeah?" Tony's definitely interested.

"You heard of Titian?"

"A tit man, is he?" Tony leers.

"Actually, a fetish for red hair, I think. Well, this duchess, the Duchess of Urbino, rather old, and rather ugly according to her none-too-gallant husband, wants her portrait done. She wants it done naked. She wants to look like a goddess, she says. Every day she comes to Titian's studio and lies starkers on his red sofa draped with a sheet—I mean, the sofa is draped, not the Duchess—and Titian tries not to show any disgust or embarrassment, or God forbid, pity, which is mainly what he feels, I expect. He's a little nervous, you know, because if she doesn't like the painting, his head will roll. Career-wise, anyway."

Tony shakes his head. "It's like these old girls who go topless on Bondi, mutton trying to look like lamb. It's disgusting. There oughta be a law."

"That's what the Duke of Urbino thought. And so did a friend of Titian's, a poet, a smart-ass man-about-town, Pietro Aretine. He rather fancied himself as a satirist, this Aretine, he wrote obscene sonnets, that kind of thing. So one evening, after the Duchess has put her clothes back on and left the studio, Aretine arrives with a nubile little prostitute in tow. 'Look, Titian old boy,' he says, 'why don't you use Lulu here as the model for the body, and stick the old cow's head on top of it? Fix the old lady's face up a bit, you know, give her the works, the red hair. Vanity being what it is, the Duchess will love it.' "

Tony laughs. "Meanwhile, the three of them are at it between the paint pots, right?"

"Something like that. But here's the joke. When the Duke sees the portrait, he says, 'If I could have had that body in my bed, even with my wife's head on it, I would have been a happy man.' And Pietro Aretine laughs so hard, he has a stroke and dies on the spot. That's the gospel truth," I say. "You can look it up in a library."

"Holy shit," Tony says uneasily. "Dying from laughing at a joke, that's not very funny."

"Maybe not. But it's the Duchess who has the last laugh, you see." Yes, it's coming to me now. "She and the prostitute have an affair. It turns out that the prostitute, who had to wait behind the curtain every day, fell in love with my lady's dignity and self-possession. She was dazzled by the way the Duchess was so at ease with her aging body, and with the way she didn't really give a damn what the famous painter and the famous poet thought. This is in Charlie's version, anyway."

"Jeez, lesbians?" Tony's a bit shocked, but very interested. "Do they . . . ? On screen? I mean, do you actually see much . . . ?"

"A certain amount is left to your imagination," I say. "In Charlie's version."

"Well, look," Tony says, willing to swim on through opaqueness for the sake of the beer because who knows what might happen after a schooner or two? "Obviously you want to talk about this bloke. There's a nice pub on the Corso—"

"I blacked out during Charlie's film," I tell him. "You know that little arts cinema at the university? There. It was full of students, I was right in the middle of them, and then bang, I fell down a black hole. You want to hear about this?"

He's beginning to think he's made a miscalculation here, but in spite of himself he's curious, and in spite of the pointlessness, I feel a compulsion to talk.

"You blacked out? In the middle of this *Duchess* film?"

"Not the *Duchess* one, no. Something else of Charlie's, a short feature. Not just Charlie's. Five Postmodern Filmmakers, it was called. I saw an ad. It was on a poster at Circular Quay."

"This Charlie, is he with the ABC or something?"

"No, not the ABC." In the sleek belly of the wake turning over, depending on the way the light falls, depending on the way I look at it, I can read ten different messages from Charlie. Seriously. Charlie believed this. It's got nothing to do with magic, he would say. We know the answers to the burning questions but we are afraid of them, and so we need a screen. We need to project explanations and read them back. "The film was a kind of telegram," I say. "It was typical Charlie."

"So does he always do X-rated stuff then?"

There's a question. "In a way," I say.

"What was this one about?"

"Well, among other things, I suppose you could say it was about the quarry."

"Yeah?" Tony gets a gleam in his eye because he's thinking of the quarry's first circle, the limbo of hot neon and strip joints and the retail trade in young girls and the little boys waiting in doorways.

But here's the trapdoor that Charlie's camera always falls through, here's the underside, here's one of the times (not the one on the film I'd just seen, but the one he called *Hungers*), here's the hole where I fell right through to an earlier time, here's the day I took him down through the labyrinth to meet Old Fury. . . .

She comes and goes, she disappears for months at a time, suddenly you may see her every day for two weeks, and then she's gone again. They say she has a niche on the Eastern Suburbs line between Martin Place and King's Cross, a cubbyhole behind steam pipes. If you watch, it is said, you can see the whites of her eyes, especially between 5 P.M. and 7 P.M., when the commuter trains hurtle through. This is what the tabloids claim. But then tabloid readers, commuters, the border people, they are all haunted by underground eyes, they see them everywhere, they see squatters evil-eyeing them when it's almost certainly cats, or rats, or possums, or simply chips of glass in the tunnels beside the railway lines. The commuters hear subterranean tappings on the undersides of their pillows at night. They are not reliable.

"Old Fury," I say. "This is Charlie. He takes photographs of black holes."

She gives him a bright fierce look. Above the bird bones of her face, her eyebrows meet and touch and she taps her index finger against her forehead as if to say: the black hole is *here*. I carry it round inside me. Her eyes, which are disproportionately large, gleam owlishly. The black hole is all that there is, her owl eyes say, though I could have the translation wrong. It is said that she prophesies. It is said that she speaks in tongues. In fact there is no way of knowing if she understands a word you utter or not, though I myself believe she has the gift of reading thought and of understanding everything that is left unsaid. She is supposed to be simple, but it could be that she sees no point in speaking except for when her Voices come. When her Voices visit, watch out! An infernal gale comes with them, it's like an oil well blowing, a black gush gurgling out of her mouth.

"Charlie thought he might know you," I say.

I wait for her to ask if he's someone I picked up on the ferries again. (I have to supply her end of the dialogue, it's good practice. Down in the quarry, if you're not careful, you can lose the knack of civilized discourse.) I've told her before that riding the ferries is something I do when I'm upset. Obsessively. I go to Manly and back for as long as it takes.

Old Fury watches. She waits. She hunches her small angular body up against the cold. God, the cold. In July in Sydney it's worse than the damp, worse than the darkness, though the latter is something down here. I expect us to evolve internal radar any day now. I expect us to start communicating by high-pitched head-noises, like bats. Any week now I expect a new crop of kids, fresh from subway trafficking and car jobs and the meat markets, to arrive with radar systems which are fully formed and which have installed themselves quite naturally within the body, possibly as cysts on the shoulder blades, or possibly tucked into a scab on the forehead, a third eye.

What am I saying, *expect*?

Already we have a whole new range of underground hearing. I believe this has to do with certain adaptations of the inner ear. I believe we have developed antennae as fine as angelhair seaweed and these filaments—so it seems to me—these filaments float about and fan out through the murk, decoding the rumble of subway trains, noting and cataloging screams, classifying the ways a knife cuts and the sound of a needle in a vein and the different sound of a spent needle falling somewhere in an empty room, registering the courting calls of sirens (these are a long way above us, of course, far above) and the car horn of johnny cruiser and the different one of the man who dispenses snow. We read the dark. We decode it and swim in it so naturally that when I wake I feel for mutations: webbing between my toes, fur, gills.

"Did you know that someone found fin prints of ichthyosaurus down here?" I ask Charlie. "So the tabloids claim. There were photographs."

"They were probably mine," Charlie says.

"I should have known. When I lived down here, I used to check my shoulders for wing buds every night. I reckoned if they sprouted, they'd be black, and they'd be barbed at their scalloped tips."

Charlie smiles. "I'll make a record of that on film."

"I know you will. Why doesn't someone nick an oil heater?" I complain fretfully. "Haven't we got any more candles? We've got candles somewhere, haven't we? We used to have. Someone nicked a whole carton, I know we've got them." I grope around. Debris collects here, particularly in the corners of the room. I find two tallow stubs. I light them. "I don't know how you'll manage for light," I say.

"I'll manage," Charlie says. "It's all done with lens opening and shutter speed. Pretend I'm not here. Just ignore me."

"Just ignore me, ignore me," sings Julie who rocks herself in the corner. Julie is queen of the rubbish heap. She trails hypodermics. "Oh jeez," I say, weary. "Have we got coffee or anything to bring her round?"

Old Fury rummages in the box in the corner where we always used to hoard what we could, a generally futile endeavor, and she manages to find not only the coffee tin but the primus stove which hasn't been ripped off yet. This is a small miracle. When she's intent on the nuts and bolts of survival, you cannot question Old Fury's intelligence. There is a feral intensity to her. Sometimes, most of the time, I believe she can read my thoughts, but at other times I accept the prevailing view that she is vacancy itself.

Look at her now. There's no heat, no plumbing, we're a few levels underground (it's anybody's guess if this was once subway, or an underground parking lot, or the remnants of warehouse storage cellars that have been extended by the squatters and blasters), but she's found some more candles. Lighted tapers bob about with her so that she's always ringed with golden cloud. She has scooped a kettleful of water from the storage bin, boiled it on the primus and made coffee, and now she's sitting beside Julie, which is, in itself, a delicate balancing act. The bed is no prize. Because it is a mattress which rests uneasily, lopsidedly, on a frame of bricks and boards—the mattress is very mangy, very lumpy, the bricks are uneven—the bed is subject to pitch and toss, the same kind that afflicts the harbor ferries in the choppy zone between the Heads. (Just the same, in its time, the bed has slept a goodly number of bodies simultaneously.) Old Fury is cradling Julie and humming something deep in her throat, a lullaby. And this is what we all come back to, you see, this is what pulls us back below the streets, this hibernation ritual, this *warmth*. It comes off the old madwoman like a kind of radiance and pulls me in.

From the dark beyond the candlelight, I hear Charlie's camera like a soft shudder of bat wings.

"Old Fury," I murmur, cuddling up. I wrap my legs around her spindly shanks, with the lumps of mattress pressing up against my right thigh and soft Julie in between us, too-pliant Julie, yielding-as-goosedown Julie, our Julie-comforter. We used to have a blanket, the last time I was here we definitely had it, but I recall Julie telling me that some fucker from a Redfern gang ripped us off. Old Fury hums, and Julie splutters and snuffles and sleeps a near overdose off, and it's cozy. I want to tell Old Fury and Julie that I love them both.

"This is what brings me back, you see, Charlie." All this love, this communion. It's very scarce above ground. Of course it comes and goes down here too. Certain substances, certain optimal amounts of certain substances, inhaled or absorbed, are more conducive than others to this state of well-being. Sometimes we can dolphin about for hours in the ocean of I-am-you, you-are-me. Sometimes not.

"Just forget I'm here," Charlie says.

"I live at Charlie's Place now," I tell Old Fury. "I don't live in the quarry anymore."

Laughter, like a visitor from much deeper down, rises out of the old woman's throat and swirls about us. Julie stirs and shivers in its spin and subsides again.

"All of us," I say reproachfully, "used to live in the world outside the quarry. Once upon a time, the quarry didn't even exist."

No. That's not true. I have to concede that from before the very first once-upon-a-time, there has always been another world, a nether world, invisible, nestled inside the cracks of the official world like a hand inside a glove, like two spoons spooning. But it didn't exist quite like this, not in quite this same form, not in Sydney anyway, and it didn't spread quite so far, and there was a time—*"Believe me,"* I tell them—before we ourselves entered it.

They don't believe me.

"Tell them, Charlie," I say.

But there's no sound from the outer darkness, I can't even hear the camera now. Maybe he's gone.

"Believe me, Julie," I say (she is trembling violently; Old Fury is massaging her bluish hands).

Down here, the other world is like shadows on the wall of a cave, like the negative prints of the photographs Charlie is taking.

As for me, I go back and forth, above and under. I cross borders. That world, this world, they coexist all the time and I move between them. It's a kind of greedy curiosity I have, a voraciousness, I was born with it, a hunger to live all my possible lives.

Underground woman, you might call me.

Yes, I am partial to the Russian novelists, who may have been mad, but who were not blind, and who did not willfully close their eyes. They saw both worlds. Perhaps because I read them very early, too early to know they were not supposed to apply in this hemisphere, too early to dilute and deconstruct, perhaps because I read them when I was still at school, when I was just an impressionable Brisbane changeling, before I'd even been taught what *not* to see, perhaps because of all this, I have always wanted to mail my own notes from underground. I want to see the nether side of our cities and send back word. Just as Charlie does.

"In the other world," I tell Julie, "people move through rooms that are full of music. They sit by windows where the light falls on a pot of orchids. They pour fine wine into crystal, they light candles on mahogany sideboards where silver gleams. They think we are just a bad dream."

A voice comes out of Old Fury's mouth, a *sound* rather, high-pitched like a boy's voice, a singsong taunting playground voice: *Dreams, dreams, dreams,* it says. (I think that is what it says.) *Objection, Your Honor,* it says. *The witness dreamed there was an ordinary world and now she thinks she's remembering it. It's cock and bull.*

I have to ponder this. I consider it only common sense to take Old Fury seriously. Playing devil's advocate against myself, Your Honor, I will record two short pieces of evidence I read somewhere.

One: Report of a Sleep Disorders Clinic. A haggard patient,

who was in a desperately insomniac state, presented himself for treatment. He was ravaged. One could have said that he was ill with desire for sleep, that sleep toyed with him, that sleep behaved toward him as a cruel mistress behaves toward an idiot lover, that he pursued her and pleaded and cajoled and promised the moon and groveled. Alas, sleep spurned him. For six straight weeks, he said. Yet the clinic's monitoring showed this: that the patient in fact slept a good eight hours each night, but dreamed, recurrently, that he tossed and turned and lay awake from dusk till dawn, and in the morning he woke exhausted.

Two (and this is something Charlie told me): Once Chuang Tzu dreamed he was a butterfly, perhaps a turquoise butterfly like the Blue Wanderer, the Ulysses, that haunter of Queensland rainforests, and that he drifted through air like light. The butterfly, needless to say, knew nothing of Chuang Tzu. It fluttered here, there, it quivered, it alighted on dawn. The dream pecked against the outer shell of sleep, the butterfly woke, and there in its bed was Chuang Tzu who was not even good-looking or mild-tempered, let alone luminous. Unshaven, dazed, rumpled, grumpy, he smelled of morning breath and of slight piss stains on his pajamas. What a falling off was there. What a metamorphosis. Afterwards, the philosopher was never certain if he was Chuang Tzu who had dreamed he was a butterfly, or a butterfly dreaming he was Chuang Tzu.

"So you have a point, Old Fury," I concede. "But the point could be this: you could be a figure in one of Charlie's photographs. You could be in one of the films I think up for him. We could both be up there, in the quarry's first circle, dreaming you."

Old Fury's heard something, I don't mean me babbling on, something else, and she pricks up her ears.

"What is it?" I ask her.

Shhh, she says, or doesn't say, but puts a finger to her lips. I can hear it. At first the sound is like the slow heavy vapor which drips from rainforest canopies after dark, a quiet sobbing coming down, coming closer. But it turns into Danny who is only twelve and very new to the quarry, and who is not broken in at all. Something is pressing down on him. He ignores us and huddles himself in one corner, whimpering. Old Fury goes to him and sits beside him and cradles him in her arms, rocking backwards and forwards, humming.

"I'm sore," he whimpers. "It hurts. They were at me all night. It hurts."

I leave Julie, who's shuddering quietly, and bring a candle over. Danny is wearing boxer shorts and a T-shirt, and even in the half-light, you can see the dried blood on his thighs and the bruises.

"Oh jeez," I say. "Clumsy buggers. How many?"

"Two of them," Danny says. "They did me all night."

Oh Danny, I think, all this for one fix? But no, he's not even had time to get hooked, he's a brand-new runaway, he's been buggered to ribbons for common old garden-variety hunger. He's starving. "And then all they give me," he sobs, "is a packet of cigarettes." He pulls it out of the pocket of his shorts, a packet of Winfields. "I tried to swap it for a pie, but the pie man wouldn't go for it. I'm hungry."

Hunger: now there's a topic. I can imagine the visual layers, the literal and metaphorical densities, that Charlie will bring to this one.

"Have we got anything, Old Fury?" I ask her, not because she'll answer. I crawl under the brick-and-board bed where I recall we used to hide a battered tin box and *please*, I say silently, *please*, and thank God, there's something there, some dry biscuits and a tin of soup. Danny is much too hungry to wait for anything elaborate like a hot meal, which is fortunate since I am not very good with the primus. It's hit or miss with me. I open the tin and give him a spoon and he gulps down tomato pulp and alphabet noodles, a cold, concentrated, gelatinous mass. "You want coffee, Danny? We've got some. I'll see if I can light this thing again, it might take me a while." He's cuddled up in Old Fury's arms and she's rocking him, crooning to him in those throaty noises she makes. "Coffee's coming," I promise. "Warm the cockles of your heart, Danny boy."

It works. I get the damn thing lit. We all have coffee and I prop Julie up against the wall and manage to get some more down her, but she's still out of it, she slumps into the mattress again like soggy bread. We sit there sipping our coffee, and I don't know what thoughts go through Old Fury's head, or through young Danny's, but whatever shape they come in, I'm willing to bet we are all entering bliss itself through the warm mugs in our hands. You see, it is difficult to find words for these things, it would be difficult to explain to the people pouring wine into crystal about the great pounding flood of joy that comes at you in this kind of situation, that comes at you through the skin, through the insides of fingers and palms, that kindly heat, the way it swamps you with happiness.

"Come over on the bed," I invite Danny, whose eyes, in *Hungers*, will one day seed nightmares among filmgoers in the other world. "I'm going to tell you a story about the time I first went on the streets."

"How old were you?" Danny asks.

"Older than you. Older than Julie. I was a university student. I lived two lives."

So we make a sort of four-headed person, all warm together, all soft, all tangled up in arms and legs, a JulieDannyOld-Furyandme kind of person, a love knot, you can see what brings me back, all this warmth, Old Fury humming her lullaby and me telling a bedtime story and urging Charlie to join us.

"Well," I whisper to him. "What do you think about Old Fury? Is she Cat?"

"No," he sighs. "She's not Cat."

"Yeah, well, look," Tony is saying nervously. "Maybe you'd rather be by yourself. Maybe some other time, eh? The beer, I mean." He's backing away toward the safety of his mates. "Nice talking to you, Lucy." He's practically falling over his feet with apprehension.

So what have I rambled on about, I wonder?

Nice talking to you, Lucy, the swift water says. It has wings and tongues and memories, and an easy fluid way with the past.

The past has heft and jagged edges. Down there, where the water licks the flank of the ferry like a lewd green tongue, I can watch the past dwindle and balloon and dwindle. I can watch it slowly submerge itself like a drowned man going under. I can watch it surface again, and sink, and spread its subterranean self from Circular Quay to the Heads. I can see rooms down there, passageways, a whole wing of recycled years, the slope of the quarry, the time spent at Charlie's Place. . . .

Oh Charlie's Place, Charlie's face, the ace up Charlie's sleeve. He was a bit of a magician, Charlie was.

The waves are sleek but memory is sleeker and the race is to the swift and that time comes washing back around me, it's a rough sea, a tidal wave, oh here it is, quick, run, hide, it's at flooding depth, drowning depth, you can never build ramparts strong enough to keep the past in its place, it skulks like the dammed-up Pacific behind North Head, it bursts, it spumes, it rampages, here it comes, here comes the first day I met Charlie. . . .

THREE

 "What I'm after," the photographer explains, "is a sense of those fishnet stockings as snare. As a trap that a man swims into."

"Oh yeah?" Lucy leans back, propped on her elbows, and coils one leg around a bedpost. "Like this?" she challenges. Her legs are like jaws, like scissors. She is mostly black mesh hose with a bit of bodysuit attached. The bodysuit is also black and cut high on the thighs.

"Talk," he says, moving round her, crouching, sometimes leaning over her like a crow after pickings. He too is dressed in black: black jeans, black turtleneck, black eyebrows, black hair. He has pale skin and dark almond-shaped eyes. "Keep talking."

"Why?" she asks. He puzzles her. He is older than she is, but she cannot tell by how much. Twenty years? Not so much? More? He seems curiously ageless, a young old man. "Why do I have to keep talking?"

"It makes a difference to the pictures. It makes a difference to which pictures I take. The pictures will show you things you don't know about yourself."

"As if I want to," she says.

"You always wear this?"

"Mostly. Unless they ask for different. Funny, this thing they've got about black. I wonder why."

"Nuns and priests," he says.

"Yeah. Could be. Most of the girls are Catholic or ex, not me though. They reckon most of the johns are Catholics too, I wonder why?" The shutter winks and winks and winks. "You a Catholic?"

"No."

"And a lot are hellfire and damnation types," she laughs. "Religious, anyway. You wouldn't believe how religion comes into it. There's this one bloke, an old bloke, I gotta sit here stark naked, reading the Gideon Bible while he jerks off. I gotta sit on the edge of the bed with my legs wide open, and he kneels on the floor and stares." She swings her legs wide open to demonstrate and balances an imaginary book high on her hands. " 'Woe to them that devise iniquity, and work evil upon their beds.' So then I let him rest his head here"—she pats her crotch— "and I stroke his hair and I gotta sing to him." She turns her palms out to the photographer and hunches up her shoulders, inviting him to make sense of such a thing. He photographs her upturned palms. "Not that I'm complaining, it's easy money. He's one of my regulars. He's a nice old bloke."

The camera records pensive reflection.

"You ever visit hookers without your camera?" she needles.

"No."

"You religious?"

The camera records question and provocation. The man says nothing.

"Christ," she says sarcastically, "what a talker you are. I'm glad I'm not working." She sits up, forgetting him, and lights a cigarette. "You know why I hate the ones who don't talk? They want too much of the other. Get them talking, you don't have to do as much." She inhales and dragons smoke from her nostrils. "I hate being touched."

He says nothing. He moves around the room, not always pointing his camera at the girl. He takes a photograph of rumpled sheets and a stain on the floor. He takes another of pillows and headboard, with the window beyond, and through it the skyline of Sydney. The pillow is grubby.

"That's why I like old blokes best," she says. "Sixties, seventies, over seventy is best of all."

"But fucking them? Kissing them?"

"Jesus," she says, shocked. "We don't *kiss*."

He photographs her disgust. He moves around, above, below, behind. He photographs the way her disgust dwindles and disappears like water through sand.

"Where are you from?" she asks.

Curiously, the question seems to throw him. He pauses and considers it for several seconds, as though testing out possible responses, and finally answers with the camera between them, "New York."

"How come you've got an Aussie accent?"

He seems disconcerted. Annoyed perhaps. But then, from the small sheepish smile, oddly flattered, oddly pleased. He says in a very New York voice: "It creeps up on me sometimes apparently." He changes lenses. "I'm sliding back into it, I guess. Especially in certain kinds of company. No, don't move. Keep your legs crossed like that." He photographs her fishnetted ankles and spike heels against the stain on the floor. "I've been away," he says. "Been in New York for twenty-five years. Just came back."

"Jesus. To live?" He is occupied with rewinding film, changing spools, and doesn't answer. He gives no sign of having heard the question.

"*Why?*" she demands.

"Why what?"

"Why would you want to come back?"

"Why not?" He takes hold of one of her ankles and lifts the leg as though it were a piece of stage furniture. He drags a wooden chair up close, puts her foot on it, takes her hands by the wrists and arranges them at her ankle. He photographs the arrangement of chair and spike-heeled shoe and stockinged leg and fishnet-adjusting hands. "Ever dream of escape?"

She laughs. "Oh, I have. I *have* escaped. This is where I've escaped to." She laughs again. "If you mean New York, I might some day, though it hardly seems worth the trouble." She taps her head. "Too much baggage that can't be left behind."

"Exactly," he says, but he looks at her differently, his eyes registering a flicker of surprise. Careful, she warns herself. She is annoyed by these little slippages from character.

"So where're you from then?" she asks, affecting bored politeness. "Before New York, I mean."

He checks his light meter, tests the flash. *Pop, pop,* it is like the sound of one hand clapping. "Okay, now at the window, leaning out. I want the buttocks." Click, his camera says. Click, click. Beyond the window, the neon glitz of King's Cross winks back, hot pink, hot purple. Jackpot, says the camera. Click, click. He stashes her fishnet buttocks in his snare.

"So where are you from then?" she persists.

"The sage is from the mountain and the fox is from his hole."

"What?"

"Keep talking." He makes a record of her inquisitiveness, of her surprise.

"Is this for a magazine, or what?" Click, click, his camera says. Click, click. "Or just for dirty pictures?" She cannot resist the guise of innocent question. Between one blink of the shutter and the next, by a clean arrangement of dark, of the absence of dark, the dirty picture settles. "You sell them? Or you keep them for jacking off?" He keeps a record of her sneer. "Jeez," she says, giving up. "Like talking to a bloody block of wood." She slumps across the bed, her chin on her hands, and broods. He keeps a record of her brooding and boredom.

Apparently listless, she demands, "When do I take my clothes off?"

"You don't."

"Yeah? What's this *for*, then?"

"What's your name?" he asks, recording the way curiosity, like a skittish breeze, quickens the dead lake of apathy.

"Which one would you like?"

"What's your working name?"

"I step into any name they want. A lot of times they don't want you to have a name at all, and I'm nobody. I like being nobody."

"What's your private name then? The one you have for yourself?"

"Fuck off," she says angrily. "Who the hell do you think you are?"

"Terrific!" The shutter licks up the blaze of a border violated. She brings her hands up like claws and hisses at him.

For a moment he looks strangely shocked. She might have struck him. He lowers the camera and stares. Then he recovers.

"Terrific," he says again, as a parent to a clever child. Click, click, says the shutter. Click, click.

"Who the fuck *are* you?" She stands up and swivels her hips and humps her crotch in slow derisive motion, thrusting toward him, back forward back, purely hostile, a parody of invitation.

"Sorry," he says. "Hey, cool it. I'm sorry. I'm done now." He finishes the film and rewinds and removes the cartridge and reloads. He grins. "Great shots, though." He sets the camera down. "As a matter of fact," he says, "I'm your new boss. You work downstairs too, in the restaurant, right?"

"You're the new restaurant manager? You're Mr. Charlie Chang?" She lights another cigarette and regards him warily. "D'you know what you're getting into?"

Does he know what he's getting into? he asks himself. Yes and no. The curiosity, the impatience even, for the tomorrows to unfold themselves is like Benzedrine sometimes (he can feel the buzz along the surface of his skin), though at other times he feels suspended in a slow dream, trapped like a fly in honey. He could say to her: I know exactly what I'm doing; I came back to nudge a train of events into motion; I came back to watch. But that wouldn't be quite correct. He could say: a chain of chemical reactions, set in motion long ago and never still, has pulled me back. Would that be any more accurate? Sometimes he feels he has made a clear choice; sometimes he feels it has been beyond his power to make any kind of choice at all.

"What did the iron filing say to the magnet?" he asks her.

"I dunno," she says. "I give up."

"We're poles apart, but something keeps pulling me."

"Very funny," she says. "You're weird."

Yeah, he thinks. Weird. Is he the stage manager or a puppet, the magician or the magician's stooge? He is never sure.

(If we come across old diaries we have written, if we find—in an attic, a locked chest, someone's desk drawer after a death—letters that we wrote long ago, we almost invariably cringe. Oh God, we think, embarrassed. Sometimes we are shocked. Sometimes we feel a stirring of tenderness for that earlier self, for its griefs, its panics, its narcissism. Occasionally we are even impressed by a ten-year-old's or a nineteen-year-old's turn of phrase or by insights we would not have expected that callow sloughed wraith of former existence to possess. Certainly we read ourselves with the same greedy curiosity and prurience that entice us through the erotic correspondence of strangers.

When we watch the self on the screen of the past, we watch a stranger, but one for whom we have complicated feelings.

I watch Charlie and myself in a room. I watch Gabriel and myself at Cedar Creek Falls, before either of us has met Charlie. I watch Charlie and Lucy, who is only myself in the most tenuous and convoluted way, and who was, in any case, acting the part of Lucy. She wished desperately to appear as a native. She wished to belong to the non-belongers.)

Lucy puckers her lips and blows smoke rings at the photographer, and the smoke rings settle. Haloes? Nooses? She keeps blowing them, batting at them with a casual hand, pushing a message across the space between them, though he cannot say if the message is playful or insulting or whether it represents the throwing down of a gauntlet. He watches her, impassive.

"This place is a wank," she says. "This place is a silk purse in pigshit." She waits, breathing smog into the room. She waits, she waits. "Just your style, maybe." As far as she can tell, neither her disdain, which is a heavy bass thing, nor the flippant smoke rings, nor the sharp little cuts her words are intended to make, have any impact. He might be an indulgent older brother or an uncle or a former fond schoolteacher, affectionately amused. He might simply be deaf. She says tartly: "We hear you're not a normal sort of restaurant manager. Into art and philosophy, we hear. High-Brow, capital H, capital B. So downstairs is right up your alley, I reckon. Right up your street. A feeding trough for rich wankers playing danger games." He smiles but says nothing. She gives up. "So where are you from, before New York?"

"Brisbane, as a matter of fact."

"Brisbane!" She whoops with laughter and throws herself back on the bed and kicks up her legs. He grabs the camera and shoots. "Well, whad'ya know?" she laughs. "Brisbane." She sits up and studies him while she finishes her cigarette. The shutter clicks. "Oh for God's sake," she says irritably, "could you put that fucking thing away?" and he sets the camera aside with a show of deference. They watch each other in a nervy, fascinated, almost drugged silence. "Me too," she grins finally. "I'm from Brisbane too. Well, whad'ya know?" Conciliatory, she offers: "The other girls call me Lucy."

He nods. Without the camera in his hands, he seems different. Like what? Like someone in a mournful intellectual movie, she thinks, a European one naturally, or else one of those slow bleak things by that Japanese bloke; like someone alone on a stage; like Hamlet. Without the camera, he is naked. Every few seconds his eyes turn to the shabby card table beside him. Every few seconds, unconsciously, he reaches out and touches the camera, lets his hand rest on it. She cannot imagine him as a restaurant manager. She cannot imagine him as someone who photographs hookers.

"How long have you been working here?" he asks.

"Is this an employment check?" There are two of him, it seems to her. There is the vulnerable one; and the armored one who operates restaurants and cameras. He interests her.

He says: "I'm curious about the ones who work upstairs and downstairs both. Any of the restaurant patrons use upstairs too?"

"Oh, lots," she says.

"What happens when they see you downstairs?"

"It's funny, that. It's really something. I used to think they were just putting on a careful act in front of their wives." She waves her right hand airily about. "Or business colleagues, law partners, girlfriends, mum and dad, what have you. I used to think they were incredibly good actors. Not the slightest sign, no nervousness, no embarrassment, nothing. I might as well be a coat rack as a waitress."

He visualizes this. He sees flesh hooks branching out of her like rainforest vines, he sees empty coats, fitted around the shapes of ghostly men, swimming like exotic fish through wet green air toward the hook. He considers lighting and shutter speeds. He calls these things photofallacies; or sometimes, singular (and his sense of the absurd is certainly singular), a photophallus. He names a possible future image *On the Rack*.

"Yes?" he prompts, into her silence.

"Well, it isn't acting at all, I've decided. I'll tell you something: there are two things that show you people as they really are, and I've done them both." There is a long gray silence, and the gray truth about people-as-they-really-are presses down on her as an atmospheric condition, though she wishes to fight her own weather. "Except, I dunno, for maybe one in a hundred." She offers this small miracle for contemplation: "You do actually meet people who make you want to keep on looking."

"Looking for what?"

"Oh you know, *goodness*, *meaning*, crap like that. One throw in a hundred."

"One in a hundred," he says dryly. "Quite hopeful really. So they're not acting, the upstairs-and-downstairs men?"

"No, they're not acting. They really don't see you. They really don't know they know you." This interests him. He has his feet on the chair rung, his knees hunched up, his elbows on his knees. He leans forward and rests his face in his hands so that his fingertips graze his temples. She thinks he looks like a genie out of some extravagant jade lamp from sing-sing dynasty, Chinatown. Through the frame of his fingers, he observes her closely. Fisheye lens, soft focus, he thinks, so the girl is the eye of the whole curved room, but blurred. "They don't even see me when they're in this room," she says. "I'm just part of the furniture. Literally. When they leave, they lock a door in their minds."

"Context," he says.

"Oh yeah. *Context.*" She mimics him, mock plum in her mouth. "That's it all right, context. Outside of this context (and what'll we call it? High Bordello? Ratbag Rococo?) outside of here, they wouldn't recognize me if they fell over me. Don't look at me like that." She feels as though he has seen through the disguise again. She feels as though she is being touched, and she hates to be touched. It's what appeals about the life, the money always between, the thick sheets of contempt, the sweet fact that you can never be touched. She would prefer the camera as partition again. She swings her legs off the bed and crosses to the window. She turns her back on him. "F'r example, would you notice that chair if I switched it with one in the restaurant? How about the pillow? How about the sheet, if you bumped into it in a pub? It's the same with hookers. And with waitresses."

"And with restaurant managers," he says. "And photographers. It's a plus, you know. It's like being made of one-way glass. You see everything without being seen."

"Yeah. You see everything all right."

"So how long have you been here?" he asks again.

"Oh, a while."

"Upstairs and downstairs the whole time?"

"Yeah."

"And before that?"

She laughs. "Oh, you wouldn't want to know. You wouldn't believe me."

"In the quarry?" he suggests.

She turns from the window. "Yeah, the quarry for one. Lived in it for three months. Quarry's a one-way trip. That's the rubbish heap, strictly for junkies." She shudders. "Last stop on the line." Disconsolate, she flops back on the bed and stares at the ceiling. "Three years, they reckon, once you're in the quarry, till snuff-out time. That's if you're hooked. If you're not, I suppose you last as long as you're strong enough to steal. There's a woman, Old Fury we call her, who looks about sixty. She's probably not. She might only be forty, the quarry does that. For that matter, three years in an up-market joint like this is about the limit. Then it's move out, or fall down the black hole fast. I'm a tourist," she says. "An explorer. These places interest me, but I can leave. I've dabbled, part of the research, but I don't touch dope."

Fisheye lens, shallow depth-of-field, he thinks; so the girl's edges are sharp as glass within the cloudy bubble of the room. "I thought girls needed dope to put up with the johns."

"Yeah. Well . . ." She shrugs. "There're other ways."

"What other ways?"

"Professional secret. Personally, I'm rather fond of silent mastication of Milton." She sits up and recites in a toneless rush: " 'Of man's first disobedience, and the fruit/Of that forbidden tree, whose mortal taste/Brought death into the world, and all our woe/With loss of Eden, till one greater So-and-so/' Et cetera et cetera and so on."

He is astonished by this and laughs, but he is looking at her differently again. She finds herself embarrassed by his delight. Self-conscious. The disguise has slipped again, she thinks, furious with herself. Without being aware of it, she pulls the sheet up in front of her and holds it around her shoulders. They study each other cautiously, tense with interest. A macro lens, he thinks; 100 mm at f/16, with flash, to get the face of a tiger caged by bedding.

"What did you do before the quarry?" he asks again. "In Brisbane?"

"Why d'you take the photographs?" she parries.

"Because the *Tao* of the photographer is like the stretching of a bow."

"What's that supposed to mean?"

"It brings down what is high; it lifts up what is low. I quote Lao Tzu."

"You're not a real restaurant manager," she accuses.

"You're not a real hooker."

"I am," she says hotly. "I *am*. I fuck real blokes for real money."

"And I manage real restaurants."

"Okay, deuce," she says, conceding. "But what are the photographs for?"

"There's a small and very unfashionable gallery in New York sells my stuff, that's partly why. But I mostly take them for myself. So I'll see what I've seen."

"So you'll see what you've seen." She gives the words a dry mocking emphasis, but he will not be provoked.

"That's right," he says mildly.

"You're very weird."

"Hmm. Now your turn. What did you do before? Tit for tat, that's fair."

"You won't believe me." She still has the sheet up around her shoulders and still feels exposed. In the contrived manner of a child on a school concert stage, she hooks her hands together and recites: " 'There was a little girl who had a little curl, right in the middle of her forehead. When she was good, she was very very good, and when she was bad she was horrid.' That's me," she says. "I'm a brainy sheila, I'm afraid. I even went to Queensland Uni. As a matter of fact, if exam results are anything to go by, I'm practically bloody brilliant."

(Would I have actually said that? Yes, I think I might have, very sarcastically, in the spirit of crossing a border and giving obedient answers to Customs and Immigration. *Do you have anything to declare?* Yes, an inconveniently busy and skeptical mind.

I would have been making full and absolute confession. I would have announced my contraband with the air of a diagnosis handed down. I would have dutifully declared an infection, a rather nasty one, and terminal, though I could not imagine where or how I had picked it up.)

"How's that for a laugh?" Lucy says. "But my true intellectual vocation is renegade."

There is no expression on his face. He imagines her in a frame of recording and examining monks, slow shutter speed to make a smoke of movement, every stylus erect, one sly gargoyle sticking out its tongue. A photophallus. He nods and shrugs, impassive. "Not so hard to believe."

She says harshly: "You're a sucker then. I make up any damn thing I please."

He smiles to himself, not patronizingly, and not in amusement. It is perhaps more like a slight wincing than a smile. It is as though he recognizes something, as though her prickliness is entirely familiar to him, and eminently understandable. "I went there too," he says, as though this explained everything. "To Queensland Uni." She has the disconcerting sensation that he knows exactly what her sudden rudeness was designed to conceal.

To be unexpectedly endorsed, to have one's angle of vision acknowledged, accepted, taken as given: it is seductive. He knows it. He knows—so it seems to her—that she is afraid of what else she may be tempted to tell him.

(*Do you have anything else to declare?*

Yes. Shape-shifting. From time to time, I find myself inside the skin of other people. I see out of their eyes. This affliction swoops down like seasickness. It changes things irrevocably.)

"So why are you here?" he asks quietly.

Why am I anywhere? she thinks.

She says flippantly: "No known antecedents or place of origin. I'm a genuine foundling, left in a home for unwed mothers, isn't that something? And beyond that I haven't inquired. I'm sure there's plenty I never want to know, but I got sent to the very best boarding schools and taken into the very best homes. I was everyone's clever Little Wonder, the emperor's nightingale."

But how would she explain that day when the air parted, when she saw suddenly that there were parallel worlds, that you could cross a line, that you could fall through a hairline crack and cartwheel giddily down and round and down in slow motion, like moondust in space? And how did you know that wasn't your real world, the one you came from and to which you properly belonged?

She was still Lucia then, on the day the fissure appeared, the day she walked right through the looking glass to the other side. She was still Lucia Barclay then, immaculate in the uniform of one of Brisbane's best private high schools for girls, a senior, a prefect, a winner of academic trophies, sports trophies, debating club trophies, a bit of a madcap and a devil but still the flower of her school where she discussed Virgil with the Latin mistress, where she asked the English mistress awkward but oh-so-innocent questions about certain lines in Shakespeare, where she had elegant Sunday dinners with the headmistress. She had yet to step on a crack.

She is still Lucia.

She is standing, surrounded by other schoolgirls, on the platform of Brunswick Street railway station in the inner-city section of Brisbane known as the Fortitude Valley. Hundreds of Brisbane high-schoolers are on the platform because they have all walked down from the Exhibition Grounds where an inter-school sports carnival has been held. In Lucia Barclay's group, there is a certain amount of simpering and giggling and coy sideways glancing toward the knot of Brisbane Grammar boys who stand nearby. The boys, conscious of being watched and overheard, discuss matters both intellectual and carnal rather loudly.

"You remember Greg Harvey who was a prefect at Grammar last year?" Barbara Williams is saying to her, pretending to be nonchalant and modest. "He's at uni now. Engineering. He's invited me to the King's College formal and I suppose I'll . . ."

And someone else is wondering if Miss Dunlop will give them extra time for the Tennyson essay because now, having made the sports finals, they will certainly need . . . And there is talk of Latin translations and basketball matches, of hairdressers, of kings and queens and history facts, of university formals and high school balls, when suddenly Diane Barbour screams.

What is it? What is it? they clamor, and Diane, embarrassed, claps a hand over her mouth and points. Lucia, frowning, turns to look.

Everyone looks.

The whole platform, crowded with shoppers and mothers and toddlers and uniformed high school students, looks.

The sight is so outside the range of what anyone on the platform might imagine happening, that it does not seem real. It is as though they are dreaming a collective dream. This cannot be Brisbane. It is like one of those European movies about the war, Lucia thinks, something by that Italian director (de Sica, was it?), that stark film they were shown in a history class, the one with Sophia Loren in a ravaged village screaming at soldiers.

Whenever Lucy remembers the scene on the railway platform, she sees it in black and white, with Lucia at one side of the screen and the woman at the other. She sees it as part of a film by de Sica. The film starts with a wide-angle shot of the woman, then gets closer and closer.

The woman appears to be in late middle age and is raggedly dressed, dirty, her matted hair sticking out around her head like short snakes. She is making a spectacle of herself. She is standing with straddled legs, holding up her dirty cotton skirts in a bunch at her waist, and pointing to the black fuzz between her legs. Under the skirts, she wears nothing. The skin of her thighs and belly is slack and wrinkled and grotesque. It is as though she has a large bearded prune between the legs. The woman is howling like a dingo.

Eerie, horrifying, the howls echo around the platform and bounce back from the iron roof. More than howls. The woman is blubbering, sobbing, gurgling, coughing up gobs of air, scuds of high frantic laughter, chunks of words, everything mixed like phlegm. Lucia lowers her shamed eyes from the woman's pointing finger (*Look, look*, the finger seems to say. *Do you know what this is?*—jabbing at her wrinkled thighs and tuft of hair).

A voice from nowhere says inside Lucia's head: *That could be your mother. How would you know?*

Lucia, lowering her eyes, is transfixed by the woman's shoes. One is a canvas sandshoe without a lace. The other is a man's shoe, black.

That is when it happens the first time. It comes like vertigo. Lucia can feel a canvas shoe on her left foot, an overly large man's shoe on her right. She can feel the ridge on the ball of her right foot where the leather sole is cracked. Through some unimaginable, unconscionable error, she is exposed, without underwear, to a mob. She looks out at them uneasily. They are all in black and white, blurred, like a ravening pack of animals straining at leashes, teeth bared. If the leashes give way, Lucia notes with terror, they will devour her. She marshals up her fear like a shield to keep them at bay. For whole seconds, the crowded platform is struck dumb and struck motionless. Lucia, the witch of the Fortitude Valley, has them in thrall. Feast your shocked eyes, her howling and her pointing demand, and they do, riveted, mesmerized.

Click. The affliction passes. Lucia is wearing neat black lace-up shoes again, regulation school shoes. She fingers the embroidered crest on her blazer pocket for reassurance. Her mouth is dry. She keeps her eyes on the woman. Feast your shocked eyes, the howling woman invites, and she does.

Then, through the turbulent weather of her sobbing, a tornado of speech racks the woman, or rather gobbets of words gush from her, strung together into something resembling speech. "Bloody," she shrieks. "Bloody fuckers bloody fuckers bloody fuckers . . ."

And this breaks the spell.

Mothers cover their children's eyes and ears, people surge forward, railway porters appear, the police surface from nowhere, the woman—struggling and kicking and shrieking curses—is restrained and dragged off.

Lucia, shaken, her mouth dry, is for some reason face to face in the melee with another girl of about her own age, a girl not in a private school uniform, not in a state school uniform, not in a uniform at all. The girl wears shapeless army-surplus pants and a torn white T-shirt and she has dirty brown hair and her eyes smolder with scorn.

For seconds, possibly minutes, they are face to face, eye to eye. Then the girl speaks. "You stuck-up bitch!" she says in a low intense voice. "No one's ever gonna lay a finger on *you*, are they, Lady Muck? No one's gonna ram his prick up your arse when you weren't expecting it, is he, you prissy little fancypants cunt!"

Lucia blinks. At school she has a reputation for saying unsayable words, but this is not a language she knows, and she attempts to translate slowly, groping for meaning, dazed. "Pardon?" she asks from polite habit.

"Oh fuck off," the girl says. "Think you're the bloody Queen of Sheba!" She spits in Lucia's face.

Then it happens again. Lucia can feel the baggy pants around her legs, and she is looking out at a girl in a neat private school uniform, an almost unbelievably ignorant foolish girl, a stuck-up bitch, a mere kindergarten child, a prissy little fancypants cunt. She feels as shaken with despair and rage as a piece of tin roofing in a cyclone. She spits in the stupid girl's face, she spits at the clucking bevy of rescuers.

Lucia, Lucia, Lucia, come *on*, Lucia, her friends are calling, because the train is in the station, carriage doors are open, someone is pulling on her arm, yes, she's in the train compartment, there's a babble of talk, the train is moving, but the howling of the woman with the lifted skirts is in her ears, and the eyes of the girl on the platform are scorching her. The girl on the platform is still standing there with her hands on her hips, leering. Her eyes follow Lucia, they dart and bother and intrude and buzz about her the way mosquitoes do. Lucia feels stunned, as though she has been hit on the head with a mallet. She thinks she might faint. I know nothing, she thinks. *Nothing*. Vaguely, she wipes a clotted wet mess from her cheek. Her hands are trembling.

Oh yuck, she sees the lips of Barbara Williams saying.

Grotesque! she sees in the shape of Diane's lips.

She cannot hear what anyone is saying, their mouths move silently, she cannot respond to them, she cannot remember how those things are done: talking, opening a train door, getting out, walking, and yet here she is at the headmistress's dinner table, the lace cloth over mahogany, the silver gleaming, the dimmed golden light of the dining room bouncing back off the Royal Albert china.

"Lucia dear," the headmistress is saying, "what on earth is the matter?"

"Don't tell *us* about woolgathering!" the English mistress smiles.

"What is it, dear?" the headmistress asks. "What is it?"

You can never step into the same dining room twice, Lucia thinks.

"So are you going to Sydney Uni on the side?" the photographer asks.

"What?"

"You wouldn't be the first MA student at Sydney to support herself by . . ."

She says vehemently: "Forget that." She lights a cigarette and smokes it violently. "For one, I can't stand academics, especially the Sydney crowd. I can't stand the . . ." She searches for a word. "They're so *tepid*, I'd rather talk to johns, that tells you something. And for two . . ." She laughs. "If I was good at being good, I just happen to be even better at being bad. I should get a medal. And for three . . ." She is searching carefully for a way to express point three, but abandons it.

"And for three?"

"Oh I dunno. *Freedom.* Choice of cages. I don't have to . . . *shut down* so much in this one as in the others. And something to do with choice of sides too. I dunno. I suppose I reckon if it's come to the Quarry versus Them, I'm not Them. I could never be Them."

He nods. Same team, she thinks; him and me. "And what about you? Where're you from?"

"I told you. Brisbane."

She waves this aside. "No, but before that. In the beginning, I mean." Her gesture implies: you've got more exotic baggage than is bought on a weekday in Brisbane. "Where were you born?"

He considers her for several silent seconds, for so long, in fact, that she looks away, uncomfortable, and busies herself with lighting another cigarette. At last he says: "One of the reasons I could breathe better in New York. Nobody asked me where I came from." She senses that she might have been dropped from his team, that at the very least she has lost crucial marks on a covert test. "Which answer would you like?" he asks politely. "I've got an old Brisbane one. As a kid, I got into the habit of saying Hong Kong. It simplified things."

"But it isn't true?"

"I've never set eyes on Hong Kong. I'm a true, blue Aussie." He smiles, certainly not in anger, not even in sorrow, simply remembering. "I said that to a teacher once, in Brisbane. 'I was born in North Queensland, Mr. Brady. I'm a true-blue Aussie.'"

"And?"

"And he said, 'Because a man's born in a stable, that doesn't make him a horse.'"

"Rude jerk." Conscious of clumsiness, but wanting nevertheless to make reparations of some sort, she says: "Would you like a cuppa? I've got teabags. Or beer, if you'd rather."

"There are compensations," he says. "It's like being a hooker or a restaurant manager. You see without being seen."

She opens a paint-chipped cabinet on the wall. "I've got Earl Grey or plain old Bushells."

It interests her, the fastidious distaste that wasn't there in his photographer's eye. He looks around the tacky room and calculates something, running debits and credits. He is balancing the room and the stink of other men against his interest in the girl, which is not a sexual interest, she is clear about that and therefore engaged. Challenged, even. Oddly excited. He is perhaps gauging the dangerous impact of that simple offer of the making of tea. She herself feels at risk. It is personal, the making of tea. It's like kissing, it's out of bounds. He is perhaps weighing the greater aesthetic pleasure and tranquillity of his own apartment, upstairs, against the invasion of privacy and who knows what breed of future threat?

Offhandedly, inviting refusal, he says: "We could upstairs, I suppose. If you really want." He begins to leave in a way that suggests dismissal. "I've taken the top floor for myself."

"Yeah. We heard." Her eyes gleam. "Okay, sure. Let's go."

38

His immediate regret is so obvious, so comic, that she breaks into a Cheshire cat smile. "Shouldn't have offered if you didn't want to."

"No."

"Fuck off then." She is affectionate almost, but exasperated with him, baring her teeth and making claws with her hands. He is transfixed. Macro lens, large aperture, slow speed, he thinks. Mock savage, she bats at him with her cat paws and he cannot move.

Curious, she says: "Jeez, just a joke."

He blinks. Focuses. Embarrassed, he picks up his camera, a piece of armor, and the detached photographer is back, a man who records the world without reaction or comment.

"What's eating you?"

"I'm not aware of being eaten."

"I had the distinct impression that I hit a nerve," she says, fascinated.

Basilisk. He raises his eyebrows and gives her the steady polite gaze of a man too well-bred to offer any response to impertinence. She puts one hand on her hip and raises her eyebrows back at him, a dare. "I hit a nerve," she insists.

"You think so."

"I know so."

"Tenacious, aren't you?" He smiles to himself, then laughs. "The second coming of Cat." He says it aloud, but not to Lucy.

"I remind you of someone."

"You do," he admits.

"Named Cat."

"Hmm."

"That why you took the pictures?"

"Maybe."

"So who is she?"

He concentrates on fitting the various lenses into the carry case.

"Another hooker?" she needles. "From the days of your Brisbane youth?"

He says dryly, "Do you want to come upstairs or not?"

"Sure," she says. "You're not getting off that easy."

"Let's go then."

FOUR

Beyond the windows, King's Cross still fizzes and roars and trumpets its brassy notes sky high, and they are certainly aware of it, but it seems to Lucy that Charlie has adjusted the lighting and fiddled with the volume controls, that a muting of noise and brightness has been achieved. What a difference is made by another two floors' remove from the street. Bamboo and rice paper screens, stretched tight as drumskins, subdue the afternoon glare and even the garish staccato shouts of neon, so that a wash of soft light, flickering, streaked with watered color, seeps through the windows and fills the space. Space. That is what the apartment celebrates: the mysterious quality of space, and the way it draws attention to single objects placed judiciously within it, and the way these isolated objects, in turn, give space a form.

Lucy feels like a traveler entering another atmosphere, like a spacewalker, like someone setting foot in emptiness, like someone returning to a lost world. Though many questions occur to her (When did you do this? How long ago did you move in? How could you have moved in without the rest of us knowing? What was it like before? How much stuff did you have to move out?), she does not want to violate the hush of the place by voicing them.

Charlie has taken off his shoes. Instinctively, Lucy does the same, and she wanders around the large main room in her stockinged feet, pad pad pad, silent. The floor is polished wood, bare, and the walls are white, and both pull the eye toward a single table, long, narrow, and high, of gleaming black lacquer, against the far wall. Here a rakish statement is made. Flamboyant and asymmetrical, six shafts of orchids, each stem crowded with flowers, flaunt themselves in a glass cylinder on the table, purple throats brushing white backdrop. By one of the screened windows are two soft black leather chairs, low slung, facing each other. Apart from these objects, and the photographs, the room is empty.

The room is full of mystery.

It is also full of photographs.

Occupying the end wall to Lucy's left, an afterimage of the world they have escaped from, is a black-and-white photograph six feet long by four feet high. In the white wall, it is a shocking window into hell. Lucy sees a great crater with pocked rock walls and rope ladders, their bamboo rungs knotted together, columns of people moving up and down the ladders like ants. The faces visible in the foreground are the faces of nightmare. They are faces which might climb staircases to rooms like Lucy's, which might come and go and leave money on the table. Lucy backs away from the photograph.

"What do you think?" Charlie asks, behind her, and she jumps. "Striking, isn't it? Wish I could say it's one of mine, but it's not. It's by a Brazilian, Sebastiao Salgado. I bought a print and rephotographed it and blew it up. Adds to the graininess, but that's appropriate, I think."

"Is it the quarry?"

"Ah," Charlie says, and she hears a burr of excitement in his voice. She hears his pleasure in her response and is momentarily pleased, and then annoyed that she has still not cured herself of a desire to please the setters of tests. "Is it the quarry?" he repeats, changing the inflection subtly, making a meditative statement. "Salgado claims it's a gold mine in Brazil."

"You know what else it reminds me of?" she asks. "Dante's Inferno. The Botticelli drawings. Have you seen them?"

"Yes," he says. "I have. And it reminds me of them too."

Lucy turns and looks beyond his shoulder into the grotto of the photograph on the opposite wall, this one in color, equally large, shadowy, full of luminous greens. "Rainforest," she says wistfully, and thinks of Gabriel and veers away quickly from the thought. She tips her head to one side, and considers the moss-thick debris of fallen trunks over which new growth rages. "It could be Tamborine, or Mt. Glorious." She walks up to it, into it, and traces the course of the water with one finger, stopping at the shush of spray around the two boulders. "I think it's Cedar Creek Falls. I know someone who . . ." She pauses and corrects herself. "I used to know someone who lived at Samford. We used to picnic at the falls. We used to swim here." She feels as though she is touching a bruise. "I used to sit on that boulder and read." She retreats into time past, pensive, her hand on the boulder.

"I'll make tea." Charlie stands close behind her, closer, until his chin touches the top of her head. Lucy flinches and moves.

"Did you take that one?" she asks, setting a question between them.

"Yes."

"It *is* Cedar Creek, isn't it?"

"Yes." He moves toward the door which is in the corner between the gold mine and the lacquered table. "I'll make tea."

She turns to the fourth wall, the one that faces the black table and the orchids. This one is a honeycomb of framed pictures, snapshots, family groups, old school photos, sepia wedding portraits (grandparents? parents?), a Chinese bride, a Chinese couple behind a shop counter, Brisbane street scenes, New York street scenes, the signposts of a life.

"God," she calls out, disgusted, noting high school uniforms. "You went to Grammar. Bloody snob, wouldn't have come here if I'd known."

(Was this any way for Lucy, former private school girl, to talk? Oh yes. It was Lucia, not Lucy, who went to that school, it was Lucia who had gone to formals with Grammar boys. Lucy was full of contempt for Lucia. She'd shed all that, the trappings of safe stuck-up bitches. She'd adopted a different history. She wanted no part of a private school past.)

"Won a scholarship," he calls from the kitchen. "Fish out of water."

A Grade 5 photograph: the boy in the middle of the front row (always the smallest kid in the class) holds an old school slate clearly chalked: *Wilston State School. Grade V.* Lucy laughs.

"Is that you with the slate? They're probably still using slates in school photos. Still used them when I was at school."

Another photograph, a composed one, catches her eye, because its enlarged central image is Charlie-with-the-Grade-V-slate. Under the curve of each arm, in the hollows of his waist, fitted to him like pieces of a jigsaw puzzle, are two girls, one on each side. The photograph is neatly titled, in India ink script on the taupe mat, *The Two Catherines*. The Catherine under Charlie-with-the-slate's left armpit is poking a face at the watcher, hissing perhaps, her finger-claws curved to strike. She seems convulsed with inner laughter and levitates, cross-legged, between Charlie's shoulder and his thigh.

Lucy runs her finger along the ranks of the Grade 5 photograph and finds both Catherines. One is in the second row, several spaces to the right of Charlie-with-the-slate. The other, like a singled-out gnome, is actually sitting cross-legged on the ground in front of the front row, at the feet of the teacher who stands to Charlie's left, at the side of the class, the grimacing gargoyle at the teacher's ankles, out of line and off-center, a mocking point of asymmetry.

The Catherine in the second row, with her plaits falling neatly over her shoulders and ending in long corkscrew curls, looks demure. Butter wouldn't melt in her mouth, people might have said of her, particularly if they failed to look too closely. She is wearing the regulation school tunic, as are all the girls, but the ribbons tied to her plaits, at the point where braiding ends and curl begins, scroll across the box pleats of the tunic in a very quiet subversion of the rules.

The other Catherine, the one in front of the front row, under the teacher's close distrustful eye it would seem, has very short dark spiky hair. If it were not for the school tunic, Lucy might have mistaken her for a boy. Everyone else in the front row, including Charlie-with-the-slate, looks solemn even if smiling, for the taking of a school photograph is a sobering and momentous event. Catherine with the short spiky hair, however, has the tip of her tongue showing through a mouth that seems to be half hiss, half clownish grin, and she is positively seismic with revolt and tamped-down mirth.

(*I remind you of someone.* You do. *Named Cat.* Hmm.)

Catherine, Cathy, Cat, Lucy thinks.

She goes to the kitchen, which is as stark and spare and beautiful as the living room, one wall a mosaic of framed photographs, and watches Charlie setting teapot and cups (small bowls, really, without handles) on a lacquered tray.

"Found her," she says. And when he looks up, she makes claws and hisses softly.

"Don't," he says.

"Who are they?"

He unplugs an electric kettle, fills the teapot, sets the kettle down. He strokes the warm bellied curve of the teapot with his hands. Lucy notes how thin his wrists are, like a girl's. She thinks it must have been hell at Wilston State School for a boy like him. She knows a little about the penalties for difference. He pours tea into the small bowls and then offers her one, holding it reverently in both hands. He might have been holding an injured bird. She takes it as though receiving communion, sips, wrinkles her nose. "What is it?"

"Jasmine," he says. "Don't you like it?"

She shrugs and takes another sip. "It's okay, I guess."

"Would you like a tour?"

"Sure."

His bedroom, the walls covered with photographs, contains nothing more than a black futon in one corner of a bare floor, except that a bunch of white arum lilies in a black vase stands on the floor below the window.

"Gosh," she says, joking. "How do you live with all this clutter?"

(But something wholly unexpected hit me then, a sharp pang of loss, a sensual vision of a room dimly lit, of crocheted lace over mahogany, of a headmistress smiling in a dining room on the other side of a great abyss. I felt something like physical pain, or hunger, and pressed a hand against my stomach, wincing.

"What's wrong?" Charlie asked.

"Nothing," I said, embarrassed.)

Bright Lucy turns away from his bedroom. "Talk about busy rooms," she says flippantly. "So what's next?"

The bathroom is completely white—white tiled floors, white tiled walls, white fixtures—except for a single blood-red hibiscus in a black vase beside the sink.

"And this is my workshop," he says of a final small room. "I've turned the cupboard there into a darkroom. Bit of a squash. You wouldn't want to be claustrophobic."

After the patterns of emptiness, this room feels crowded, not just because of the workbench and the developing trays and stacked frames, but because of the shelves crammed with books and tapes, the television, the VCR, the chair. Lucy sets down her bowl of jasmine tea and picks up a videotape.

"Charlie's Inferno," she says, reading the neat lettered spine. "Sounds like either Beckett or Monty Python."

"Not exactly."

"Hookers in motion? Soft porn?"

He frowns, but in thoughtfulness, not irritation. It is maddeningly difficult to ruffle him. "It's something new I'm trying, hard to describe." He searches for words and disappears into the enterprise itself, cuddling the little cup of tea in both hands, sipping, breathing the jasmine steam. "A sort of photographic decomposition," he says carefully. "The declensions of an image. Not sure if it'll go anywhere, but New York seems interested. I'm still working on it. The subject matter keeps changing."

The desire to touch the frail wrists that cradle the cup frightens Lucy.

"So who's this?" she asks brusquely, flicking one finger at the boy on the workbench. The boy is wearing a Grammar uniform, he is a blow-up from one of the high school photographs, but across the surface of his body the jigsaw outline of a puzzle has been inked, black lines, interlocking tabs and slots. Some of the pieces have been removed by scissors, so that the boy has a hole where his face should be, another at the left thigh, another at the blazer pocket skimming straight through school badge and prefect's crest, another shearing off part of one hand. The missing puzzle pieces have been stuffed into the boy's other hand which is cupped and held up for show in a way that seems slightly frantic, slightly comic, as though, heroic school prefect that he is, he hangs grimly on to the shreds of a desiccating self. *See, not a single piece lost or unaccounted for! Aren't I a good little boy!* he seems to say. In the original group photograph, Lucy suspects, this hand held a football, or a cricket bat perhaps. "Who is he?"

Charlie looks at the puzzle-piece boy as though the question has long baffled him, as though the question is the meaning of the photograph.

"Is it you?" Lucy prods.

"Sometimes."

"And other times?"

"Another boy."

"What happened to him?"

"Oh, he's very much in one piece. A pillar of the community. A judge, as a matter of fact."

"Don't tell me," Lucy says, rolling her eyes. "I'm on intimate terms with a couple of judges."

"Yes," Charlie says. "I know."

Lucy bridles. "Jesus," she says, annoyed. "Talk about Big Brother. Next thing, we'll need permission slips, I suppose. Have the johns sign the visitors' book as they pass through the restaurant on their way upstairs." She hisses and makes claws and lunges at him.

Very quietly, but swiftly, he reaches up and takes hold of her wrists. They stand braced against each other, deadlocked. Seconds pass.

"Fuck," Lucy says in a nervous whisper. She feels a hunger for Gabriel so acute, she can scarcely breathe. "Oh fuck."

Charlie leans in against her and kisses one of her wrists.

"Oh fuck," Lucy says, and pulls away. She wrenches free of his grasp. "I'm going."

At the apartment door, she turns back. He has not followed her, and the emptiness of the living room seems immense. She cannot bear it. "Who are they?" she calls out, to fill the emptiness.

He does not answer.

When she goes back to the workroom, he is sitting huddled on the floor beside the bench, rocking himself, his arms folded across his chest. He holds his sides as though he is in terrible pain, as though his ribs are bruised and flayed, as though he is stopping up the bloody openings from which the two Catherines have been ripped.

"Who are they?"

"They are part of me," he says.

"Fuck," she says wearily, ridiculously and violently jealous (but of *what*, exactly?), hardly able to stomach her own idiocy. Gabriel is certainly *not* part of me, she tells herself. Nobody is part of me and they never will be.

"I'm off," she says savagely. "I'm *working*. Can't stand around talking all day." At the door she calls: "And keep your bloody hands to yourself. If there's one thing I can't stand, it's touchers."

FIVE

Yes, where the road crosses Cedar Creek, you must make a sharp turn, and follow the unpaved detour until it ends, and then you must leave your car and enter the dark wood on foot and keep going until the straight way is lost.

When I said that I came to myself in that dark rainforest, I meant it literally. I blacked out. Shock hit me in a cinema full of strangers, once in London and then a second time in Sydney, in dark rooms full of those projections of moving light where Charlie regularly cobbled together time past and time still to come.

I remember once in Charlie's apartment commenting on a large blow-up of a hooker, done not in black and white but in sepia, so that the girl looked as tawny as one of the great cats. Stripes of shadow fell across her. In standard bodysuit (long sleeves, backless, cut high over thighs and buttocks) and fishnet pantyhose, she had her hands in front of her face like rapacious claws. The image was elongated, not quite human. The mouth was distorted in a feral hiss, the bedposts were like bars of a cage.

"God," I said, awed. "Is that Cat?"

"No."

"Who is it?"

"I call it *Wildcat*."

"It's horrible." Because of the way he looked at me, I said uneasily: "It's not me, is it?"

"It's *Wildcat*," he said. "It is itself."

That was the maddening sort of non-response Charlie hid behind when you tried to pin him down. Catherine and I expect to bump into him again in New York shortly, and when I see him I'll insist on a proper answer. Would it shock me? The johns thought I was unshockable. Quite frankly, from that day on the railway platform in Brisbane until I lost my way in the dark, I myself thought I couldn't be shocked. (*I myself.* What a riddle that is. Where, in the grab bag of costumes and masks, does the self hide out?) Insatiable, invulnerable, beyond the reach of dismay, that was what I thought. That was in the time of the Second Innocence, before Charlie, before I got tangled up in Gabriel's riddle, before I stumbled into the way Charlie saw things. Sees things. Saw. He's thrown it all away now, he's stuffed the past in a bag and dumped it somewhere and shot through to New York again. He left his camera in the workroom where someone else lives, his photographs are in boxes under Sheba's bed, he's through with all that, he doesn't care to see like that anymore, but he used to juggle coincidence, he used to shuffle incongruities and hold them up to the light and show that their contours matched.

This was part of his black magic. This was part of his uncanny power. Second sight, intuition, precognition, I don't know what to call it. He himself would have had an artist's explanation, which would have been self-deprecating and a little flippant, almost offhand, but would have hinted at bemusement too, as though he found his own magic puzzling. People are always telling me they see themselves in my work, he would shrug. People I know nothing about, people I've never even met, insist I've got their lives in my lens.

Must be my negative perspective, he'd joke. Or my overdeveloped angle of view.

At any rate, *Charlie's Inferno* is part of the body of work which has now made him a cult figure in New York, and even, belatedly, in the Australian art world as well, in certain enclaves of the avant garde. *Chang* is a byword in some quarters. (This was after the hidden ideogram signatures were discovered on photographs, and reassessments were made. Looking through a different glass, the critics solemnly pronounced that the Chang eye was not at all a common expatriate eye, nor was it just one more migrant eye or ethnic eye. Not at all. The Chang eye sees us in its own authentically foreign light, the critics said. The Chang eye has visited and dwelt among us and has seen what it has seen. The Chang eye has integrity. The Chang eye makes us all seem willfully blind. The Chang eye is valid in a unique and remarkable way.)

Particularly since its disappearance, the Chang eye's validity has grown.

(*Bull's eye!* Charlie would laugh. *Chang-eyed* and *shang-haied*, I've got them both ways.

The Chang eye sees a congregation of vapors, he would say, a jostle of hot-air balloons.)

Making an effort to be suitably detached, I will say only that the particular short feature to which I refer—I once held it in my hand in videotape form—is an early example of a Chang-eye technique to which the critics, as critics will, have attached a label. "Mutational collage" is what they call it.

In the undersized overheated cinema (London or Sydney? Both, it seems to me now), some pompous doctoral candidate from Film Studies explains this to us. Of the five postmodern filmmakers whose work we are privileged to experience in this festival, he says, blah blah blah . . .

And then it is running.

There is no soundtrack at first, and the blurred arrangement of black and gray is deliberate, I have no doubt. Oh Charlie, how typical. You and bloody Gabriel: riddles, games, puzzles, conundrums, the world as Rubik's Cube.

Charlie's face, a finger to his lips, appears hazily on screen. Be patient, his finger says. Wait.

"*Now,*" his voice murmurs, and my body lurches and spins.

"Note how the shifting pattern of blackness is transgressed," he says. (His voice is eerily disembodied, an offstage whisper, distorted, fed through synthesizers, but it is Charlie's voice. It is unmistakably Charlie's voice. It reaches me from outside of time, it echoes, it causes vertigo and pain.) "Note," he says, "how a thin line of light reaches down from the top of the screen like God's bony finger."

(*Charlie*, I plead. *Charlie!*
Am I sobbing?
I *will* him to step out from his screen.)
But he falls silent.

There is no voice now, only electronic music, and I note how radiance leaks out into the image until I can distinguish rocks and water and trees, the soft murk of Cedar Creek Falls. I note how color bleeds into the black and white. The lens catches the braided water where it twists into a whorl around two boulders. I am looking into the eye of the whirlpool, two seconds, five, ten, the effect is hypnotic. Freeze. The water goes suddenly still. It moves again. Now, as though swaying or drunk, I seem to lose my footing and perspective, painlessly, languidly, and I seem to slide down the outside of the whorl and see the translucent funnel in profile.

(How did you do that, Charlie? At what dangerous angle, on slippery rock, did you and your camera lie to get that shot? What magnification was used? Did you get drenched? Did you slide on the moss?)

The image goes still again: portrait of a waterspout, an impossible aqueous ballerina *à pointe*.

(Very clever, Charlie, though you're making me lose my sense of balance. Which you always did, damn it. You always did.)

Vertigo drains out of me, color is drained from the image.

Then, as subtly as a spill of ink disperses itself in clear oil, the cone of water is smudging at the edges, growing fur, putting forth angular roughness. It is no longer water, but something else. What? It looks vaguely medieval, or more ancient, like a diagram from a book on the plumbing of Roman bathhouses. Text appears at the bottom of the screen: *Sandro Botticelli's drawing of Dante's Inferno.*

I am hanging in space, watching the funnel of hell entire, and it begins to spin like a top, faster, faster, so that I grab the arms of my chair to stave off giddiness. Mercifully the dervish-thing slows down, it stops again, I have the sensation of flying toward the vortex, the zoom takes me closer, and where before the corded water of Cedar Creek Falls made its screw turns, now I see the spiral ledges of something like an open-cut mine. It is a black-and-white image, swarming with ants, no, with people, I am swooping down into the slope which is spinning again, I feel nausea, streaks of color are spinning past me like spittle, I clutch blindly at armchair supports, I stabilize things, I slow down, I am now in the eighth circle of hell.

Get off here, Lucy, Charlie whispers. (He speaks silently now; privately; for my ears alone.) Get off where the two gowned figures stand, one in scarlet and one in purple. Yes, you have your bearings now, he smiles, you recognize this famous landscape of paint and charcoal on white vellum. It is Sandro Botticelli, yes, from the drawings housed in the Berlin and the Vatican museums, the ones in a book on my shelves, the tourist's illustrated guide to Dante's hell.

(You remember you commented, Lucy? You remember you thought of Botticelli?

I remember, Charlie. Do you remember what *I* said when I picked up your videotape? Beckett and Monty Python, I said. I wasn't so far out, was I?

Pay attention, Lucy. Two gentlemen are waiting for you.)

Here, then, are Dante and Virgil. Beneath their frail rock bridge, boiling excrement bubbles, froths, cords itself, piss-curls, shit-swirls, slips, slops, turd-twirls, putresces, a foul slippery flush of cosmic diarrhea; and here the Flatterers (recyclers of sewage, panderers to Presidents and Prime Ministers and Supreme Commanders, flaunters of the Queen's birthday honors), here they cavort in acrobatic, scatological pain.

Now the camera distances itself, backing away from the stench, so that the striations and rocky niches and rock ladders, the whole diabolic honeycomb, can again be seen entire. Colors stream down the funnel and are sucked out like water running down a plughole (the flushing of hell?). Mutations again; something subtle is going on, too minute to decode. Is that still Dante's and Botticelli's hell or an open-cut mine?

(Everything reminded you of the quarry, didn't it, Charlie? It was a Venus flytrap, it sucked you down.

Wait, Lucy. Wait.)

Wait. Wait. I move slowly closer, riding the eye of the camera like a gull on a slipstream of air. The scene in my gull's eye is steady, motionless, its colors gone: the same pits and ledges and rock pockets, the same ladders busy with tormented souls, but it is no longer Botticelli. It is the same pit all right, and yet it is also another, a black-and-white photograph that looks familiar.

(Do you recognize it, Lucy? Charlie whispers.

Is it the quarry?

Not yet, he says.)

Text flickers across the base of the screen:

Since a peasant found the first nuggets there in 1980, a mountain has been reduced to a hollow 600 feet deep and half a mile wide. It has yielded 42 tons of gold. Bars, brothels and stores have sprung up nearby; 100,000 people now live alongside the pit. Photographer Sebastiao Salgado captured this image of the Serra Pelada gold mine in northern Brazil, where fortune-seekers have moved a mountain on their backs.

(*New York Times Magazine*, June 7, 1987)

(Okay, I say. The photograph on the wall in your living room. Yes, he says, you remember it now. You remember that you thought of Dante, and I'm willing to bet you thought of various other landscapes of nightmare too, of the desolate craters made by desert storms, of mines and quarries and clearcuts and man-made hells. You were idly riffling through an old magazine in your upstairs room, and there it was again: the traffic up and down the ladders of hell, the fanatic eyes. You closed the magazine quickly. Remember that, Lucy?)

The camera moves slowly across the screes and pocked walls of the pit, pausing here and there so that first one tormented face then another fills the screen in stark black and white. At the point when I cannot bear those maddened dilated eyes a second longer, the pit recedes, a languidly falling ball. I am somewhere high and suspended, uninvolved, a remote high-tech bomber pilot, a spectator, a newscaster in the first circle.

This respite is brief. But when I descend the scarp of the pit again, something has changed, something I can't quite pinpoint, a change so slight that at first only a sense of mild disorientation assails me. How shall I explain it? It's the kind of malaise you feel on returning to a home that has been burgled. No vandalism, nothing spectacular, but your eye snags on a hook near the back door that should have a coat on it. Odd, you think, pausing. But then you shrug; probably you hung the coat in your bedroom. A drawer in the kitchen is slightly open. You close it, frowning a little. A tiny splinter of unease scratches one corner of your mind, but it's nothing, probably nothing, certainly nothing of consequence. When you see your lover's running shoes and his pillowcase on the living room sofa, you are annoyed *(How many times have I asked that man . . . ?)* but you are also puzzled. Pillowcase? Why the pillowcase? Then you notice the space where the television set should be. And then it hits you.

In the same gradual way, looking at the black-and-white still, I come to realize I am no longer looking at the Serra Pelada mine in Brazil, but at the granite cut that surrounds the railway station of Newtown in inner Sydney. I am, at last, in the quarry. It is difficult to ascertain just when this photograph would have been taken, but clearly it was some time after the squatters moved in, after the buildings were burned out and the digging began, after the construction of the warren of tunnels that turned Newtown and Redfern into something resembling the Pueblo cliff dwellings of New Mexico. Probably the photograph was taken at about the very time the newspapers began to speak of the quarry. Just as I recognize one of the places where Old Fury used to scavenge for food, color surfs in like a fast king tide, relentless, a splash of all the harsh bright sunstruck colors of Sydney.

(So, Charlie, what's this? The Big Dipper tour of the quarry? Visceral involvement for the audience? You want to induce actual nausea?)

I am in the pit, at the heart of a fisheye lens, and I feel dizzy because of the languid curving zoom, as though the lens and I are swinging at the end of a rope. I am on a ladder that will not keep still, I am going to fall. Other bodies on other ladders are falling with me, this is unbearable, I close my eyes.

(Stop it, I cry silently. Stop it, Charlie.

Be patient, Lucy. Wait. I haven't told you anything yet.)

Alone in the dark, sheepish, I remind myself that I am, after all, not on a ladder but very comfortably settled in a chair. There are people around me. Charlie himself is in New York. I open my eyes.

How long has the screen been spinning like this, a giddy blur? Am I still on the ladder? I hold tightly to the arms of my chair, my ladder. When the image comes to rest, the whole scene has been turned on its side, and from this perspective, the ladder looks like a railway line with someone lying prostrate on the tracks, other figures bending over it, watching. No faces can be seen. The figures are cowled and stooped, the mood is stark but also mysterious: these hooded forms are keepers of a horrible secret.

(Oh Charlie, I don't think I want to know what you're planning to tell me about this.)

What is the queasy sensation of decomposition, of dissolve, which follows? The rails and the sleepers are growing green fur, growing moss, growing slack, sucking color into their spongy limbs, turning organic. The figures, all except one, slump into soft rotted logs. We are back in the grotto of Cedar Creek Falls where a young woman, wearing jeans and T-shirt and a battered straw hat, sits on a boulder, knees hunched up, chin on her clasped hands. It is not possible to see her face, but her eyes are fixed on the dark hollow between the boulders. The shadow spreads.

(Foreboding drops, shadow out of shadow, a sense of dread. What explains this? What is it you're dabbling in, Charlie? When you made this, you had no inkling of where the bones would be found. When you made this, didn't you believe the body was warm and vibrant, its heart beating, its hopes high?

And when I saw the film I too still hoped that all was well, I didn't know death hid in that place, and yet I felt such dread, such dread, to watch that screen. Why? What explains this?)

It is not possible to see the young woman's face. The shadow spreads, the sequence ends, all returns to patterns of blackness, and begins again.

This time the order of events is speeded up and the effect is that of a time-lapse nature film, the kind where before your eyes the rosebud appears and swells and opens and loses its petals, all in a matter of seconds. Conscious not of movement nor of any actual detail of change, but only of mutation, I watch the rain-forest deconstruct and remake itself, I slide down the declensions of Cedar Creek Falls into the vortex of water which is the funnel of Dante's hell which is the Serra Pelada mine which is the New-town quarry which contracts to one of its ladders which is a railway line which is Cedar Creek Falls in the middle of a dark enveloping wood. This happens in the space of twenty seconds. And happens again, and then again: three time-lapse mutations which by now seem so natural that the audience could believe any plughole drops straight into hell, any railway line will grow moss and will harbor a fallen body.

(Okay, Charlie. Point taken.)

Begin again. The fifth cycle is in slow motion. . . .

Yes, it was during this final sequence that, for myself, there set in those little burrs of visual disturbance that add up to panic. Small alarms went off in my mind. There was nothing I could put my finger on until the railway line scene, and then I felt a buzz of excitement and agitation because I recognized a particular house and overhead bridge. I stared. Yes, I knew that bit of railway line, I knew the bridge near the embankment cutting, and I began to think I knew the tiny figures on the overhead bridge. They were leaning over the parapet to observe the prostrate body on the rails and to monitor the hooded figures who were a dark Greek chorus. The mourners. Or vultures. They could have been anyone, those tiny figures. They could have been—I was almost sure they were—Catherine, and Charlie himself.

As grit bothers an oyster, something else kept scratching at my mind. I closed my eyes and mentally replayed the film until I found the eighth circle of hell within the slow fifth cycle of the film. I held the image steady in my mind. I didn't know what I was looking for until I saw it: the face of Charlie himself under Dante's hood.

So Charlie was Dante, speaking in code and turning history into allegory. I kept staring at the image in my mind, scanning every profile, every averted face. Ahh. The figure floundering in the bog of sewage just where it went under the bridge, was it not . . . ? Yes. Yes it was. It was a young man in a school blazer with a prefect's crest on the pocket.

Of course, I could have been seeing what I was looking for. I could have been, as they say, *projecting*; but then all of us see what we expect—what we *want*—to see, don't we? Is seeing what the rest of the audience doesn't see, seeing against the grain, reading against the grain, therefore more intelligent? Is it more intellectually rigorous? Is it more moral? Or is it, in fact, *less* so:

a murky private enterprise of the ego? Is all exegesis of necessity eisegesis in disguise?

At any rate, an answer came to me then, or *leapt* at me, it would be more accurate to say, an answer to Gabriel's riddle hit me between the eyes and I told myself I read that answer in Charlie's film. Perhaps this was true. Or perhaps, as Charlie would claim, I had known the answer all along. Perhaps I always had an explanation for the missing people and for Charlie's hasty departure for New York. Perhaps I even knew what happened before it happened.

Perhaps Charlie knew. Yes, very likely Charlie sensed what had happened and was bound to happen, and that is the explanation for the film.

Then I thought I was quite simply crazy. I rejected the answer out of hand. It was the wrong answer because it couldn't possibly be true. It was preposterous. And absolutely nothing was certain.

When I saw the film a second time, especially that slow final cycle, I stared at the image of the eighth circle of Botticelli's hell and was certain only of two things: that the faces of Dante and of the man doing shitstroke under the bridge were deliberate photographic impositions. In fact, the methods of film collage drew attention to this, for the face circled by sewage was torn from a group photograph in a newspaper, you could actually see the rough edges and a neighboring arm and a few newsprint words. The face was peripheral, almost hidden under the bridge in the manner of carvings on the undersides of pews in Gothic cathedrals, gargoyle faces where no one can see them, subversive jokes, a mere trace of the countertruth.

But when I go to New York, when I next bump into him, I know what Charlie will say. Total strangers are forever insisting I've made raids on their lives, he'll say. It's the occupational hazard of the artist. Listen, he'll laugh. If it doesn't happen, it probably means you've failed.

But you've used actual photographs, I'll argue. You deliberately superimposed on Botticelli a picture torn from the *Sydney Morning Herald*.

Did I? Pure accident, he'll say; or more likely, punning away as usual, pure graft. Or maybe: Must be the unkindest cut of all.

That is the sort of joke he'll make. All art is accretion, he'll say. I use random found matter all the time. I can't be held responsible for what you make of it.

Besides, he'll say, the world is crammed with messages. We'll never have time to read them all.

Perhaps, perhaps. All art is reception, that is certainly true. But on the slow projection of my mind I found everyone. Yes, I knew I could be putting them there, the way the gullible do with Tarot cards, but I also knew, I *know*, the faces that haunted Charlie.

And what does it have to do with me? Nothing, really. Or so I used to believe, so I told myself. I am nobody. I'm a mere bystander who got sucked in, who got infected by Charlie's obsessions and Gabriel's riddles, who lost my footing and nearly drowned in their nightmares and bumped into all the floundering people in Charlie's dream: the latest dream I ever dreamed, or ever want to, on the cold quarry side.

Well, they are all gone into the world of archive now.

Into archive or underground.

And I am awake, and I find myself here alone, and no birds sing, and I stumble about in a dark and trackless wood.

So.

Once upon a time, having been so lost in thought and grief that I was oblivious to the ending of a film, I found myself sitting alone in an empty cinema, in London, in Sydney, wherever, waiting for the second showing. No. Wait. Before that I opened my eyes into someone else's film, not Charlie's I mean, one of the other postmodern offerings, a jazz-beat concoction of cartoon and real figures mixed. I watched it blankly. I can't remember a thing. I think I sat through three features, four. Then the theater was empty. Then it was full again. This time I knew what I was waiting for.

It began again, it begins, it goes on beginning.

The entire thing (first cycle, three fast cycles, slow-motion fifth cycle) takes only ten minutes. At the last slow dissolve of the girl in the rainforest, a young woman sitting just where I myself had often sat, a young woman sitting on the very boulder below which the bones were found, at that last interminable slow-cycle image, the sense of foreboding began to suffocate me (although I cannot tell why). It was the old sense of entering a burgled house, the wariness, poised at the brink of something you do not want to know. I wanted to close my eyes, I wanted to leave. I had a sense of dread about it. The figure could have been any young woman, any woman at all, a university student on a field trip or a local slut or a young mother whose toddlers play behind the ferns. The face was hidden in shadow and it could have been any face. People were always seeing themselves in Charlie's work, it was ridiculous really. I don't know what I was nervous about.

Just before the smudges of blackness spread to touch one another, in the last gleam of that high bony line of light, the camera came close to the girl and she looked up at the photographer and the light fell on her face.

Lucy, meet Lucy.

I could feel myself falling, a cloudiness swimming across my eyes.

My right hand (the one on the screen) was extended, gesturing, and from the tip of the index finger dangled a thin gold chain. The final close-up was of the pendant at the tip of the chain, not a pendant in the ordinary sense, but two small gold rings, earrings, each threaded with a tiny glass bead.

A black dizziness, like a sack over my head, descended.

When I came to in the dark room, when I came back to myself in that dark wood, I thought first of this: that the last time I had been at Cedar Creek Falls was long before I met Charlie, and long before I ever saw that thin gold chain which I had never held in my hand and never touched.

Was it a memory I then dredged up, or an invention, that vision of a small hiking party, tourists evidently, smiling Japanese businessmen with cameras, or maybe Chinese, how does one tell? Or here's another memory, or invention: two solitary wanderers, strangers, bump into each other near some falls. "Beautiful, isn't it?" the girl says. And the man says, "Yes. I grew up near here." And the girl says, "Really? So did I." And the man explains that he's been away for years, been away in New York or China or somewhere, but the place still haunts him.

At any rate, someone with a camera asks politely, "Do you mind?"

And the girl shrugs, "Feel free," not paying any particular attention.

And was that Charlie? Did we stare at each other idly, as polite strangers do, before we met? Or did Charlie simply clip the photograph from somewhere, a Qantas flight magazine, the *Geographic*? Did Gabriel give it to him? Did he pick it up in some secondhand shop full of other people's bric-a-brac? And which coincidence would be more strange?

Or is it just a piece of technical wizardry, a bit of cutting and splicing, the normal cinematic black magic? After all, Charlie had plenty of photographs of me, plenty of negative footage. I suppose, for someone like Charlie, inserting a moving figure into a different backdrop is nothing very remarkable.

Not that it matters. Because at the time he used it, when he made this particular collage, when it was first lying as a neatly labeled videotape in his workroom, we had still not yet met—though of course, of course, he could have added to it, changed it; I could have changed it: the observer brings images to the screen.

But I couldn't reassure myself, I felt afraid, I felt that all my bearings had gone haywire, I knew I was somewhere in the middle of a pitch-dark rainforest and all straight paths went in circles and ate their own tails and they all went down the plug-hole of the quarry or of Cedar Creek Falls.

I cannot start with that, I cannot start there.

I will start somewhere in the middle, in Sydney. I will start somewhere shortly after Charlie's return from New York, shortly after the first time I met him, and I will try, like any archivist or reader of entrails, to salvage the future and to predict the changeable past.

Six

A name, I think, tugs its owner in its wake as a string tugs a kite. That is why, when we overhear the name of someone we have not yet met, we may feel a curious shiver of premonition. That is why we pause, the wineglass an inch from our lips. It happens that there are people we have not yet met who are on their way toward us bearing gifts: chaos, perhaps; or desire, or transformation. It happens, sometimes, that their names reach us in advance, telegraphing upheaval the way stillness in stringybark scrub foretells dust storms; the way milfoil stalks thrown properly, in accordance with ancient rules, will trace a map of the future in the dust of a Sydney pub.

That was what Gabriel, overhearing stray words, had sensed. And before that, something had caused Charlie to stand stock still when he first heard Gabriel's name. It must be that random sounds move through the air by instinct, that they unerringly lodge in the niches where meaning will find them. Is that the explanation? I direct these questions at one of Charlie's grainy photographs of Cat, who continues to be her deeply silent enigmatic self.

It might be possible to adduce theories thrown up by the new mathematics. If turbulence, freeway collisions, and downswings in the market can all be shown to obey strange cluster compulsions, how can I discount an abstruse mathematical curve which might pluck four people out of Brisbane, scatter them, and pull them together again years later in Sydney? Attraction-repulsion-attraction, that would be the rule. They might be some sort of quadratic equation: Charlie and Cat and Catherine and Robinson Gray, Australia's golden boy, the Grammar School prefect, the man who became a judge and ascended into the Order of Australia.

What would that make Gabriel and me? Where would we fit in that theory? Scrap that. In any case, none of it really concerns *me*. It's not my story, though it's odd, is it not, and interesting, and revealing, the way the teller inserts herself into the tale, even when she's trying to avoid it. A funny thing happened on the way to the telling, but in truth I'm scarcely in the script at all. Marginal notation is my style. Notes from underground. (I imagine Charlie raising an eyebrow. *Art thou there again, old mole?* I imagine him saying.) So. Scrap mathematics. I lean toward the instinct to invest sound with meaning, because it wasn't enough that the four of them surfaced again in Sydney. It took Gabriel too. He was the catalyst, everyone came to believe that, and it even seems possible that I, quite inadvertently, had something to do with the way in which Gabriel became the ignition switch. The whole course of events, it seems to me, was nudged into motion the day Gabriel walked into Charlie's pub and ordered his beer and sat staring down the slope of Bayswater Road, where King's Cross begins to slide into Rushcutters Bay; though I suppose you could say it began before that. I suppose you could say it began with an erotic encounter at Cedar Creek Falls, or with a different sort of encounter at Brisbane's Shamrock Hotel and with a girl who ran away partly because of pain and partly because of the pull of that underground jazz which sounded like freedom to her, or perhaps she ran because of certain obscure fears she couldn't quite put her finger on, and you could say, I suppose, that it began with Gabriel looking for her and following her to Sydney. Or it might have begun with Charlie luring Gabriel to his pub. Or with Gabriel seeking out Charlie.

Where do interlocking circles begin?

Answer: at arbitrary points.

It all began, then, a day or so before Gabriel arrived in Charlie's pub, with two nameless students sitting at the bar.

"Gabriel's back," one said.

"Yeah? Couldn't hack Queensland, eh?"

"A few years planting pineapples, enough to drive anyone to drink."

"Pineapples? Heard it was sheep at Cunnamulla."

"Nah. Brisbane. Market gardening round Samford. Supposed to be doing law at Queensland Uni, but you know Gabriel, can't get him to lectures when there's action on the side. Took on the Queensland police is what I heard."

"So'd he hafta clear out of Brisbane, or what?"

"Dunno. Wouldn't surprise me. He's on the lookout for a job, so give us a shout if you hear about anything, okay?"

What was Charlie thinking as he stacked beer glasses in the dishwasher? He was surely exploring the concept of Gabriel. The name would have come to him as visual image, a man in white samite herding sheep at Cunnamulla, or great swooping moonshine wings folded over pineapple plants. Gabriel. What kind of a name was Gabriel for an Aussie kid? Charlie Fu Hsi Chang had a particular interest in names, and he was well aware that a name like Gabriel would be an affliction. A photograph composed itself in the lens of Charlie's mind: a young man is tapping draft beer from a keg in a pub. The young man has blond hair and long lashes and that kind of disturbing beauty which calls masculinity into question. Two great shafts of sunlight bounce off the mirror above the bar and rise from his shoulders like wings. The photograph is called *Gabriel*.

A different photograph composed itself. A young man in black jeans and sleeveless black muscle-shirt sweeps up slops and broken glass from the floor of a pub. The young man has an incongruously angelic face, but he wears a bike chain around his waist. On his upper right arm there is a tattoo of a foot crushing a serpent, and below it, the words HELL'S ANGEL. Behind the young man, sitting high on a bar stool, an old drunk reading the *Sun-Herald* has managed to set the paper alight with his cigarette. Flames swoop up and the angle of vision is such that burning newsprint wings spring from the shoulders of the young tattooed sweeper. The photograph is called *Hot News of Gabriel*.

Of course, I am interpreting backwards, from artifact to conception. Both of these photographs exist.

It came to Charlie, holding a beer glass up to the light to check for smears, that he needed an extra bartender. The awareness was brand new, blinding, but seemed to him urgent.

"This Gabriel," he said casually to the students. "If he's looking for a job send him here. I've got an opening."

And so Gabriel came, walking into a shaft of light, preoccupied. He accepted a beer and a bar stool from dumbstruck Charlie. "But what's really strange, Mr. Chang," he said, from the middle of some discussion inside his head, "the really strange thing is the way a name like that gets its hooks in. The way it sets up shop in your mind, bloody well takes over." He laughed, and shivered a little, and shook himself in a curious way, like a terrier. Charlie thought to himself that people who emerged from Queensland were forever embroiled in debates inside their own heads; it was the only safe place to argue in Brisbane. Charlie thought that a young man who looked like Gabriel might talk to himself all he wished, and perfect strangers would sit at his feet and listen. "Next thing, you find yourself certain that you know what she looks like," Gabriel said. "Next thing you're *watching* for her." He gulped down half his glass at one go. "It's got bloody claws, a name like that."

"A name like what?" Charlie was registering the way Gabriel's fingers drummed against the thick lens at the bottom of his glass. Something more than a name has got its claws in, he thought; something the name is pulling behind it, something Gabriel can feel along the tips of his nerves. There was sexual arousal, but also nervous excitement, maybe fear, maybe even dread, in the sweat on his palms. Yes, I believe Charlie detected all that. It was astonishing—to Charlie, at any rate, even after all those years, even after half of his lifetime spent on the kindergarten side of world history—it was astonishing what Australians would broadcast through the large-print magnifications of the bottoms of beer glasses.

Charlie said little, he saw everything, it was a lifelong habit.

Charlie read small print and invisible signs.

"Jesus, mate!" customers used to say, unnerved, after he'd translated their throw of the milfoil stalks, or the yarrow sticks, or three Australian coins thrown six times. "How'd you *know* that?"

If he'd said that their secrets were written all over them, that he read pages and pages of their past and inner lives before they even took the coins in hand, if he said that his knowledge was only startling because Australians are illiterate when it comes to a text that is not written down (the text of a life, for example; or the text of a disarming lie), if he said any of that, they'd get resentful. They'd turn nasty in that quick belligerent way Australians have. *Got tickets on yourself, haven't you, mate?* they'd challenge, and he'd see their knuckles turn white.

So he used to shrug and smile enigmatically. "Ancient Chinese secret," he'd say, which was what they wanted to hear. Which allowed them to laugh it off, to demystify, to make crude jokes. "Bloody Chink mumbo-jumbo," they'd grumble affectionately. "Ought to ship the whole bloody lot of you back. Where you from anyway, Charlie?"

"Brisbane," he'd say.

That was a good one, they loved that, they killed themselves laughing over that one. You even *sound* Australian, you bloody two-bob magician. You don't even have an accent, you little Chink cheat.

This is the measure of love in Australia, Charlie used to say. The blunt edge of insult. The blunter the blow, the greater the level of acceptance.

"No, but before that," they'd persist. "Before Brisbane."

"Hong Kong," he'd say. "Family of merchant princes. They sent me out to God's own country to go to school."

"Yeah? And you could never bear to leave again? Good on yer, Charlie."

"So yer people got rich from tin watches and plastic junk? Half their bloody luck."

"You blokes and the Japs are gonna have us all in your pockets if we don't look sharp, we got our eye on you, Charlie."

"Heard the one about Dad and Dave and the Chinaman, Charlie? See, the three of them kicked up their heels in King's Cross with three very well-stacked sheilas, and afterwards Dad says: 'Well, Dave, I may be getting on, but I'm not over the hill yet. Lulu and me, we did it three times last night. What about you?'

"An' Dave says: 'Well, Dad, I can't tell a lie. I reckon I was feelin' me oats last night, I reckon we managed six times.'

" 'An' how'd the little Chinaman do?' says Dad. 'He's look-ing mighty pleased with himself. How'd you do, mate?'

"An' the little Chinaman smiles from ear to ear. 'Velly velly nice,' he says. 'One hundred and twenty-six times.'

" *'What???'* says Dad. 'Now, hold your horses a minute. You count the same way we do?'

" 'Velly careful count,' says the Chinaman, smiling. And he makes his fist go up and down, up and down, like a piston, see? 'One-two, three-four, in-out, in-out, five-six, seven-eight, in-out . . .'

"You get it, Charlie?" they'd ask, falling over the bar in raucous laughter. "You get it, Charlie? You count the same way as us?"

Charlie couldn't keep count of the number of times he'd been told that joke, but he used to smile and say nothing and serve another round of drinks.

"So what do you think, Mr. Chang?" asked Gabriel, on that day when the chickens began to fly home to roost. He was res-tive. He slopped his Tooheys on the bar and puddled in the spill with an index finger. "I hear you have a bit of a gift. What do you read in my beer?"

"You're just back from Queensland," Charlie said.

Gabriel laughed. "No prizes for that one, Mr. Chang."

"Charlie."

"Pardon? Oh. Thanks. Tell me something half the world doesn't know."

"This name you bumped into is going to lead you a merry dance. You are looking for someone. She is going to bewitch you and lure you and lead you into the pit."

"Hell," Gabriel said, alarmed, and knocked over his glass, precisely because Charlie had told him something he already and instinctively knew. "Hell, Charlie, what kind of rubbish is that?" He brushed his soaked shirtfront with agitation. "I admit I'm looking for someone. Well, in a sense I'm looking for two peo-ple, and one reminds me of the other in some way. I was hoping it was her, of course. It's just the kind of name she'd choose."

"A whore's name?"

Gabriel frowned. About some things, he was quaintly old-fashioned in a way that bemused his peers. He could be posi-tively perverse in his refusal to face certain facts. "She tries to be, but she's not. She plays at it. She plays with names. She hides behind them. I heard this one last night in the quarry. That's where she'd go."

Ah, the quarry.

"You saw something horrible last night." Charlie mopped up the spill and refilled Gabriel's glass. "You'd like to forget it, but you can't."

"Come off it, Charlie. People see bloody horrible things all the time in the quarry, don't they? Doesn't seem to disturb anyone's sleep. It was just a striking name, that's all. And for some mad reason I got excited and I thought, it's *her* again."

Names have potency, this is ancient and unassailable knowledge. Charlie's name, for instance, his real name, was Fu Hsi, though no one had ever used it. Can you imagine how Fu Hsi would go down in Brisbane? You're Charlie Chink, the kids said, because they do that in Australian schools, bash the difference out. Deviation from the ordinary is not permitted here except as a source of amusement *(What'smatter, can't you take a bloody joke, mate?)*, bewilderment is no excuse, certainly not in frightened little boys encumbered with arcane social rituals and bafflements and bed-wettings and sheer *foreignness*, which is a terrible liability in Australia. So Fu Hsi began to become someone else, he began to become Charlie Chink who could always be a good sport and take a joke.

A name that goes underground, however, continues to have a life of its own.

"*Your* sleep is disturbed by the quarry," Charlie pointed out.

Gabriel laughed uneasily. "I was warned you were a bloody oracle, Charlie. Inscrutable, people say."

Inscrutable. That word used to get tossed around fairly often, in various tones and accents, for all strata and creeds and colors used to mix at Charlie's Place (well, not such a great range of colors, to be scrupulously accurate; for certain reasons, for certain—what shall I call them?—*historical* reasons, persons of darker persuasion were always underrepresented, at least on the ground floor where the pub and the restaurant were). Still. The mix was decidedly eclectic, for that was one of the dispensations attaching to outsiders, a general moratorium on the rules. Nothing *counted* at Charlie's establishment, you see. When I call it Charlie's establishment, I do not, of course, mean that he owned it. None of us knew who owned it, not even Charlie, who was paid from a numbered account. No doubt the profits flowed, as they usually do, to some consortium of entirely respectable people, pillars of society no doubt. Charlie merely managed the place for a nine-digit number. He had his own reasons, the reasons of a professional voyeur, which is what a photographer is when you get right down to it, and he had his own apartment and darkroom on the top floor. The floors between . . . ah well, they were out of his control. In style and substance and tone, however, the restaurant and the pub, both at street level, were decidedly Charlie's.

Government ministers came to Charlie's Place, and so did the people whose faces appeared in newspapers and on television, and so did the anti-establishment establishment. (You know who I mean. The university people and the arts bureaucrats and the literati: that distinguished group who look after culture and host conferences and play safe games of subversion in the literary journals and newspapers.)

Quite other sorts of people also came. For example, the girls from the Cross and from the quarry itself came (though to different floors, of course, to different floors; if there was any going up or down stairs, it was not something on which anyone used to comment). Carlton and South Melbourne would fly up for a visit, Vaucluse and Bellevue Hill and Balmain and the university crowd, in short, used to mix with riffraff, with people of dubious standing, with the vibrant, dangerous, highly charged, illegal visitors from underground.

When Charlie was proprietor of The Inferno (that was his name for the place, but hardly anyone else called it that; they usually called it Charlie's Place, though there were many who referred to it simply—not in polite company of course—as the Cat House), when Charlie was there I imagine many of you dreamed of visiting his fizzy enterprise in the combat zone between city and quarry. You always wanted to come, did you not? You imagined coming. (Ah, and many of you *did* come, many of you nodded to me as you handed me your coats; many of you talked to me, upstairs, as you took off your clothes. You won't remember my face, but I remember yours. Indeed, it's entirely possible that your face is on record in Charlie's archives.) The *idea* of a place like Charlie's has always lurked in the shadows of your mind, although by most standards the place was far from shadowy. It was, in the opinion of many, *the* place to be seen. Charlie's was the pub where significant discussions took place. And with respect to secret desires, with respect to those scenarios that you visualize hazily in unguarded libidinous moments but dare not put into words, with respect to those encounters you do not even permit into conscious thought, with respect to covert hungers that visit even the elect and are no respecters of age or gender or status, with respect to unplanned, spur-of-the-moment, absolutely innocuous visits to the upper floors, the arrangements were impeccably discreet.

Charlie was situated, you might say, in the first circle of the quarry. He occupied the border lands. He looked both ways.

The view from here is always interesting, Charlie used to say.

"It's true," Gabriel acknowledged quietly, surfacing from his own preoccupations. "I see horrible things every night and every day." He hunched forward and hugged himself as though the things he had seen were lodged painfully behind his ribs, a knot of angina. "I don't know what to do. I don't know if there's anything that would make any difference." Gabriel was like the little boy who kept his finger in the dike all night, a frail buffer against inundation.

"I heard that there's been more blasting," Charlie said casually, as he might have said that more rain was on the way. "The quarry's spreading. I hear there's more talk of the courts taking tougher measures."

Gabriel brushed this aside, distracted. "Has it ever happened to you? Have you ever been obsessed with something . . . or with someone . . ." He rolled up his eyes, mocking himself. "And everything you see or hear seems to have something to do with . . . You're always convincing yourself you've bumped into a clue, that the person you're looking for is actually watching you, waiting, luring you on. Of course it's crazy."

Charlie smiled and turned away. He composed a photograph inside his head: *Gabriel Comes with Clouds Descending*. The photograph shows the gloomy cellar beneath a pub, and between the cobwebs and small pyramidal mountains of kegs, in the darkness, are three huddled figures, Cat and Catherine and Charlie himself. Gabriel stands in the open cellar doors, at the top of steps, the sun and a cloudbank behind him. He seems to have wings but they are merely pure shafts of light.

This photo exists. It's the illusion of control, Charlie told me; a kind of sympathetic magic; the frail hope that you can benignly influence a course of events that is already under way.

He said neutrally: "What name did you hear?"

"It just seemed as though the name had something to do with her, that it meant something I already knew," Gabriel said thoughtfully. "Of course, in one sense the reason's obvious, but I don't mean for the obvious reason." He laughed, shrugging off portents. "What's *déjà vu* for sounds? It's like a dream you can't quite remember." He stretched upwards with both arms, a self-mocking dismissive gesture, so that Charlie saw the winged figure he'd imagined the day before. "Anyway, except for this premonition that came with it and won't go away, this is about nothing. I overheard a few words in a pub and it was a very strange conversation, that's all."

A sharp moment of knowledge came to Charlie, not the kind he invited. They arrived like little pieces of heartburn. Gabriel is too physically perfect for this world, he thought; too passionate, and too stupidly given over to goodwill. He will invite violation as surely as we did, Cat and Catherine and me.

He felt angry. He felt an urgency to hang a bike chain on Gabriel, to construct the Hell's Angel photograph by way of protective charm.

"There was a fight in a pub in Newtown," Gabriel said. "And a stabbing. There was a hell of a racket." He drifted inside the noise. "And then these bits of conversation reached me, I couldn't even tell who the speakers were. I heard one man say: 'They reckon she's a witch.' And then his mate said: 'She's got bloody claws, I can tell you that, a raging maniac when she's up and going.' And then the first one said: 'That's why they call her Cat.' "

The spigot on a keg of draft ale snapped upright and bit Charlie's hand. If Gabriel could have read the texts Charlie read, he would have known much from that. He might even have remembered why the name sent seismic tremors across his own synapses, why it gave off echoes (quite apart from the obvious ones; quite apart from the description of someone who could have been me). He might have smelled the name in his own blood, since it must have come down in his genes, it must have traveled round his veins before birth. Knowledge travels on unnoticed routes; it sprints along so much faster than thought; it leaps along images and sensation and unremembered memory the way a possum leaps from branch to branch.

Everything is foretold of course. The text of everything that is going to happen is written somewhere. That was what Charlie believed. My ancestor Fu Hsi, he used to say, first of the Five Emperors of the Third Millennium B.C., who taught his people how to split the wood of the t'ung tree and how to spin silk and how to read the history of what has not yet happened; my ancestor Fu Hsi, who invented the sixty-four hexagrams of the *I Ching*, the Book of Changes as my father called it, the Book of Secrets my mother said, my ancestor who spoke once of a young man at a distant border who would meet a shining messenger at the edge of a pit, my ancestor already saw, at the shimmering edge of his future dream, the building on Bayswater Road and Waratah Street from whose upper-floor windows both Sydney Harbour and the quarry could be seen. (Did Charlie believe a word of this? He did and he didn't, I think. I think the ancestors and their gnomic predictions were safety and consolation, both, like his hiding behind the lens of a camera and composing kaleidoscopic truth.) But when he heard the mention of Cat's name, he did feel that a die was cast. He believed that Gabriel had been sent.

And if it became true, what does that mean? Perhaps simply that Charlie made a choice at that point. Whatever is going to happen, will happen, he said. It is already known somewhere. I wait and I watch.

But is it true that the future is unalterable? Or can a watcher, a mere watcher, influence the course of events?

I have come to think so. Watchers, after all, make choices; they choose what to see. And certainly the course of events changes the watcher.

Of course, this is hindsight. Yet it seems to me that the body does instinctively recognize turbulence. I have read that the oscillation of butterfly wings in Brazil may set off storms in Texas. More colloquially, more domestically: a goanna moving its tail on a rock near Perth, by a long and escalating chain of air displacements, can unleash flooding in Queensland. Certainly, then, it is mathematically possible that the speaking of a name can cause cyclonic disturbance of a different and more dangerous kind. In a dizzy instant, Charlie saw—no, he *felt*—the unstable convergence of past and future, the storm warnings, the betrayals, the old and new deaths.

But it passed, of course. Such moments pass. We reel and then we steady ourselves. We rub the back of a clammy hand across our eyes. We forget what we saw, we convince ourselves we saw nothing. It is not a gift, it is a curse, to read ahead. Charlie was as human and lonely as the next magician. He told himself that he was talking to an extraordinary young man in a pub, nothing more.

Gabriel talked his way through glass after glass of Tooheys.

("They drink by reflex, Australians," Charlie said. "They have genetic immunity to toxins that would savage the livers of the foreign-born.")

Gabriel talked as people always will talk to a silent listener. (Silence, Charlie said, seduces.) With a kind of greedy languor, the talkers stretch themselves out in the voluptuous cushions of quietness—something priests and prostitutes, something therapists and interrogators, something bartenders know all too well—the burdened talkers settle in and colonize silence with their unburdenings.

Gabriel talked and talked and Charlie listened, both to what he said and what he didn't say.

The sages tell us, Charlie said, that when doubts about great matters arise, consult the tortoise shell and the milfoil stalks.

In his own way, he kept the records as meticulously and as creatively as his ancestor, Fu Hsi, recorded the cracks in the dermal plates of muddy reptiles and wrote down, in his Book of Secrets, the arcane translations of scattered stalks. Like Fu Hsi, he was also an interpreter of the gaps and the spaces. When it was necessary, he read between the cracks. He saw the negative print. He underexposed and overexposed as he saw fit.

"So," he said to Gabriel at last. "Would you like the job?"

SEVEN

So she reappeared to him first in the form of her name. Gabriel, angel of the annunciation, brought word of her, and her absence filled the pub and the restaurant and the stairwells and the waiting emptiness of Charlie's apartment. Absences were potent for Charlie.

If the potter takes clay, he said, to make a pitcher, its usefulness lies in the hollow where the clay is not. I am quoting Lao Tzu, he said.

There were absences that had never left Charlie, and he believed that his own absence would have clung to Cat, to all of them, like a second skin. He believed that Cat was fishing for him, that she was using her name as bait. He believed that just as twenty-five years in New York had done nothing to stop them all surfacing and resurfacing in dreams, in the same way they would *know*, they would in some sense be aware of his return. Cat and Catherine certainly would, though he was less certain about His Honor the judge. Much less certain. In fact, the more he thought about it, the more he realized that part of the thing that would not be dislodged (he did not name it in so many words; Charlie did not think in words exactly; words were visual objects for him, shapes and colors; he saw a cloudy black tumorous mass behind his own ribs which would translate roughly as "the thing that would not be dislodged"), the more he thought about this thing, the more he realized that part of it lay in the fact that it was all too likely Robinson Gray would remember nothing at all, not Charlie's name, not his face, not Catherine or Cat, nothing. Robinson Gray's eyes would be cloudless, untroubled, smiling, full of charm. But Cat and Catherine would sense his return; most certainly Cat would. Yes. She had sent her messenger.

(*Had* she sent her messenger to Charlie? Or had Charlie sent for the messenger? Or was someone else altogether leaving a trail of clues for Gabriel to follow, someone who finds it safer and less painful to avert her eyes from certain shadowy corners? Here is my dilemma: an intricate web existed, that much is definite; perhaps Charlie was spinning it as he went along, perhaps he was its still center. Only now, in his absence, do I sense the full dimensions of his power. Absence is potent, unanswerable questions are the ones that engage us, the silences are thick with story. All I can do is feel my way, advancing, retreating, positing theories, testing, rejecting, going in circles and always covering new ground. Everything I say is provisional. A hapless fly in Charlie's web, fleeing from memories of my own, I spin my webbed translation as I go.)

So a messenger came or was sent for.

At any rate, Charlie did not invent her annunciation in the pub (though since this is my record, my history, Charlie's thoughts curl up inside mine just as my ideas take shape from his photographs. His words flow into the shapes of my words just as the thought of Fu Hsi reaches us through the commentaries of the Duke of Kau, and through many subsequent scholars). It is written: the water that flows into the earthenware vessel takes on its form. So Charlie said. So he showed in a black-and-white photograph. And it is noted that Charlie Chang nursed a deep and abiding respect for annunciations, whatever he called them.

He was waiting for Cat herself to reappear.

After the last table was cleared and the last drunk shunted out of the bar, in the hours before dawn, Charlie went looking for manifestations. With Gabriel as guide, he set out for the pub where her name had appeared. He crossed the line. He sat with his camera in the bar of The Shaky Landing in the quarry's first circle, and watched and waited. Sometimes he took photographs, sometimes not, he let his eye decide.

✧✧✧

The quarry is far larger than appears on the map. Far larger. Nobody knows exactly where it begins or where it ends, most people have only hearsay and their fears and nightmares to guide them. Everyone knows certain details of course, the quarry brushes us like cobwebs in unused rooms, some of us descend into it and climb back out (and yet our memories remain very unclear, our memories are instinctively—*protectively*—fuzzy), some merely descend, everyone has felt glancing blows (panhandlings, muggings, fights, stabbings, sexual assaults, drug transactions, break-ins, the numerous small acts of arson, the blastings and tunnelings) but it is difficult to pin down facts.

In Sydney, it is said that the quarry began in the rift valley of the Redfern railway station, though some claim the Newtown station, when squatters (*the Mole People* as we began to say, *a permanent and willful underclass* as the newspapers intimated), when the Mole People began tunneling into the rock cliffs. Homes for the homeless, they chanted, chip-chipping through the back passages of the city. And the newspaper dirge, antiphonal, responded with a slow black tolling of headlines: honeycomb hovels, shit holes, rat traps, rabbit warrens, cankers, the deadly lace-trace of white ants, the underminers. That was the beginning.

Others date the quarry from the year when inner-city insurance became untenable, when burned-out buildings were boarded up, left to decay, left to squatters; when the squatters began digging in the burned-out shells, tunneling their way down beyond basements and into underground parking lots, occupying the zigzag layers of concrete, setting up camps, invading the subways and sewers.

But what does anyone know? Even underground, no one knows. I used to live there. We used to grope about on the underside of Sydney, we used to put our ears against rock, against concrete, against earth, we would hear the world. I have only black misshapen memories and Charlie's photographs and Gabriel's obsessions to guide me. Poor Gabriel, afflicted with the conviction that atonement must be made, that the futility of action does not absolve from the failure to act, alas poor Gabriel, he knew the quarry well. Sober and clear-eyed, he probably knew the quarry—in one sense, anyway—better than I ever did. I imagine them, Gabriel and Charlie, in the quarry's first circle.

Now let us descend into the blind world down there, began Virgil, deadly pale. I will be first, and thou second.

Let's go, Gabriel says. I'll go first and you stick close to me, Charlie.

In the bar in the quarry's first circle, noise inhabits Charlie, he breathes it in and out. Through the soles of his feet, through the nerves of his bar stool, through the skin on his face, he ingests the music of a heavy metal band which might conceivably launch earthquakes. Two men in black leather pass a rag doll of a woman back and forth. She is limp with dope. Charlie is strobe lights and sound waves. He watches himself being shredded into particles of colored glitter and reassembled on the opposite wall. He tastes amplifiers, drums, electric guitar, the quick slash of deals contested. Soon he may piss knives and sweat blood. He paws at the air in a vague distressed way, as a dog with its guts on the street might do, wanting to breathe, wanting to clear a little space in the fights, in the smog of noise. And a voice slips through the clearing.

"Shit, the way that cat moves."

Noise smashes and flows, and spumes around the words. Then another tiny lull, a bobbing phrase: "She'll be the death of him, she will." Do these splinters have anything to do with Cat? Unlikely. The mind gathers up what it wants to, it picks and chooses sounds as children choose shells on a beach.

But Charlie takes messages as they come. A photograph composes itself: a woman, sinuous as a cat, slinks along a bar on all fours. Her thighs are bloody. Louts surround her, catcalling. She turns her face back toward the camera, exposing a man's head in her tiger jaws. The photograph is entitled *Catcall*. It exists.

It is written, Charlie said, that the ruthless man, oblivious to what he has bred, will step on the tail of his own palace tiger and be devoured.

He leaves Gabriel and strikes out on his own. He pushes his way past the black-leather thugs, past their limp rag doll, past the door, past the boarded-up buildings. His nerves listen. He skirts the small craters and shanties of the Prince's Highway. A kid shoves someone who shoves back, a knife moves, and the kid teeters there for whole seconds before falling like a swallow. You'd think the little rifts and canyons sucked him down.

Behind Charlie's shoulder, someone leans out of the charred skeleton of a building and his nerves feel it, see it. There is another head inches from his. An absolute stillness hangs within the uproar like a bubble.

"Cat got your tongue, darling?" A feline voice, scarcely audible, comes slinking into Charlie's ear. The voice purrs, it tastes of syrup and hate. "Cop's like a piece of rotten meat," it says sweetly. "Smell one a mile off."

"I'm no cop," Charlie says without moving. "But I'm looking for someone."

A thin young woman (they are all dreadfully thin) leans over the blackened sill. "Who're you looking for, luv?"

"A woman named Cat."

"Fuck you, darling," the woman says in her honeyed whisper, leaning close. She spits in his face, then she withdraws behind the wall.

Behind the wall, there is nothingness. Behind the wall, an old construction site corkscrews dizzily downwards, stripmining its way, circle by circle, into hell. Behind this wall, behind the next, behind every burned-out shell of a building: a grand canyon of random blasting and burrowing by quarry squatters. Lights float about the crater like small moons. Just below the sill, Charlie can feel the struts of a ladder, he can feel it sway as the woman climbs down, he imagines her looking up, waiting for him, mocking him, daring him, lithe as a kitten, a gaunt siren. Not gaunt, he thinks. No, not exactly gaunt. Wiry, or feral, perhaps. He imagines reaching for the scruff of her neck as a tomcat might. He shivers and swings himself woodenly, deliberately, with a show of indifference, across the sill and onto the rungs.

Down, down. He passes rock ledges where people are still

swinging hammers and scraping with scrapers, savagely, mind-lessly, maybe they do it all night long, maybe they can't stop. The hammers fall one microsecond after the other, a jazz riff with syncopated words: *she'll be the death of me, Cat will, Cat will, Cat will, and the way, and the way she moves.*

There is order and disorder, both, he thinks, mesmerized. His eye speaks to him, he adjusts lens opening and shutter speed, he hooks his legs around the ladder to leave his arms free. He sees: *The Grid System of Chaos.* This photograph exists.

The photograph is heresy, but Charlie calibrates the spillage and run-off daily, in files and negatives and dreams. The quarry is leaking into the city, and the city is seeping quarrywards. Everyone knows this, but everyone denies it. The quarry is growing, imperceptibly, relentlessly, inch by inch. This is held to be inevitable, given the times, the nature of the times, the limited wars here and there, the worldwide recession, the un-employment, the migrant problem, the angers, but infiltration of the city proper is denied and the spreading is not a problem, not a problem at all, officially speaking. Officially, there is a policy of containment. Conditions with respect to the quarry, the government announces daily on national television, are sta-ble. The boundaries and demarcation points are clear, although they cannot be shown on a map. Between city and quarry, the division is absolute.

In one sense, this is true. Of course the funnels of the quarry, when compared to the spread of the city, are minuscule, a neg-ligible area, but it is feared that the separate vortices in the capital cities might now have serpentine underground links, illegal, un-traceable, and alarming. This is what is widely believed: that the quarry is not only chipping away at the walls of its cauldron, gnawing at the flanks of settled suburbs, the quarry is tunneling its way beneath the streets, there are miles and miles of intestines winding below the larger urban lots and landscaped gardens. Nothing can be done about this. Rumors fly: that the quarry tunnels have entered the subway system, that its feelers have merged with city sewers. As far from the quarry boundaries as Toorak and Vaucluse and Ascot, in those manicured suburbs where alarm systems blink their electronic eyes, people can hear a tap tap tapping at the undersides of their pillows at night. The sound is faint, like a parakeet pecking at soft wet wood, but the dreamers stir uneasily and thrash at their sheets and wake and lie waiting for dawn. It's nothing, they tell themselves resolutely, listening to the soft thump thump of their fears.

The concept of seepage is not countenanced by the honorable members of parliament, the directors of public welfare, the rulers of straight lines. *"Triage,"* they say earnestly, on the Prime Minister's behalf, "in such times as these, is a moral imperative. For the greater good, for the healthy growth of the body politic as an organic whole and a flourishing plant, a certain pruning is essential. The burning off of dead wood is required."

Sometimes one or another of them, someone with tousled hair and boyish charm, a judge perhaps, an officially sanctioned cultural figure, someone who doesn't rock boats unnecessarily, someone who can be counted on to want his oceanfront hideaway on the side, may pause in an informal game of rugby or Aussie Rules, reaching for a pass in a city park, drop-kicking the ball to his darling little sons and their mates. He may wipe his sweaty forehead with the sleeve of his guernsey and smile into the camera. "There is a tough rightness to our policy with respect to the quarry," he may say, "that can only be compared to the rightness of a good clean catch in footy."

(Sometimes I have tried to remember exactly when newspapers, when all of us, stopped referring to the sinkhole or the cesspit and fled into euphemism. The quarry, we began to say neutrally. The people from the quarry, we said. Or the Mole People, we said, of those who lived in the tunnels and subways. And when did *triage* first appear in political speeches? Was there once a time when people had to scurry to dictionaries and look it up, when they didn't kick the word around like a football at backyard picnics?

TRIAGE: a system of priorities designed to maximize the number of survivors in times of crisis and natural disaster.

Designed by whom? That is the interesting question, it seems to me. It seemed an interesting question to me very early. In high school, quite suddenly, on a railway platform in Brisbane one day, it seemed to me the only question worth asking.

Charlie made photographs of triage. For *triage*, he felt the fascination of a man for whom words are live and squirming. They were creatures that crawled into his brain, he could taste them, smell them. He wrote in light. Here's one of his words, black and white: the entire photograph swarms with ants. A magnified lens has been used, and the ants are a horrifying writhing war-ring mass. It is a dark photograph. There is an out-of-focus grayish blur from the top right-hand corner of the print, reach-ing diagonally toward the center, and only at that still center, within a small bubble of light, does the blur reveal itself as the fang of a snake. The elect, the handful of chosen ants, wait in the bubble of light. *Triage*, the photograph is called.)

Charlie photographs the swaying lanterns in the rift valley below a gutted building in Newtown: *The Descent into Sydney*.

He descends. Down, down, down, past the honeycombed pitface, how many caves per circle, how many bodies per cave, how many new tunnels per body if each has a hammer and a trowel and one little, two little, three little, four, five little, six sticks of quarry-made dynamite, seven sniffs of glue, eight of smack, nine hypodermics, ten tokes of dynamite crack?

The flares and the transistors and the steady percussive ham-mering mesmerize him. This is how they cope, he thinks. With this and the dope.

They choose this, the government ministers and the busi-nessmen and people from the university and the wise judges in their cascading wigs all say. They want it this way. Down there they are more like monkeys than like us. They are not at all like people who do not live in the quarry, they have chosen to be there, and for the good of those of us who do not so choose, *triage, triage, rhubarb rhubarb, triage*.

It is not altogether unpleasant, Charlie thinks, the pattern of hammers and lights, the rhythms which can be felt through the rock face. There is something hypnotic . . . perhaps he will stay for the night, perhaps he will take photographs later, perhaps the work . . . it is difficult to remember what work exactly, it is difficult to remember why he is . . . A shape, as of a cat slinking along a wall, passes across the rungs of the ladder, climbing up. It is that woman again, he thinks for no logical reason, the one who taunted me, the one who perhaps knows Cat. A hot flash of erotic hunger shakes him. On all fours at the edge of his rock shelf, he cranes his neck up into the glow cast by a flare and he thinks he can see the length of her smooth brown legs and the shadow where they meet. Then dizziness. He has to crawl back, he has to lean against the cliff face, he has to stare at the opposite wall of the pit.

Across from him, ladders bow under the weight of his watching. The fluid bodies of men and women and children are climbing the ladders, the long swaying dangerous ladders, hand-made, knotted imperfectly with rope. Which is the woman who taunted him? And which one is Cat?

An image of Cat forms in his mind, as he had first seen her when they were nine years old in Brisbane. She has the body of a tomboy, she moves with feral grace, she is a witch. He imagines the way she might be now: still ugly, still small and wiry, cheekbones high and gaunt, eyes set in deep smudged sockets, a forty-seven-year-old witch. He wants to find her.

His eye settles on a body climbing through a haze of flood-lights on the opposite face of the pit. How crowded those ladders are, how insanely long, how constant the jostling is. The woman who might be Cat enters an area of turbulence, there is a scuffle. Involuntarily, Charlie flings out a useless hand to save her. She falls as a cat falls, her body flaccid, and though the fall seems to take an inordinately long time, he watches with a lunatic hope that she will land as a cat lands, miraculously light on her feet, unharmed.

But this is no such catfall. This is a perfectly ordinary quarry fall, there are scores of them every day and more every night. Somewhere down there, a ledge or a ladder or the galvanized iron of a shanty roof or some dealer with a knife breaks the fall. There is a sick thud as of an overripe melon bursting, and the scream, which must have started when the fall began, doesn't reach Charlie till after he sees the blood splash into the lights.

He pushes his back against the rock, breathing raggedly. What if he should vomit? Head down between his knees, something watery and bitter in his mouth, he feels both feverish and clammy. The ladder fills him with dread.

He has to picture himself as a figure on videotape to be able to move. He has to visualize the top of the ladder as a narrative ending he can reach and rewind and rereach at any time. The risk of falling into a black void is real, the long arduous climbing away from the pit has always been real, but he needs to invent the image of Virgil (with Gabriel's face) reaching back to take his hand, he needs to invent the woman at the top of the ladder, Beatrice with her gleaming Cat eyes, beckoning, waiting.

So he reaches across the screen of his imagination and climbs. Cat watches. Gabriel waits. Charlie reads the signs. In a pub on Main Street in Newtown, Gabriel waits.

"Thought I'd lost you, mate," he says with relief, and they strike out on foot for King's Cross and Bayswater Road.

EIGHT

Set down this: a conversation had already lapped at Gabriel's edges years before. He had paddled in it inattentively, he was just a child, he certainly didn't remember that he'd heard it.

There are many things people don't know that they know.

Once, when I asked Charlie why he took photographs so constantly, so obsessively, why he collected *other* people's photographs, why he scavenged in secondhand shops and bought, by the shoe-box full, old cracked brown-and-cream records of other's people's pasts, he said: "So that I will see what I've seen."

Of the *Ch'ien* hexagram, he said, his ancestor Fu Hsi had this to say: *Within the earth, there is a mountain.* He smiled, apologetic. "I'm afraid Fu Hsi had a maddening and elliptical style." Charlie frequently spoke in the maddening elliptical manner of Fu Hsi. He spoke on rice paper in brush strokes that had to be laid down in a ritually specified way. The mountain, as Charlie saw it, was that intractable thing that was always blocking one's view. It was the thing that would not be dislodged. The mountain, according to Charlie, is an obstruction that we partly create, it is the thick solidified lava of the things we know but don't realize we know. Our task, if we want to clamber over or round the mountain, Charlie said, is to observe more sharply, to set everything down, to record the minutiae, to add to the documentation on premonition and coincidence and chance, to know what we know, so that we may inch ourselves toward that place from which everything will be seen and understood.

"That is why I take photographs," Charlie said.

"At least to know what we know: that would be a start," he said.

I think he was right.

Consider this recent item in the *Sydney Morning Herald*: a woman was assaulted and robbed late one afternoon on a side street in Darlinghurst. In these days when the quarry seems to dilate and distend itself like a jellyfish in the shallows, when it can pass as invisibly as a virus into the world of order, when the residents of Darlinghurst shelter themselves as from the plague behind high garden walls, no one saw the incident.

A black car pulls up (these things can only happen in the present tense, they go on and on happening, they never recede, they are always now), the rear door opens, a man leaps out, he holds a knife to the woman's throat. After that, confusion. Touching her bruises and cracked ribs, the woman conjectures: "I think I screamed, I think maybe I struggled, I think I wouldn't let go the strap of my purse, I seem to have been in the backseat of the car, but that can't be right." Pain like a hot poker is all she remembers, and gutter dust in her mouth, and herself as a comma of shock against the curb. As the car drives off, she stares after it dully. Why does no one come running?

"It happened so fast," she tells the police from a hospital bed. "I never saw the driver at all." She seems to have a sharp vision of the cracks in the leather of the backseat, though this can't be right. Of the backseat assailant, however, she recalls with eerie clarity the color of his eyes, the brown spiky hair sprouting above his forehead, the freckles, the blister on his lip, the dark hair on his arms, a scar on the third finger of his right hand, the mole at his wrist, and the fact that the knife was a large kitchen knife, the kind used for cubing steak or peeling and chopping pumpkin. Its blade was mottled and old. She remembers having a sharp memory of her grandmother making beef stew and of a long conversation in the kitchen about one of her uncles.

And what about the number plate of the car? the police ask.

The woman is embarrassed and furious with herself. "I must have stared at it as the car drove away," she says, frustrated. She remembers what her grandmother was saying about her uncle, but not the number of the car.

A police hypnotist is engaged and his lullaby voice cradles her, seduces her, leads her back down the velvet shaft of time to where she lies huddled on the curb. Can you see the number plate on the car? the hypnotist asks. Yes, she says in a sleeper's voice. Read the numbers, the hypnotist commands. And she does. Now you are struggling with your attacker again, the hypnotist says. The woman jackknifes into a self-protective curve, she throws her hands up in front of her face. The man with the knife cannot harm you, I will not let him harm you, the hypnotist says. Now tell me, can you see the driver of the car? I am watching the man with the knife, the woman says, but the driver is in the corner of my eye. Describe the driver, the hypnotist says. Uhh, the woman cries, doubling up again, her hands over her face. He is too close to see, she says. What is the driver doing? the hypnotist asks. He is hurting me, the woman sobs. We are in the backseat, he is hurting me. I do not permit him to hurt you, he cannot hurt you, the hypnotist says. Describe the driver, he insists. She describes the driver in detail.

Let us suppose, however, that there had been no hypnosis. Remember: the woman has told the police that she never saw the driver at all. She is quite certain of this. Let us suppose, however, that the driver of the car had entered her hospital room as a medical orderly. Would she not have recoiled? Would she not have felt a violent jolt, an apparently unaccountable and irrational spasm of panic? She might tell herself: I've never seen this man before in my life; but her body would retain the knowledge of harm.

Charlie, an intelligence gatherer himself, a kind of interrogator, a man who had been on both sides of harm, knew that this sort of thing could happen. He knew that it happened all the time. He knew that censors, both hapless and cunning, guard all the doorways of memory.

On a different night altogether from the night of the childhood conversation he didn't remember, on a night shortly after he began to work for Charlie, Gabriel was serving at the bar of Charlie's Inferno when the judge arrived.

I was working, so it must have been a Tuesday or a Wednesday or possibly a Thursday, those were the nights I worked downstairs. Weekends, well, that was upstairs, that was heavy traffic time.

It was a Wednesday, I think.

Gabriel was already in some distress, I remember that. There had been words between us, between Gabriel and me, all the more distressing for their quietness. Anyway, I was aloof and he was upset.

And then the judge arrived.

"My regular table, Charlie?" the judge asked, and I remember how Gabriel twisted round rather fast from a shelf of spirits at the sound of the voice. I remember that the judge glanced idly, as one does, in the direction of the movement and that the judge's hand, which lay lightly on the sleeve of the coat he was handing to Charlie, then registered something: the fingers clenched themselves into the palm, and four cords stood up like guy ropes across the back of the judge's hand. Then the fingers uncurled and splayed themselves, stretching, and then they relaxed.

"Gabriel." The judge's tone, as always, was cordial and measured. There was a nod of polite but restrained acknowledgment in Gabriel's direction, the kind that people with power give to underlings. There was a smile. To me it seemed that the smile implied not only distance and the habit of easy courtesy, but also a warning. Or perhaps I thought so because of the tone of that "Gabriel," the civil finality of it, the way it made clear that a passing comment on any matters of shared knowledge was not to be thought of.

Although we had met before, in quite other circumstances, the judge and I, he did not seem to be aware of me at all. He turned back to Charlie. "My wife's coming separately. And our other guests."

"They're here already, Your Honor," Charlie said, and the way he said it fascinated me, the way the voice seemed like a thing apart from Charlie, a synthetic voice, the voice of a robot, a voice acting the part of a voice.

And then the judge moved on quickly—unnecessarily quickly, I thought—through the small lush atrium corridor, to the restaurant.

Charlie was watching Gabriel.

"What was that all about?" he asked.

"Nothing," Gabriel said.

Inscrutability is, in fact, a tactical skill, a habit of survival. Charlie had acquired it in childhood. I mastered it quickly, naturally, given the nature of my profession; I mean, once I had embarked on my calling. Gabriel being someone who found truth puzzling, sometimes even painful, but not yet dangerous, was just a learner. Although he tried valiantly to hide it, you could tell he was rattled. Through practice, one can experience shock like a slow wave of sleeping medication; one can delay one's reaction for hours or days, even years. I went on making careful notations in the reservations ledger, watching Gabriel and Charlie. After what must have been at least a full minute, Charlie said casually: "You know the judge?"

"Mnh," Gabriel grunted noncommittally, moving glasses around.

Minutes passed. Charlie disappeared through the swing doors into the kitchen. Gabriel mixed two Bloody Marys, placed them on a tray, and took them to the two women at one end of the bar. Charlie came back from the kitchen.

"Do you?" Gabriel asked.

"Do I what?" Possible elided verbs slid through Charlie's mind like stops on a lottery wheel.

"Know him."

Of all the possible moments, the one that came back to Charlie with a sick thump (so I choose to think now, from this distance, from my vantage point) was the two of them in school uniforms (himself and the judge) going into Chang's Grocers and Greengrocers on Newmarket Road in Brisbane, and there was Cat, as well as Charlie's own parents, behind the counter. But it could as easily have been a picnic at Cedar Creek Falls that he saw, or the railway cutting, how would I know? Any splinter had a dangerous edge.

Charlie pulled down a shutter. "The judge eats here often," he shrugged.

Gabriel tapped off two beers for the restaurant and held them out toward Charlie. He smiled. "Why don't you read the judge's tea leaves, Charlie?"

Charlie said nothing. He was watching Gabriel's fingers against the beer glasses, and I was watching Charlie watching Gabriel.

His table for eight was the table Judge Robinson Gray always reserved. No doubt his preference stemmed from the habits of a legal mind, from that scrupulous attention to fine points which a judge must cultivate, for he had given standing instructions about many aesthetic details and about placement of the table at the center of the glass-canopied courtyard. At first this surprised us. Most diners want privacy, intimacy, the romantic, all of which were available off the courtyard, in the fenced enclaves with their glimpses of Rushcutters Bay. Some patrons, however, do not mind being observed.

At times His Honor had requested, in his charming way, that an earthenware pot be shifted a little. Its waxy trail of orchids, perhaps, was obscuring another diner's view; or possibly the showy clusters of bougainvillea were a bother. His Honor would lightly touch the arm of a young waitress who was passing, he would put his hand on her wrist, she would feel constrained to bend close and listen to his whispered request, so that, with their foreheads almost touching, for a moment the two would seem to be lovers. He might even lift the fall of her hair from her cheek and hold it gently aside in a manner both suggestive and . . . well, judicious, quaintly formal, certainly irreproachable, in order to murmur his order privately. Singled out in this way, drawn into the aura of his conferring of special notice, the waitress would glow a little and blush. Watching, you had the sudden certainty that it had never crossed the mind of Judge Robinson Gray, not even fleetingly, not even once in his life, that a request of his would not be instantly carried out. You had the certainty, in fact, that being chosen to cater to the judge's whim was—in the judge's own mind—a distinction of the highest order.

"Of course, Your Honor," the waitress would say. "It's no trouble at all." And the orchids would be moved.

There would always, then, be someone across the courtyard, some woman whose view was now unobstructed by translucent commotions of mauve and pink, who might glance at the judge and away. By chance, by sheer coincidence, the judge would become aware of her at the very moment she glanced back again, that moment when she half turned to look vaguely across the room at something on the opposite wall. Ah, the soft accidental collision of their meeting eyes. I used to think of light hitting pillows of dark water. With such surprise, such pleasure, the judge would raise his glass. The woman would smile, flattered and a little embarrassed, and lower her gaze, though the judge knew she would steal glances all evening. He knew too that the little waitress who moved the orchids would be solicitous to gratifying extremes. Every time she reappeared, he bestowed on her the warmth of his artless and boyish smile. It reminded me of the smile of an adored child who knows a fond circle of grown-ups is always watching. It was the smile of a tribute collector. Render unto Caesar, it said silkily, the things that are Caesar's. It was the smile of someone you expected to see pausing in a game of football somewhere, brushing away sweat with the sleeve of his guernsey and saying to the camera: "In these times of *triage*, our response to the quarry is both a sad necessity and a moral imperative."

People like myself could write lengthy commentaries on smiles like the judge's smile, but then people like myself can't be bothered. What would be the point? People like Charlie, however, will save photographs of a man with just such a smile, a man pausing in a game of football somewhere, winningly, to murmur *triage, triage* to the eye of TV. People like Charlie can show you a black-and-white photograph of a smile like the judge's smile and make you shiver.

The knowledge that comes from meticulous and ceaseless observation is a kind of power, is it not? Shadow power. And yet it was not power that interested Charlie. The thing that would not be dislodged was like a riddle without a solution that held a knife to his throat; your answer or your life, it demanded. It gave no quarter; the fact that there *was* no answer meant nothing to it.

Here is a photograph of a man studying an X-ray photograph with a magnifying glass; the X-ray shows a cumulus mass of tumor behind a ribcage; within the magnified circle of the glass, two ribs cross a hump of blackness. The photograph is called, enigmatically, *Obstruction: Railway Line.*

Here is another photograph of a man with a magnifying glass studying the photograph called *Obstruction: Railway Line.* This one is called, in the words of the *Chi'en* hexagram, *Within the Earth there is a Mountain.* The mountain grew behind Charlie's ribs, and he lived inside it, he breathed it, he could feel its shifts and momentums, it was a dense mass that had pulled him back across twenty-five years. He had to find out what he knew.

"... the same rubrics," the judge was saying to Catherine Reed, leaning toward her, "the same rubrics. The patterns came over with the First Fleet, maybe they imprinted themselves, maybe they slid into the genes, I don't just mean here. Take the way the czars turned into Supreme Soviet Commanders, or the Shah of Persia into Khomeini. Increasingly, I find myself absorbed by this, by the way all cultures return to their ancient grooves, to their own inherited taxonomies. ..."

What interested Charlie was the intimate relationship between Robinson Gray and his image. He, the judge, knew exactly where it was at all times, he kept a discreet eye on it in various mirrors. *I have a little shadow that goes in and out with me. ...* He liked the way it sounded, its rehearsed sonorities. He communed with it frequently. Furtively. It was some sort of guarantee. When the potted orchids were moved, he was able to salute the woman at the other side of the courtyard and simultaneously drink a discreet toast to himself in the mirror above a sideboard. He collected tribute and the benediction of his own approving smile.

See him now, on the night I am conjuring up, see him leaning closer toward Catherine Reed. Having placed her at his right (he, of course, is at the head of the table), observe the subtle diagrammatic way he illustrates his point, marshaling cutlery on the tablecloth, moving a saucer, accidentally bringing forearms into contact. Observe the way he is excited, subtly goaded, by Ms. Reed's casual withdrawal of her arm and her politely interested lack of interest. Catherine does that to people.

"... history as palimpsest," the judge is explaining. "The

penal colony, you could say, was our seedbed, the mulch of all that which is distinctively Australian."

Catherine reaches for the oysters. Beverley someone, from across the table, remarks: "Tom says you can't grow peaches on the North Shore anymore, it's all mangoes and lychees. The climate's shifting, he says."

"Ah . . . yes." The judge is only momentarily thrown off course. "The climate *is* shifting. But it's almost like a geographical trace laid down, isn't it? The first felons, the quarry, it's as though Sydney Cove . . . I mean, you look at those convict striations on the rock of The Cut and it's like a prophecy. And we can't underestimate the contribution of the First Settlement to the kind of people we are. Thank you, yes I will." He accepts a smoked oyster. "Moral causality, a sharpened instinct for what it takes to survive, that's part of it. And what I like to refer to as *psychomachia*, our own distinctive and nationalist form of *psychomachia*, that abiding conflict in our cultural soul, the convict and the law enforcer still locked in combat. When I go back over my articles and constitutional essays and the pieces I have written for newspapers and academic journals, I'm struck by this most of all, by this almost lyrical *leitmotif* throughout my work."

A man rises from his words, said Fu Hsi, as mist rises from a marsh. Or so Charlie claimed. The discernment and translation of mists was not something Charlie chose, it was not something he could prevent, it was something that trailed along with his name, his real name, like the tail of a kite. The mists rose and settled onto his photographs. And so—it was plain to Charlie in the eddies above the judge's words—he knew unexpectedly how it would be with Robinson Gray alone in his bathroom. He knew how, before and after his shower, the judge would stand in front of the full-length mirror, how he would turn a little, first to one side, then to the other, how he would move away and glance back over his shoulder, trying to surprise himself, trying to get a candid view of himself as others saw him. Charlie knew how, in the spirit of radical and earnest inquiry, the judge would strive to be that passing casual stranger, that objective eye, and how he would search for the perfectly apposite word to describe the body he (as the passing stranger) could see in the mirror. *Eumorphous?* he would hazard. No. Eumorphous might capture the earthy, the rugged, the weekend footballer quality, the purely bodily, but not . . . *Insouciant?* Possibly. Insouciant would intimate the boyish Pan-like nature, the Papageno-like innocence of the . . . but not that dimension of torment . . . not that rarefied malaise which must always surround the moral being, must always keep him . . .

Promethean?

The search would go on until the judge's wife, a highly intellectual woman but a little insensitive perhaps, a little impatient, not sufficiently attuned to the philosophical and metaphysical . . . a little philistine, in truth, in a particular kind of intellectual way . . . until she rapped on the bathroom door.

Oh, were these Charlie's words? Let me be scrupulously honest. Whatever Charlie divined, and Charlie's powers of divination were unnerving, he kept between himself and his camera. But I myself was not without experience in decoding hot air.

I knew, for example, how it would be with Robinson Gray and a woman (and here, I happen to have more substantial information), I knew how he would rise to smooth down the bed covers, or move to pick up the clothes and fold them on a chair, or how he would cross to the window where the light would gild him, how he would do these things with studied unself-consciousness, absorbed and abstracted, granting to the woman on the bed the pleasure of observing him from multiple points of view.

"Pardon?" he would say to her, startled. "Oh, sorry, I thought you said something." And carelessly: "I still play football, you know."

"Are you joining us for the football tomorrow, Catherine?" Roslyn Gray asks, apparently benign. "A motley crew of Sydney Grammar Old Boys (with a few Brisbanites thrown in) versus a ragtag team from Sydney Uni. My loyalties are divided." She raises her glass in wry salute and from the other end of the table the judge makes a modest gesture of repudiation. Small ritual sighs scuffle about, token commiseration, token envy. Roslyn accepts them graciously. She accepts them as legal tender. They are diligent bookkeepers, she and the judge. They know their due. "Robbie's playing," she says disarmingly. "He keeps in frightfully good nick. He puts me to shame." She takes a sip of wine. "No, really," she says, as though someone has strenuously demurred. She is given to letting slip that she was trained as a classical dancer, "a frivolity of my pre-feminist youth."

Roslyn's cheekbones and causes are immaculate, and she is intimate with great minds. "Irigaray," she will murmur over the soup. "As Foucault says," she will remind. She has a particular intimacy with things French. She presides over a small cultural circle and deservedly so. Roslyn is smiling, passing the lemongrass sauce down the table to Catherine. "It's a benefit game," she explains. It goes without saying (although Roslyn does in fact say it at some length) that the cause is important. "I hope we can count on you, Catherine." She frowns as Catherine, absorbed in the task of spooning lemongrass sauce on fish, gives no sign of response. "Catherine?" she repeats, a trifly sharply.

"Pardon?" Catherine says, blinking. "Oh, I'm sorry, I wasn't paying attention."

Is this happening now or was it a long time ago? I have difficulty with that question, you see. I do not find it a simple question. I find that the past lies in wait, just ahead, around every corner. "You need a particular blinkered angle of vision," Charlie said, "in order to sustain belief in linear time." Linear time, he said, was a filmmaker's gimmick, an *inferior* filmmaker's gimmick, and before that a gimmick of nineteenth-century novelists. It was a thoroughly Western superstition. It seems that Fu Hsi had words on the subject: *When the sun goes, the moon comes; and when the moon goes, the sun comes; of waxing and waning there is no beginning and no end.* So Charlie said. And now there is something behind my ribs (an infection I picked up from Charlie), something which won't be dislodged. It induces giddiness, it tells me time is a Möbius strip and we all go round and round the mulberry bush, and I find that on the night under observation, the night which meant nothing in particular to me when I carried plates back and forth, I find that on that night, Roslyn Gray is still passing the lemongrass sauce, and signaling to me and indicating: "Another bottle, if you wouldn't mind, Miss."

Particularities do not impede the moral flood of Roslyn's political commitment to women. "Miss," she says to me, as to a chair politely treated. "I wonder if you wouldn't mind keeping a sharper eye on the table and removing the dinner plates."

Roslyn Gray's mind, of course, is preoccupied with loftier

matters than waitresses and the removal of plates. She is writing a revisionist biography of Christina Stead, deconstructing Stead's unseemly passions, showing where a certain strain in the writing of Australian women began to go awry.

"Miss," she says to me again, for alas I have gone daydreaming, wandering into a story by Katherine Anne Porter, a woman almost certainly not politically correct. I am afraid, though I cannot imagine why, that certain lines of hers have floated to the surface of my mind and interfered with the removal of plates, certain memories of Braggioni, that "good revolutionary," that Braggioni who had *the malice, the cleverness, the wickedness, the sharpness of wit, the hardness of heart, stipulated for loving the world profitably.*

"Excuse me, Miss," Roslyn says with increased aspersion, "I wonder if you could manage to be a little quicker off the mark. . . ."

There are, of course, other members of this cast, other guests at Robinson and Roslyn Gray's table, but as they are merely fashionable and powerful in the usual uninteresting ways, I cannot remember them. I am watching Charlie, invisible behind the polite costume of the *maître d'*. There is a white linen cloth, starched and folded, over his forearm. I am watching the way he pours wine for Catherine Reed.

You would never know, to look at Catherine, Charlie thinks, that the muddy paths around Cedar Creek Falls retained fossil imprints of their childhoods. He has photographs to prove it. He has a photograph of two boulders interrupting the falls; on the boulders are delicate traces of children's bodies, thin outlines, maps of their veins.

What went through Catherine's mind when she looked at Charlie? Was there a third person, always absent, who walked beside her? What did she see when she looked at Robinson Gray?

You would not guess at any answers to these questions from watching Catherine return the sauceboat to Roslyn Gray. "No," Catherine apologizes. "I'm afraid I can't make it. I'll be working."

"Ahh." Roslyn sighs meditatively. She concentrates on the

sauce and a flake of barramundi. "Mr. Chang, your chef is excelling himself." Roslyn can behold infinity in a grain of freshly ground coriander or in well-prepared fish. This is something she is able to do in a Blakean sense, not at all incompatible with Irigaray. "Wouldn't you say, Catherine, that Mr. Chang does the best barramundi in Sydney?"

Beverley from across the table, beckoning me with her finger, interrupts. "Another dish of black olives? I wonder if you wouldn't mind?" She has that curious rising inflection of so many Australian women (though not of the ones who move in the upstairs rooms), an inflection that renders all statements tentative.

Roslyn frowns. Roslyn does not approve of female tentativeness, and feels it incumbent upon herself to instruct when instruction is due. "Beverley," she says, smiling. She offers Beverley many significant names and articles. "Perhaps that sounds puritanical and pompous," she says sweetly, pausing, giving the murmurs of denial time to settle. "But I do think this disturbing lack of self-confidence is perpetuated by some of our writers. I fear this tendency set in with Christina Stead. I really cannot approve of women who think that noting down the events of their own lives without any understanding of recent theoretical work on language"—this, I'm afraid, is the way Roslyn talks, the way she writes—"without any understanding of theoretical work, especially that of the French, I cannot approve, she says, I cannot *rhubarb rhubarb rhubarb*, don't you agree?"

A different sort of smile, which she is at pains to conceal, flickers on Catherine's face. She half glances upwards so that the smile reaches Charlie who waits on the other side of the table, an attendant lord. Does her smile indicate discreet shared mirth, or merely politeness? She gives no indication of knowing Charlie beyond the context of this moment, no suggestion of having played in long grass with him, of having witnessed things best forgotten.

Does she remember? He is never quite sure. He knows it is impossible, as well as essential, to forget. He knows it is entirely likely that she doesn't know she knows him. Sometimes, with his back to her, watching her in a mirror over a sideboard, he thinks he catches her studying him with what could be genuine puzzlement. But then too he has observed how she disconcerts other guests, acquaintances and colleagues of hers, from time to time. "Oh," she will say with a vague smile. "I don't believe we've met before, have we?" And then, embarrassed, "Oh dear, have we? Forgive me." Some people make allowances, some do not.

"I was between wives at the time," Judge Robinson Gray is saying with a self-deprecating smile. He moves crumbs across the damask surface with his fingertips, illustrating something, deploying facts, and manages once again to brush Catherine's hand. How interesting it is, the way Catherine flinches, that momentary thing. Her face is politely expressionless. Robinson Gray notes the flinching, he was not elevated to the bench without cause, there is a moment when his fingers hesitate as though losing their way before they begin methodically reassembling the crumbs. "I've had rather bad luck with wives," he says disarmingly to the table at large, expecting absolution, implying that when all is said and done he is preoccupied with rather larger issues than the bric-à-brac of marital accord. "Until now, that is," he adds smoothly, raising his glass. Roslyn gives him the smile of those who share a private joke.

Into a slight strain that seems to be felt, not by the hosts, but among the guests at the table, someone says lightly: "Third time lucky."

The judge murmurs to Catherine: "It was a time of personal turmoil, when the appointment was made." He makes a neat pathway through the crumbs with the blade of a knife. "A painful time."

Roslyn says comfortably: "Painful for both of us, really. She just couldn't cope, I'm afraid." She shakes her head, marveling, and takes a thoughtful sip of wine. "The second, that is. Of course, we have no contact at all with the first."

Catherine passes the judge the salad bowl just as Beverley, determined to lighten the mood, chips in brightly: "By the way, what's your son doing these days, Robinson? I heard he was back from Queensland."

"Ah yes?" The judge concentrates all his attention on the salad bowl, but it is Catherine whom Charlie watches, and I am watching Charlie. Charlie is unreadable, but Catherine forgets to let go of the wooden bowl.

"He drifts," Roslyn says. "His mother's in Brisbane, that's

Robbie's first, you know, and she dominates him. The oldest battleground." She spreads her fingers in bemusement at the things certain women will still resort to. "We don't see much of him. He gives us a wide berth, I'm afraid." One does not have the feeling that this devastates Roslyn Gray. "It's hard on Robbie," she says.

Catherine and the judge are still holding the salad bowl between them. Beverley laughs. "Are you two meditating on artichoke hearts, or what?"

As though a pause button has been released, Catherine relinquishes the salad and I have the curious sense that the weight of the bowl alarms the judge. He sets it down, forgetting to help himself to lettuce, and is intent on making small levees in a continent of crumbs with his knifeblade. "Children go their own way," he says.

Catherine, surprising everyone, muses without inflection: "Why is that, I wonder?"

On a zigzag route, the judge sees himself framed by ferns in the mirror above a sideboard, an elegant gentleman in the prime of life, approaching fifty to be precise, a man of private sorrows and public distinction, a man of whom biographies will surely speak well, a man for whom his difficult son will surely one day write an anguished posthumous lament. Something restorative comes to him from these reflections. He says to Catherine in an easy, wry, avuncular tone: "Thus the world turns."

Catherine smiles, and Charlie waits, fascinated. Catherine's smile is that of the Brisbane child, it is the smile she used to give long ago when she felt cornered, when she slipped in the knife. Charlie feels prickles along the back of his neck, he watches for the blade. "I thought I saw your son when I came in," she says. "Is he bartending here?"

Robinson Gray makes an ambiguous gesture, but Roslyn is clearly taken by surprise. Kitchenhands and waiters silently appear to sweep up splintered glass and spilled wine, people push back chairs in consternation. Movement, anyway, much movement, but Charlie is extraordinarily still at its center. His stillness is a measure of amazement. How mysterious chance is, he thinks. How unnerving the apparent coincidence is.

(Is that what he thought? Or did he think: *Now it begins.* Sometimes I choose the former, sometimes not.)

Perhaps something inappropriate has been said at the restaurant table, some fine line crossed, by Roslyn perhaps or by someone else; perhaps the judge or one of his guests, with the usual private school aplomb, is rescuing the table from awkwardness. If I was aware of Robinson Gray's reaction, or of Roslyn's, it is part of that mountain, the things I don't know I know. The dinner party must have wandered on to dessert and coffee, but the tide has moved me, I'm in the bar with a tray, I'm aware of Gabriel at the bar as the kind of disturbance one gets on a television screen in a storm, people are signing chits, collecting jackets, people are discreetly disappearing into the Ladies, the Gents, except for Catherine whom I see in the mirror over the bar, still alone at the table.

She is still there when everyone else has left. She is still there when Charlie, as stranger, as deferential *maître d'*, goes to offer another round of liqueur.

She turns to him very slowly. She stands as a sleepwalker stands. She stares at him as though he is part of a dream that is slithering rapidly out of reach. She says in a flat drugged voice: "Why did you come back, Mr. Chang?"

Dizziness, yearning, grief, memory, what a dangerous mix, Charlie is swaying, he's losing his bearings, here's yesterday . . .

"Catherine," he says.

"Where have you been?"

"Away."

She nods and nods.

"Can I take you home?" he asks.

"Charlie," she says, very faintly, as though she is at one end of an infinitely long corridor but does not really expect the person at the other end of it to hear her. She seems to be in a trance.

It could be minutes or hours before Charlie reaches to touch her cheek momentarily, then drops his hand. "Catherine?" he says again.

"Yes?"

"May I take you home?"

She considers this, her eyes unfocused. "No," she sighs. "I don't think that would help." She extends her hand, formal, and shakes his. "Good night, Mr. Chang." And then, with a flicker of satirical life: "You do the best barramundi in Sydney."

NINE

Upstairs the women come and go, speaking of nothing—or nothing of consequence—and never sleeping before five in the morning. Until then there is no time for sleep, and no beds for it either, for the landlord has intimated that an idle bed is not a luxury he can afford, and that idlers will swiftly lose lodging privileges and will have to forgo their lavish entitlement to the five entire hours of sleep—unproductive hours, from the landlord's point of view—which they get for a pittance, for a mere thirty dollars per night, from dawn right through the hot drugged headachy Sydney mornings till 10 A.M. Disseminated along mysterious channels, this rule is common knowledge. Straight from the mouth of the nine-digit number himself, the girls will say if pressed (and men do press them, in many ways, and for many reasons), but no amount of foraging can finger a name behind the number.

Upstairs, where the men come and go, half-hour by half-hour, hour by hour, averting eyes at the turning of the stair when they pass one another, upstairs it is understood that sleeping, buying enough hours, enough bedtime, to *sleep*, is an inordinate extravagance for which they must pay dearly. Some do. There is never any telling what they will want. It is not at all what you think. Sex is not what you think, not at all.

Consider, for example, the two gentlemen who visit Lucy on the first Thursday of every month. Order is important to them, and schedules, and the quiet midweek discretion. They are orderly men, and they are certainly men of absolute discretion. She calls them the peanut-butter-and-raspberry-jam twins, but they are not, in fact, twins. They are not related at all, though they went to school together (a private school for the sons of graziers, a boarding school) and they went to university together, and studied law together, and were received at the bar together. There they parted company and now practice with different firms, not infrequently facing each other on opposite sides of a courtroom case. They are married to quite different women, and between them they have five children, whose pictures they carry proudly in their wallets. Lucy knows this because in the latter stages of each monthly visit (they are affluent and extravagant young men, and pay for much of the night), in the latter stages, when she has to discipline them, they have shown her the photographs and have often wept over them and have become, if the truth be told, a trifle maudlin.

Knowledge is a kind of power, and sometimes Lucy wonders if it is shadow potency to which she is addicted. No, not addicted exactly, but she does find it endlessly seductive simply to discover what will be required. She is a scholarly observer, an expert of sorts, on the lonelier intimacies. She is dumbfounded, grieved, humbled, moved, by how *trusting* the men are, how vulnerable, how . . . well, the extent to which they will humiliate themselves. And sometimes she ponders the relationship between this and the fact that so many of her clients are tangled up with the law. They are policemen, lawyers, Queen's Counsellors, judges. Does the strain of juridical power, the weight of order, exact this toll? An eye for an eye? An abject citizen in the dock exacting the abjectness of the locker-up? It is clear to Lucy that the risk the lawkeepers take is part of what holds them in thrall. It is also clear that the lawkeepers like to believe that risk itself is subject to their control, that they are experts (as they from time to time point out) when it comes to undermining the credibility of a witness—Lucy, for example—in court. Even so, even knowing the considerable dominion of their safety, Lucy is overwhelmed by revelations. By no means is she blind to the meaning of their view of her, the meaning of their choosing her as a safe receptacle for revelation. It is not a flattering meaning. Even so, she is overwhelmed.

(In another sense, she sometimes thinks, it *is* a flattering meaning: *Here, where it doesn't count, the unvarnished truth will serve.* That is why Lucy continues to make do. That is why she is here—though she is in transit, a tourist, someone who could, and eventually will, leave. That is why, in choosing one cage over another, she finds more leg room here. For the time being.)

And perhaps the very infantile nature of so many of the legal disclosures is brilliant, perhaps it is not reckless but cunning, an intuitive *tour de force* calling forth, as it invariably does, a maternal instinct. When Lucy thinks of the twins, her primary urge is protective.

(And when I think of Lucy and the twins? Lucy, or at least that particular Lucy, Lucy-upstairs-at-Charlie's-Inferno, was a costume I wore for several years. I stepped into that costume and out of it. Sometimes, mentally cleaning house, telling stories to Catherine in London for example late at night after several brandies, or talking silently to my reflection from the ferry railing, I pull the costume out of the back of a closet and look at it. I step inside it for a moment to look again at Lucy's visitors with Lucy's eyes. I think this: What a piece of work is man! How needy in all seasons, how infinite in abasement, in action how like a child.

What *is* this quintessence of lust?

And Lucy remembers from that time: lust is a frightened manchild in the dark.)

Upstairs at Charlie's Inferno the men are safe, and they sense it, for the very nature of the power of the women upstairs weakens the women. They are moved to pity. And are they also moved to contempt? Rarely, in fact. *This is what we are*, the daily singularities tell them. The women are moved to awe, they are often moved to a kind of fear. Ask not for whom the games are played, for whom the whips prepared. Upstairs the women are silent, keeping the secret of communal shame.

What the twins require is simple. It's easy work, Lucy says, though not without its distressing side. Specifications have been made with an exactitude befitting the legal mind. Lucy must wear the white button-front uniform, the thick pearl gray stockings, the flat lace-up shoes with crepe soles. She must add a hairnet and synthetic braids which coil themselves around her head and then snake their way into a bulky knot on the nape of her neck. "My name is Miss Montmorency," she must say, "school matron. There will be no hanky panky while I am around." She must then stand by sternly and watch while the twins undress, and she must bring them peanut-butter-and-raspberry-jam sandwiches.

From this point, her role in the script remains passive until the third act. Sitting cross-legged on the floor, facing each other, the twins eat the sandwiches while playing with each other's pricks. Lucy must watch. The twins giggle, they sway, they duck and dodge, they rub jam on each other's faces, they sometimes escalate to bread fights and raspberry cocks which must be licked. *Ride a cock horse to Raspberry Cross*, they sing. Lucy must keep supplying them with peanut butter and raspberry jam. Her face is stern, it must always be stern and deeply shocked, but the twins are deliciously free to defy her in a fever pitch of nervous mirth. When their playful torment reaches climax, however, Lucy must fetch the switch. Act Three. This is reckoning time. The switch, significantly, is of lawyer cane, a withy of great suppleness and bite, a two-edged sword. Bent over the footboard of the bed, side by side, the naked legal bottoms receive six of the best and take their punishment like staunch little men.

And then? Then Matron Montmorency tucks them up in bed and brings hot milk and turns out the light. Furtive movement in the dark, furtive cuddling, subplots hatching in the dark, secrets, secrets, oh no, oh help, oh please, matron is back, the light is on, the bedding is thrown back to reveal the naughty boys who must be switched again and made to sit in the corner where they subsist on prisoner rations of peanut butter and raspberry jam, poor little bad boy shenanigans going off half-cocked and having to begin again begin again begin again.

So it goes.

Mr. Prufrock has quite different needs.

It is because of Mr. Prufrock that Lucy watches certain television programs she would never otherwise have time to see. For Mr. Prufrock, preparing a face to meet the faces on the screen, television is a flickering tingling electronic cave of carnal possibilities, all of them safe. Certain faces on television arouse Mr. Prufrock to paroxysms of derring-do, and in the soft safe darkness of a curtained room there is nothing to stifle his murmured Do I dare? and do I dare?

Anything, it transpires, absolutely anything, can be the mysterious machinery of desire, can be eroticized, fetishized, tantalized, sandwiched between peanut butter and raspberry jam. Mr. Prufrock is intimate with a number of women, all of them newscasters or hosts of forums where cultural and political events are aired. He has his current affairs.

Mr. Prufrock, who feels naked even when neatly dressed in suit and tie (his collar mounting firmly to the chin), is not the kind of man who can be easily imagined without clothes. Perhaps a vision of pale flabby stomach, an incipient paunch, confronts Mr. Prufrock in his morning shower, but he banishes it instantly. In his own inner notion of himself, he is always clothed. Fully dressed therefore, except for the shoes carefully aligned beneath the chair and the tie which he folds in quick expert coils and places on the card table, he sits on the bed in his black-socked feet, with the pillows behind his back and the remote-control channel-changer close to his left hand. Lucy, naked, sits on his right and keeps his other hand occupied, his fingers languidly stroking her smooth young body, exploring cavities and creases, assessing textures. Being a man highly sensitive to touch, Mr. Prufrock translates and transmits through his fingertips, giving his entire visual attention to the screen.

Mr. Prufrock is in love with Catherine Reed. Though he has never met her, and would indeed be terrified of doing so, he finds in the weekly watching of "Catherine Reed Presents" a sort of Arabian Nights. She is his Scheherazade. Who knows where she will take him? Who can predict what intimacies she will lure him into? Fearless Catherine Reed travels the nation and the world, where danger lurks she will be there, talking to rice-farming guerrillas in the Philippines, to Palestinians on the West Bank, to Koori protesters in Kakadu, to rebels in Afghanistan, to Kurdish caravans fleeing across the Turkish border from Iraq. . . .

Ah, but I am mixing the Now and the Then, Catherine Reed presenting last night, Catherine Reed presenting last year, Catherine Reed presenting a decade ago, I am mixing time as a television special does, as "The Decade in Retrospect" does, as Charlie did, as memory does, one image bleeding into another, Lucia taking off her neat school uniform and putting on Lucy, Lucy seeping by degrees into me, but who am I?

There is a woman who pauses in her writing, puzzled; a woman without a name, without a face, without a voice. Underground woman, who lives below the text, a misinterpreter, a mischief-maker perhaps, a faulty retrieval system which sometimes presumes to call itself an "I."

The woman pinches her left forearm with the thumb and index finger of her right hand. She watches an old scar turn bright red and then fade. She touches the imprint of perpetual Nows of pleasure and of harm, of joyous fucks and Lucy-fucks, of pain.

She frowns. She observes her mind, which sits there like a derisive crow on a fence, changelessly monitoring her changing body, doggedly discriminating between Now and Then. *Then,* her mind says with elaborate and withering patience, you were earning money in a grubby room. *Now* you are someone who shies away from speech, who dreams of writing without language since language deceives, who wants to give the silences their say, who watched Catherine Reed last night, live, and who also last night watched Catherine Reed in re-run, "The Decade in Retrospect," who watched the mostly silent Catherine Reed giving time past and time present their cues, pulling history onto one little pocket-handkerchief screen, letting other people speak, giving airtime to Queensland Greenies and Albanian democrats and Bangladeshi flood victims and the quarry riots in inner Sydney and the anti-quarry demonstrations in the suburbs and rival black factions in South Africa and antiwar activists in Melbourne.

"*Now,*" Mr. Prufrock warns, as the camera curves away from the marchers on Lygon Street. "Any second now," he says. For always, in those brief moments when Catherine Reed fills the screen, silent, listening, she speaks directly to Mr. Prufrock.

"Do you notice," he asks Lucy in his fastidious voice, "that she practically never talks? That is what I like about her. She *listens.* That is why people tell her so much, that is why they trust her. She is not one of those tiresome celebrity hosts who have guests as an excuse for showing off, who cut in and control and cannot be induced to shut up."

Lucy marvels at how talkative Mr. Prufrock becomes during "Catherine Reed Presents," since he is otherwise such a shy and retiring man, a professor of literature. This too surprises Lucy, for she rarely sees academics. Academics, as a rule, don't need the services of Charlie's Inferno; they have so many bright young bodies at their beck and call.

"She hardly ever speaks," Mr. Prufrock says in a thrum of excitement, his fingers paddling frenetically in Lucy's crotch. "Do you notice that? She's so *intimate* with her guests, there's this . . . you can feel the electricity between them. Just the same, waiting for her voice, it's almost *unbearable*. I don't know why her producer keeps giving us crowd scenes like this."

"Hush," Lucy soothes, stroking his thinning hair, motherly, leaning toward him.

Mr. Prufrock sucks Lucy's breasts. "Catherine," he moans.

Catherine Reed fills the screen. "Tonight," she says, "we'll be exploring the psyches of prisoners of war, the powerlessness and the sense of abandonment and the loss of self, and the long, long aftermath."

To music, Catherine fades from the screen. Two film clips succeed her, they are film clips that Lucy, and indeed the whole watching world, has seen a number of times already. Lucy knows she will never forget those faces, the young American one and the older, haggard, darker British one. . . .

(*Did* Lucy see these particular film clips with Mr. Prufrock? What year was Mr. Prufrock a client? What year did the prisoners' faces grab the world by the scruff of its fears? Retrieval systems are faulty. Press the wrong button, you get the wrong rerun. Then what? Then you get Virgil wandering through Christian cosmography and discoursing on Florentine affairs, you get Plantaganets sounding like Tudors, you get Cordelia keeping silence for us all, you get Henry V's foot soldiers, on the anti-romantic eve of battle, as ghostly voices on "Catherine Reed Presents."

> But if the cause be not good, the king himself hath a heavy reckoning to make; when all those legs and arms and heads, chopped off in a battle, shall join together at the latter day, and cry all, "We died at such a place"; some swearing, some crying for a surgeon, some upon their wives left poor behind them, some upon the debts they owe, some upon their children rawly left. I am afeard there are few die well that die in a battle. . . .)

Catherine Reed fears there are few live well who are captured in time of war.

"Now," Mr. Prufrock says. "Any second now, they'll get back to *her*."

Lucy wonders if she will ever forget those soldiers' faces, the young American one, a boy's face, plump-cheeked, pocked with peppershot wounds; and the British one, darker, older, bruised, his shoulder (possibly dislocated) hunched into the camera in pain.

The voice of the young American is that of a bewildered child, a frightened child who no longer has any confidence that black is black and white is white, who will dully, abjectly, listlessly—if required to do so—state that black is in very truth white.

Then the British pilot speaks. His voice is different, it hangs grimly onto its truths, it will resist surrendering them, though it has no illusions about the cost of this stubbornness. A shock of black hair shields the exhausted eyes, the shoulder braces itself against coming pain.

"I can't bear this," Lucy says. "I can't bear to see those faces again."

Mr. Prufrock is agitated. "Wait," he says. "Wait. She'll be back."

Catherine Reed reappears, her brows knit, her face strained. "I think all of us," she says quietly, "have flinched on behalf of these men. Tonight I will be talking to someone who remembers that condition of powerlessness. . . ."

Music, a view of the dusty western suburbs of Sydney, a neat front garden, a modest house, a curtained window, a man behind the window staring out at nothing, at the unfocused distance, the past, the bamboo cage, the Burma jungles.

"Mr. Rex Kenney," the unseen voice says, "was a prisoner of the Japanese during World War II, a worker on the notorious Burma Railway. At one point, in retaliation for his shouting at a guard who was kicking a fallen friend, Mr. Kenney was kept in a bamboo cage for several weeks, with only ricewater for food.

"Mr. Kenney, when you saw the captured pilots on television, can you tell us what your reactions were? Can you give us some idea of what they are going through?"

We are inside Mr. Kenney's living room now, an ordinary sort of room with a couch and two armchairs and a beige carpet and a TV set in one corner. Mr. Kenney does not face the camera, but looks across the room, apparently studying the intricate pattern in his wife's lace curtains. He looks like a man under constant and exhausting siege from nightmare.

"To tell you the truth," he says, coughing—it's a smoker's cough, a dreadful hacking sound which occupies several seconds—"to tell you the truth, I couldn't watch. I mean, I did see them the first time, but I got the shakes so bad that I had to . . . I had to . . ."

There is a long silence. Mr. Kenney runs the fingers of his right hand back and forth across his forehead, kneading the skin, as though a fierce headache is yanking at the nerves of his eyes and twisting them, braiding them into thoughts he cannot hide from. Lucy suffers for him, intimately aware of his thumping blood and snarled nerves, running her cool fingertips over his temples, massaging his neck.

Mr. Prufrock's caresses have become sharply rhythmic, staccato, playing demi-semi-quavering needs. "You can *feel* her, can't you?" he asks, intent. "Even when she's not on the screen at all, you can see her there, just off the edge, with those eyes. . . . You see, she won't cut in, she lets him take his own time, she'll let him take all the time in the world if he needs. . . ."

"The first twenty-four hours is the worst," Mr. Kenney says suddenly, vehemently. "It's the not knowing, you see. It's the not knowing if anyone will ever know. . . . You see, it's not the beatings themselves, it's waiting for the next one, not knowing how many nexts, not knowing what they *want* from you."

He drags the back of one hand across his eyes and coughs again and fumbles for a large slightly grubby handkerchief. He blows his nose, and surreptitiously rubs his eyes again with the back of a wrist.

"I'll tell you what I was thinking," he said. "You mightn't believe me, but I was wishing I could do it for them, see? I wish I could spare them, change places, because I've got the knack now, see? Those poor buggers, right now, they don't know what's hit 'em, they don't know there's all that everafterwards, wondering what you said to them, frightened of what you might've said, hating yourself, blaming yourself. I'm stuck with that, see? I'm shot." His body suddenly and visibly relaxes as though this acknowledgment, this realization, is a great relief to it. "It's criminal to give 'em brand new fodder," he says. "It's like throwin' babies into a cement mixer, there oughta be a rule . . ."

He begins coughing again, helplessly, shockingly. His eyes are streaming from the coughing fit. He blows his nose vigorously.

"After the first twenty-four hours," he says calmly, "things settle down. Once there's a pattern, see? It's the not knowing that flattens you." Mr. Kenney retreats into memory, forgetting the camera. There is a long, long silence.

An intimate silence, Lucy thinks, her breast against Mr. Prufrock's cheek.

From just off screen, Catherine Reed's voice, gentle and respectful, asks: "And after the war, Mr. Kenney. After your release and safe return home. Were bad dreams a problem?"

"Yes," he says, wincing. "Yes, bad dreams." The ghosts of bad dreams smoke around him. "It's funny that," he says frowning. "Not while you're a prisoner, at least not me, I didn't dream at all. Or if I did, I never remembered them. But afterwards, yes. My wife will tell you. It's hard to tell, you see. . . ." He shifts awkwardly in his armchair, embarrassed. "Sometimes it's hard to tell if you're dreaming or if you're back there, sometimes even after you wake. . . . My wife can tell you."

"And how long was it before you stopped having nightmares?"

Mr. Kenney presses his hands together, the fingers splayed out, until the knuckles crack. "I still have them," he says.

"How long does it take, then, for the worst after-effects of the trauma to wear off, would you say?"

Mr. Kenney, startled, looks directly at the point where it can be assumed Catherine Reed is sitting, off camera. He raises his eyebrows in a kind of shock, as though she has asked: And when do day and night stop arriving? When do birth and death disappear? Then he looks away again. He twists himself in the armchair to turn his face as far from the camera as possible. His left hand gestures vaguely behind him, pawing at the cameraman in distress. Impassive, the camera records. There is a long, long silence. Mr. Kenney's body trembles like a tuning fork.

"I can't bear it," Lucy says. "It's cruel. It's cruel to keep shooting."

Mr. Prufrock, half on top of Lucy, her breast in his mouth, his eyes intent on the screen, sucks noisily.

"I'm sorry," Mr. Kenney mumbles. "I can't seem to . . . Could you take that thing away please?"

Mercifully, the camera shifts around the room.

"Thank you, Mr. Kenney," Catherine Reed, in profile, says in her low quiet voice. "Thank you for speaking to us." Then her face fills the screen and she looks directly at Mr. Prufrock. Her eyes soften, she turns on him her small sad smile. "Good night," she says, and Mr. Prufrock, a little clumsily, messily, reaches climax.

TEN

Lucy has a recurrent dream. Sometimes she is in the lower left-hand corner of Charlie's photograph of the Serra Pelada mine, and sometimes she is at the bottom of the quarry. She has a sense of urgency about climbing up the rockface and escaping, but the ladder sways precariously and no matter how many rungs she negotiates, the top seems ever further and further away. She can never, in fact, see the top, only the endless vertical wall of pocked rock. Besides, it is dangerous even to look up, since throughout the dream it is raining birdshit from unseen birds. On her arms, in her hair, on the nape of her neck, running slimily down inside her clothes, she can feel the wet, viscous ammoniac-smelling coating. When she looks up, it falls in her eyes, putrid.

Knock, knock.

An ordinary sound from the ordinary waking world invades the dream, and a door appears, dimly visible through ladder rungs, fantastically cut into the rock, neatly surrounded by pine moldings and chipped white paint, its brass handle dinted with age.

Who's there?

Lucy does say this, and she does actually open the door of her room (of the room where she works; the room where she is permitted to sleep, for a fee, between five in the morning and ten). It's early. It's only eight o'clock. She is still half inside the dream and half out.

Gabriel leans against the wall of the upstairs hallway at Charlie's Inferno, his arms folded, waiting.

Oh God. And here she is covered in birdshit, stinking; the last thing she wants is to be seen. She slams the door shut, or tries to, but Gabriel—bloody persistent Gabriel—sticks his foot, then his body, inside the frame.

"Go away," she says, pushing him, pitting her weight against the door.

"Why don't you lick the pus from other people's boils, Lucia?" he asks mildly. This is cheating, using her own words against her. This was something she had told him, those stories of saints passionate in their rituals of self-mortification, the ones who cleaned convent floors with their tongues, the eaters of spiders, the wearers of burrs against the skin. "Why don't you just let people shit on you, and be done with it?" he wants to know.

"Go away, Gabriel. Please."

"Last night," he says, "I saw a friend of my father's, an old professor, coming downstairs from your room. He couldn't look at me. If he comes here again," Gabriel warns, "I'll just drop in, in the middle of things, for a chat, Lucia."

"Don't call me that." This is what happens when worlds and incarnations intersect: vertigo. And how does one ever know what Gabriel's verbal intentions are? Satiric? Accusatory? Grieving? Take your pick. Shoulder against the door, her weight backed up against his, she is brushing at herself to scrape off the lingering skin of the dream. Black spots float in clusters in front of her eyes. As usual, she has not had enough sleep, and feels dizzy. She flattens her palms against the door. "Listen to who's talking," she sighs. She is closing the gap, squeezing him out. "The judge's son himself, all dressed up in his hairshirt, atoning for the sins of the fathers." Under his quick surprised pain (but is that what it is? *Is* it?) she digs at what might be a wound, but the power seesaws. "You never told me he was Robinson Gray," she accuses, probing, stabbing, giving ground and sliding back into the room with the opening door. "It's interesting how you avoided ever actually mentioning his name."

"Did I?" he says, surprised. He is in the room now, and closes the door behind him. "Well, I wasn't making any attempt to hide the fact. Funny thing, that, the way people generally say 'my father' instead of using their father's first name." He is watching her with a mixture of tolerant amusement and sadness, but also with a sharp eye. Nothing escapes Gabriel's careful interest. "I gather you've met my father in other circumstances, Lucy."

Lucy. She notes that shift. Of course it is what she wants (birdshit is birdshit, a spade should be called a bloody shovel, a new mask should be acknowledged when the wearer demands it) and yet a small grief, perversely, lodges itself behind her ribs. "If you weren't hiding something," she says defensively, "why did you tell me you were Gabriel Brennan, not Gabriel Gray?"

"Ah," he acknowledges. He is miles away now, lost in thought, examining his own motives with the attentiveness of a trial lawyer. "I never thought of that as concealment," he says. He wrinkles his forehead, concentrating, sifting through the evidence for and against himself. "It was a statement of allegiance. My mother's name." He begins to nod at some inner point raised by the prosecution, he nods at Lucy as though conceding something, as though acknowledging her non-hoodwinked eye and her acuity and her superior translation. (He sees me, Lucy thinks with another sense of vertigo, as I see him: as the dispassionate observer who can't be fooled.) "But perhaps you're right. I think you may be right."

She can never, at any time, and certainly not first waking thing, late in a headachy morning, unravel the muddle of what she feels about Gabriel though she knows it is composed of love and panic and a sense of betrayal and desire. She sets bluster between them as protective barrier. She opts for attack. "How come you're here? How come you're working for Charlie?"

"I thought I would ask you that."

Now he has his back against the door and stands watching her with his arms folded, reading her carefully, noting changes, decoding her, doing some kind of interior translation, implying (so it seems to her) that nothing she might be thinking or feeling is foreign to him. This partly infuriates her, partly makes her feel wary. She fears it is true.

"Lucia." He reaches out and touches her cheek.

"Don't!"

He lets his hand fall but stands close enough that she is aware of a faint smell of stale tobacco from restaurant patrons on his shirt, and something else, a pleasant familiar smell of Gabrielness that transmutes itself instantly into hunger. It is not any kind of hunger she can readily put a name to, or not a name that makes sense. It is intensely physical and sexual, but that seems such a small part of the ravenousness. It is certainly composed partly of nostalgia for those languid days at Cedar Creek Falls, those long intense discussions and silences. *Coming home*, her mind tells her. *Sliding back into myself.* But what kind of nonsense is that? She feels dizzy with the desire to touch him and the determination that he will not be aware of her desire; and yet she knows that such elaborate emotional subterfuge is pointless. Gabriel will know already, will take it as unremarkable, will be neither flattered nor *not* flattered by it, neither sexually excited nor *not* excited. He will not be immune, he will not be indifferent, but nor will he be affected in any of the predictable ways.

Or perhaps it is she who invests him with such enigmatic and intuitive powers. Perhaps he is simply preoccupied with other matters all the time. She feels nervous; almost ill.

"Hey," he says, concerned. "Are you okay?"

"I'm fine. Not enough sleep, that's all."

"Let's go somewhere where we can talk."

"I don't want to talk to you, Gabriel."

"Yes you do."

"I want to sleep."

"I'll buy you breakfast on the ferry," he says. "C'mon, let's go."

Of course, I haven't been fully honest. I haven't told you everything. I glossed over the nature of my response to coming downstairs one day and seeing Gabriel tapping off beer behind the counter.

I was thunderstruck, needless to say—and yet in another sense, his presence seemed inevitable and utterly unsurprising.

Is there further evidence against the reliability of the witness Lucy?

Yes, Your Honor.

Are her intentions honorable?

As to intentions, Your Honor, she is not at all clear about them herself, but as far as she can determine, through rigorous self-analysis, they are to find a needle in a haystack, and to follow a thin thread of truth through a dark wood. She is not at all sure this will lead to a way out, or to anywhere. Given the messy and provisional nature of her enterprise, Your Honor, her intentions are honorable.

She may have neglected some peripheral details about the dinner party in the restaurant, some of the activity offstage, for example, and certain reactions in the wings at the very moment when Catherine Reed caused a slight stir while the salad was being passed.

I haven't told lies, Your Honor—no; you have my word on that—but there have been, perhaps, little sins of omission (sometimes intentional, sometimes not; sometimes conscious, and sometimes, undoubtedly, not; but then how would I know about the latter?). On the other hand, I am well aware of bits of embroidery, indirections, avoidances, digressions and subplots (but these are because I am going in circles myself, stalking the meaningful coincidence, sniffing at possible connections, leaving no meander unwandered). And sometimes, because all the implications are still unclear to me, or are troubling, I will admit that there have been careful skirtings of certain revealing moments.

For instance, the following exchange, a few days after Gabriel materialized behind the row of taps in the pub.

"Who the hell do you think you are, Charlie?" Lucy asks, quietly furious, deeply uneasy, a little panicked perhaps (and perhaps, on some level, relieved, but afraid that her pleasure will show). "Are you auditioning for the role of Big Brother, or what?"

Charlie, always mild, raises his eyebrows in surprise.

"Oh, very touching," Lucy says dryly. "Very convincing, I'm sure."

Charlie smiles his polite inscrutable smile. He never fails to be amazed at the powers people ascribe to him. The less he says, the more they insist he knows. He asks patiently: "What are we talking about, Lucy?"

"Why's Gabriel here?"

Charlie raises his eyebrows. "He was looking for a job so I offered him one."

"That's not what I meant."

"I gather you know him, Lucy."

"I would like to know what's going on. For instance, why are you taking photographs of him?"

Charlie raises his eyebrows. "For the same reason I took photographs of you."

"But that was just one session. You follow Gabriel round like a shadow. Why?"

"Surely that's obvious. It's like having Michelangelo's David roaming around."

"That's not what I meant either. And *why* did you offer him a job? Why *him*?"

Charlie stares at Lucy, fascinated. The more questions a man is asked, he thinks, the more pieces of the answer he has.

"You're playing some sort of game and it makes me nervous," Lucy says, blundering helplessly into further self-revelation. "And I hate it when you just smile and say nothing like that. You *are* playing a game, aren't you?"

The thoughtful way in which Charlie fails to answer, Lucy notes, pulls a whole hatful of questions out of air.

"I don't like to have anyone keep tabs on me," she warns. She and Gabriel are both leaning on the ferry railing, staring into the water that rises like a sleek fin and curls outwards and melts back into shapelessness. Gabriel, watching the wave shift shape, thinks: Lucia, Lucy, lucent, loose end, lost.

"Charlie says your customers call you Wildcat."

"Oh *Charlie*." She rolls her eyes. "It's news to me." She watches the shavings of the wake curl away from her, she notes the way the same shape is always there and always vanishing. "But I'm sure you gave him the third degree. I'm sure you've both got a dossier on me that would put the KGB to shame. I'm sure you're going to tell me what your old professor and I talk about between the sheets and TV. What is it, exactly, that you're fishing for, Gabriel?"

"Who's been fishing for whom, Lucy?"

"What's that supposed to mean?"

"Who got Charlie to offer me a job?"

"Not me," she says hotly. "I thought it must have been your idea of irony. Who came sniffing along my trail from Brisbane to Sydney?"

"Well," he says. "That wasn't the reason I left Brisbane, but it's true I was looking for you. And who dropped clues and invitations like a trail of crumbs?"

"Not me," she says. She can be definite about that. She was running away, leaving Lucia and Gabriel behind for good, shaking the dust of Brisbane from her shoes. She was done with all that. She was crossing the bridge from past to future and blowing it up behind her.

She smells Brisbane streets, she smells the green yeasty smell of Cedar Creek. She says quickly: "You've got tickets on yourself, mate. Believe me, I don't want *anyone* on my case. I fly solo."

"Hmm. The lady doth protest too much, methinks."

"Oh yeah?" she says belligerently. "The gentleman is not what he seems, I think."

Gabriel raises his eyebrows, interested. "What *does* he seem, exactly? And what is he really, in your opinion?"

This was pure disorienting Gabriel: the fact that he could, and would, ask such questions seriously, that they would bubble out of him, they would grab him, and then he would buttonhole you for an answer. But this odd habit had nothing whatsoever to do with vanity or arrogance or self-consciousness. In fact, it was as though Gabriel was without consciousness of a self at all; no, that was not the way to put it, since that suggested insecurity or neediness, and he was none of those things. He was, as far as Lucy could tell, fearless. He had, as far as she could see then, as far as I can see now, that rare and enviable form of confidence which simply accepts what it is without pride or embarrassment, and so requires none of the subtle rituals of preening or self-justification or self-aggrandizement, none of the discreet denigration of others that most egos require. Gabriel's integrity, too, was of the daunting kind: he could never quite understand the dishonorable action, nor quite comprehend it as temptation. I would describe Gabriel as one of the Holy Innocents, except that he was by no means uninformed or innocent of an awareness of the seamy underside of things. Gabriel lived inside a moral riddle. The riddle breathed him.

He says gravely: "Your opinion matters to me, Lucia. It interests me."

But Lucy's opinion of him is chaotic, and so is mine. I can't pin him down, I don't quite know how to describe him, and never did, then or now.

And so Lucy was in awe of him, and was made uneasy by him, and she resented him. Like Charlie, she feared for him. And she resisted him with instinctive irreverence.

"The gentleman," she says, "the right honorable Angel Gabriel, is really just a common old tomcat sniffing round."

Gabriel grins. (That was disconcerting too, the sudden slides, the easy switching to her terms, the affectionate teasing as though she were a fish on the hook and might have all the line she wanted, and all the time in the world, because, after all, if he wanted to reel her in, what could stop him?) "Naturally the local cathouses were on my list," he says easily. "But to be offered a job in the very place . . . ? It stretches credulity, Lucy."

"Exactly," she says. "You're not going to convince me that was pure chance. I find it pretty bloody curious that you show up, and next thing it turns out we're both waiting table on your father."

"I found it pretty bloody curious too," he says. "Lucia, why did you run away from me in Brisbane? Why did you disappear?"

"Because."

"I was frantic at first," he says, "until I got your message from Sheba. And then I was stunned. I simply couldn't make sense of it."

The doors to synchronous time and parallel space are everywhere, and between one word and the next, a crevasse can open. You can step into nowhere. You can fall through an abyss between yesterday and today, you can walk into The Shamrock in Brunswick Street in Brisbane on a Saturday afternoon and hear a young man say to a barmaid: "It's curious, watching you."

"Yeah?" The girl flutters heavily blackened eyelids as she taps off his beer. "Why's that?"

"Because you're acting. The pub's not your natural element."

Her hand, pushing down on the spigot, pauses. "That's where you're wrong." She looks him directly in the eyes, and plonks his glass of Four-X on the counter. You have no idea, she thinks. This *is* my natural element.

"Ah," he says, raking his fingers through hair the color of pale mustard seed. The gesture suggests slight malaise, but it is not that he feels rebuked or is conceding error. It is more that he seeks to be polite while contradicting. "Well. I've seen you in other places."

"Like where?"

"Like the university library." He smiles. "I've got a file on you, Lucia Barclay."

"Really?" She monitors the way the shock of fair hair keeps falling across his forehead, and the way he rakes it out of his eyes. "Well, if you don't mind, I'm *Lucy* here, and as it happens, I've got a file on you too."

"I thought you noticed me," he says.

Blue eyes like that, and long lashes: they seem almost improper in a man. "You must be rather used to being noticed," she says dryly.

He doesn't seem to get the point of this. Is it possible he is unaware of his effect on the beholder? Perhaps those who turn heads from birth take it for granted. Perhaps they don't notice it. "So you know who I am?" he asks.

"Oh, I don't know your name, or anything about you. It's not that sort of file. I've traced you through the Quattrocento and the High Renaissance though. Masaccio, Fra Angelico, Uccello, Michelangelo, Botticelli, you show up quite a bit in Siena and Florence."

He frowns for a minute, then laughs.

"I like to look at you," she says boldly. Elbow on the bar, chin propped on her fist, she smiles lazily and runs the tip of her tongue around her lips. She lets her eyelids droop.

He rests his elbow on the opposite edge of the bar, knuckles under chin, and grins back, not a come-hither smile but a grin of collusion. "It's the way you do that kind of thing," he says. "The bit of melodrama. I recognize the phenomenon. That's what interests me."

In the act of sucking one fingertip, Lucy goes still, as though she has suddenly backed into an iceberg in blood-warm Barrier Reef waters. "Mind you," she says evenly, withdrawing her middle finger languidly from her mouth and tapping off another pot of draught, "looking is all that's called for, I reckon. Much too pretty for eating."

He is not at all provoked. He considers her with indulgent amusement and considerable fascination. "I'm not implying that you don't mean it," he says. "The sexual innuendo and all that. It's the style, the campiness, that interests me. Certain patterns I recognize."

She would feel slapped in the face, except that his manner is not arrogant or rude. She does not know what his manner is. She feels caught in a searchlight.

"You're atoning for something," he says.

She waits to see if he will be able to explain the ferment, to see if there will be a *click*, to see if some inner bodily shift will occur and she will be able to take a deep relieved breath and say, *Yes, that's it, that's exactly why.*

"Upper middle class," he says thoughtfully. "Private school education, academic prizewinner, high distinctions in every course. Your English tutor happens to be—"

"Oh, old Sparky," she laughs. In an instant, she somehow rearranges the shape of her body to indicate a nervous, intro- spective young man. "I don't think he likes the way I argue in tutorials."

He is very much amused by her mimicry. "You do him well," he says. "He's a friend of mine, he says your mind scares the pants off him. It'll get you into no end of trouble, he says." He rakes his fingers through his hair again and grins. "I told you I had a file on you."

She can imagine. "And now we get the sermon on how I'm throwing away my life."

"Are you?"

She is deeply disappointed in him. "And who the hell are you, darling?" she asks with exaggerated motherly disdain.

"Gabriel Brennan." He simply sits there, elbows on the grubby Formica bartop, watching her. She doesn't know what to make of him. It's not small talk, bar talk. Perhaps he will not be a total disappointment after all. Abruptly, for no reason she can think of, she wants to give him a real answer.

"It's not a case of throwing away or *not* throwing away," she says. "It's like finding a secret cupboard under the stairs. You have to open it. It's like Columbus or Cook finding a whole continent that isn't on the maps. You have to explore. You *want* to explore."

He nods.

"Hey, Luce love!" another customer calls. "Do I hafta wait till bloody Judgment Day for me beer?"

She moves away and blows a kiss at the impatient customer. "Sorry, Jack. Got a talker over yonder," she says.

"Ah, Luce," Jack says lovingly, taking hold of her shoulders and leaning across the counter, "yer a wonder, love." He plants a slobbering kiss on her bosom, the upper half of which is exposed by her barmaid's dress.

"Go on with ya, Jack. Ya know I hate touchers." But there is touching and touching, and this kind doesn't bother her. This *is* my natural element, she thinks, pushing a foaming pot across the bar. I go for beery uninhibited warmth. She has discovered pleasant fevers in her blood. Her own body and its sensations are a miracle to her. Daily, she feels full of joy and recklessness.

When the brisk traffic in beer and repartee brings her back to Gabriel, she whispers hotly: "It's *not* an act." Under his steady gaze, she amends: "Well, maybe being a barmaid is. But the play itself, the real play"—she waves her hand to take in the men on bar stools, the whole pub, Brunswick Street—"the cupboard under the stairs, that's real."

"And when did you discover the cupboard under the stairs?"

"Oh . . . a few years ago. Not far from here. On Brunswick Street station one day. There was this woman . . . there was a girl. . . ."

"Circe," he says.

"Yes," she agrees, startled. And in this elliptical way, they appear to understand each other completely. She feels as though she has been waiting for Gabriel. She has been waiting to tell someone. "Yes, it was like that. Circe. Well, Sheba in actual fact." She gestures with her thumb at the lounge beyond, where another barmaid moves between tables. "Sheba spat at me. She called me the bloody Queen of Sheba and spat in my face." She puts her hand to her cheek. "She put a spell on me till I found her again. Now I call her bloody Sheba, and it's stuck."

"Hey, Luce!"

"Coming." She moves along the bar and he watches.

When she drifts back, she says: "It's impossible to be just a student, if that's what Sparky wanted you to tell me." He shakes his head and begins to demur but she barrels on. "The thing is"—and she can feel anger rising, a waste of energy, something to flee from—"I've taken a hard look at women in the university." She shudders. "It's not a safe place for a woman's mind. Besides, I've got something *here*." She knocks lightly on her own ribcage with one fist. The voraciousness, she means. The hunger. The passion to explore, to know everything. She wishes she knew where it came from, this frenzy, and where it will take her.

"Yes," he says, laying the palm of one hand against his own ribs. "Well, I told you I recognized the phenomenon."

"Hey, Luce!" the far end of the counter calls again. "We got a bloody drought on down here."

She moves away, she laughs, she teases, she flashes energy.

Gabriel watches.

When she returns to his end of the counter, she says to him: "You're like a bloody detective, the way you watch every move." He smiles and says nothing. She leans across the bar and asks in a low urgent voice: "Have you ever felt as though you could *eat* each day? As though you could gobble it up, every single day, the entire thing, morning, noon, and night, but you'd still be *starving*?"

"Look," he says. "How'd you like some weekend work picking pineapples?"

"What?" She has to laugh.

"I live out near Samford. My mother and stepfather have a farm at the edge of the rainforest—well, a market garden to be more accurate. We give street kids jobs, give them a place to stay."

"Rescue the perishing." She's affronted. She's disappointed again. Maybe he hasn't understood at all. "Fuck you, love. What if it turns out that the perishing are the ones who found El Dorado and never bothered to send back word?"

"Maybe that's why I lure them out to the farm," he says. "But rescuing you is not on my mind. Just telling you there may be people you know out there. And maybe not. They come and go. You interested?"

"Maybe."

"When do you knock off work?"

"Another hour."

"I'll hang around then."

She considers him carefully. Finally she says, "Okay, mate. You're on."

Perhaps it was that time, or perhaps it was the next time, or maybe the one after that, when he turned off Samford Road just after it crosses Cedar Creek and followed the unpaved detour until it ended, and then parked the car. I suppose we were so busy talking that I barely noticed walking through rainforest or reaching the falls. It is odd how certain memories trail streamers of connecting detail and others have sharp diamond edges against a void, entire in themselves.

This memory presents itself complete, inside a bubble, or like a sudden frame in a darkened cinema, a young woman sitting on a boulder, a young man slightly further downstream, just off camera, his body comfortably wedged into a crevice not far from the great rock on which the girl sits. Around them, cold clear mountain water cords and ruffles itself noisily, so that it is something of an effort to talk; or rather, talking itself is in consequence particularly private and easy, but the effort to hear, and to be heard, demands energy.

Sometimes the garrulous scrub turkeys interject. They are cheeky birds, not at all afraid, and they come in little clusters to the edge of the creek to eavesdrop and comment.

"I'll be honest," Gabriel says into the green clamor. "You remind me of someone. I've been watching you for weeks."

Déjà vu, she thinks. No. *Déjà vécu.* I have already lived this. This feels strangely familiar. I have always known him.

But that is absurd. That is patently ridiculous, she tells herself irritably.

And yet how odd. Two strangers, believing themselves unobserved, watch each other for weeks, circle each other, and suddenly find themselves cocooned in rainforest, sharing secrets. How odd that she is not at all surprised. She thinks of the way she had to find the girl who spat at her, had to find the old woman, *had* to. She remembers how the next weekend pulled at her, compelled her, how it was like a magnet dragging her back to Brunswick Street, how she walked for miles and hours, peering into back alleys, into fish and chip shops, into pubs, until at last the girl looked up and said matter-of-factly, "Oh it's you again, is it?"

And then she had to ask: "Why me? Why did you pick me, of all the people on the platform, to swear at and spit on?"

"Dunno," Sheba shrugged. "You're the one I noticed, that's all." She laughed. "Maybe because I knew you'd ask barmy questions." She chewed her gum thoughtfully and blew a bubble and snapped it. "Tell ya somethin' funny, though. I knew you'd come lookin' fer me. I had a dream about it, only in me dream ya come waltzing right off the train while it's chuffing off to Mayne Junction and come walking back between the railway lines cool as a cucumber."

Lucy says to Gabriel: "Do you think we live in magnetic fields or something?"

Gabriel thinks obsessions create their own magnetic fields. "We go round and round on our treadmills," he says. "We plaster meaning over everything the way tradesmen slap paint on a wall."

"Yes," she says. "I suppose that's it. But you know, till that day on the platform, I never gave gutter people a thought. I didn't really see them, and then quite suddenly I felt they were my natural kin."

"Must have been something there, though, some dormant memory, for you to react the way you did." Gabriel puts a fist against his stomach. "In my case, certain things trigger this . . . this *buzz*. When I said you remind me of someone, I don't mean you look like her. I can't really remember what she looks like, not clearly, it's one of the things that drives me crazy, trying to get her face in clear focus. But I think I see her all the time. I have to tell you you're not the first woman I've watched and followed, and I don't suppose you'll be the last. It's a *type* that . . . an archetype, I suppose. When I see it, I'm hooked, I get this compulsion, I have to speak to the woman."

" 'It is an ancient Mariner,' " she murmurs, " 'And he stoppeth one of three.' "

"Yes. And he does have to talk. Unfinished business, a therapist would say. Unresolved pain."

She recites:

> " 'Since then, at an uncertain hour,
> That agony returns:
> And till my ghastly tale is told,
> This heart within me burns.' "

"Yes," Gabriel nods. "That's exactly how it is." She murmurs on:

> " 'I pass, like night, from land to land;
> I have strange power of speech;
> That moment that his face I see,
> I know the man that must hear me:
> To him my tale I teach.' "

"The first time I felt it," Gabriel says. "I was only six years old." He crosses his arms and runs his hands up and down from elbow to shoulder as though monitoring electric pulsations on the skin. "And yet I can remember as clearly as if it was last week." He frowns, pondering this. "Of course, what I'm remembering at this point are my own endless replays, and there's no way of knowing whether they've altered subtly over the years. I keep going over them in case there's something I've missed.

"I was six years old," he says.

Book

Two

Cat

In ancient Rome the cat was a symbol of liberty.
No animal is so opposed to restraint as a cat.
Brewer's Dictionary of Phrase and Fable

ONE

Gabriel's father was with them because of the imminence of the funerals for the trams. TRAMS DEAD, one headline read. TRAMS GET THE AXE read another. By the end of the year, reported the *Courier-Mail* (this was in 1969), Brisbane would be free of the dragging past, free of antiquated road-clutterers, free of traffic jams; and suddenly people who had used nothing but cars for a decade were griefstricken, people who could not even remember the last time they had rumbled along Adelaide Street in a "silver bullet" were lining up at the tram stop outside the City Hall. Petitions were signed. Aldermen were telephoned. AN ERA PASSES lamented posters on the newsagents' stalls. In the tabloids (the *Truth*, the *Telegraph*) there were front-page spreads of whole families leaning from tram windows. The *Sunday Mail* ran an entire supplement of photographs.

It occurred to Gabriel that his father was with them because his father rather hoped to be spotted by a reporter. Dr. Horvath, their neighbor, had been on the front of the *Telegraph* with his wife and three daughters. *"Part of our heritage," prominent doctor says.*

"Look, Dad!" Gabriel was excited. "Ruthie's in the paper." Gabriel and Ruthie fished for tadpoles together in the gully behind her house. Ruthie had soft golden down on her arms and at the nape of her neck. She wore her hair in plaits tied with blue ribbons.

But to Gabriel's bewilderment, the photograph did not please his father. Gabriel was the apple of Robinson's eye—he knew that—and anything that gave Gabriel pleasure automatically pleased the man who spoke with such boyish charm and warmth to the mothers of all his friends. Gabriel's friends and their mothers were extremely fond of Mr. Robinson Gray. So it was something quite new that his father should frown and become agitated, taking a book down from the shelves of his study, sitting in his armchair, reading a page, jumping up again, putting the book back, taking down another. This went on for some time while Gabriel watched, mystified but fascinated. His father seemed to have forgotten Gabriel's presence entirely. Then, abruptly, his father went outside and got the lawnmower out and began mowing energetically.

At dinner that evening his father announced: "I think we'll take a tram ride on Friday afternoon. We'll go out through The Valley to New Farm."

Gabriel's mother was astonished. "*Friday* afternoon?"

"I'll take the afternoon off," his father said.

"But why?" she asked.

"To take the tram to New Farm."

Gabriel's mother stared blankly as though trying to translate. Every Thursday she and Gabriel took the bus into the city from St. Lucia, and then, because she always shopped at McWhirter's, they took the tram from the city to Brunswick Street in The Valley. Gabriel's father had sole use of the family car (his mother, like most Brisbane mothers, did not yet have a driver's license) and his father drove every day to the law courts in George Street. "To go to New Farm Park?" Gabriel's mother asked, puzzled, trying to imagine why they would not use the car.

"To ride in the tram as a family." Robinson spoke with a certain amount of impatience. "A keepsake for Gabriel. It's something I want him to remember." He moved into the tone he frequently used when speaking to Gabriel's mother. It made Gabriel think of the way teachers spoke to you at school. "It's a momentous occasion," his father said. "The present crosses the Great Divide and descends into history."

Unbidden, an image popped into Gabriel's mind of a future

grainy picture in the *Telegraph*, three faces behind the bars of the tram-car window, six-year-old Gabriel in the middle, his mother on one side, his father on the other. *"Momentous occasion,"* prominent lawyer says. *"The present crosses the Great Divide and descends into history."*

Gabriel felt strangely furtive and uneasy about this thought. Where had it come from? He felt as though he had done something wrong, and any minute now his father, stern but grieving, would send him to his room. He turned the sentence over again in his mind. *The present crosses the Great Divide.* It had such a lovely murmuring kind of sound, as though it had rolled under and over the pointed arches of a church. Another deeply disturbing thought zipped into Gabriel's mind the way nasturtium pods pop their seeds. *Zing! Pok!* He saw his father mowing the lawn again, the strange jerky way he had pushed the mower past the nasturtiums and round the mango tree to the Horvaths' fence and then turned and crossed back again and turned. He suddenly seemed to hear the voice inside his father's head, trying out different comments for the reporters, testing how they sounded, imagining how they would look on the front page of a newspaper.

Gabriel was so confused by these dreadful thoughts that he jumped up and ran to fetch his father's slippers from the bedroom. When he brought them to the table, he could see how silly this was, so early in the evening, but it was such a relief when his parents both laughed at him and his father tousled his hair and his mother kissed him and he felt, rather than saw, the smiles that passed over his head. He felt that warm glow, which was getting rarer now, that meant both his mother and his father were happy.

And now they were all on the tram. His parents sat opposite, on the gray-painted slatted curved seats, facing him across the small alcove. He loved the trams. He loved watching the straphangers as they clutched at the overhead leather loops, the way they swayed together, now this way, now that, not quite in unison but as if a wave moved along them, like a row of passionfruit runners on the side fence when the wind was in them. He loved the sound of the *ding-dong* when the conductor gave the cord two quick tugs after a stop. How unbelievable it was, how appalling, that the City Council wanted to axe the trams.

He tried to imagine this scene of carnage: a mob of city councillors swinging weapons above their heads, the sound of splintering, the silver metal ripping and squealing, the trams bleeding to death.

A sudden question arose.

"What will they do with the dead trams, Daddy?"

Gabriel's parents looked at one another and smiled. Gabriel's father took hold of his mother's hand. "The makings of a barrister, Constance. A quirky imagination and the ability to mull over a riddle from new angles."

"But what will they do?" Gabriel persisted.

"Bury them, I'm afraid, son," his father said, and his parents smiled at each other again.

Such happiness flooded Gabriel. He looked at their interlaced fingers lying lightly against the navy cotton of his mother's dress. The dress had a soft lace collar and the way her throat rose from it made Gabriel, for some curious reason, want to stand guard for her with his wooden sword. There was something precious and frail about her neck. It was like the neck of the porcelain shepherdess on their living room mantel. His mother's hair was light brown and brushed her cheeks like feathers. She was very beautiful, Gabriel thought, and he was filled with happiness to see the smile in her eyes. Lately, it seemed to him, she had become quiet, quieter, and her skin seemed stretched more tightly across her delicate bones, almost as tightly as the cellophane across the jars of new homemade jam. Impulsively, he stood and leaned across the space of the small alcove and kissed his mother.

"Gabriel," she said softly, smiling, touching his cheek with the hand that was not interlaced with his father's.

Gabriel sat down again and then, *crash*, the lovely glow was in splinters. That look was on his father's face again, that edginess in the way his father uncrossed his ankles and shuffled them on the floor and then recrossed them the other way. Gabriel was in an agony. There was nothing he could do. It was not permissible to give his father a hug and a kiss in public. If he had done it, his father would have said in a stern but kindly way: "Now Gabriel, that's for girls and sissies, not for grown-up young men who are six years old." But his father was hurt, Gabriel could see that. His father wanted a hug and a kiss, and he also didn't want it. Gabriel said urgently, guiltily: "Dad, where will they bury the trams? And what will they do with the tram lines?"

It was like turning on the rugby game on Saturdays. It was like watching the yabby water leak into the bays he and Ruthie made in the creek bank, the way his father's body soaked up energy again. Such relief flooded Gabriel. I must watch more carefully, he told himself. I must be more careful what I do.

His father said boisterously: "The trams will mostly go for scrap metal, I'm afraid, son. When I said 'bury' I was using a figure of speech. We call that a metaphor. That's when we say something dramatic, for effect, but we really mean something else. Do you understand?"

Gabriel, a little foggy, nodded solemnly.

"Though there'll be some for the museum, no doubt," his father added. "When you have a son of your own, you can take him to the museum and sit in a tram with him and say, 'Son, when I was as old as you are now, I rode along Queen Street on a tram like this with my dad. The old tram lines ran down the middle of the street in those days.'"

Gabriel laughed with pleasure and his mother smiled and his father squeezed his mother's hand.

"As for the tram lines, they'll probably have to pull them up, though they might be able to run asphalt right over the top," his father said. "And we won't have any more of those wretched traffic snarls or that crawling along and getting held up at all the tram stops. It's good for the flow of traffic, Gabriel. That's progress."

A reporter with a camera who had got on at the last stop and had been moving along the car paused at their alcove. "Excuse me, sir," he said, "but are you Mr. Robinson Gray?"

Gabriel's father looked enormously surprised. "Why, yes," he said. Gabriel's mother blushed a little, and pressed her lips together, and looked out of the window because she hated having her photograph taken. A cloud passed across her eyes. Into Gabriel's mind another nasty little cobblers-peg weed of a thought intruded. *How did the reporter know we would be on this tram?*

The reporter's camera sprouted a silver pudding basin on a black neck. *Pop, pop,* it said, and lightning flashed across the tram. "Just another with the little lad in the middle," the reporter said, and Gabriel was half-sitting on their laps, an idiotic grin on his face. "And do you have a comment, sir?" the reporter asked in a deferential tone.

"Well, it's just something I want my boy here to remember," Gabriel's father said solemnly. "Something he can one day say to his own son in a museum somewhere." He patted Gabriel on the head. "It's a momentous occasion," he said. "The present crosses the Great Divide and descends into history."

"Oh very good, sir," the reporter said. "And ma'am?" he nodded to Gabriel's mother. "Do you have a comment?"

Gabriel's mother smiled shyly and brushed her hair a little nervously out of her eyes. "Well," she said, "I've always used the trams, I like to go to McWhirter's every—"

"Gabriel has a comment," his father said jovially. "Tell the man from the newspaper what you wanted to know, Gabriel."

And so Gabriel dutifully repeated: "What will they do with the dead trams?" and the reporter laughed, and pop, pop, pop, he flashed lightning again, and "Just this way a bit, sir, father and son, that's wonderful. Chip off the old block, eh Mr. Gray?"

"Time will tell," Gabriel's father laughed, ruffling his son's hair. "But I think this young fellow may well leave his mark on the Queensland courts in time."

Behind him, Gabriel could feel the way a warm rash was moving up his mother's throat, fanning out from the white lace collar, mottling her face. When he sat down opposite again, she was smiling fiercely at him and her eyes were very, very bright. His parents were no longer holding hands.

"Mummy," he said, desperate, "when we get to McWhirter's, can we buy sugar doughnuts again?"

She smiled and nodded, grateful to him, her eyes full of love (*It's all right, then*), and the reporter handed his father a card. "Ted Bixby, sir. *Sunday Mail.* It's up to the editor, of course, but I think you'll find . . ." And his father swelled with such well-being (Gabriel—oh he wishes he didn't, but he does—Gabriel thinks of the frogs on the back porch at night) that it was going to be all right after all. There was such happiness again.

Now, in fact, Gabriel's father was bubbling over with energy and helpfulness. "See the tree?" he pointed for Gabriel at the triangular junction with Eagle Street. The Moreton Bay fig, at least a hundred feet high and a hundred across, stood serene as a pagan colossus in its own shaggy green light. "That tree was there when Captain Cook sailed up the coast."

The tiniest of looks and an unsmiled smile passed between Gabriel and his mother. Every Thursday he would say to her: "Do you think Captain Cook could have seen the tree, Mummy?" And she would say: "I'm sure he might have through his telescope, darling."

"There's the Story Bridge," his father pointed, crossing the alcove and sitting next to Gabriel and leaning across him, excited as a boy.

"McWhirter's is soon," Gabriel said. He thought with pleasure of the amazing doughnut machine in McWhirter's, how watching was as much fun as eating, how the little circles of white dough plopped down out of the metal chute into the river of burning oil, sizzle sizzle, and the slow wheel with its twenty metal gates slowly turned and the white dough got puffier and firmer, and exactly halfway round a magic lever rose from the burning oil like Excalibur and flipped the doughnut over, and lo, the underside was golden brown and the circle kept turning, slowly, slowly, toward the avalanche of sugar, the final gate, the final flip, the hot sugary doughnuts popping into little waxed-paper bags and then into desiring mouths. On Thursdays after school, Gabriel and his mother sat at the café table in McWhirter's and laughed together and ate and licked their sugary lips and wiped their greasy fingers on paper serviettes. "Two more stops to the sugar doughnuts," Gabriel, veteran of tram rides, sang joyfully.

"Two more stops to what?" his father said.

"To the sugar doughnuts," Gabriel said. "At McWhirter's," he explained, since his father looked a little blank. Then a trifle uncertainly: "That's where we get off."

"We most certainly do not," his father said. "We're going straight on to New Farm wharf. We can ride the ferry across the river and back if you want."

"But Mummy said . . ." Gabriel began, and bit his lip.

"Constance?" his father said sharply. "You haven't been buying the boy rubbish, I hope? It's very bad for his teeth."

Teeth were a big issue for Gabriel's father, whose smile was crowded with them, dazzling white. Brushing was a big issue too, and so were dentists.

"Just occasionally," Constance said meekly.

"Well kindly don't do it again," his father warned.

Gabriel, budding rugby player under weekend tutelage from his father, made a quick feint to the right. "It's not fair, Daddy," he grumbled. "You and Mummy never let me have sugar doughnuts when I want them."

"That's because your parents know what's best for you," his father said. And Gabriel saw his mother's eyes, expressionless, rest on him and stay there and he looked back at her and smiled sadly, knowing that both gratitude and surprise lay behind her expressive non-expression.

He loved his mother. He loved her so much that when she was unhappy he could feel it like a bruise on his arm.

He worshipped his father. Nothing made him happier than the feeling of his father's hand tousling his hair.

Right now, he felt as though his skin was being stretched across his bones by two dogs who would not let go. He was angry with himself. He thought that he must be more careful, that he must watch very carefully indeed, and that he must think very very carefully before he said anything. When the tram lurched round the corner into Brunswick Street and The Valley, and he saw McWhirter's loom large and then dwindle from view, he found himself wondering how the doughnuts felt being flipped out of burning oil and sliding down the chute toward somebody's mouth.

It seemed to him that the wonderful hot sugary taste was something he would never know again; that next Thursday, when he and his mother sat in McWhirter's café, something bitter would be in the little wax-paper bags, spoiling things.

It was two stops after McWhirter's, as the tram began to rumble by the huge old gone-to-seed houses with the rotting verandas, as it stopped outside the shabby old Empire Hotel, that the thing happened. It was this event which, more than the death and burial of the trams, more than the sandpaper edges of his parents' unhappiness, more than the loss of sugar doughnuts, would fix the day forever in Gabriel's mind.

At the stop outside the Empire Hotel a woman got on the tram. She entered through the wide door in the middle, and came down the aisle toward Gabriel and his father who was, in the wake of posing for photographs, still sitting next to him. Instantly she had all Gabriel's attention. For one thing, she had shorter hair than he had ever seen on a woman, and for another, she was dressed very oddly, and for another, she had such sharp darting eyes. She made him think of a magpie. She sat across the aisle from the alcove where Gabriel and his parents sat. She sat level with his mother, diagonally across from Gabriel and his father.

Gabriel was not at all surprised that she attracted his father's attention instantly too. What did surprise him was the bold and unwavering way the woman stared back at his father. He thought with great interest about the fact that someone who ought to feel self-conscious, someone of whom it was possible to imagine the whole tram smiling and whispering behind its hands (in fact, he could see people doing exactly that, raising their eyebrows at one another), someone who ought to feel embarrassed and ashamed . . . that person could act, in some mysterious way, as if she were queen of the tram. Perhaps it was the way she held herself, with her back very straight and her head high.

With her wiry hair—it was black, jet black—in a strange spiky fuzz around her head, she should have looked absurd, but she did not. She was old, at least as old as Gabriel's parents, maybe more. Her arms were browner, more leathery, but were crisscrossed with the strangest patterns of lines. Were they scars? Some were ghostly white, as though ferns had imprinted themselves long ago, and some were vivid and new. She looked like a woman warrior from some unknown tribe. She looked, Gabriel thought, magnificent in some wholly new way, in spite of the fact that she wore white bobby socks like a little girl, and a dreadful yellow cotton dress of the kind you could see in Woolworth's windows, and—on the left lapel of the front opening—a plastic brooch, a turquoise Ulysses butterfly, a Blue Wanderer as Gabriel's Grade 1 teacher called it in Nature Lesson. It was the kind of brooch you could buy in tourist shops, the kind little girls wore.

Gabriel was becoming aware of a curious throbbing, or humming, coming off his father's thigh which was pressed against his. It was as though he were sitting next to a dynamo.

Because Gabriel and his father were so obviously mesmerized, Gabriel's mother glanced sideways. The woman, who had been looking at Gabriel's father as a queen looks at a slave, caught the slight movement to her left and turned. The two women stared at each other for a moment, and they both seemed a bit startled, then Gabriel's mother smiled slightly, very shyly, and the woman gave a most wonderful radiant smile in return and did something quite odd. She leaned across the aisle to shake hands with Gabriel's mother.

Gabriel's mother took the hand and the strange woman pumped it up and down, very vigorously (Gabriel thought of a magpie again, that chirpy energy, those darting vibrant eyes), and Gabriel's mother said hesitantly: "I think I met you once, at Catherine Reed's party, didn't I? Catherine and I were at high school together. At Clayfield College."

The woman never spoke, but she laughed a most wonderful belly laugh, as though the thought of Clayfield College was a huge joke, and Gabriel's mother laughed, and Gabriel laughed too because it was such a rollicking boisterous king-sized breaker of hilarity rolling and surfing over them, sweeping them up, rushing them along, foaming and spuming and over-and-overing them, a laugh so infectious that other people joined in and the reporter came back and pop, pop, he flashed lightning at them all again, he caught the strange woman and Gabriel's mother leaning in across the aisle toward each other.

Then Gabriel became more intensely aware of the vibration against his thigh.

"Daddy?" he said alarmed, because his father was clearly trembling now, visibly and violently. This did not help, this drawing of attention to his father.

His father flashed a very toothy smile at everyone, a very dazzling white smile. "Crossing the Great Divide into history," his father boomed in a strange tight voice, and the reporter pop-popped again, and everyone laughed and cheered, but Gabriel could still feel his father's thigh against his, and his father's hand in his, and his father was vibrating like a jackhammer doing roadwork. He would not look at the woman in the yellow dress, but the woman looked at Gabriel's father and the way she looked at him frightened Gabriel. He did not know the meaning of her look, but it made him feel queasy and dizzy. It was as though someone had told him that when you step off a footpath you fall straight through a grating that goes to the bottom of the world. And had proved it to him.

He felt as though he was going to be sick.

He supposed they stayed on the tram until the terminus at New Farm. He supposed they went into the park and the woman went in some other direction. Perhaps she took the ferry across the river to Norman Park, or perhaps Gabriel and his parents did. He could recall nothing whatsoever from this part of the day. It was blank. He remembered his father's trembling, and the unreadable look on the woman's face. The next thing he could remember was the feel of his own sheets against his skin and the murmur of his mother's voice and then the blank of sleep from which he was jolted awake to the sound of his father shouting and shouting and then the crash of something being thrown.

He could hear, but he could not remember what the fight was about. He seemed to be watching from his bedroom doorway, he was frightened, there was a glimpse of his mother in her white nightgown, his father was shouting something, his mother's hands were in front of her face, then he couldn't remember anything more. He could only see a shut door.

The next morning when he woke, his father had already gone out, and Gabriel found his mother crying silently in the garden. There was a large red mark on her cheek and one eye was purple, but otherwise her face was frighteningly pale. Gabriel tiptoed up to her and put his arms around her, and she held him very tightly for a long time.

Then she dried her eyes on the back of her hand and smiled brightly.

"Whatever happens, Gabriel," she said, "you must remember that Mummy and Daddy both love you more than anyone else in the world."

And he did remember that. When his father took him to

Sydney the next weekend, he remembered it. Through the weeks and weeks of muddle, the hotel rooms, the changing schools, the three months in the rented terrace house in Paddington, he remembered it. When his father took him finally to the school with manicured lawns and verandas and paneled rooms, when his father showed him the new house with its view of the harbor, he remembered. "No more changes, mate," his father promised. "This is your school from now on, and this is our house."

Gabriel, remembering, asked timidly: "When's Mummy coming?"

"Mummy's not coming, old boy," his father said.

On the balcony of the house in Point Piper, he sat in a wicker chair and pulled Gabriel onto his knee. "I'm going to tell you something, man to man, Gabriel. And I expect you to behave like a man and not cry." Through the treetops, Gabriel could see the curve of the Harbour Bridge, and when his father sighed, very heavily and sorrowfully, he connected the sighs with the steel girders. He saw his father's breath looping through the gray struts, crossing the water, heading northwards for Brisbane. "The truth is, Gabriel, your mother is not a very stable woman."

Gabriel didn't say anything. He watched the way the sun caught the steel girders of the bridge and bounced off them again.

"Well, there," said his father with immense joviality, tousling his hair. "That's that, then, and you've taken it like a man. I'm proud of you, son. We'll have a bonzer time in Sydney, you and me. We love doing things together, don't we, old chap?"

"Yes, Daddy," Gabriel said.

He did. He adored his father. He certainly did.

It was fourteen years before he saw his mother again. From time to time, he would hear his father comment sadly at dinner parties: "She just couldn't cope, I'm afraid. Biochemical, the doctors think."

He always associated the strange woman, and the marks on her arms, and the yellow dress, and the blue butterfly brooch, with cataclysm. He would remember that wave of laughter that had engulfed the woman and his mother and himself. He remembered the way the woman had looked at his father. There was no one he could ask about this. The smell of hot sugared doughnuts could still make him ill with grief and longing. There was a riddle that smelled of McWhirter's café and of sugar and hot oil and waxed-paper bags. The riddle kept eating him. He was ravenous.

Two

"It was Cat," Charlie says, excited. "He saw Cat."

Lucy watches with awe as inscrutable undemonstrative Charlie paces up and down the room of the photographs, his face in his hands. If I touched him now, she thinks, I would be jolted across the room. The air around him would spit blue lightning.

"So she was still in Brisbane in '69," he says. "When did Gabriel tell you this?"

"Oh, I don't know. The very first time I met him, I think. The first time we drove out to Cedar Creek. You should ask him about her."

Charlie shakes his head, but throws himself into one of the low black leather chairs and sits hunched up in it, staring at the wall of his neatly framed past. Lucy goes to the kitchen and finds the Scotch and pours him a drink. She pours one for herself, she pries ice cubes from the tray in his refrigerator, drops three into each glass, and goes back to the living room. "Why not?" she says, as she puts a glass into his hand. "Couldn't you give each other answers?"

Charlie gulps his Scotch. "If he comes and asks me, perhaps," he says. "But you can't . . ." Whatever ambivalence Gabriel feels toward his father, Charlie is thinking, one of his emotions must be love.

"You can't what?" Lucy prompts.

"I don't want to tell him what happened, that's all. I don't want to be the one. Other people could tell him. Probably his own mother could tell him. She went to high school with Catherine Reed, they were friends. Besides . . ."

He sips his Scotch and stares at his wall of photographs.

Lucy follows his line of vision. He is not looking at the collage of *The Two Catherines* but at a grainy photograph of a laughing woman with short spiky hair. "Oh my God," she says quietly, going over to look more closely. Behind the woman, she sees now, are the slats of a tram seat. A chrome pole rises from behind her left shoulder, a leather loop hangs from above. Someone is hanging on to the leather loop, curving with the sway of the tram, making a kind of bracket round the woman. She is leaning out from the seat, laughing at someone unseen across the aisle. The photograph has been cropped so that the people across the aisle are missing.

"My God," Lucy says. "That's the very day . . . ?"

"It was in a box of old *Sunday Mail* rejects," he says. "I bought it this year at an antiquarian shop in Regent Street."

"Incredible," Lucy says. "Now I see why you scavenge in secondhand shops."

He becomes silent for so long that Lucy prompts: "Will you show Gabriel?"

"What?" he says, dazed. Then, as though he were still locked in conversation with someone else, he says: "Yes. You're right. You're right. You were right about that all along. And we had to get out, you were right."

"Who was right? Who are you talking about?"

"Catherine," he says. "She was right. We had to get out."

"Is that when you left?" Lucy asks.

"What?"

"After this?" She taps the photograph. "After the trams went. Is that when you left for New York?"

"I'd already been gone more than six years."

"So you never saw this in the *Sunday Mail*?"

"It was never in the *Sunday Mail*. It was a reject. I found it in the antiquarian shop."

"That's positively spooky," Lucy says. "So when did you leave?"

"After her twenty-first, we knew we had to."

"After whose twenty-first?"

"Catherine's."

There is a long silence. "She didn't stay with the *Manchester Guardian* very long," he says. "She started moving round the world. She couldn't keep still."

"But you've always stayed in touch?"

"What? No." It seems to Lucy that the mere acknowledgment bruises Charlie. "No," he repeats sadly. "Well, in a sense of course. I read her articles. I saw her on television from time to time. I wrote, but she never replied. Then I read that she'd come back here."

He drains his Scotch as though it were water and barely seems to notice when Lucy brings him another. "We tried to see Cat again before we left," he says. "But she'd gone."

"Charlie, who *is* Cat?"

"She's part of me."

The boy looks strange, even to Charlie, from this distance. Something about the way he walks draws attention, though that is the last thing he wants: that is, in fact, the very thing his rituals are designed to deflect. After every sixth step, the completion of a hexagram, he slides his right foot sideways, brings the left foot across to touch it, pauses, slides the left foot back again, transfers weight to it, slides the other foot across, then steps forward. It is essential to begin every hexagram with the right foot, since only by the most scrupulous attention to proper detail will he be rendered invisible. (When there is necessity for stealth, the sages say, the wise man moves as the dragonfly moves.)

There are further refinements. The boy must not step on a crack in the concrete footpath, nor must he fail to touch hedges as he passes them. Since meaning attaches to the number of feet which approach, he must keep a careful count and he must also keep classification by type: male feet or female, bare feet or shod, adult or child. If someone were to walk toward him, to block his path, he would stand stock still, his attention fixed on the person's shoes, then, a hexagram having been broken, he would do his foxtrot side-slides around the obstruction and begin again.

Charlie, describing him for Lucy, looking back at him, can

hardly bear to watch as he approaches the three boys on the corner. He wants to intervene, but what could he say? Suppose he said: Your oddities make other schoolchildren nervous, your oddities speak to them of obscure threat, all the more dangerous for its obscurity; your oddities excite gestures of self-defense in response to this threat: first verbal mockery, then public humiliation, then savagery.

The boy is only nine years old, but already he knows all these things. He knows more: he knows that there is nothing he can do, or fail to do, to change his status or his original crime, which is that of *difference*. Might as well be hanged for a sheep as a lamb, he thinks; especially since the rituals are a corridor to somewhere else.

So even now Charlie averts his eyes as the boy walks into the un-gentle hands waiting on the corner, just as the boy himself averts his eyes. The boy is, after all, invisible. There is nothing to watch. Charlie feels nothing as they move in on him, just as the boy, having vanished down his private corridor, feels nothing. But Charlie finds it harder to protect himself from the boy's walk, and he describes for Lucy its bizarre zigzag progress down a Brisbane street with embarrassment, with a kind of pain, with the same helpless mixture of anxiety and pride that his parents feel, watching from the window of their shop. Charlie watches the parents as they watch the boys on the corner. The boys on the corner play with dragonflies, plucking wings off for sport. Afterwards, the boys on the corner swagger into the shop to buy licorice sticks, and the parents smile and smile and serve them, always placating.

The boy embarrasses Charlie and amazes him. Where did he get his ideas? There is nothing I could tell him, Charlie says, although I wish I could make a voice in the crowd call out: *Good on yer, mate, you're a tough little bugger.* I wish I could reassure him. I wish I could say: Look, mate, in its own strange fashion, your system works. You are on your way to my vantage point.

Charlie wants to invent a comforter for him, he wants to invent friends. Just hang on for a bit longer, old chap, he wants to say. At this very moment, Cat is watching. At this very moment, Cat is on her way to meet you. Catherine, though more distant, approaches. Robinson Gray waits to befriend.

Charlie sighs and is silent.

He wishes he could promise the boy that they will then live happily ever after. He wishes Cat didn't have to prick her finger on the spindle, that Catherine didn't have to get the glass splinter in her eye, that Robinson Gray would always be Prince Charming and would always be true. But that is the way of things, he thinks. That is the way all stories go, following unalterable laws. We find, we lose.

(But Charlie, I could say to him now, keening for him, hugging myself and rocking backwards and forwards, grieving for the absent people who are part of me. You've done the same to me, Charlie. You and Gabriel have done the same thing that Cat did to you. You've buggered off, you've absented yourselves, and sometimes I forgive you and sometimes I'm furious and sometimes I storm and weep, but I've learned something too. There is something I could say to the little boy with his curious walk. You will find Cat and lose her, I could say, but loss is a kind of permanent presence. I could tell him all this. But he will learn it around the next corner anyway.)

Already he has been applying the salve of thrown coins, from whose configuration has emerged the first hexagram, the *Khien*, which tells him: *The dragon lies hid in the deep.* And his father explains: The solitary person can experience disapproval without trouble of mind. Though sorrowing, he is not to be torn from his root within himself. This root, his father says, is "the dragon lying hid."

Though solitary, the boy sits curled up at night on his bed in the closed-in veranda at the back of the shop. Within him, the dragon stirs. He could reach through the glass louvers of the sleepout and touch stars. He could step into China. He feels his body webbing its way down through the mattress and the veranda floor and into the warm mud of the crawl space, feeling its way, stretching, touching the couch grass and paspalum, dropping into the hollow where the ferns crowd the mango tree, burrowing deep below the pawpaws. He feels omnipotent, drunk, euphoric. He feels *rooted*. The stars, it seems to him, recognize his power. There is nothing the boys on the corner can do about it.

He opens the Book of the Emperors that was given at his last birthday. He enters the court of Fu Hsi, his other home. In the court of Fu Hsi, on a certain page of the Book of the Emperors, is a painting by Wang Wei, *Clearing after Snowfall on the Mountains along the River*. He enters the painting. In the cabin among the firs on the headland, he meets with friends, he records adventures, he consorts with swordsmen and courtesans. He consults the Book of Secrets where the glittering future is revealed.

Out of a quick brash sunset, night drops. Safety. Corner encounters are swallowed up by darkness and by calls from sundry front doors. The boy with the dragonfly walk comes home for tea, for what his parents—following local custom—call tea, although it is a concoction of rice and beansprouts and whatever is left in the green-grocery section, not what anyone else has for the evening meal. One of the boy's theories hinges on this fact: it is because his food is different, that is where the problem lies. At the back of the shop, after tea, his parents count the day's cash, write out their order for the dawn visit to the farmers' markets, and make a list of the number of tins of soup and packets of dried peas and cakes of soap to be replaced. They sweep the shop and wash down the counter. The boy is not required to help. His task is to read and study, to win scholarships, to be the hope and salvation of the family line.

When matters of doubt or uncertainty arise, a prescribed ritual ensues. We will ask the milfoil stalks, the parents say. What they actually do is toss three threepenny bits, lucky threepences, the coins kept wrapped in a scrap of silk in a lacquered box.

Questions are specific. Should we buy a freezer and sell paddlepops and vanilla buckets and family ice cream bricks? Will the landlord extend our lease? Will the new supermarket on Enoggera Road ruin our business? Will Charlie come top in his exams? Will he win a scholarship to Brisbane Boys' Grammar School?

"Grammar," Charlie tells them. "It's just called Grammar." This was knowledge painfully gained from the boys on the corner whose opinion of Grammar is not particularly high. The mothers of the boys on the corner buy their groceries at Mr. Chang's shop, and Mr. Chang has confided to them his dreams. "Charlie is very very clever," he has told the mothers proudly. "In Innisfail, his teacher say Charlie is brilliant, must come to school in Brisbane." The boys on the corner, who are much older than Charlie, who are in Grade 8 in fact, tell Charlie he has tickets on himself, for which he must pay.

"Where're you from, Charlie Chink?" they demand.

"Innisfail," he says. A vivid memory of paradise lost assaults him: the sugar cane, the thick yeasty rainforest smell, the pearling luggers off Flying Fish Point, coral cays against the line of sky. Home. His own place, the great wide untrammeled preschool place before difference arrived.

"Where's Innisfail, Chinkie Charlie? We never heard of Innisfail."

"Up north," he says. "Near Cairns."

"No, it ain't, Charlie Chink, you ain't from there. You're a yellow wog from China, Charlie Chink." A song evolves on the spot.

> Charlie Chink is a yellow wog,
> He was born in China under a log.

"No, I wasn't," he says, a slow learner. "I was born in Innisfail."

The leader of the boys on the corner affects surprise. "*Where* were you born, Charlie Chink?"

"Innisfail."

"Wrong." There are penalties which must be paid for wrong answers. "You're a yellow wog from China, Charlie Chink. Where were you born?"

"China," he says, learns to say, learns to believe. In time, he will improve on the right answer, he will build extensions for it, new wings, cantilevered bridges, turrets, drawbridges, a portcullis, moats, secret passages, elaborate maps. The right answer will fill a whole book, he will spend a lot of time coloring it in.

"Where was I born?" he asks his parents.

"Innisfail," they say. "You are true-blue Australian, Charlie."

How many right answers, he wonders, can questions have?

When questions arise, Charlie's mother tosses the coins and recites the results. Two heads, one tail. Three heads. Two tails, one head. Whatever. She throws the coins six times. With a soft lead pencil, very black, Charlie's father constructs the hexagram, converting the statements of the coins into solid or broken lines. The Book of Changes (or the Book of Secrets as his mother calls it) is consulted and gives this advice: *The feudal prince with his bow shoots at the hawk, which falls to earth.* Quietly elated, Charlie's father tells him: You will win the scholarship, you will be accepted by the Brisbane Boys' Grammar School. We will buy a freezer.

The best answers, the safe answers, are riddles, Charlie notes.

The boy takes six steps forward, carefully avoiding the cracks. If he touches the hedge with his left hand eighteen times between here and the end of the block, will he see the face again, the one that sometimes watches, the one that sometimes sits in the front row of his class at school? If he resolutely refuses to look as he passes that space, that hole in the wooden fence, matted with orchids and trumpet vine and lantana hedge, will the face be there when he finishes the hexagram and looks back over his shoulder?

The face is there.

It vanishes.

The boy stands uncertainly in front of the hole in the fence. Jungle is behind those rotting pickets, the kind of front yard he loves, the kind people had up in Innisfail, the kind that stretches back forever from the fence, reaching all the way to China. Pawpaw trees poke up all over the place like scaly stakes in a vegetable patch, circles of banana clumps bump into each other, a rubber plant threatens to engulf the whole house. Perhaps it *has* engulfed the whole house, since, in fact, only a bit of rotting veranda can be seen, but the boy assumes there is still a house behind the dark galloping green. What he likes best: the grass is waist high, the sticky heads of paspalum brush the trumpet vine. There is something thrilling, defiant, deliciously unruly, something full of illicit promise about an unmown lawn. When a breeze moves across it, secret pathways are revealed, tunnels are hinted at. There is a murmured suggestion of hidden loot: rubber tires, rusty iron, lost tennis balls.

The face is there again. It is a grubby face, framed by short spiky hair. It has green eyes. There are two tiny gold hoops in its earlobes, and hanging from each hoop, like a teardrop, is a blue glass bead. The ends of a yellow ribbon tied around the head droop over the forehead and into the green eyes. The mouth blows them off, but they flop into the eyes again. He has seen that face in the front row of the classroom and in the playground, he has heard many stories about it, but boys and girls live in different territories at school. They don't look at each other. Besides, the face comes and goes. Sometimes it doesn't appear for weeks.

"Whad'ya staring at?" the apparition asks.

"Nothing."

"Were so. Where ya from?"

The boy thinks for a moment. "China," he says.

"No, yer not. What's yer name?"

"Charlie Chang."

"I'm Cat. Yer wanna come in?"

"Yes," he says. When he crawls through the hole in the fence and the lantana, he feels that he has crossed a line similar to the one he crosses when he enters the painting by Wang Wei. On the trek toward the rotting veranda through the waist-high grass, Cat leading the way, they pass a rainwater tank, several stacked boxes with rusty grilles on one side (they appear to be birdcages), and the rusted corpse of a car resting legless on its axles. Charlie stops with wonder.

"It's me dad's old Holden," she calls, amused, having mislaid him and coming back for him. "You wanna get in?"

"Yeah," he breathes, awed.

She opens the door for him and he sits, kingly, behind the wheel. He has never been permitted to sit behind the wheel of his father's utility truck, which is used strictly for bringing vegetables and fruit from the farmers' market. She stands on the running board and hooks her arms over the glassless window and grins at him. He is oblivious, driving to China. Then she goes around and gets in the other side. His absorption interests her. She watches him, amused.

"I seen you in the shop sometimes," she says. He looks at her, surprised. He cannot remember seeing her in the shop. "Round the back," she says. "I climb yer mango tree. I seen yer with yer books in the sleepout."

This makes him uneasy, to know that he has been observed in that private space. He says carefully: "I've seen you at school sometimes." *Half wild*, he has heard teachers say. *A little tart*, they say, *with those shameless pierced ears*. And from other children have come certain facts: she lives in a loony bin, her family is nuts, her dad is raving mad when he's drunk, her dad's drunk all the time, her dad'll kill you if you go too close, they live in rubbish tins, they eat pig slops, she's a tart, only whores and tarts wear rings in their ears, she smells of manure, she can put a hex on you. "But you don't go to school much," he adds.

She grins. "I nick off. They catch me sometimes, but."

"What do they do?"

She laughs, and he feels invited into her conspiracy, into the funnel of her power. What, after all, can they do? "They come and see me dad and he tells them to bugger off, and then they tell me I gotta go to school."

"Where do you go," he asks, "when you don't go to school?"

"I play with Willy," she says. "We go fishing at Breakfast Creek. Or else Dad takes us out to the farms."

"Who's Willy?"

"Me bruvver. He's potty, but we don't care, Dad and me. You wanna come and see Willy?"

"Okay," he says, reluctant to let go of the driving wheel, but very much under her spell, willing to do anything she suggests. She laughs at him again, then gets onto her knees on the passenger seat and leans over and puts her arms around his neck and kisses him on the lips. He feels as though he has been pitched over the cliff in Wang Wei's painting and is soaring through the sky. He has never been kissed on the lips. His father, very occasionally, touches him on the shoulder. When he goes to bed, his mother puts both hands on his shoulders and presses her lips lightly and briefly against his forehead.

She has put a hex on me, he thinks. He feels lightheaded and full of a wild happiness.

Cat laughs and kisses him again and he kisses her back.

"C'mon," she calls gaily, and is out of the car and off through the long grass like a rabbit. He goes pelting after her. He is flying.

Two of the steps up to the veranda are missing, and the rest are so soft with rot he is afraid he will sink right through. On the veranda, sitting playing with an arrangement of stones, is a child who must be about five. Charlie, who is nine years old, suspects that Cat might actually be ten, though she is in the same grade as he is at school. He has heard that she was "kept back," because of her frequent absences, perhaps. (Because she's thick, other kids suggest, tapping their foreheads.)

"That's Willy," Cat says, and flings herself on the child and covers his cheeks with kisses. Charlie is greatly tempted to do the same. There is something about Willy that makes one want to cuddle him. He is quite unnaturally beautiful. His skin is translucent, his hair is wheaten blond, his eyes are the watery green of rainforest pools, a paler green than Cat's, a limpid blue-green. "Willy's cracked," Cat says lightly.

"What's the time, Mr. Wolf?" asks Willy.

"It's three o'clock," Cat says, smothering him with kisses again.

"No it's not," Charlie says. "We get out of school at three and I've been home for ages. It's five o'clock maybe."

Cat laughs. "Doesn't matter," she says. "Willy always asks the time. He's cracked. Dad says he's got the holy spirits in his blood, coz he was drinking too much the night he made Willy, or else Mum fooled round with an angel, he doesn't know which."

"Where's your mum?" Charlie asks, peering into the dim interior beyond the front door.

"She buggered off," Cat says cheerfully.

"Where'd she go?"

"We dunno. There's just Dad, but he's out on the farms."

"What farms?"

"Ferny Grove. Or maybe Samford or Cedar Creek, he works at all them places."

"What does he do?"

"*Farms*," she says, exasperated. "He mucks about for the farmers. You know, manure and stuff, and picking pineapples and veggies, and the pigs. He takes us sometimes. You wanna come?"

"When?"

"Tomorrow, if me dad'll take us."

"You mean miss school?"

Her eyes glitter. "Yeah."

Charlie is awed. He feels the lure of breaking the rules, but says uncertainly, "I'd have to ask my father."

Cat wrinkles up her nose. He cannot tell if she is disgusted with him, or simply puzzled.

"Who looks after you?" he asks curiously.

Cat wrinkles up her nose again. "I look after me."

"You mean," he asks, in a hushed voice, "there's no one here?"

Cat looks puzzled. "We're here," she says.

"But I mean, no grown-ups?"

Cat lies on the wooden floor of the veranda and kicks her legs like a frantic beetle on its back and laughs.

"You'll get splinters," Charlie says, embarrassed and excited by the sight of her grubby panties. There are loose boards, and oddly slanted ones, and strange warps and bumps and missing planks. Through one of the spaces he can see the dark crawl space thick with cobwebs. He shudders.

"You wanna play the railway line game?" she asks suddenly, sitting up.

The dangerous thrill of the forbidden seems to rise from the cobwebs in the frightening black space below them. It occurs to Charlie that he is sitting on top of hundreds of spiders. Underneath him, they are moving in their noiseless silken way, and some of them are redbacks and some are funnelwebs and they carry secret little pouches of poison.

"You wanna play?" she asks again.

"Play what?"

"I *told* ya. The railway line game."

In the shadowy cutting in the railway embankment, his parents have warned, lurks death. Can Cat seriously be suggesting . . . ? What does she mean by the railway line game?

Charlie's shop and Cat's overgrown house are both on Newmarket Road, and both face the railway line that runs from Brunswick Street to Ferny Grove, the end of the line. On the other side of the road from their houses, a high embankment separates trains from cars. There is an overhead footbridge—it is not far from Cat's place—that leads up to Wilston Heights where the snobs and the nobs and the private school kids live. On the other side of the line, the Wilston Heights side, the lawns are always mown and the fences do not lean or sway or have missing planks. There are no rusted cars in long grass. There are two ways to go from Cat's and Charlie's side of the railway line to the other side: by the overhead bridge, or through the cutting which is quite close to the bridge.

Charlie has been absolutely forbidden by his parents to go anywhere near this cutting, but he has seen the boys on the corner, his Grade 8 tormentors, duck under the fence and stand there in their loose gigantic bodies to watch the trains rush by. From the far side of the street, hidden behind bushes, he has observed, awestruck, that when the trains go by, the wind they make flattens the grass in the cutting and whips his tormentors' hair about their heads.

"C'mon, Willy," Cat says. She grabs Willy's hand with her right, Charlie's with her left. Her hand is wiry and hard.

"I'm not allowed," Charlie says.

"You don't have to do it if you're scared. You can stay with Willy and watch."

She does not, however, as he learns with alarm, mean that he can stay on the other side of the street, or even on the footpath outside the fence. As soon as they reach the cutting, she ducks under the sign that says DANGER. ENTRY FORBIDDEN BY ORDER, BRISBANE CITY COUNCIL, and Willy bobs under with her.

"Well, c'mon," she says impatiently, and Charlie hesitates only for a minute. His desire to please Cat is greater than his desire to stay beyond the fence. And he finds, in fact, that he is no longer afraid because he believes Cat could step on the lines and raise her hand as a policeman might, and the trains would brake and rumble to a halt, or would vanish into thin air. She has holy spirits in her blood, he thinks. When she moves, the yellow ribbon bobs about like a kite tail and he can see a fizzing glow around her, the kind you see around a light bulb when you squint.

"You hold Willy's hand," she says. She draws an X in the ground with a stick. "Now Willy, you know you gotta stay right here," she says. "Don't you move or I'll clobber ya."

Charlie, his heart racing, stands in the valley of the shadow of the cutting and takes Willy's hand. It is soft and plump and Willy looks up into his face and laughs and asks: "What's the time, Mr. Wolf?"

"It's five o'clock," Charlie says, and kisses Willy on his soft silken cheek. Willy tastes delicious, and Charlie kisses him again. From the corner of his eye he can see Cat, but he can hardly bear to watch. It is not exactly fear that is coming back into that place in the stomach where butterflies breed. No. He knows Cat is all-powerful. It is more the frightening mystery of the exercise of her power, of not knowing what might happen next, where he might be taken, what he might see. She is doing what the boys on the corner do: walking between the lines on the wooden sleepers. His heart is beating so fast, he thinks it may leap up into his mouth like a fish. What time *is* it? Is it time for the 5:30 train to come through?

"Cat," he calls nervously. "I think the train's coming soon."

"Course it is," she calls back. "Hasn't got to Wilston yet, but. You can hear it whistle."

Yes of course, he thinks, feeling foolish. His parents' shop is opposite Wilston station. He knows perfectly well that the train whistles as it leaves. He knows you can hear it from here.

"Fifty-one, fifty-two, fifty-three," calls Cat, stepping from sleeper to sleeper, turning, coming back past the cutting, turning.

"What's the time, Mr. Wolf?" Willy calls, jumping up and down with pleasure and tugging at Charlie's hand.

"Train time, Willy!" Cat calls. "You stay right there or I'll smack you."

The train whistles and Willy calls excitedly *What's the time Mr. Wolf what's the time Mr. Wolf what's the time Mr. Wolf?* and Cat claps her hands and laughs. Then she does something quite mad, quite terrifying. Directly opposite the cutting, she lies on a sleeper, her head propped against one shining steel rail, her feet on the other. Charlie gives a strangled cry and lets go of Willy's hand and rushes forward, but stops transfixed at the edge of the mound of crushed bluestone on which the tracks are laid. In the distance, down the long shimmering silver line, he can see the train leaving Wilston station, belching smoke, its black mustache grille almost scraping the rails.

He is weak at the knees, he cannot move, he cannot speak. "Cat!" he tries to call, but no sound comes. Cat says to him calmly, "When it gets to the bridge, I get up."

The overhead footbridge is fifty yards from the cutting. Charlie, paralyzed, watches the train streak toward it. Oddly, it takes much longer than usual, it takes forever, it is coming in slow motion without a sound and Charlie is in a dream now, he is moving through water or through honey, this is not real at all. Sobs of laughter come up out of his mouth like hiccups. He feels a small warm hand clutch his and wants to tell Willy to go back to where Cat drew the X on the ground or he'll smack him, but only the bubbles of laughter come out of his mouth. They should step back, they should run, but he cannot move. He can feel something warm and wet trickling down his legs. Willy murmurs in a singsong voice: *What's the time, Mr. Wolf?*

And then the train is at the bridge and Cat jackknifes up and catapults herself across the gap, and she is pulling Charlie and Willy and they are all rolling over and over in the grass of the cutting like tennis balls rolling down a hill and the train is like a rushing mighty wind and the roaring of the end of the world is in his ears and Cat and Willy are laughing and Cat is kissing him on the lips. He has never been so frightened or so excited in his life, he has never felt so powerful. If he snapped his fingers, the train could roll over them like a cloud passing and not a hair of their heads would be touched. He kisses Cat back and wants to go on kissing her forever.

"You wanna marry me?" she asks.

"Yes," he says. "Yes yes yes."

"Okay," she says. "Willy can marry us."

And the three of them, laughing and shrieking, kissing and hugging, roll around in the long soft grass of the cutting like nestlings waiting for the mother bird's return.

THREE

Five children played in a deep rock pool at Cedar Creek Falls: Charlie and Cat and Willy and Robbie Gray and Catherine Reed.

It is not difficult for me to picture this scene, knowing the place as I do, knowing the people as I came to know them, knowing the way the green closeness of the rainforest folds people in on themselves, knowing the way it holds secrets. They became part of me, those people. I met them in the dark wood of Charlie's memory and in his photographs, I swam in the looped rock pools of Gabriel's dreams. Dreams hang around in the rainforest. There is not enough sunlight to lift their fog.

I don't think I could go back there now. No, I'm sure I couldn't. And yet that place is always with me. I am never absent from it.

When Gabriel and I swam there, and talked, and made love, he used to say he felt his father's childhood watching him from the damp clumps of ferns. Sometimes when we were making love, things would go awry; he could not function in front of those paternal eyes. In the rainforest, things stay in the drugged air, they drip back out of the warm green fog, they cling to the ladders of climbing pandanus, they lodge under rocks. Moss grows over them. They steam and ferment.

Gabriel said he sometimes thought the only thing his father minded about the divorce was losing the Samford farm and the falls. Not that he actually *lost* them. He disposed of them rather, his motives tangled, and then later regretted it. Indeed, so anxious was his father, at the time of the settlement, that the farm not fall into his ex-wife's hands that he sold it off hugger-mugger to Gil Brennan, a neighboring pineapple farmer. But creepers snake their way up to the light and things that passionately wish to connect do connect. This came to be one more thing Gabriel's father held against his mother.

"She belonged out here," Gabriel said. "This was just our weekend place when I was a kid, but Mum took to it the way a bowerbird takes to scraps of blue."

I had a vision of Gabriel's mother as soft and feathery, her liquid eyes darting about on the lookout for blue, coveting blue, stealing blue socks and scraps of blue T-shirts from clotheslines, snapping blue foil milk-bottle tops from open rubbish bins, lining her nest, turning an inhospitable clutter of sticks into paradise. I relayed this fanciful vision to Charlie once and he said: "It's the *male* bird who makes the bower. The bower is a trap."

"Did you ever meet her?" I asked. "Gabriel's mother?"

"I think I did at a university formal once," he said. "She was a friend of Catherine's. They went to high school together, I think. She was a shy little bird, and I remember thinking how typical. Robbie was peacocking all over the place as usual, and I reckoned he'd want a drab little peahen to set himself off. And I must have met her at Catherine's twenty-first, I suppose."

"I think," Gabriel said, "when the marriage began to go wrong, she could come out here to the farm and the rainforest and it didn't matter."

After the fall, and the freefall, she flew into Gil Brennan's life and they built a nest. To watch his mother and his stepfather moving absorbed along the spiky rows of pineapples, Gabriel said, or just walking through the rainforest, or picnicking at Cedar Creek (though she wouldn't go near the falls anymore as she used to when he was a child; she wouldn't go anywhere near the falls), to watch his mother with her young second family was to know the sheer simplicity of happiness. Poetic justice, he said. He hadn't known, all those years away from her, that his mother was happy. His father had led him to believe otherwise. "She can't cope, I'm afraid," his father had said, "and we both think it's better if you don't . . . She just wouldn't be able to cope with you, you see. She just doesn't want you right now."

To discover her tranquillity when he was twenty, Gabriel said, to walk into the peaceable kingdom of the sweet ordinariness of her life with Gil Brennan and their ten-year-old daughter and their eight-year-old son, was a miracle. And to find that it was not true that she had banished him . . . ! But he must not be harsh with his father, she said. Behind every lie, she said, there is a wound. One should be gentle with the bloody gashes in other people's lives.

And what was this bloody gash in his father's life? he wanted to know bitterly.

Be gentle, Gabriel, she said.

He was eight or nine, Gabriel thought, and they were living in Sydney when his father, fuming, and pacing up and down, told him: "Your mother's got hold of the farm."

He wanted to ask if he could visit her now, but was afraid to say anything.

"It's her way of getting back at us," his father said.

"It's funny," Gabriel mused. "I never thought he even liked the place much. Mum and I used to come out here every weekend, and all the school holidays, but Dad used to stay in town and work. Well, he had to, I suppose. But I never thought he liked the place much."

Gabriel, I remember from those green and golden days, used to turn suddenly and look behind him (perhaps once every half hour or so), or stare intently downstream where the churning water bumped under thick low-slung vines. I never teased him about it.

It was a disturbing stillness.

"Once," Gabriel mused, "when he realized Mum and I used to come here to swim . . ." Gabriel, perched on the boulder like a gnome, knees crooked up under his chin, hands clasped around his knees, was staring into the whirlpool that the water made between the two boulders. "He hadn't realized it. I suppose he simply hadn't thought about it. The falls aren't on our land."

In the whirlpool, I could see our reflections whizzed into concentric circles of color like clothes in a washing machine. You could not look into the whirlpool for too long. You had to look away or you could lose your balance and fall.

"He threw a tantrum," Gabriel said. "Not at me, of course, he was never angry with me, only with Mum. He said it was dangerous, and Mum was never to bring me here again."

Sometimes I would wait silently, never interrupting, never prompting, for half an hour before Gabriel would dredge up another bit of his life. It was like a vast jigsaw puzzle to him. He was always picking up one small piece or another and holding it up to the light and studying it and trying it out in different places, but never quite finding where it belonged.

"Then one day he brought me here himself," Gabriel said.

In the whirlpool I could see the other Gabriel, maybe four years old, maybe five, the apple of his father's eye, the angel child, the dryad in the pool, still down there in the swirling water's black eye, the plughole where everything went.

"It's strange, isn't it?" Gabriel asked me, "that I can remember these things so vividly when they all happened before I was six. He took me to Sydney when I was six. And yet I see them as clearly as if . . . The trouble is, I can't remember the in-betweens." It was, he said, like having a drawerful of photographs without any captions or any known sequence to them. He looked behind him and stared into the deep green–black shadow. "Did you hear something?" he asked.

"Only scrub turkeys."

"Yes, I suppose so." In the whirlpool, I could see his brooding face race and spin and stretch itself into a funnel. Those are stones that were his eyes, and those are merely pitted dimples in the rock, those hollows that look like eyesockets gouged. "The day he brought me here, he behaved very strangely. I thought he was frightened of the place. No, not exactly frightened, that's not right. But tightly wound, the same way he would get on the footbridge near Wilston station." New water keeps coming and keeps coming, racing into the same spinning circle and then on. I suppose it was possible, somewhere in the millions of years of climatic history of the world's oldest land mass, that there had been droughts of sufficient length to make the whirlpool disappear. "He kept looking behind him," Gabriel said. "He was in a strange state of nervous excitement. He kept turning around suddenly as though someone was watching him from in there." Gabriel, looking over his shoulder again, gestured into the murk where someone unseen could indeed be silently watching, where strangler figs and epiphytes and she-oaks and creepers fed off each other and fought a deadly silent fight in the quest for sun.

Gabriel closed his eyes, concentrating. "He must have had his camera with him. I keep trying to see him with the camera in his hand, or in the knapsack, but I can't seem to . . . it won't show itself. I can never remember the camera. But he has a photograph of me sitting on this boulder, and he had it enlarged. Once I woke up at night because I heard something and I crept down to his study (we were still in the terrace house in Paddington then, it wasn't long after we'd moved to Sydney) and he was sitting with just the reading lamp on, staring at a photograph. He didn't hear me. I stayed there for ages watching him, until he put it in his desk drawer, and then I tiptoed back to bed.

"The next day, when he wasn't around, I looked. It was the photograph of me at the falls.

"It's funny, though. I never thought he liked the place when I was a kid."

Once, when Gabriel and I were picnicking and I had gone back to the car alone to get a jumper (it turns cool very quickly in the rainforest if the sun goes; I think the moss and the damp black earth suck warmth out of the air), I came back to find Gabriel kneeling on the boulder, his back to me, holding his hands out toward one of the trees a little upstream, the one that has been choked by the strangler fig whose roots make a thick mazy ladder up the old smothered trunk to the sky. We climbed that ladder once, Gabriel and I. It was not very difficult, not difficult at all really (so long as you didn't look down) with so many woody rungs for the feet, so many vines to grab. We climbed up to where the tree orchids and the wheel-of-fire flowers run amok. We looked at each other and couldn't say a word.

So at first I thought Gabriel was praying to the strangled tree. (I don't mean literally; I mean the way the pagan privacy of the rainforest affects most people.) Then I thought he was placating someone. I waited quietly. I never told him I'd seen.

"Dad told me the worst mistake he ever made was selling the farm," Gabriel said. "And yet I can always hear him shouting at Mum and telling me the falls were dangerous and I must never come here without him."

He looked behind him. He stared into the whirlpool and

watched his spinning history doing cartwheels. Five children played in the pool beneath the boulders: Charlie and Cat and Willy, and Robbie Gray and Catherine Reed. *With a down, hey down, hey down.*

There were five children played in a pool, with a down, derry derry derry, down down, and here we go round the mulberry bush, the stinging bush, the banyan tree, the merry-go-round.

Oh yes, it's easy for me, having lain beside Gabriel on the boulder in the sun, having listened, drowsy and happy, to the murmur of his voice, to picture those five children in that place, to know the way the dark green wall of the rainforest shut them in on themselves. I can hear their shrieks as the chilly water that comes from under the mountain splashed shock on their young bodies.

It was not a schoolday, it was a Saturday, but nevertheless, for Charlie, it had all the trappings of forbidden enchantment. Cat had waved her wand. She had put a hex on everyone, on Charlie's watchful protective parents, on her own unpredictable father, on Robbie Gray and Catherine Reed, and here was Charlie in a place as beautiful as the lost paradise around Innisfail in North Queensland, here he was with people who would in other circumstances ignore him, or even torment him.

"This is Robbie Gray," Cat said. "His dad owns the farm, but *my* dad does all the work." She laughed. "Robbie's just Lord Muck like his dad and he lives up on Wilston Heights with the snobs and he goes to snob school."

"Grammar," Robbie Gray explained. "Brisbane Grammar School."

"Robbie's old," Cat said.

"I'm twelve," Robbie explained.

"This is Charlie," Cat said.

"Pleased to meet you." Robbie Gray put out his hand the way grown-ups did, and Charlie, a little overwhelmed, extended his. The two shook hands solemnly, quite as though they were a pair of aged scholars in Wang Wei's painting, bowing to each other on the low curved bridge beside the willow tree. "Samford's just our weekend place," Robbie Gray explained, as though Charlie were a person of substance to whom careful explanations were due.

(Charlie, telling Lucy this many years later, is momentarily overcome. He walks up and down his spartan living room and stops in front of the large photograph of the Cedar Creek pool. I loved him at that moment, Charlie said. I was moved to the point of tears. When you are so used to being treated more or less like a dog by other kids, especially by other boys, so used to it that you don't even think about it, it's just the way things are, and then suddenly . . .

I loved him, he said. I would have died for him.)

But Cat made a face at Robbie Gray. "Robbie's got a plum in his mouth and he tries to talk like a bloody Pom. They make them talk that way at snob school." She pinched Robbie on the arm and he blushed and tweaked the dirty yellow ribbon in her hair. "Ouch," Cat said. "Cut it out." But she liked it, Charlie saw. She liked Robbie Gray, and Robbie Gray couldn't take his eyes off Cat. There was a wall around them made of all the times they had played at the farm and at the falls. There were secrets between them. Charlie passionately wanted to step into the circle that ran around them.

"And you know Catherine," Cat said. "She's in our class."

"Yes," Charlie said, swallowing. But he wouldn't have said he knew Catherine. He wouldn't have dared.

"She lives next door to me," Robbie explained. "I said she could come."

Charlie noted the way Catherine let her eyes rest on Robbie for a moment then move away. "Hello, Charlie," she said. She gave him a small shy smile and dropped her eyes.

"Hello, Catherine," he said awkwardly. He felt exposed. Catherine had heard the chanting in the playground. *You're a yellow wog from China, Charlie Chink.* So had Cat, of course, but that was different; he and Cat were two of a kind, there were songs about her too, though people were more wary about teasing Cat. They were more likely to do it behind her back.

Catherine moved in a different orbit. It was, in fact, hard to believe that she would walk onto the same piece of earth as himself and Cat. He felt as he had felt the first day the boys on the corner arrived at the railway cutting and began to add new rules to the railway game. They had seen the dark stain on Charlie's pants (it appeared every time Cat lay on the tracks, he couldn't stop it) and they jeered and pointed and made up a new song on the spot. *Last one home is the one who snitches, Charlie Chink has wet his britches.* Cat, who always lay on the rails longer than the boys did, Cat who was always the last one up before the train came through, Cat flew into the boys like an avenging little wheel of arms and legs. They had a certain respect for Cat. Charlie thought they were afraid of her. And there was something else in their eyes; he couldn't tell if it was love or hate, but whatever it was they let her be. Charlie, however, was always terrified they would break into the wet-britches song in the playground and his disgrace would be complete. He felt as though Catherine brought the knowledge of such shames with her, and that it was between them, smoking like a compost heap. They were both embarrassed by it, he thought. Yet she simply smiled shyly and said: Hello, Charlie.

Although she and Charlie were in the same class, they had never spoken to each other before. They had never looked at each other, except furtively. Catherine was the cleverest of the girls, and Charlie of the boys—so it transpired after various tests and exams, and after the visit of the school inspector. Therefore only an aisle separated their desks in the back row, but they might as well have sat on different planets.

Charlie was not at all certain of what to do, confronted with Catherine Reed in a swimming suit.

"C'mon," Cat called. "Last one in is a rotten egg."

She jumped off the boulder, hugging her knees up to her chest, and made an explosive fan of water leap high into the green air. It sounded like a shot from a gun. Willy shrieked and chortled and went waddling in after her from the edge of the pool like a plump duckling, burbling *What's the time, Mr. Wolf?*

Charlie, too timid to jump in, watched Catherine and Robbie with interest. They were timid too, he saw instantly, worried about the stones on the bottom of the swimming hole, worried about the depth of the hole, worried about the whirlpool. Nevertheless Catherine, pale and determined, stood on the knob of the boulder where Cat had stood and closed her eyes and jumped. She did not hug her knees in elastic joy, but went straight down like an anchor being dropped. When she surfaced, she spluttered, but she paddled about gamely in the pool with

Cat and Willy, ducking when they smacked the surface of the water with their hands, copying them, smacking water back at them, laughing with Cat.

Charlie was fascinated. At school, Catherine could have held court if she wanted to but she didn't seem to like company much. A bevy of girls followed her around, but she would slip off and disappear. He had seen her in the school library—one of his own retreats—a number of times. She never looked up when he came in. She kept her head buried in a book. Charlie very much wanted her to lift her head and look at him now, on the boulder. He wanted Cat and Catherine, both, to look at him and to approve.

He climbed on the boulder and looked down. It seemed very high and the stones below all had edges like razor blades.

"Look out, I'm going to jump," he called, and Cat and Catherine both stopped splashing and backed away from the center of the pool and looked up. Cat had to keep paddling with her hands to stop herself from being moved back over the rock lip and into the sucking mouth of the funnel between the boulders. Charlie felt giddy. He could see their faces, pale as the underside of leaves, turned toward him, Cat and Catherine smiling, both of them waiting.

Waiting.

"Come *on*," Cat called, impatient, and he wrapped his panic around himself like a blanket and closed his eyes and jumped.

What a strange and thrilling world he torpedoed into. The inside of the rainforest hummed in his ears and the churn of a washing machine was pulling him through to the other side of the earth. He was so surprised by the sense of weightlessness and euphoria that he opened his eyes and the water was crystal clear. He saw each dimple in the great basalt slabs and he saw moss waving itself like flags, and he saw the pale ghostly legs of Cat and Catherine, twin mermaids, trailing above him. When he popped above the surface like a cork from a bottle, he was spluttering but laughing too. He thought his laughter might take him up above the water, past the boulders, past the laddered fig, past the canopy itself. He was flying.

He looked at Catherine and he knew that she knew. She knew from the high breathless gasping way he laughed that they had discovered the same thing: there is nothing quite so thrilling as leaping into the very teeth of your fear. She smiled at him. He smiled back. Cat splashed them and duck-dived beneath them and tugged at their ankles. Down they went again, and Catherine's wafer of a face, pale as pearl-shell, was inches from his, her long fair hair streaming upwards like a drowning woman's cries.

Time ticked differently underwater. Charlie didn't care if he never drew a breath of air again, he was floating in the orbit of Catherine's eyes. When she reached out and touched him and he took her hands, he expected fins to form themselves, and gills. He thought they would stay forever with the flags of moss and the white stones that did a slow minuet toward the lip of the whirling.

Shaboom! Like champagne corks, they were up in the pool again, the three of them gasping and spluttering in a knot of limbs, he couldn't tell where Cat ended and Catherine began. They duck-dived, they surfaced, they dived. He wanted to stay in that fluid place where shapes undid themselves. Sometimes, in later years, it seemed to Charlie they spent that whole hot summer under the skin of the pool. Years later, he could close his eyes and summon up the bodily memory at will: the weightless drift of it, the green filtered light, the ghostly floating presences of Catherine and Cat, the champagne fizz building and building in the lungs, the torpedo resurrection. He would sit alone in rooms in New York, in Sydney, rocking himself in clear undercurrents, hugging the hollows in his sides where Cat and Catherine coiled their long mermaid tails.

In this memory, Robbie Gray was never underwater with them, but was high and distant on the boulder.

Robbie Gray was sitting on the boulder, king of the pool, the sun king. How selfish happiness is, Charlie thought. It might have been hours that he spent tripling and dippling in the pool with Catherine and Cat, with Willy happy as always in his strange solo world, before it occurred to Charlie that Robbie might be lonely up there, and before an even more disturbing thought occurred: that Robbie might be afraid to jump. He remembered that his recklessly happy heart rushed out to Robbie Gray. He wanted to say: Look, just close your eyes and do it. Catherine was scared, and I was scared, but we did it. He wanted to say: Trust me, Robbie, there's nothing like it. There's nothing to equal tilting your lance at fear and charging in.

But it was not the sort of thing he felt a yellow wog from China could say to the sun king.

There was a moment when silence fell, except for the scrub turkeys and Willy's warbling in his private cocoon, and he and Catherine and Cat climbed out, slithering on the rock, and sat with Robbie and didn't know what to say. Well, Charlie and Catherine didn't know what to say. Cat said: "You're the rotten egg, you silly drip."

"I've already been swimming this morning," Robbie said. "Before you came." Charlie watched Catherine, who had arrived with Robbie, give him a quick sideways look. "While my dad was showing you the barn, Catherine," he said. He jumped up. "Let's explore. Let's climb up the falls." And he was off, the leader of the pack, though the others followed happily enough. Cat had to scamper back and forth between Willy and the forward scouts. Sometimes they walked up the watercourse itself, stepping across the flat rock platforms; sometimes they had to take the boundary paths, clambering over fallen tree trunks gone soft, watching for the dreaded stinging tree. Robbie Gray was a ferocious climber. He was determined to stay in the lead where indeed, Charlie thought, he rightfully belonged. In particular, he thought that Robbie became upset whenever Cat got ahead of him, and this friction between two such adored beings distressed him terribly. Charlie did not think Cat was aware of Robbie's irritation; she simply darted back and forth, checking on Willy in the rear, barrelling up ahead of all of them and back again, because that's what her energy made her do. He wondered if she ever slept at night. Or did she go stalking the back alleys with other cats, climbing his mango tree, spying on him as he sat at his little table in the sleepout reading a book? It made a difference to him, knowing that.

Cat is watching, he would think happily, looking out into the night.

When they came to the base of the steepest stretch, where the falls were really *falls* for a quick short drop of fifty feet, Robbie announced suddenly: "Okay, last one back is a rotten egg," and swung about and went crashing his way back downstream.

And Charlie would have instantly obeyed except that Cat called out: "Poohey! I'm going to climb the falls first."

Looking upward, Charlie bit his lip.

"You mind Willy, Charlie," Cat said. She hoisted herself up to the next rock ledge, lithe as a possum, and grabbed at trees and reached for handles of rock. She got about halfway up. "Okay," she shouted, panting. "I quit. I'm coming down."

She planted herself on a ledge to rest, and Catherine, gritting her teeth, called out: "Wait there for me."

Charlie could see the muscles in Catherine's arms and legs bleating with fear. When she hoisted herself past the first great ledge and walked her fingers up the rockface feeling for something to grab on to, her straining ankles made him think of desperate flies bucking about on the struts of a funnelweb.

He couldn't look. He sat on the rock platform and put his hand in the water, against the rock, and prayed to it: *Don't let her fall.*

He had not felt frightened for Cat. He knew now that Cat was invulnerable. (In the cutting, it was the train he didn't trust.) He knew that if Cat lost her footing she would simply sail across space the way glider possums did, she would settle as lightly as a puffball on the next ledge. But he felt himself enter Catherine's frail and trembling body and could not bear it.

Willy put his arms around Charlie's neck and cooed in his ear: *What's the time, Mr. Wolf?* and Charlie pressed his lips against the soft delectable cheek and held Willy like a pillow and prayed *Don't let her fall don't let her fall please don't let her fall please don't.* He only looked up when there were loud halloos and there they were, both of them, waving at him from halfway up. "Look, Willy!" he yelped with excitement. "Look up there!" And he and Willy laughed and hugged each other and he covered Willy with kisses and told him over and over again: "I love them, Willy, don't you? I love them all." He was awash in love, he floated in it for one entire summer, duck-diving, and surfacing, and submerging himself again and moving languidly through that weightless space where everything connects with everything else.

He could not remember the trip back down to the pool; that is, he could not separate it from the water or the green air or the climbing or the swimming and diving or from other times and other days, except for the clear sharp moment when the three of them and Willy were lying on their stomachs on the great boulder, staring down at Robbie who floated on his back with arms outstretched, king of the pool.

"You're all rotten eggs," Robbie said.

Charlie thought of the elegant Grammar School way Robbie had shaken his hand and he wanted to make an offering from out of the rich cloud he moved inside. "Cat and Catherine climbed up the falls," he called out. "You should've climbed up with them, you would've won."

Robbie ignored him. "It's best in the pool when you're by yourself," he said. "You can jump further off the boulder then. I only like to jump off it when I'm here by myself."

"Eenie meenie minie mo," Cat called, sliding on her belly on the boulder like a lizard. "Look out, here I come!" She went in like a water snake, and Charlie and Catherine could see her wreathing a slow coil around Robbie and then yanking him down. There was a spluttering thrashing game, and laughter, and they could see Robbie kissing Cat and Cat kissing back.

Charlie, on his stomach on warm rock, wanted to kiss all of them. He most especially wished, however, that Cat was dunking him in the pool and kissing *him*. Catherine touched his arm, and he turned sideways to look at her. "Cat loves everyone," she said.

He laughed happily. "Everyone loves Cat."

She smiled at him and he smiled back. How beautiful she was. He loved her. He would have kissed her if he'd dared.

"*I* love Cat," she said. "And so do you."

"So does Robbie," he said.

Catherine looked at him without blinking for three seconds, four, five. "*Here* he loves her," she said.

Charlie, startled, could not sustain the weight of her gaze. He watched Cat and Robbie in the water. When he turned again, Catherine was still looking at him. She frightened him just a little. With Cat, you knew exactly what to expect. With Catherine, you didn't quite.

"I love Robbie," he said.

Catherine raised her eyebrows. She kept looking at him, unblinking. "Not as much as Robbie loves Robbie," she said.

"Don't you like him?"

She watched Robbie, expressionless, for several seconds, then she looked at Charlie again. "Not very much," she said.

In front of the barn there were two fathers and two cars. It was like a game that teachers gave you in school, Charlie thought. Which father belongs with which car? It wasn't hard to guess. Cat's father owned the battered red utility truck, a much scarred vehicle. There were a number of places on its body where Cat's father, after too many beers, had had close encounters with lampposts and curbs and various other immovable objects and with other vehicles. In these places he had daubed applications of lurid pink metal primer, so that the car had a fevered chicken-pox look. Robbie's father stood beside a sleek black Buick.

As soon as the children came within sight of the cars, Cat and Robbie, propelled by some unheard starting gun, broke into a run and pelted toward the two fathers. Robbie won by a whisker. "I won!" he announced, and then grandly: "But for the second prize, you can have a ride back in our car, Cat. Dad, can everyone come in ours?"

Robbie's father frowned a momentary frown, looking askance at the wet swimsuits and at the always-slightly-grubby face of Cat, but graciousness fell so quickly as a veil that Charlie wondered if he had imagined the frown. "Certainly," Robbie's father said mellowly. "You won't object, Reilly, if your young-sters ride in the Buick? I'll drop them off at your place on the way home."

Cat's father turned his head to spit a wad of tobacco. "No skin off my back," he shrugged. "If they wanna be posh and la-de-dah."

"I don't wanna," said Cat, unhooking the backboard of her father's Holden and pulling it down. "It's more fun in the ute. C'mon, Willy." She hoisted him into the back. She pulled herself up as easily as possums do.

Robbie, only fleetingly thrown off stride, said graciously, "You can still come with us, Charlie, but you'll have to sit in the middle, that's all. I always let Catherine have the other window."

Catherine smiled her demure smile at Robbie. It was a smile

that already made Charlie hold his breath. "Thank you, Robbie," she said, her gaze resting on him until he looked at her and smiled in his gracious way. "But you can let Charlie. Mr. Reilly, could I come back in the ute too, please? It's more fun."

She took Charlie's breath away, her sheer delicate savagery, the smile, the look in her eyes; and he couldn't bear to have Robbie's feelings hurt. He wanted to offer tribute, he wanted to give himself in homage to Robbie who had shaken his hand and who had spoken to him as though he were another Grammar boy. He also wanted to be with Cat and Catherine and Willy.

Mr. Reilly laughed, and Charlie saw his mouthful of yellow and uneven teeth. "Right you are, luv," he said to Catherine, and picked her up and set her down next to Cat. She might have been a piece of dandelion fluff. "Not as posh as you look, little lady." He nodded approvingly. Mr. Reilly didn't have much time for posh.

Cat and Catherine sat on the dirty floor with Willy between them, their backs against the driver's cabin. Charlie wanted to join them, but he also wanted to please Robbie Gray.

"Utes are for girls and little kids," Robbie said. "The Buick is for boys. We'll still let you come with us, Charlie."

We'll still let you. . . .

"Thank you, Robbie," Charlie said.

Ah, and he felt important—more than that, he felt like an ambassador at the court of the emperors, sitting next to Robinson Gray who lived on Wilston Heights and went to Grammar. He could not deny that sinking into that pillowed backseat and fingering leather as soft as Willy's cheek filled him with wonder. He could not deny that he savored that excitement on his parents' faces when the black car pulled up at the shop door, and he got out and went inside and said casually: "I got a ride home in Mr. Gray's Buick. He lives on Wilston Heights." He could not deny the thrill of feeling the power beneath him, of soaring down the hill (it felt like flying), of overtaking and gliding past every other car on Samford Road, on Kelvin Grove Road, on Newmarket Road. Oh, and he had to admit he was quite profoundly grateful that the boys on the corner just happened to be in the shop in full rude domineering flight over his parents when the black car stopped and he got out.

Nevertheless, when Robbie's father overtook Mr. Reilly's

leprous ute and Charlie stuck his head out the window and waved madly to the three in the back—the three who swayed together and laughed together and sang, their hair whipping about their heads like flags in a storm—he knew that was where he really wanted to be. And he knew from the moment he pulled himself back inside the Buick that Robbie Gray would rather have been there too.

It was Cat who made the difference, he thought. He and Catherine and Robbie Gray all wanted Cat to touch them with her wand. He thought Robbie Gray was baffled that the Buick did not exert a stronger magic. Robbie Gray gave him a look whose meaning he could not decipher.

"Very immature, isn't it?" Robbie Gray said. "The way they behave."

Charlie swallowed. That was the elegant sort of way Grammar boys talked. He did want to agree with Robbie. Yes, he allowed, it was a bit immature.

At the shop, Robbie Gray shook hands with him. "See you again," he said.

Something warm and rich stirred within Charlie. "Would you like to come in?" he offered. His mind raced across possible attractions he could offer. "My father can read the *I Ching*," he said. "You throw three coins and he can tell you your future."

Robbie hesitated. Charlie thought Robbie wanted to be liked. It was a miracle, but Robbie wanted to be liked by Charlie. He hesitated for a second, and Charlie always kept that second in his mind.

"Maybe some other time," Robbie said.

But that second was there like a warm little seedling between them all summer, floating between them in the pool at the falls on weekends, germinating slowly in the car on the long rides home.

It was a pity, Charlie thought, that though it put forth a fragile green shoot, it never did come to bud.

FOUR

Across the railway line there was a footbridge linking Wilston Heights with the humbler side of the tracks and it kept on showing up in Charlie's nightmares and photographs. Not only Charlie's. Once, after I got to know Catherine, after I began to follow in her footsteps, moving around the world with my own TV crew, we found ourselves collaborating on a documentary in London. In Willesden and Harlesden, to be precise. There was talk of Mole People, there were rumors of underground coils of settlement, there were whispers about the murky urban ravines along the Bakerloo line.

"There's the perfect place for the shot," our cameraman said, pointing to the overhead footbridge with its steps down to the platform at Willesden Junction. "We'll get an aerial view of the station without comment, the faces on the platform will say it all, and we'll pan along the cobweb of lines from there." Catherine nodded, but on the bridge she began to feel dizzy. She hung on to the railing and put her head down on her hands. She told the crew she thought she'd have to go home. "I must have picked up something in Asia," she said.

Nightmares are infectious, I am certain of this. There are virulent strains which go on the rampage, which move around like the Hong Kong flu, which have no regard whatsoever for borders, which enter the genes, which cross generations and visit their harm on the sons of the fathers and the lovers of the sons, which possibly persist even unto the third and fourth generations.

I know the footbridge that is roughly halfway between Wilston and Newmarket stations. I know it because it was part of the riddle that swallowed up Gabriel. On the way out to his mother's pineapple farm at Samford we used to drive along Newmarket Road. We used to stop at a little grocery store, the kind that hardly exists anymore, and we would buy ice creams and then we would walk along the road to the footbridge and we would climb its zigzag steps and lean over the railings and watch the trains rushing beneath. We would lick our ice creams and talk. It was one of our rituals.

"It was a kind of habit with my father," Gabriel said. "Whenever he came with us to the farm, he'd drive here with me—just with me, he never brought my mother here—and we'd stand on the bridge and watch the trains. I suppose I do it because it brings back that time before they split up. There was an old Chinese couple running the shop back then. They were always very obsequious toward my father, very pleased to see him, smiles all over."

Gabriel would lean over and stare at the lines as though they were telegraph wires, as though if he looked at them long enough they would yield up some message. "I suppose we came here because the house Dad lived in when he was a kid was up on the hill there," he said. "It was strange, though. I thought he was almost frightened of the trains, actually, but it was like an addiction. He'd get very agitated, or very excited in a strange sort of way when the trains came through. Did you know people can be addicted to their fears? I read about it somewhere. It's got something to do with endorphins.

"After we finished our ice creams, we used to cross over and walk up the hill past the old house. In the front yard next door, in a pen where people passing by could look at it, there was a huge tortoise that was supposed to be a hundred years old. 'A hundred and thirty now,' my father would say. It was supposed to be a hundred when he was a kid."

"I wonder if it's still there," I said. "We should go up and see."

"I suppose that's why we came. Me and Dad. Nostalgia."

But he would frown and stare at the rails as though something about the ritual puzzled him. There was a piece missing and he kept looking for it.

"It was a very strange state he got into. Looking back from here, I'd be tempted to say it was sexual excitement, but I suppose that's the adult twisting the child's memories. Reading something into them."

There was something his father always said to him on the bridge, a rather pompous and formulaic thing it seemed to Gabriel now, part of the ritual of ice-creams-and-bridge. "The law is like railway lines, Gabriel, straight and true. The law protects the truth. What the law decides *is* truth."

"I suppose," Gabriel said, "it's the kind of thing fathers say to sons, especially when they've made up their minds their sons will study law. I suppose it doesn't mean anything." But in fact, everything seemed cryptic to him, any platitude could have been a code, any cliché, looked at from the proper angle, might turn into gold.

"Of course," he said, "it did leave an imprint. Straight and true, I've discovered, is exactly what the law is not." Gabriel was already making a name for himself as a dropout from law, a legal maverick, a brumby, combing the city's underside, keeping a meticulous file on certain policemen and judges and politicians, hawking his investigative services *like a vulgar fishmonger* his father said (deep in his disappointed cups, full of grief). Gabriel's capacity for moral outrage seemed limitless.

"Your boyfriend's nuts, you know," Sheba used to say. She couldn't figure him out. "He probably still believes in Santa Claus," she said. "You'd better warn him," she said. "He's gonna get himself killed if he doesn't watch out. He's making some of my best clients very angry. He doesn't understand the way the world works."

"He's more like his father than he likes to think," Gabriel's mother confided. "He gets a bee in his bonnet and he can't leave it alone. His father was a man of strange obsessions." She put her hand on my arm. "Be very wary, Lucy, about a man who's obsessed. He has no space left for someone else."

I said brightly: "Don't worry. I'm a congenital soloist anyway." I laughed, but she didn't. She looked at me for so long, in such a sad kindly way, that I felt uneasy. "Look," I said, jokey. "Don't worry about me. I don't bruise."

"I hope it will be all right," she said. "I hope neither of you will be hurt."

"I'm unhurtable," I said.

"I do know this, Lucy. I've discovered there isn't anything, there simply isn't anything, that you can't survive."

She was moving among the orchids in her greenhouse, a tranquil woman, a woman one could imagine putting forth leaf and lateral root systems, attaching herself to the earth.

"Were you . . . ? Did you and Gabriel's father . . . ?" I stammered about, curious about the dislocations and scars in my lover's life, curious about the sudden absences, but unable to frame a question that might not cause pain.

"The years without my child," she said quietly, "were like an amputation." She was dividing the roots and nodes of two orchids, using a penknife and her fingers, patient, meticulous, never hurrying. When they came apart—I would never have had the patience myself—she packed them lovingly into two separate pots. "But what's past is past," she said. "I couldn't ask for greater happiness than I have now. That is the thing I've learned," she said. "You think you can never be happy again. But then you are.

"Some people," she said, "seem to get it right the first time with marriage, but I think it must be a fluke. Sheer luck. You're too young to know what you're doing. Anyway, for us it was a mistake, that's all, and yet it brought me here, and it gave me Gabriel. I can't regret it." She tamped the earth around her orchids with her fingers. "Poor Robbie," she said. "He's such a haunted man. I think he'll be throttled by his own demons in the end, and yet, you know, I'd like him to find peace. I loved him once."

"Why is he haunted?" I asked.

But she was concentrating on her orchids and didn't answer.

"Catherine," I asked years later, on a London night when we were talking late, our tongues loosened by brandy, "is Robinson Gray haunted, would you say? Has he got demons on his back?"

"I don't know about haunted," she said. "But I know about demons."

"When we were kids," she said, "there was this tortoise that was supposed to be a hundred years old." She has her fingers hooked through the old front fence again, watching the armored hump, apparently headless, move in its slow weird waltz across the lawn. Its head is tucked under its shell. It won't stick its head out when Robbie wants it to, and suddenly Robbie is red in the face and his eyes are a violent purple and he is smashing smashing smashing at the shell with a mallet and Catherine puts her hands over her ears and screams. . . .

"Were you afraid of him?"

Catherine thought for a long silent time. "Not for myself," she said. "Because he's afraid of me."

"Who were you afraid for?"

"Lucy, don't ask me anything. I won't talk about it. I can't."

They used to congregate at the bridge after school. Charlie could never quite remember the sequence of events that led to the railway game being a regular thing, or to its awful escalation, or to the bridge as the gathering point, and not just for the five children who had spent so much of the summer at Cedar Creek.

The railway game was simply there as a full-blown regular event, part of Grade 5.

What he did remember was his own obsession with the nature and varieties of power. That was mainly what he watched in those years—the workings of power, its instinctive groupings and alliances, its varieties, the people who were polite to his parents and the people who were rude to them—and that was what he pondered afterwards, alone in the sleepout at the back of the shop, staring out through the louvres at the mango tree and the stars.

There was Cat's kind of power, which came from not caring if you got hurt and not caring what people thought of you. Which came first? he wondered. Cat's not caring? Or her knowledge that for people like herself there was no point whatsoever in caring? In its way, Cat's power was absolute; and yet people with a different sort of power (teachers, for example; or the kind of people who lived up on Wilston Heights; but also the boys on the corner whose power was simple brute strength), those people despised the kind of power that Cat had, they snapped their fingers at it, they did not acknowledge that it was any kind of power at all. And yet, it seemed to Charlie, they were also afraid of her power. They ignored it because it made them uneasy, because it didn't acknowledge *their* kind of power.

Not that Cat gave a fig about whether they acknowledged it or not. But Charlie minded, and Catherine minded too, and in both, the increasingly frequent revelations of discrepancy between Cat's power and other kinds of power gave rise to a terrible intensity that was partly composed of euphoria and partly of fear. It was as though they could both smell tumult coming, it was as though Cat stank of something that was either cataclysm or omnipotence and they knew it. Charlie knew that Catherine knew, and she knew that he did, and they shared this fevered excitement-and-anxiety, and the unexpressed shared secret bound them in a telegraphy of quick exchanged looks in the classroom and on the long walk home from Wilston School over Wilston Heights and on the footbridge.

In the classroom they both suffered for Cat constantly, though she herself gave no sign of being bothered in the least. The classroom was high comic drama for Cat. When she was made to read aloud from the Grade 5 Reader, which she was made to do every day, her halting mumble and long pauses and mispronounced words were painful to hear. Hopeless, Miss Oswell said. Cat clowned about her hopelessness. Cat would, in her ignorant way, sometimes substitute shocking and forbidden words for others which bore only a slight resemblance. The class would guffaw, a sound like a pressure cooker letting off steam.

"What else can we expect?" Miss Oswell would ask the air. "Water finds its own level and guttersnipes find the gutter."

Catherine found herself fantasizing that Miss Oswell would fall down the steps and be killed, or that a car would hit her and she would be paralyzed and would send a letter of apology to Cat from her hospital bed. Catherine was frightened by this violence inside her mind; all the more so since Miss Oswell invariably treated Catherine with the greatest affection and respect. Often Miss Oswell would ask Catherine to stay behind and help her with the stacking of school readers in the press or the filling of inkwells. She would stroke Catherine's long fair hair and say: "You must brush it, you know. Let me brush it for you." And she would take a hairbrush out of her desk drawer and Catherine would look stonily out the window while Miss Oswell drew the brush through her hair. Catherine could see Cat and Charlie dawdling along the road, still separate but gradually approaching each other the way railway lines, when you follow them into the distance with your eyes from an overhead bridge, eventually touch. They were waiting for her, and she wanted to be with them.

"It does credit to you, Catherine," Miss Oswell said, "to show pity on the Reilly girl."

Catherine closed her eyes. Cat and Charlie would be in the big dip of Wilston Road by now, taking the shortcut through the spare lot where the wattles were in bloom.

"But it's wasted, I'm afraid," Miss Oswell said. "She's a bit of a sewer rat, I'm afraid. She'll drag you down. As for schoolwork, she's hopeless, you know, and you'll win a scholarship to university."

Miss Oswell always required the class to laugh about Cat's hopelessness, which the class readily did with the most boisterous relief. Catherine and Charlie never laughed. They never even smiled during obligatory Rat-on-Cat time. (This was Catherine's term and it startled Charlie, but he noted it as further evidence of Catherine's unexpected way with a knife.)

"The guttersnipe strikes again," Miss Oswell would say, and the class would laugh.

"Now if only everyone could read as well as Catherine," she would say. Or: "If only everyone could do mental arithmetic as well as Charlie."

Both Catherine and Charlie began, during that Grade 5 year, to feel ashamed of the ease with which they excelled, to feel there was something dirty and disloyal and even obscene about it.

("Do you know," Catherine said to me in a dazed voice in London on one of our drinking nights, "when I think back, I realize that schooling in Queensland in the fifties and sixties was still as bad as anything in Dickens. It scarred all of us. It scarred us even if we were teacher's darlings."

"Do you know," I said to her drunkenly, "that if you put two Queenslanders together anywhere in the world, you get a cabal. Once Charlie and I were talking in the bar at the Inferno and some visitor from Melbourne says: Oh God, not two Queenslanders, get me outta here. God's chosen idiots, he says. I upended his glass on his head."

"If any of that smug, self-righteous, tepid, supercilious lot from Melbourne or Sydney starts Queensland-bashing," Catherine said, "that's it. They're off my list."

And we laughed till we cried.

"You should have had Miss Oswell in Grade 5," she said. "Or Mr. Brady in Grade 7."

"I did," I said. "They had different names, that's all."

And we laughed till we cried again. We laughed till we made ourselves sick.)

Though she herself did not administer the cane, Miss Oswell was a frequent sender of boys to the headmaster's office for any talking in class, any horseplay, any look that could be construed as "cheeky." Two or three times a day, boys would depart and return, sometimes pressing their lips hard together for it was obligatory to be nonchalant and to signal to the class, during the first moment that Miss Oswell turned to write on the board, the number of cuts received: two, three or six. For mysterious reasons these were the unchanging coordinates of punishment, with six cuts the most favored dose.

For small misdemeanors, such as a mistake in spelling, an error in tables, the capital of Western Australia not known, the products of the Atherton Tableland not memorized, Miss Oswell herself would administer a thump on the shoulder or a quick whack of the ruler across the palm. These latter were the punishments meted out to girls at all times, both for the aforementioned major crimes (talking, horseplay, cheeky looks), and for the further, and apparently exclusively female, felony of sulking. "I cannot abide sulking," Miss Oswell said. So strongly could she not abide it that it was quite possible for a girl, looking as though she were on the point of tears from a shoulder thump, to receive a second thump for sulking.

It was not surprising, Catherine and Charlie thought, that Cat came to school infrequently, rarely more than three days in five, because when she did come Miss Oswell devoted a considerable amount of her considerable malevolent energy toward making certain that Cat hated being there.

"Do I smell something?" Miss Oswell would ask when Cat arrived, sniffing the air with delicate distaste. "Do we have someone in the class who didn't have a bath last night?"

"But I did have a bath, Miss Oswell," impetuous Cat could never learn not to say.

"Don't be cheeky to me, my girl." Miss Oswell would raise her eyebrows and look heavenward as though she could never quite believe the extent of Cat's insolence. On cue, the class would laugh. "What is the rule in this class?" Miss Oswell would ask.

Speak when you're spoken to, the class would chant.

"Precisely," Miss Oswell would say. "Come here, Cat Reilly. Hold out your hand."

Cat collected many red stripes across her palm and she would wink at the class as she sat down. She had a devastating way of mimicking Miss Oswell when the teacher's back was turned, and the class would grin and press its lips together in silent glee. "Do I detect horseplay?" Miss Oswell would demand, whirling. Cat would be still as a statue, the class frozen in solemnity.

Once, however, Ross Johnson spluttered audibly with laughter and Miss Oswell whirled and pointed and said with magnificent rage: "To the office with you, my boy."

"I'll go, Miss Oswell," Cat said. "I made him laugh."

Ross Johnson paused.

"So we have a namby-pamby little mummy's boy who wants a girl to take his cuts for him, do we?"

"No, Miss Oswell," Ross Johnson said, his eyes flashing. He left the room.

"And tell the headmaster I said six of the best," Miss Oswell called after him. "As for you, my girl, come here."

There was something about her tone that made the class, inured though it was to the wraths and ragings of Miss Oswell, take a collective swallow and hold its breath.

"Hold out your hand," Miss Oswell said.

Cat obediently extended her arm, palm upwards, and looked Miss Oswell in the eye, her face carefully blank of expression.

"Don't give me that cheeky look, you bold girl," Miss Oswell said. The ruler descended, side on. This, everyone knew, was forbidden. It was required that girls be disciplined with the flat of the ruler. Cat flinched, and looked with surprised eyes at the sharp red line across her hand. The ruler descended again. And then again.

Catherine looked at Charlie, and Charlie looked back, but what could they do? From desk to desk, furtive glances were exchanged. It was rumored that a rule existed about hitting girls: if a teacher did it more than twice, one's parents could report the teacher to the Board of Education. There had been a celebrated case involving a Grade 7 teacher. It could be safely assumed, however, that Miss Oswell was not too worried about the parents of Cat. It was clear to the hushed class that Miss Oswell had crossed some line and was possessed by passions which were galloping without any reins.

On the sixth stroke of the ruler, something happened, and what happened would live in school legend. On the sixth fall of the side-on ruler, Cat closed her palm around it and took it. Miss Oswell was totally unprepared. Thrown off stroke, she opened her mouth and her mouth seemed to hang there in front of the class in a large silent O as though whatever sound Miss Oswell intended to make stuck in her throat. She simply stood there, and it began to occur to the class that she looked distinctly foolish, though no one was stupid enough to smile. Cat returned to her seat and placed the ruler neatly along the top of her desk.

Miss Oswell's voice, almost unrecognizable, came back to her. It was like a mute placed in a trumpet. "Leave the room," she said.

Cat did.

She didn't come back for a week.

When she did come back, it was as though the incident had never occurred, as though she and Miss Oswell had agreed to wipe it from the book of memory. But there was a change, and it could not go unnoticed by the class. From this point on, Cat was invisible, and the change seemed to disturb Cat as much as anyone. No matter what Cat did, no matter how rowdy or impossible she was, no matter how many tables she got wrong, no matter how badly she read, no matter how her mimicry stirred the class to spluttering mirth, Miss Oswell ignored her. She might as well not have been there. At first Charlie and Catherine were immensely relieved, but there was something eerie about the change. They both noted that this eeriness seemed to affect

Cat. She seemed to get wilder. There was an almost desperate edge to her recklessness.

All this, it seemed to Charlie, was part of Cat's power and part of the mystery of its potency and of its impotence. All this came with her every day to the footbridge and to the cutting beside the railway line.

On the footbridge over the railway line, what fascinated Charlie were the unexpected alliances. He thought he could remember a time when just the five of them—Cat and Catherine and Willy and Robbie Gray and himself—used to gather there. He and Cat and Catherine, officially strangers at school, would converge somewhere along Wilston Road, they would walk home together over the hill, past Catherine's place, past Robbie's place, past the ancient tortoise which was said to be a hundred years old. They would wait on the bridge. Sometimes Catherine came late; sometimes she had to stay and help Miss Oswell put the books in the press. Cat always went home for Willy and came back; and on the days when she didn't bother to go to school, she and Willy waited on the bridge. Robbie Gray would join them. In the beginning, Charlie was fairly sure, Robbie Gray would come alone, after he got the tram home from Grammar and walked from the tram stop toward Wilson Heights. Charlie could never pinpoint a time when the boys on the corner also showed up on the bridge as a regular thing (he always thought of the boys that way, long after they stopped molesting him on the corner nearest his parent's shop). The boys on the corner— there were three of them—went to Wilston School but they were bigger and older. They were the same age as Robbie and were in Grade 8. He never knew their names, or if he did the names disappeared behind their boys-on-the-corner masks. He had trouble remembering their faces. In his nightmares, they had long hairy arms and deep eye sockets and large black jaws like apes. When he put them in a photograph, they held gorilla masks in front of their faces. And somewhere early on there was another boy from Grammar, older than Robbie and the boys on the corner, someone else who lived up on Wilston Heights. Charlie must have known his name, Catherine knew him, but he remained an extra, a walk-on part, in recollection.

Here was the puzzle: the boys on the corner hated Grammar School types, but not as much as they despised girls and wogs.

Charlie knew that Robbie was caught in the middle and felt sorry for him. He thought Robbie must feel the way he and Catherine did when the class laughed at Cat.

He supposed there was a progression of events. Certainly he knew that the older boy from Grammar and the Wilston boys hated Cat's reckless way with the railway game, and that Robbie felt somehow aligned with it, felt a sort of possessive pride, rather as though he were the circus trainer and Cat his clever performing seal. Robbie was proud of her, Robbie boasted about her, and whatever Robbie boasted about, Cat would do.

Charlie thought there were strange sorts of pride around the way the game developed: Cat's pride, and Robbie's pride, and certainly the determination of Catherine and himself not to be found wanting. He was sure the game was Robbie's suggestion, though the other boy from Grammar, older than Robbie, a senior whom Robbie clearly admired, was in charge. What puzzled Charlie and absorbed all his attention was the way the Grammar boys and the Wilston boys automatically clubbed together and declared themselves ringmasters, and what bothered and disturbed him afterwards (for the rest of his life, in fact) was the way he and Cat and Catherine consented to the circus act. Willy, of course, made no decisions at all. Pliant Willy loved everyone and smiled and sang his Mr. Wolf song, and Cat and Catherine and Charlie, and sometimes Robbie too (when the other boys weren't around), bestowed hugs and kisses on him constantly. The Wilston boys and the Grammar boy paid no attention to Willy at all.

Charlie knew that, for himself, the decision to lie on the rails was made by his body. He remembered that his body stored the knowledge of earlier encounters with the boys on the corner, and that lying in front of an approaching train seemed the lesser of unpleasant options, especially after you had done it once or twice and learned there was nothing to it. It seemed, also, a small way of thumbing his nose at the boys on the corner. He could frighten them. There was something about his body lying on the tracks that pulled their punches and stilled their kicks. He was buying a kind of safety, but he also sensed this: the more untouchable he became, the more they hated him.

He did learn that danger was addictive. As he and Catherine lay beside Cat on the sleepers, their heads against one steel rail, their feet on the other, he learned how quickly one learns to feel nothing. They were not allowed to get up until the boys said they could, until Robbie and the Grammar boy and the boys on the corner said *Now*. And then he and Catherine vaulted up like corks from champagne bottles, neat as flies evading a swatter, but Cat always waited. She always waited till the boys were nearly wetting their pants with fright. The engine would be past the bridge and she would stretch and sit up as though she were waking from a nap.

The boys were furious. You wait too long, they said. The driver will see you and we'll all get into heck.

But the train never stopped, and Cat waited longer, and the boys cheered and berated her with a strange kind of intensity.

Charlie and Catherine began to taste Cat's power. You could *frighten* the ringmasters, they learned. The longer you waited, the more you saw your power in the cold sweat on the ring-master's brow. But Charlie and Catherine tempered that power with the knowledge of oncoming pistons and wheels. Cat, Charlie thought, was indifferent to them. Was it because she trusted her own reflexes the way a possum does? Or was she drunk on her own kind of powerless power? Did she think she was omnipotent?

Afterwards, Robbie would act as though the triumph were his. "I told you," he would say. "I told you she doesn't know the meaning of fear."

The trouble with Cat's kind of power, Charlie saw, is that there are people who develop a passion to break it. And the trouble with people like Cat is that they always have some point where they are vulnerable, and the ringmasters have a sixth sense for sniffing it out.

Cat's vulnerable point was Willy.

Charlie could not remember (and if Catherine did, she would never speak of it to me) why, on the particular day the railway game was played for the last time, he and Catherine were still on the bridge instead of down in the cutting. Perhaps they had stopped at Catherine's place on the way; perhaps Miss Oswell had brushed Catherine's hair longer than usual, and Charlie had waited for her. Whatever the reason, they felt responsible.

It could not have happened if I'd been there on time, Charlie said, because I would have held Willy. I wouldn't have cared what they did to me, they could have punched and kicked all they pleased, I would never have let them take Willy.

Catherine thought: I should have stopped it earlier. I knew something was going to happen, I could smell it. I could smell it on Robbie. It was like the time he tried to smash the tortoise, the same kind of smell. I knew Robbie's fear of the boys on the corner, I knew his desire to please that Grammar School senior was making him crazy. I knew he was terrified they'd make him lie on the rails. I knew it. It was like Miss Oswell hitting Cat that day. You know something has snapped. You feel sorry for them in a way, for people like Miss Oswell and Robbie. You know you should do something, but you can't think what to do. They are like springs that wind themselves tighter and tighter and tighter and you close your eyes, waiting, because you can't bear to watch, because you know if you beg them to stop, they'll ignore you.

"I think that's what happened," she told Charlie. "I think because we weren't there, they ganged up. I think they wanted Robbie to lie on the rails."

It was Robbie who suggested Willy, Cat swore to that. It was the boys on the corner who held Willy down, and Robbie who held down Cat. They used long forked sticks, no, not sticks, small branches of stringbark trees.

Cat struggled and screamed. "I'll kill you, Robbie," she yelled.

The wave of pleasure Robbie felt was so intense, he thought he might choke on it. He felt drunk. He forgot he was afraid of the rails. He threw himself down on top of Cat and kissed her full on the mouth. She bit him. He was in a frenzy of excitement, struggling on top of her, kissing, being bitten and biting her back. Her wrists were manacled with his hands but she fought against them and reached up and yanked his hair. He gave a yelp and laughed in triumph, but vaulted back and held her down with the branch.

"I'll clobber you, Robbie!"

"But I knew they'd let Willy up in time," Robbie protested. "And I knew Cat would get up in time, she always does."

They did let Willy go in good time—Catherine and Charlie, watching from the bridge, had to testify to that fact. They let him go while the engine was beneath the bridge, while Charlie and Catherine still had a clear view of the tracks, while there was plenty of time. But Willy, not frightened in fact, probably prattling about the time and Mr. Wolf, Willy didn't get up.

"Get up!" the Wilston boys screamed, suddenly panicked, too mesmerized by the approaching train to run and grab him.

"Get up!" Charlie screamed from the bridge.

"Willeeeeeee!" Catherine screamed.

And after that, they couldn't see anything. The train, like an evil black slug, was underneath them, filling the space from the cutting to the bridge. The engine braked with a great hiss and a dreadful shuddering of buffers, and Cat's scream curdled around them like soot.

FIVE

It was not so much Willy's death for which Charlie blamed Robinson Gray. The death was an accident. Even Cat knew it was an accident, she knew no one wanted Willy to die, she didn't blame Robbie any more than she blamed herself, though he was the one she tore at with her nails when he wouldn't let her look below the train. Robbie held her and she fought and screamed and kicked until she was exhausted, and then she went limp and howled in his arms.

It was not the death they blamed him for. It was for what happened afterwards.

Between the accident and the afterwards was a blur. People came across the road from the houses, the engine driver kept saying *Oh Jesus Christ Jesus you stupid bloody kids oh Jesus Jesus*, Catherine was sick, the Wilston boys and the Grammar boy were pale and trembling, Robbie was shaking, you couldn't tell if he was holding up Cat or she was holding up him, Charlie could feel his bowels turning to gruel, an ambulance came, police came, cars came, blur came, more blur, and blur. It was blur for days. Charlie could never remember how he got from the railway cutting to his parents' shop, though he must have gone in someone's car, a police car in fact so his parents said, and he must have gone by way of the police station because he read what he said in the *Courier-Mail*, though he had no recollection of saying it.

186

A tragic and senseless accident, the paper said. A terrible game of dare. CHILDREN PLAY WITH FIRE AND GET BURNED.

Cat was in hospital. Cat was under sedation. Cat's father, who went on a roaring drunken binge, raged up Wilston Heights and smashed the windows of Mr. Gray's Buick with a cricket bat and slashed the tires. Mr. Gray was very gracious about it. There was a picture of him in the *Courier-Mail*. Understandable grief, he said, and no of course he was not pressing charges. As a matter of fact he would vouch before a court of law (and he himself, after all, was a member of the judiciary), he would vouch for the fact that Mr. Reilly was a good man, salt of the earth, a trusted laborer on Mr. Gray's own weekend farm, a bit immoderate with the drink perhaps but under the circumstances . . . and the Reilly children were practically like a son and daughter to him. He himself was in shock, his own son was suffering as much as anyone, he said. A terrible awful thing. A tragedy.

The *Courier-Mail* could not print what Mr. Reilly said.

At Willy's funeral, Cat and her father looked like shadows. Charlie was there with his parents, and Robbie Gray with his, and Catherine with hers. There were acres of space between them all. It was all a blur. It was like floating under the skin of Cedar Creek at midnight, Charlie thought. He was drifting, everything was blackness, there was no fixed shape to anything, there was a feeling that something dark and heavy like tar would drown them all. Cat wouldn't look at any of them. He looked at Catherine and she looked at him and her eyes seemed like two black holes. They frightened him.

Mr. Gray went to shake Mr. Reilly's hand and Mr. Reilly spat in his face.

Robbie came over to talk to Catherine and Charlie.

"Poor Willy," he sighed. "And poor poor Cat."

"Poor Robbie," Catherine said silkily, and Charlie and Robbie, both startled, looked at her but her expression was unreadable.

There was blur and drifting and then there was the inquest, and that was where Cat broke some unwritten rule. It was odd how the inquest turned into the trial of Cat. Replaying that inquest for the rest of his life, Charlie thought that what was curious was that he and Catherine and Cat all blamed themselves. It was an accident, yes. Everyone agreed it was an accident. But just the same they blamed themselves. They were responsible. They would never be free of guilt.

But Robbie Gray, and the boy from Grammar, and the Wilston boys, they did not blame themselves. They did not feel responsible. They felt it was all Cat's fault.

They seemed to fear, however, that some sense of their culpability was in the air, in the press, in the eyes of others, and this awareness bred in them a particularly volatile anger which they kept demurely hidden (like pet poisonous snakes in plastic bags) in the pockets of the neat suits they wore in court.

They themselves knew they had been goaded and put into the wrong. They knew Cat had it in for them.

She started it, they told the judge. One by one they said it. She started it, they said. And she wouldn't stop. She loved it, she kept egging us on, she *made* us do it, it was her idea.

The judge, with his kind fatherly face, was looking directly into Charlie's eyes. "Did Cat Reilly start it?" he asked.

Charlie wanted to explain about Miss Oswell and the ruler, and about the playground songs and the jokes about Cat not being clean, and the things the boys on the corner did. "They made her do it," he said.

"They made her do it," the judge repeated very carefully and solemnly. "And did they make you do it too?"

"Yes, sir."

"They held you down, did they? So you couldn't get up?"

"N–no, sir. But they made the rules."

"I see. What rules did they make?"

"They said we couldn't get up till the train reached the bridge. Till they said."

"But they didn't do anything to stop you getting up?"

Charlie thought about the way the ghostly shapes of former punches and kicks hung in the air. "I was afraid they'd hurt me if I did, sir."

"Who were you afraid would hurt you? Which of the boys did you think would hurt you? Could you point them out to me, son?" The judge was so kindly, so fatherly, so understanding.

Charlie looked at the faces of the Wilston boys. They looked back with bland neutral eyes. Between their eyes and Charlie's, a regiment of boots and knuckles marched, left right left right left right, he could see hobnails and knuckle-dusters and sharp brass rings, he saw broken windows in his parents' shop, a promise of future harm. "I don't know, sir," he said.

"You're a foreigner in this country, young man," the judge explained, "and I make allowances for the fact that you do not, perhaps, fully understand our Australian commitment to fair play. Australian boys seem a bit rough to you, perhaps, but I believe there is no Australian boy alive who won't give his rival a fair go. In fact, a fair go is something we believe in quite passionately. Would you say you've had a fair go since you've been in this country, son?"

"Yes, sir," Charlie murmured obediently.

"And is it true that in fact you often *didn't* get up when these young gentlemen said, but you waited longer?"

"Yes, sir," Charlie said.

"Thank you," the judge said. "That will be all."

"And how did you come to be lying on the railway lines, little lady?" the judge asked Catherine. You could tell he would have liked to brush her hair. You could tell he thought she was there by some freakish accident.

Catherine looked him right in the eye. "Because I want to be as brave as Cat," she said.

"You like Cat, do you?" asked the kindly fatherly judge. "I like her better than anyone else in the world," Catherine said in a clear steady voice.

"I see," the judge said. You could tell he thought the matter very grave. "You like her because she does dangerous things."

Catherine frowned, as though this was not quite correct. "Because . . ." she said, faltering.

"Thank you, my dear," the judge said in a kindly way.

"Because she doesn't pretend," Catherine blurted.

"Thank you, dear," the judge said. "That will be all."

"And what were you doing at the railway cutting, young man?" the judge asked Robinson Gray. Robbie was wearing his Grammar uniform and looked very smart.

"I tried to look after Cat, sir," Robbie said. "I felt responsible for her. She doesn't know the meaning of fear."

"But you went along with the game, I understand?"

"I pretended to, sir, but it frightened me."

The judge nodded sympathetically. "As it would any sensible person," he said. "Indeed yes. Anyone with a grain of common sense."

"We couldn't stop her, sir," Robbie said. "I think she loves danger, sir."

"Yes," the judge said. "It would seem so."

"And you, young woman," the judge asked Cat sternly. "What do you have to say for yourself?"

Cat stared at him silently.

The judge frowned a little. "Did you, or did you not, start this game?" he asked.

Cat said nothing.

"Young lady," the judge said sternly. "Your attitude to authority is very revealing, I'm afraid. Very revealing indeed. This tragic death was clearly an accident, but I fear a long trail of family negligence leads to this sad place. A runaway mother, I understand. A father who leaves his children to run wild. A reckless little girl, product of a broken home, who has no sense of responsibility for the younger brother left in her care, no sense whatsoever, a wild little ruffian addicted to danger it would appear—"

There was a crashing sound from the vicinity of Mr. Reilly, a chair knocked over, a bloodcurdling string of words not often heard in the presence of juridical gowns and wigs.

"I would ask the constables to remove Mr. Reilly from the courtroom," the judge said, though Mr. Reilly was not disposed to be removed until his daughter, catching everyone by surprise, said quietly but clearly: "It's okay, Dad. I'm okay." She addressed herself to the judge: "But I got somethin' to say before ya cart me dad off."

The judge raised his eyebrows. "I'm pleased to hear it, young lady."

"It was an accident," she said. "It wasn't Willy they wanted to hurt, it was me. They couldn't've ever got me, but." She flashed her eyes at the five of them, the Wilston boys, and the Grammar boy, and Robbie Gray. "They knew they could never get me," she said witheringly. "It made 'em wanna spit chips." She flung back her head and her dirty yellow ribbon jabbed the air, and the little glass beads on her earrings flashed blue fire. "It was my fault they got Willy," she said. "I shoulda thought of it, but I never." She pointed at the Grammar boy. "He was the boss," she said. "He told them to grab Willy." She pointed at the Wilston boys, one by one. "And they grabbed Willy and held him down," she said. "They knew he was simple. They knew he didn't even know he was supposed to get up." She pointed to Robinson Gray. "And he held me down so I couldn't get to Willy in time. He wanted to see if he could make me cry."

Charlie, transfixed by Cat, flicked his eyes to Robbie's face in time to see the disbelief, the shock, the blank baffled look, and then the rage. All of these zipped across Robbie's face like shadows on the pool at Cedar Creek. Then they were gone. Then there was Robbie wearing his mask of "poor poor Cat" for the kindly judge.

"Thank you, young lady, and I think that will be enough," the judge said. "Would the constables please remove Mr. Reilly from the room."

"It's okay, Dad," Cat called to him. "I won't let the buggers say nothin' behind yer back."

"That will be enough, young lady," the judge said.

"Good on yer, Cat, tell the fuckers orf, luv," her father called back, but then he began sobbing in a noisy helpless blubbering way, the way children do, the way drunks do outside hotels after closing time.

When the shuffling subsided the judge addressed the room. He spoke sorrowfully of the decline of civilization and the decline of the family. He spoke of the corrupt effect of modern music and films, the cheap taste for excitement, the lack of respect for authority. There was no one person to blame, he said. There was the acknowledged tendency of boys to be boys, but (with a slight rueful smile) there was no one who could be a boy like a wild tomboy could. He paused for the smiles and the rueful shaking of heads. Beyond that, he said, there was a long trail of sorry neglect, a long sad trail. And this sort of family breakdown was like a disease, he said. Like a cancer. Unless it was stopped, it would spread and infect others, even those whose family circumstances were entirely admirable. (Here, he let his eyes rest briefly on the parents who lived on Wilston Heights.) His finding was that the tragic death was wholly an accident, but in order to prevent further harm, and for her own future good as well as that of society, he ruled that Cat Reilly should be removed from the inadequate home and desperately inadequate parental situation in which it was her sad fortune in life, through no fault of her own, to find herself. He ruled that she should be placed in the Holy Family School for Little Wanderers where, by God's grace, she would learn the proper deportment required of a young lady on the verge of puberty. In such a setting, he believed, there was every reason to hope she would learn discipline and moral rectitude before her life was beyond all repair.

Charlie saw a little jolt to Cat's body, as though a pellet had hit her, then she was still.

Nobody needed a translation of Holy Family School. Everybody knew what it meant. Reform school. Delinquent girls. When the judge asked Cat if she had anything to say, she did not answer him. But she turned toward the boys, toward Robinson Gray in particular, and lifted her hands up to her face like claws, and made a soft hissing sound.

Afterwards.

Charlie was never sure how much time elapsed between the inquest and the afterwards. It could have been the same night. It could have been the next. He thought the worst thing was that they came into Cat's place, into that magic untouchable kingdom of long grass and old tires and the rusted skeleton of a car.

There were four of them and three of us and they were all much bigger than us, he said. It was dark. God knew where Cat's father was.

Charlie and Catherine had gone to Cat's place by instinct after school. Cat sat on the rotting veranda and stared at nothing. She didn't move, she didn't speak to them. She had finished with words.

Of course, at the time, they simply thought her silence was temporary shock. They didn't know that the last words she would ever speak were those she had tossed across the court: *I won't let the buggers say nothin' behind yer back.*

They sat one on each side of her and held her hands, but she could have been a rag doll. It was this, Cat's listlessness, that stunned Charlie. A tidal wave of grief hit him, he floundered, he felt he would drown. That the fire could be extinguished in Cat: it made the world falter in its orbit. It seemed to Charlie they sat there for hours, not a word being said. And then, when it was nearly dark, the others came: Robbie and the three Wilston boys.

It was, Charlie thought, almost certainly an accident that they arrived together. It was entirely possible that Robbie was on a pilgrimage of remorse or a consolation mission of his own. (This was what Charlie thought. Catherine, I discovered years later, was much less sure.) It was virtually certain, Charlie thought, that Robbie, disconcerted by the presence of the boys on the corner, aligned himself with them out of fear.

"What did they do?" I whispered into the long silence in Charlie's room on the top floor of the building in King's Cross.

"There were four of them and three of us," Charlie said.

I waited and waited. I stared at the photograph of Cedar Creek Falls. I could feel myself floundering in Charlie's grief and his memory of fear. I could feel myself going under. This drowning sensation had as much to do with Gabriel as with Charlie, as much to do with my fear for the way he kept ferreting around in the underside of respectable lives, my fear of the riddle that lay between him and his father, my fear. Charlie stared at his blow-up of the Serra Pelada mine.

"I remember lying on the grass in front of the veranda," he said. "I remember seeing into the crawl space in the dark and knowing it was full of cobwebs and spiders, ladders and ladders of cobwebs and furry spiders. It was too dark to see them but I could see them anyway. I felt as though Cat and Catherine and I were at the bottom of a bottomless pit and we would never climb out."

"What did they do?"

But he could not speak of it. Nearly forty years later, all he could say was, "They taught us a lesson."

He can hear the hissed whispers: *We'll teach you to dob us in. We'll teach you. We'll teach you a lesson you won't forget, you little slut, you little wog, you little stuck-up bitch.*

After a long long silence, I asked: "Did they hurt you?"

He looked at me as though I were a stranger inexplicably in the room. "At first," he said—but he was speaking in a sort of trance, he was thinking aloud—"at first, the worst pain was *why?* They'd got off scot-free, but they were furious, they wanted revenge." He shook his head. *"Revenge,"* he said, mystified, still incredulous. With his fist, he made the motion of a knife twisting and twisting in his lungs. "It used to bore into me. *Why?*

"I've thought and thought about it," he said. "I've decided there were two things they couldn't forgive. They couldn't forgive what Cat knew about them, and they couldn't forgive her for being articulate. They wouldn't have minded if she'd screamed and sobbed. They didn't mind her dad, that was okay, they expected the Reillys to make fools of themselves, they could forgive that any old time. But they wouldn't forgive Cat for despising them."

"What did they do?"

He walked to the window and moved aside the pearly paper of the shoji screen. The Sydney sun and the King's Cross neon came into the room like gaudy pimps. He looked down at the street: "You know," he said, "to be stabbed by some stranger in a drug deal, that's nothing. It's quick and kind." He pulled the screen back across the space. "Shame is more deadly and permanent," he said. "If an attacker shames the person he attacks, he can do whatever he wants and get off scot-free, because the attackees won't speak of it, and he knows it."

He stood in front of the photograph of the Serra Pelada mine. "It was their faces," he said. "It was Robbie's face. I'll never forget Robbie's face."

I don't know why, but I had a terrible nauseating sense of premonition, I wanted to rush out and go downstairs and find Gabriel and say, Let's leave here. Let's go and live with your mother and stepfather and plant pineapples and never come near the quarry or any sort of harm again. Let's flee. But I knew it would be useless. I knew the riddle and the need to atone wouldn't leave Gabriel alone.

"Charlie," I said, "what did they do?"

"They taught us a lesson."

He stood in the window again and stared at the opaque screen and said over his shoulder, with his back to me: "I can't talk about it. That's what was so brilliant about it, you see." He turned around and said urgently, "We weren't meek, mind you, we weren't passive. But they were bigger."

He turned his back to me again and said in a low quick monotone, "They pulled our pants off and they did things. And then the Wilston boys pissed on us, and one of them shat on us." He said it in such a rush, in such a quick low voice, that I had to play it back in my mind to hear it properly.

He turned round and his face was stricken. It was as though he had fouled himself in front of me. "If you ever tell anyone," he said, "I'll . . ."

"Oh Charlie," I whispered, instinctively moving toward him, but he flinched and hugged himself, his crossed arms a fortress. Don't touch me, his body said.

"And Robbie watched," he said. "He didn't do anything. He just watched."

"Oh Charlie."

"It was their faces," he said. "The looks on their faces. I'll never forget Robbie's face."

Book THREE

Photograffiti and Silence

*Picture taking is first of all the focusing of a temperament,
only secondarily that of a machine.*

Susan Sontag

*Where can I find one who has forgotten words?
That is the one I would like to talk to.*

Chuang Tzu

ONE

The loudest and most chilling scream in the world is the silent one in Edvard Munch's painting. It is composed of every scream the viewer has ever heard, every fear he has ever felt, every nightmare that has ever jackknifed him out of sodden sheets. It cannot be shut off, that scream. It is deafening. It is not just the open *rictus* of the mouth which screams, but the skull, the hands, the whole body. The body is at risk of imploding, the scream sucks the body into itself. The giddy sky screams too, and the contortionist earth writhes in the grip of the same endless shriek.

Only the geometric grid of the bridge suggests, by its parallel railings, that there are in fact two side-by-side worlds in *The Scream*. There is the world that is only scream, and the world where the scream means nothing and is not even heard. They occupy the same space, but one world fits inside the other like a hand inside a glove.

The bridge rails bisect the painting. They warn that the hunters are coming, those two elongated figures, the stalkers, the black birds of prey, the executioners. They warn that the executioners are deaf, indifferent, sinister, grim as reapers with black scythes, as schoolteachers looming above young children, as bullies hanging about on a corner, as judges. They are unmoved but moving closer, their intentions unswerving, straight as railway lines, straight as the law, relentless as death or the black fact of power.

And the screamer puts his own hands over his own ears but the sound which shreds him will not abate.

I have never seen Munch's original painting, which hangs in the National Gallery in Oslo, Norway. I have only seen reproductions in books, and I have seen Charlie's photograph of it, taken (in violation of copyright, I suppose) from a book on modern painting and incorporated into several collages of his own.

In one of Charlie's photographs, the Grade 5 class at Wilston School in one particular yesteryear (that one in which Cat and Catherine and Charlie sat at the feet, as it were, of the wise Miss Oswell, paragon of good exam results and discipline, that old-fashioned virtue), the Grade 5 class in that year is somewhat incongruously posing for its photograph on an overhead railway bridge. The photographer, as was the case in those distant days, is also on the bridge with his tripod and with his black cloth over his head, almost as though he were the hangman rather than the archivist.

His right hand is held aloft and one expects to see the shutter-trigger attached to cord, but in fact he holds a hand mirror up by its wooden clasp. Look at the birdie, he seems to say, and when the class does so, the reflection that it sees is Munch's loud silent scream.

In another of Charlie's photographs, the class sits in front of a blackboard and the blackboard is full of Munch's scream. Miss Oswell, leaving a cutout silhouette behind her in the class photograph, stands at the blackboard and points with her long teacher's pointer right into the open ellipse of the screamer's mouth. Miss Oswell is tall and gaunt and dressed in black and looks remarkably like the long figure of one of the stalkers at the far end of Munch's bridge.

Silence seduces, Charlie said. People cannot resist silence. They fill it with confession, he said. This is something therapists and prostitutes and bartenders know all too well.

And photographs also seduce, he said. Their seeming passivity and their silence is irresistible, it invites transgression. Certainly Charlie would know. He lusted after photographs, his passion for them was unbridled. He bought them in droves from junk shops and estate auctions, he saved them from newspapers and old school magazines and illustrated weeklies, he scavenged in abandoned rooms and rubbish bins for them. He hoarded them and studied them. You can read infinity in a grainy snapshot, he said.

And he himself took photographs obsessively in order to see what he had seen.

He arranged and composed, but he did not believe that these arrangements lied, or that they refashioned the truth. All photographs lie and they all tell their own particular truth, he said, the truth of their own lie. They reveal and conceal, they enlighten and deceive, they hold steadfast and they manipulate the truth—but all this is beside the main point.

Photographs *beckon*, he said. Photographs seduce.

The relationship between a photograph and its viewer is one of seduction, and like all seducers, photographs know how to enthrall. It is what is *not* seen that tantalizes us. It is what is excluded from the frame that we desire. It is the figure in the photograph with her back to the camera, her face averted, that we cannot forget, that young woman, scarcely more than a girl, only partly visible in a doorway on a city street.

It is the thought of what would have happened if the photographer had focused a few feet further to the left, the thought that perhaps he in fact did do just that, that perhaps a photograph already exists somewhere which would, let us say, reveal the face of a man about to approach the young woman.

I'll tell you a story, Charlie said. I'll tell you why I suddenly came back from New York after twenty-five years. Actually, I'll tell you two very strange stories, he said. They are both true and they are both about photographs and death.

The first story. A car salesman who lived in New York City took his family (a wife, two teenage daughters, a younger son) to Florida for vacation. They had two weeks of Daytona Beach and body-to-body sunning, they opened themselves up to pleasure as unguardedly as day lilies do, the teenagers had five beach romances between them, the boy and his father went fishing, the mother read thirty paperbacks and had an epiphany out there alone in the salt waves where she swam into a beatitude which stayed with her on the beach, and hovered above the trailer in the campground, so that she knew life would be irrevocably different henceforth. All these poignant little hedonisms were crammed into the family's Kodak Instamatic and hoarded for the return to the mundane world.

When they got back to New York, they found their town-house had been ransacked. The back door had been forced, the microwave, the TV, the VCR, the compact disc player had all been taken. Drawers and boxes had been emptied, their contents apparently dumped into T-shirts and sweatshirts and carried out like laundry in a basket. One of the shirts, in the burglar's haste, was left on the living room floor. Tax receipts (why on earth had the thief bothered with that desk drawer?) from five years past were spilling out of the hammock of an overlarge New York Yankees T-shirt. There was an iron-on badge proclaiming *John Lennon Lives* on one sleeve. At least they brought their own shirts, the mother said with a forlorn attempt at dry wit. It's not one of ours.

It was a horrid end to a wonderful vacation, and chaos and depression ensued for some time. Weeks later, when the tedious business of insurance claims and replacements was behind them and the family was more or less back to normal (except for that queasy sense of unsafety which visited them daily like shadows falling on the kitchen wall), the mother, cleaning out a sandy beachbag, discovered four rolls of undeveloped Kodak film.

Our happy Florida time, she thought, with a certain forgivable excess of sentimental regret. That beatitude, that happy family time, safe and sound.

She had the film developed and over supper the family slipped under the fence of the burglary and retouched that Florida joy. Oh look, they laughed, Jerry's fish! And the one that got away from Dad. And Nancy's romance. Oh look, there's that gorgeous hunk on the motorcycle, that Tim, who took Maggie to Disneyworld. He said he'd come and visit back here, he said he lived in Queens, remember? We thought he was really stuck on you, Maggie. Oh well, *qué sera*, he must have found someone else.

Maggie sighed. "I gave him our phone number and address," she said. "You never know. He might call me one of these days."

The whole family studied gorgeous Tim on his Yamaha, his blond curls falling to his shoulders, his leather boots high and polished, his tanned and muscled arms protruding from his Yankees shirt, the perky *John Lennon Lives* badge caressing his delectable bicep.

"Oh my God," Maggie said softly.

They all stared at the T-shirt, then they stared at one another. Oh my God, they said.

"Did he give you his address?" they asked Maggie.

"Just a phone number," she said.

That was enough, and the police did the rest. Unfortunately the beautiful suntanned Tim, being part of a busy professional ring which specialized in vacation-emptied houses, panicked when the police showed up in Queens and there was a shootout and he was killed by an officer's bullet. Most of the stuff had already been fenced, of course. But there were a couple of incriminating pieces of jewelry and the microwave, microwaves having become so cheap at the discount stores that they cannot be easily fenced anymore.

To die for a T-shirt and a microwave, Maggie thought, stunned that someone who had so recently groped inside her jeans could be dead. In dreams, her beach lover came to her wearing nothing but John Lennon glasses, and he parked his motorcycle on her bed and revved it and posed for his photograph.

Almost all burglaries, almost all acts of assault, and almost all murders, the police told the family, are committed by people the victims know. A house is virtually always burgled by someone you or your children know, and in eighty percent of murders, perpetrator and victim are related or known to each other. An act of violence is an intimate act, they explained.

The greater the violence, the greater the intimacy. And vice versa.

In fact, they said, when we get a mutilated body, twenty stab

wounds, a head beaten to a pulp, a limb cut off, stuff like that—
begging your pardon, young lady, we didn't mean to upset
you—but when we get stuff like that, we know right off it's
family or a lover, they said. Only love does that. Strangers kill
quick and clean, but family is vicious, they said, and love is a
savage beast.

Funny thing, the police said, but statistically you're safer on
the streets than at home, and safer with a stranger than with
family or friends.

"I read all this in *The New York Times*," Charlie said.

The second story. In my apartment building in New York,
Charlie said, was a music director from one of the city's most
exclusive private schools. He was a gregarious chap with a wife
and several children and a passion for music. I liked him enormously. I didn't know him well, but every so often he'd show
up in my restaurant, or come to my exhibitions, and I'd go to
his concerts, and we'd meet on his balcony or mine to have a
few drinks and discuss music and art.

We used to look over the balconies at a children's playground
and it was during one of our conversations, as a matter of fact,
that I suddenly got the idea of doing a series on children at play.
I began to sit in the playground with my camera and watch. I
was fascinated by the paradox of angelic faces and sheer jungle
behavior, the little group cruelties. I was thinking of my own
childhood, I suppose. I did a whole series of the more striking
faces against a backdrop of jungle gyms and sand pits and swings.
I had an exhibition, and my musician friend came to it. He
seemed profoundly affected. He said something very odd to
me at the end. He said: *So you know.* And I thought it was
a statement of our shared artistic sensibilities. I thought he
meant we were both aware of this paradox of the angelic and
the cruel.

Then just a week later, out of the blue, stupefying me, there
was a suicide and mass publicity. The musician's body was found
in the East River. Just in time, the papers said. There had been
insistent allegations of patterns of sexual abuse: of boys in the

school orchestra, of friends of the musician's own offspring, of children in the apartment building where the musician lived.

It transpired, Charlie said, that every single face in my series was in fact the victim of regular abuse. It transpired that the musician, this friendly family man, had got more and more reckless in his predatory habits, more and more coercive with his prey, and more and more confirmed in his sense of personal invulnerability.

It is hubris, a criminologist said on the local evening news, that eventually does the repeat offender in. They get away with it so many times, they begin to think they have magic powers. We were gathering evidence, we would soon have been in a position to lay charges, but he pre-empted us. He was getting careless, the detective said, the way they always do in the end. He thought he was invulnerable, he thought he lived a charmed life, he thought he had magic powers. That's when we get them, he said.

In fact, Charlie told me, still half incredulous, the musician had once made a tasteless joke about a scoutmaster who'd been jailed. ("Got his fingers caught in the honeypot," he'd snickered. "Too fond of fingering little boys, the old perv, and serve him right.") So I had no idea, Charlie said. Not the slightest clue. I couldn't believe it when I read the papers. In fact, I *didn't* believe it at first.

That's what protects them, the detective told Charlie. These people are safe for astonishing lengths of time. They are protected by our capacity for denial, you see, by our need not to know. And so they come to feel they are immune. This fellow, now, we knew he thought he was a magician, but I guess you trumped him. I guess you were the last magician, the detective said. You must have had an inkling, eh?

But I didn't, Charlie told me. I didn't. I suppose I had a need not to know. I was grateful, I suppose, for someone in my building I could talk to about music and art. There was a link, you see, he said thoughtfully. We were both attracted to the most angelic young faces. But I didn't have the slightest shadow of a suspicion about him. And yet, when he saw that line-up, he thought I knew. And that out-magicked his magic. He panicked and killed himself.

Do you see what I mean? Charlie said.

After the death of Willy, he said, Cat disappeared into the barred world of reform, and Catherine was whisked off to private school by her parents for safety, and Charlie himself retreated into the magic rituals that had protected him and kept him company before the days of Catherine and Cat. "I never talked about any of it to anyone," he said, "and nor did Catherine. In its different ways, silence swallowed the three of us up."

Everyone's parents wanted to expunge the whole event, Charlie said. Cat wasn't allowed visitors at reform school, because visitors would have a bad effect. So the officials decreed. Charlie saw Catherine occasionally, fleetingly, accidentally, but her parents forbade all contact.

There was that day on the tram however. He sees her sitting next to her mother at the far end of his tram, on another planet, in outer space, forty feet away from him. She feels his gaze. They are so powerfully aware of each other that he can smell her hair. Her mother speaks. She looks away. They get off the tram.

Charlie didn't see Robbie Gray for three years.

Then he won a scholarship to Brisbane Grammar.

He recalled the strange mixture of excitement and anxiety he felt, going there for the first day, knowing he'd see Robbie again. . . .

❖ ❖ ❖

Charlie tosses all night. He imagines every conceivable scenario for a first encounter. Robbie will go rigid with shock and remorse. Robbie will be icy and distant. Robbie will give him a wide berth but there will be little telltale signs of nervousness because Charlie *knows*. . . . Robbie will come unstuck and will turn into the wild thing he was that last night at Cat's, a red-eyed lunatic, raving, drunk with either blood or fear.

Charlie has the recurrent nightmare again (it has dwindled in frequency over time). He and Cat and Catherine are thrashing about in a river, drowning, being sucked under. The river is boiling hot. It is not water they swim in, but shit. They cling to each other. Robbie sits on the bank enthralled, his eyes glowing like coals, a manic rictus of pleasure on his face, pushing them under with a long stick every time they reach for the bank.

Charlie wakes and paces. He stands at the window and holds the talisman Cat gave him before reform school swallowed her up. (She gave him her gold hoop earrings with their blue glass beads; he wears them on a thin chain about his neck at all times; they are safely hidden under his shirt.) Does *he* have nightmares? Charlie wonders. Does he ever wake with a thudding heart and go to his window to look for Cat? Will I know? Will I see telltale signs? Will it *help* if I see telltale signs?

He closes his eyes and thinks of Cat. He is sometimes able to believe that behind the barred windows of her school, she knows when he does this. When he puts her earrings to his lips, he smells her hair and her funky body perfume.

But nothing at all happens at Brisbane Grammar School. It is such a civilized place.

"Hello, Chang!" Robbie Gray says brightly, courteously. "I think we've met before, haven't we? You came out to our farm in Samford once or twice, years ago, didn't you? Your parents, wasn't it? For produce or something?"

Oh, Robbie Gray is invariably gracious to him. Robbie Gray is a charming sort of person, well liked, a senior now, a prefect, a pillar of the school community. Other boys like to be in his company. He treats Charlie as though they had perhaps met casually once or twice at his weekend farm, at someone's tennis court, in someone's pool.

This confuses Charlie. It baffles him. Sometimes he begins to doubt his own memory; at other times, he finds himself wondering if in fact the punishment was just and if this explains Robbie's easy conscience. Were there nameless and unspecified crimes of which he, Charlie, was guilty? There *was* the death of Willy, yes. And Robbie had loved Willy, they had all loved Willy, and Robbie had especially loved Cat. Yes, Charlie is definite about that. He remembers the way Robbie always glanced about to see if Cat was watching him, the way Robbie looked at her, the way his eyes gleamed.

Sometimes he thinks his memory of the whole event is feverish and not to be trusted. At other times he feels a helpless rage. He wants to see Robbie lying on the tracks with the train coming closer. He wants to hold him down and see the fear in his eyes. At still other times he feels a black hopelessness, as though Miss Oswell held up a white stick of chalk and asked Charlie: "What color is this, black or white?" And he said: "White." And she said: "Wrong," and sent him straight to the office for the cane.

The most disturbing thing of all is that he still feels seduced by Robbie Gray. There is a cachet to being recognized by the golden boy. He notes its effect on other students, he notes that because of it, Charlie Chang has ceased to be invisible. People listen to his opinion simply because he is one of those who gets a nod from Robbie Gray. He cannot pretend that he doesn't in some sense enjoy this. It is like arriving in front of his parents' shop in a black Buick. He feels both grateful and unclean.

Charlie's nightmares are frequent again. There is a cloudy thing, a kind of tumor, thick and heavy, behind and beneath his ribs. He gets used to it. It is simply always there. Its name is bafflement.

"Then one day," Charlie told Lucy in his room above King's Cross, "we both saw Cat in my parents' shop...."

It was an incredible coincidence. Or perhaps it was not. Chance was thick with message for Charlie.

"We both saw Cat," he said, "and Robbie bolted. He went white as a sheet and he *bolted*. We were with a bunch of Grammar boys, he would have had to account for it later."

So then Charlie knew that things weren't necessarily as they seemed. He had a brief cessation of bafflement. "I can't tell you how it eased the pain," he said. "For a while."

"I wouldn't count on a conscience." That was Catherine's opinion, expressed to me at another time, another place. "Wounded vanity, that's my guess. It's the only way he can be touched."

"I don't know," I said. "He's quite vulnerable in a way.

Maybe all that bland charm is a form of protection, a sort of shell."

A tortoise shell, Catherine thought, remembering the boy with the maddened eyes and the mallet, smashing, smashing. "But there's no one inside," she said.

When in doubt about great matters, Charlie's ancestor believed, *consult the milfoil stalks or the tortoise shell.*

"For twenty-five years," Charlie said, "I stuffed up every hole where the past might show through."

Then he read about the family photographs and the burglary in *The New York Times*. Then his neighbor said *So you know.* Then the police spoke to him of hubris, of people who come to think they're invulnerable, of people who overplay their hands.

And Charlie thought about Robbie at Grammar, and about Robbie bolting at the sight of Cat, and it seemed to him the play had still not reached its final act. It occurred to him that all he had to do was wait, though the taking of photographs, he knew, was germane to the plot.

I thought that maybe if I came back, he said, I'd precipitate something. So I came back. Perhaps I nudged things a bit, he admitted. I read the social pages, I knew he'd be advertising himself, I studied his watering holes. But all I'm doing is watching and keeping the record, he said.

And waiting.

And now I'll tell you one more story the way I heard it told in my own pub downstairs, he said. It's a story about waiting and death.

Once upon a time, said a bloke in the pub at Charlie's Inferno, Madame de Sévigné was writing a letter to her daughter, the Comtesse de Grignan, a thing she did just about every day. Epistolary addiction, the doctors said. Not a thing they could do.

"Oh *Gawd*," said Clancy. "He's off again. King Bluey Kuttorze."

At the time of this story, King Bluey said, Madame *la mère* was in residence at Chantilly, and she wrote at the top of her letter in a neat round hand: April 26, 1671.

"Once upon a bloody long time ago," Clancy said, "you blokes used to stay in the university pub where you belonged."

Madame was at Chantilly, said King Bluey, and so was the king, for it happened that Louis XIV and his entire court were visiting the Prince de Condé, and festivities were planned for the prince's château: a stag hunt by moonlight, lanterns in the woods, a promenade, banqueting under the stars, music, fireworks, the whole shebang.

"The whole bloody shebang," Clancy groaned. "We're stuck with the whole shebang."

Paparazzi and gossips were on the scene, King Bluey said, and Madame de Sévigné, all décolletage, wore a divine little thing in blue silk. The king ogled her breasts and Monsieur le Prince chatted her up and Monsieur Vatel, the most sought-after cook in the kingdom of France, that astonishing Monsieur Vatel whom the good Madame knew *personally*, the gifted Vatel surpassed himself.

"He has fucking surpassed himself," announced Clancy to the pub at large.

The banquet, continued King Bluey, was fit for a king. So pleased was Monsieur le Prince with the groaning board that some time after midnight he himself went to Vatel's room. "Felicitations," he said. "Congratulations, libations, and bouquets. Nothing could have been more perfect. You're a true-blue bobbydazzler of a *maître d'*, and you bloody well did the château proud. Good on you, mate."

"Good on ya, mate," Clancy said. "There's no stopping you, I'll give ya that."

But Monsieur Vatel was distraught, King Bluey said.

"I will die of shame, Monsieur le Prince," he wept. "My honor is at stake. I am disgraced, I am in agony, I am having a king-sized bout of the watery shits."

"Merde!" said Monsieur le Prince. "Pull yourself together, man. What the devil's got into you?"

"Woe is me," wept Monsieur Vatel.

"He's pissed as a newt," Clancy said. "He's bloody crying in his bloody beer."

Because of unexpected extra guests, King Bluey said, two of the tables had been without a roast. Not the king's table, and not the next, but certainly the twenty-fifth table from His Majesty, and also the twenty-eighth, had been meatless, ruined, undone.

Après moi, King Bluey declaimed, no lamb, no venison, no roast suckling pig.

"Pardon my French," Clancy said.

But Monsieur le Prince was kindness itself, King Bluey went on. "Look, mate, relax," the prince said. "His Royal Highness thought it was A-1 grub, he told me so himself. And tomorrow, you can go for the gold."

But all night Monsieur Vatel could not sleep. He paced and worried. He was one of these perfectionist types, he couldn't bear the disgrace of two roastless tables at the royal spread.

At dawn, still sleepless, he began at last to turn his thoughts to a new day's meals. He paced, waiting for his orders to arrive. Seafood, seafood, the call had gone out. The orders had been placed, the shopping lists drawn, the runners sent to every port in the realm. Monsieur Vatel paced and paced. At last, by the sun's early light, a man arrived with baskets of fish. One basket. Two. Monsieur Vatel, pale about the gills, held fast to the kitchen table for support. "Is that all there is?" he asked faintly.

The poor bloke, knowing nothing of the army of runners converging from fifty other fishing towns, told him yes. Two baskets, *oui, monsieur, c'est tout.*

"Mademoiselle from Armentières," Clancy sang, off-key, at the top of his lungs, and the barroom chorus joined in. "Hasn't been kissed for forty years," they roared. "Inky pinky parlez-vous."

Thanks, mates, King Bluey said. I appreciate the concern for atmosphere. But Monsieur Vatel was frantic. He moaned to his kitchen crew in a low stricken voice: "I'm done for. My honor is destroyed. I am up shit creek without a paddle. I am dead."

"Glory hallelujah," Clancy cried.

His *sous-chef* urged him to calm down, King Bluey said, and have a cup of coffee while they waited for the day's catch to catch.

But this was no joking matter to Monsieur Vatel.

He went up to his room, planted his sword in the floor, and fell on it.

"He *what*?" Clancy asked.

He fell on his sword.

"Shit," Clancy said.

And then, said King Bluey, almost immediately, shipments of fish and lobster began to arrive from all directions, seafood seafood everywhere, all over the bloody kitchen and not a cook near the sink. These goddam perfectionists, the *sous-chef* fumed to himself. These damned slavedrivers, these neurotic bloody *prima donnas* who get a fit of the vapors at the very moment you want maximum elbow grease. Swamped with mussels and carp, he sent hot words and a kitchen boy rushing upstairs for Monsieur-the-Worrywart-Vatel, but alas, alas, Monsieur Vatel was hooked on his own grim line, he was dead in a pool of bright blood.

"Bloody hell," Clancy said, fortifying himself with a drink. "Then what?"

Then they all wept salt tears, King Bluey said. The king, and the prince, and Madame de Sévigné, and the rest. The king said he was awfully sorry, and so did the queen and the prince.

"Cooked his own bloody goose," Clancy offered.

The End, King Bluey said.

And the moral of the story, Charlie said, is patience. You have to *wait*.

Silence, exile, and cunning, he said.

And patience.

And photographs.

TWO

There is no order, no sequence. Charlie's photographs spill out of boxes with the randomness of memory itself. Sometimes there is a caption, sometimes not. The sequence is determined by the viewer, a magician of sorts, who must shuffle the crossed destinies and read the cards. Meaning is in the eye of the beholder, and I sift through an avalanche, picking up random pieces of the jigsaw puzzle, trying them out here, moving them there, looking out at the photographer, trying to make circles intersect and dead ends meet.

Photographs seduce, Charlie said, and studying them is a passionate act of transgression. It's a dangerous pastime, he warned.

Violence Is a Persistent Weed

This is postcard size, in color, its title scrawled across the back. It shows a paddock that stretches into the distance and is covered in dandelions as far as the eye can see.

In the foreground, her back to the camera, the stooped figure of a woman in straw hat and gardening gloves (it could be Catherine, I think) removes the dandelions one by one with a small knife.

The Three Judges

One of Charlie's frequent collages. Rouault's painting of the three judges appears on the pocket of a blazer where the school crest should be. The photograph is eight-by-ten, the pocket occupies most of the space, though part of the lapel and a brass button can also be seen.

The judges have fleshy red faces and bull necks and little pig eyes.

Sex in the Head

A large photograph of a white skull. Through the eye sockets, one sees that the back of the skull is the wall of a quarry, pitted with blastings and tunnelings and laced with long swaying ladders.

Through the gaping mouth, one sees the bottom of the quarry, crossed with a railway line. A naked man and a naked woman are locked in sexual embrace on the rails.

Blind Justice

A papier mâché head, wearing judicial wig and a blindfold, is at the left of a postcard-sized photograph. The figure (only its black-gowned shoulders and head visible) stands at the edge of a large picture window, its back to the glass. Through the window one can see the city of Sydney. The photograph appears to have been taken from perhaps the eighteenth floor in one of the new high-rises near the Opera House. We can see the Harbour Bridge in the background, the water and Circular Quay in the foreground, and, in this view, the quarry occupying everything south and west of the quay.

The Quarry

A view of a path corkscrewing its way into a pit. Two figures in black, furtive, one stalking the other, descend into the funnel. Because of the circular nature of the paths and the optical oddity of the aerial view down into the quarry, it is impossible to tell who is stalking whom.

214

Untitled

The three famous monkeys (hear no evil, see no evil, speak no evil) sit on a boulder in the rainforest somewhere, except that each one has its hands over its mouth.

Mute Testimony

An enlargement of the Grade 5 photo. There are three absences, three white cut-out silhouettes. In the space where Cat would otherwise be is a photograph of a panther's head. In place of Catherine is a TV screen on which appears a tiny image of Catherine hanging as an earring from the ear of a talking head. In place of Charlie is the blank black eye of a camera.

The Hollow Man

A man stands in front of a mirror, his back to the camera. There is no reflection in the mirror. A neat caption across the bottom reads: *Don't worry, this is no reflection on you.*

(There is clearly a witty double homage to Magritte here, and a witty double reversal with special reference to Magritte's *Ceci n'est pas une pipe.*)

Untitled

This is simply a snapshot of Charlie and Catherine at a dance. In the bottom right-hand corner there is a logo: *Cloudland Photographers.*

The photograph beckons.

Catherine is wearing a long gown with shoestring straps. Her hair is shoulder-length and stray curls wisp across her forehead and into her eyes, Charlie is wearing a rented evening suit. They are holding hands and are turned slightly toward each other, their shoulders touching. At the time of the photograph, they have recently completed degrees at the University of Queensland. The event is the Graduation Formal, but neither Catherine nor Charlie gives the appearance of being at a festive dance. There is a haunted look to their eyes, their faces are drawn. One might be forgiven for thinking they were on their way to a wake or a funeral in fact.

The relationship between a photograph and its viewer is an act of seduction, Charlie said.

They did not, in fact, go to the formal together. They had other partners, officially. In fact, Charlie hates these things, but friends have fixed him up with a girl because it is really not acceptable, in his graduating year, not to be part of the final extravaganza at Cloudland, Brisbane's ballroom palace on the hill. Needless to say, his partner is shy and awkward (why else would she be available in this blind and demeaning way?). As they shuffle miserably through a fox-trot together on the mercifully overcrowded floor, and as the girl chatters nervously about her father's peanut farm in Kingaroy, Charlie mentally calculates the number of minutes before escape.

And then he sees Catherine. He feels her eyes actually. In that press of people, he feels something warm and compelling on his left cheek. He half turns, and there she is, and there they are in the pool at Cedar Creek, the warm sun fingering them through the canopy, the water linking them, their blood warm in each other's veins.

He supposes they managed to be polite and keep to formalities, he hopes so, he hopes he wasn't rude to the awkward little girl from Kingaroy, but here he is with his cheek against Catherine's, here he is in the dimmed light with his lips against the hollow of her neck, here he is flowing into Catherine, curve to hollow and hollow to curve, her thigh against his crotch, his leg between hers, two people in one space, his twin. They do not speak. They do not dance with anyone else all evening.

Here they are in the taxi, here they are creeping into the sleepout at the back of his parents' shop. Here they are occupying the same space in his narrow bed, floating in a Cedar Creek haze. It is perhaps not so much ecstasy as a cessation of pain. He is floating in remembered happiness. He realizes: this is the first time he has felt happy since that summer. He had forgotten what it was like.

Catherine begins to cry. "We're like war veterans, Charlie," she whispers. "We can only talk to each other."

"I talk to you all the time in my head," he whispers back. "And to Cat."

"Yes. Me too. Not with words."

"Shh," he murmurs. His parents will hear sounds, but will say nothing. They will ask no questions. Beyond the louvres, he sees the mango tree and the stars. He kisses the soft skin of Catherine's breast, which feels like Willy's cheek, the silken skin of innocence. She undoes the buttons of his shirt and reveals a thin gold chain and its pendant: two small hoops, each threaded with a blue glass bead. Catherine kisses the earrings. "She gave me something too," she says. "She gave me her hair ribbon. I keep it in a jewel box in my room." He puts his finger against her lips. Shh. He unfastens the chain from around his neck and puts it on Catherine, so that Cat's earrings hang between her breasts. He would like to eat her. Starting at her lips and working down, he licks and sucks and nibbles her creamy body. She tastes of the pool at Cedar Creek.

"I'm a virgin, Charlie," she whispers.

He kisses the hollow between her legs, then rises to kiss her on the mouth again. "So am I."

Charlie thinks, though he loses all track of time, that they simply lie there for hours. They lie together naked, holding each other, and Catherine cannot stop crying though she doesn't make a sound. Then he licks the tears from her face. He licks her neck and her breasts and her belly. He licks her between her legs till she cries out and stifles her cry in the pillow and clutches at him and he comes to her and they both come and cling to each other and cry soundlessly.

"I'm going to London, Charlie," she whispers. "My parents are having a twenty-first birthday party for me in a few weeks and I'm going right after that. I've got a job with a newspaper, I can't stay here."

Of course, he thinks. We can't stay here. He decides on the spot. "I'll come too." But she puts her finger against his lips and shakes her head. "I want to have amnesia, Charlie." Then I'll go somewhere else, he thinks. New York perhaps. Anywhere. It doesn't really matter where as long as it's away.

She unfastens the chain from her neck and gives it back to Charlie. Then she asks: "Have you seen her?"

"Once. One of her escapes. She came here, to the shop. Well, she came to see her dad, I suppose."

"I tried to visit her at that school," she says. "They wouldn't let me."

"Yes," he says. "Me too. She was let go, you know, when she was eighteen. She got a job at The Black Pussycat."

"Yes," she says. "I heard that. She's, um, a dancer, I heard."

"Yes," he says. Neither of them wants to say the word *stripper*. "I've heard other students, engineers, talk about her. She's very popular."

"Yes," she says. "Robbie goes there a lot."

"So I heard."

"Have you seen her?"

"I can't bring myself to go and . . . not like that," Charlie says.

"No."

"But I tried to make contact. I mean I went there during the day and left messages, but they always said she wasn't around."

"I tried too," she says. "It's not . . . you know, women don't go into places like that. They told me she'd gone to Sydney, I don't know if it's true or not."

"She still doesn't talk," he says. "That's what I heard. Ever."

"No," she says. "That's what I heard too."

Giacometti's Foot

An eight-by-ten black-and-white photograph with the title neatly lettered in white ink at the base. The photograph is simply a close-up of an earlobe and an earring. The earring is a plain gold hoop with a small glass bead like a teardrop at its lowest point. Since the photograph is black and white, one cannot tell what color the glass bead is.

The ironic title needs some explaining, and I recall the anecdote Charlie told me about Alberto Giacometti, 1901–1966, the famous sculptor of those striking elongated forms. When Giacometti was a young student at art school in Geneva, Charlie said, the nude model for figure-drawing classes was the generously endowed and luscious Loulou. To the instructor's exasperation, however, Giacometti never moved higher than her ankle. He religiously and obsessively drew endless studies of the model's foot. The secret of all her sensuality is in that foot, he implied.

Charlie had reason to find the whole of Cat encoded in the fleshy tip of her ear.

On the last night before she was taken away to reform school, the night after the violent events in her own overgrown yard, Charlie lay awake in the sleepout, staring out at the mango tree and the stars. There was a tapping on the glass louvres and Cat was there.

"Wait," he whispered. "I'll come outside."

They sat together among the ferns, leaning against the mango tree, holding hands, looking at the stars, saying nothing. A hot damp breeze stirred the ferns. From time to time there was the screech of a flying fox, and a banana or a mango would fall to the ground with a soft thump. They sat there for hours. They sat there until it was almost dawn.

A cock crowed.

Cat flinched violently.

She stood, and he could not bear the look on her face, so he closed his eyes and put his arms around her and he felt her go limp, with her head tucked under his chin. He held her fiercely.

She broke loose suddenly and began running away, stopped, ran back, with a quick movement of both hands reached up and pulled her earrings sharply from her ears. She simply tugged, so that the gold circles cut through the lobes as piano wire cuts. She put the trinkets in his hand and then she fled.

Neither of them ever said a word, but after she had gone he clung to the mango tree and sobbed. He howled like a dingo for her.

When he looked at the gold hoops by daylight, he saw the dried beads of blood as well as the blue glass beads.

Holy Family School for Little Wanderers

Black-and-white photograph of complex of gray cement-block one-story buildings surrounded by high chain-link fence and barbed wire.

Running Wild

Newsprint pasted on white paper. Clipping from *Courier-Mail*, subheading, small black caps, RUNNING WILD. A million black and gray newspaper dots congregate into the approximate configuration of Cat's face. Her spiky hair has been cut so short that she looks like a prisoner of war. Photo credit: court records.

Item: *Catherine Reilly, aged 15, nicknamed "Wildcat" by police and social workers, has escaped from Holy Family School for Little Wanderers for the sixteenth time in five years. Reilly holds the record for the number of escapes from a Queensland institution. A spokesman said Reilly is obdurate and non-reformable. "You get a certain hard-core type which has never had any respect for authority," the school spokesman said, "and there's nothing to work with. Nothing that can be done, I'm afraid."*

Chang's Grocers and Greengrocers

A small black-and-white snapshot of the shop on Newmarket Road.

What is not visible in the photograph is a knot of boys in Grammar School uniforms. They constitute the debating team and have been on a trip to another school for a tournament. The four boys on the team (which includes both Robbie Gray and Charlie Chang) are in the elegant black Buick owned by Robinson Gray's father, who is one of the volunteer drivers for school trips. There is no reason to go anywhere near Newmarket Road, but Robbie has graciously invited the team back to his place on Wilston Heights where there is a backyard pool, and on the way it occurs to him that he needs a particular kind of gum eraser, very difficult to get these days, available only from old-fashioned family shops like the grocer's on Newmarket Road.

Charlie feels something like nausea. He feels unclean. He feels that he has become one of the boys on the corner. He knows the glances, the raised eyebrows, the quietly polite comments and their snide subtexts that will wing their way around the dingy cluttered confines of his parents' shop. He knows how friendly and obsequious his parents will be. He feels the thoughtless good humor of Robbie Gray like a constriction in his chest. A strong undertow of intuition tells him that this thoughtless good humor is in fact malice, but as usual there seems too much evidence to the contrary. What would be the point of the malice? And if Robbie felt malice, why would he bother to confer the golden benefits of his endorsement on Charlie in the first place?

Mr. Chang is at the counter and when the four boys enter, he registers first amazement and then radiant joy. He calls excitedly to his wife who is in the rooms behind the shop. "Charlie has brought some of his friends to visit us," he calls.

Charlie can feel rather than see the repressed smiles of the debating team. He feels in equal measure a rush of embarrassment and a rush of fierce protectiveness. Not one of you, he wants to say hotly to the boys, deserves to polish my father's shoes.

But the debating team takes its cues from Robbie Gray, and Robbie is the essence of courtesy. "Delighted to see you again, Mr. Chang." Robbie's voice is as pleasing as a caramel. He extends his hand as gentlemen of substance do, and Mr. Chang, enchanted, takes it warmly in both of his and bows over it, smiling and smiling. He calls to his wife again.

When she comes into the shop, Charlie can tell instantly from the turbulent mix of pleasure and anxiety on her face that the visit at this particular moment is disturbing. Her actions are those of someone forestalling danger. They are camouflage actions designed to deflect entry into the shop. She comes out from behind the counter, she comes toward Charlie to embrace him, she is instinctively shepherding the visitors toward the door. Images rush through Charlie's mind, a riff of snapshots from the past: if she had not finished preparing accounts when the tax inspector came, if she did not have the cash in hand when the city rates-collector came, if she were not properly dressed when an important visitor arrived, she gave off that same charged aura of disturbance.

"G'day, Mum," Charlie says quietly, greeting her in front of those boys who register everything, who store everything as fodder for future witticisms, exposing himself and his mother, putting his hands on her shoulders and giving her a quick kiss.

"Oh Charlie," she says softly, a barely perceptible tremor in her voice. She manages to encode a whole treatise into the two words.

Robbie Gray, standing between Charlie and his father at the counter, watches with intense and apparently benign interest.

"Right, Mum, good to see you too," Charlie says lightly. His eyes say: Message received. I'll stay behind and you can tell me what it is.

But what it is abruptly makes itself manifest.

Because of where he is standing, Charlie sees simultaneously the faces of two principals in a drama. Robbie is watching him. Behind Robbie's head, in the doorway which leads to the back of the shop, an opening flimsily covered with a bead curtain, a figure appears.

It is, of course, so startling and so overwhelming for Charlie to see Cat with almost-shaven head standing there, that he is transfixed. And naturally Robbie turns to see where the fireworks are.

Which means that Charlie has an uncensored, unmediated view of Robbie's reaction. It is as though Robbie has been hit by a pellet from a gun. It is as though some powerful vacuum cleaner has sucked all the blood and all the color from his body in one split second. It is as though invisible pincers have taken him by the head and by the feet and put him into the machine which shakes up oil paint in hardware stores.

Then, white-faced, trembling, apparently blind, he bolts.

He rushes out of the shop, they hear the car door slam, the Buick drives off.

Charlie never does learn what face-saving explanations Robbie gives to the rest of the debating team. He doesn't care. He feels as though the pain of a bleeding ulcer has been momentarily staunched for the first time in years. Pouf! It is as though a magician has waved a wand. He realizes that he has become so used to a certain kind of ache that he cannot remember not having it. Now, for a moment, it has vanished. The difference is immense.

But Cat has vanished too. She is not in the back of the shop, she is not at the mango tree. When he pelts down the street to her old house, he thinks he sees her on the veranda and he crashes through the hole in the fence, through the waist-high grass, sobbing, calling to her.

He hears police sirens. A car pulls up at the gate and Charlie leaps over the side railing of the veranda and races along the backs of the houses to the shop. He has a mad hope that she will be waiting in the sleepout for him, or up in the mango tree, but she is not.

"Who called the police?" he asks his parents.

Ah who?

The *Courier-Mail* said she eluded capture for two days.

A pernicious and total lack of respect for authority, the police said. The way she clawed them upon recapture, more like an animal than a young woman. Beyond reform, they said.

Triage

School magazine photograph. Two debating teams. In school blazers, side by side in the front row, the two captains, one with prefect's crest on pocket. Night of the intramural debate.

Topic: TRIAGE—that in times of crisis or natural disaster, it is legitimate, in the interests of a stable society (whether macro or micro) and for the greater good of the majority, for the authorities to establish a system of priorities; that is, it is legitimate to ask, *If all cannot be saved, who then should be saved?*

Team arguing in affirmative captained by Robinson Gray.

Team arguing in opposition captained by Charles Chang.

Statement of Headmaster acting as judge: Though both teams advanced powerful and well-argued cases, reason wins over passion. Successfully argued by Robinson Gray that the ability to be intelligently "cruel" when the occasion demands is the hallmark of enduring civilizations. Award given to affirmative team.

Lost and Found

This photograph, taken in a bathhouse or in the locker room of some school swimming pool, shows two adolescent boys, naked, their backs to the camera, toweling themselves. Their school uniforms hang from pegs on the wall. Small duffle bags are visible near their feet, tucked under the wooden bench that presumably runs the length of the room.

The title of this photograph, printed neatly on the back, would not make sense except for something Charlie once told me.

I always had to remember, he said, at Grammar, to take off the chain with Cat's earrings before swimming lessons. (These were compulsory, twice a week.) You know what would happen to a boy seen with a necklace on, he said.

But he hated to take the chain off. He had such primitive, intense, superstitious feelings about Cat's earrings. He needed to feel them against his skin. So he used to wait until he got into the locker room, and then he would remove the chain quickly and surreptitiously, before he took off his shirt. He used to slip the chain into the pocket of his pants and then remove the pants and hang them on the peg.

Once he forgot.

He was in his swimsuit, under the obligatory shower, about to walk outside the pool.

"Hey Chang, you sissy!" someone yelled. "Is that from your girlfriend or your mummy?"

Charlie felt instant fever. He turned to face them, stepping out from the shower. "It was a dare," he said lightly, his survivor's instincts racing. "I had to keep it on till someone noticed. Thought you were all bloody blind."

But he saw the way Robbie, very close to him, stared at the gold rings and their tiny blue beads. He thought Robbie was going to strike him. He saw that mad red-eyed look come and go, the look he associated with Cat's veranda and spiders and shit.

Robbie turned away. "Wouldn't have picked Chang for a queer," he said.

Everyone laughed.

Charlie yanked the chain from his neck, breaking it, and walked back up the locker room and stuffed his shameful bit of Woolworth's jewelry into his duffel bag.

He didn't dare look at it after the swimming lesson, but at the end of the day, when he got home, it was gone.

He felt so ill, he was unable to sleep. He crept from the sleepout and spent the night sitting under the mango tree, his back against the spot on the tree trunk where Cat had leaned on that long-gone night.

Two days later, after the next swimming lesson, the chain and its earrings reappeared in his duffel bag.

After that, he was more careful. On swimming days, he left the chain at home in his underwear drawer.

The Black Pussycat

Snapshot of sleazy nightclub in lower George Street in Brisbane, a notorious place of ill repute. To call a spade a spade, it was a cathouse.

Ah, how legends billow from the photograph.

Once upon a time a woman of enchantments walked the catwalks of the night. When she moved, men swayed as the grass sways for the wind. She wore seven veils of silence and perhaps for that very reason, by some instinctive urge toward balance, men were particularly noisy when she appeared—though the sounds they made were not the sounds of rational discourse.

Was she beautiful? This was passing strange. All the evidence indicates that she was very far indeed from being beautiful. She was not even pretty. In fact, patrons would say in a puzzled kind of way, if you had to find a single word, *ugly* would be closer to the mark. There was something scrawny about her, something that made you think of an alley cat, something quite remote from beauty, something feral and sinuous, something that stretched itself toward you, green eyes glittering, until your skin began to catch fire and your body began to purr and you began to smell the sharp primitive musk of your underwear and your secret desires. You began to want her, you began to feel convinced that she was keeper of some powerful secret, you believed she was luring you, compelling you, you began to move toward her as cats move, motion flowing like a slow spill of perfumed oil from brain to nerve.

Yes, she was quite ugly really. She had short spiky hair, feral eyes, hollowed cheeks, small breasts, the body of a wild underfed boy. She looked frail and tiny but she was a wafer of dynamite and she held men in thrall. Under the enchantment of her Circe eye, they were turned into swine and they certainly behaved like pigs. Though she was under a curse of silence, it was rumored that her tongue could speak the whole of the Kama Sutra and every item in the Kinsey Report. Men had wet dreams and blew a week's wages on a tongue-lashing from the witch at the Pussycat.

Did she dance? Ah, when she danced, men saw fire as they had seen it the first time, when Prometheus filched it from the gods. It flickered with defiance and pain, it tantalized, it licked at their hopes.

She lived by theft and by enchantment, it was said. At night, you might see her moving like a possum from roof to roof, a cat burglar against the moon. She would slide noiselessly through the openings in your house and make off with your valuables and set up camp in your sleep. Once her eyes fell upon you, you were marked. You would never be free. You would feel compelled to put your sign on her, oh and men did, they felt challenged. You cannot make her cry out in pain, it was said, and there were those who went to unusual lengths to verify the truth of this claim. Who could resist?

Yes, she was certainly ugly. There were many scars on her arms and legs and on other more intimate stretches of her skin: cigarette burns, razor blade scars, the marks of whips. Some of the slashes she had administered to herself with rusty razor blades, or broken beer bottle necks.

"You do it when you need to scream but you can't," another self-slasher from the Holy Family School for Little Wanderers told *Truth*. "It doesn't hurt when you're doin' it. You don't feel nothin'. You don't notice it. You're just tryin' to cut away all this other pain, see? It's like pus, and you're tryin' to let it *out*."

This is the kind of sensational thing the tabloid newspapers print. It's in very bad taste. Respectable people avert their eyes, and rightly so. Let us return to modesty and social decorum, they say, for these are the proper hallmarks of our time, and of civilization, that delicate flowering tree. Let us return to lapdogs, let us examine the angst of the dinner party, the distressing intimations of the tap-tap-tapping of the quarry's tunnels beneath mahogany sideboards and against the undersides of pillowcases of pure combed cotton, handkerchief-fine; let us consider the disturbance of a shiver passing through the frail stemmed crystal, the exquisite prose of lamentation for the falling off in the quality of wines. These are the modest details of our lives—of the lives that count—and therefore let us read only of such matters, let us have a literature that is unassertive, limpid, economical, and lean. Let those with gothic taste and vulgar memories keep a proper silence, please.

And rightly so.

The woman of the catwalks, the alley cat dancer, is not the stuff of literature. There is something far too excessive about her. Let her keep silence. Let those who would speak of her silence keep silence too.

Let us turn instead to those who discuss Chekhov and Irigaray over wine.

For Cat was ugly and vulgar and absolutely non-literary, and ideologically she was definitely unsound.

She was a dangerous woman, but a challenge. How men loved it, how intoxicated they became, when she silently fought and scratched. On dirty beds, they wrestled with their turbulent fantasies, they dreamed of belling the cat, they had visions of breaking the unbroken colt and taming the shrew.

This is the sort of trashy fantasy that is reported in tabloid newspapers.

Odysseus on the Island of Circe

Newspaper clipping on white card. The title, *Odysseus . . . etc.*, printed beneath in Charlie's hand. Photo credit: *Truth.*

What is truth? asked a smiling judge.

Truth was a tabloid newspaper in Brisbane, Your Honor. It was not read by respectable people, and rightly so.

What does the photograph show? It shows the frontage of the infamous Black Pussycat in George Street. Through the large picture window the bar can be seen, and along the bar the fuzzy line-up of the backs of a number of men. Some are wearing suits, some are in working-class shirts. One can safely assume that the men are ogling the scantily clad woman who walks along the top of the bar.

Newspaper caption: BACK TO BASICS. Does Brisbane know where respectability and prestige go on their odd night off?

In Charlie's handwriting: *When men act like pigs it is entirely the fault of Circe, naturally. But Odysseus draws his sword and sticks it in Circe's mouth, and lo, he may leave unscathed.*

It could be at The Shamrock in Brisbane, it could be later at Charlie's Place. Whichever. She worked in both joints. Golden in the light that streams through stained-glass Four-X and Swan Lager signs, the Queen of Sheba presides over the bar with a languid contentment that has been known, on occasion, to break into runnels of flame the way a bushfire does. Then her anger will lick and scorch. A few quick sparks of contempt for the great cloud of unknowing that hovers above the comfortable, above those who live at very safe removes from nether worlds, a few sparks, and *whoosh*, her disdain may leap out of control.

Mostly, however, Sheba accepts the world as it is, and deploys her energies in its many pleasures, and sets her compass for survival. That is why she says to Lucy: "Your boyfriend's gonna get himself killed."

Ah. The Shamrock. In Brisbane still. "He's making a lot of people very jumpy," she says. "Taking pictures, keeping records like that, asking too many questions. You just don't do that sorta thing around Brisbane."

"I thought that's what you were after, Sheba, when you first put your hex on me. Someone to shake things up. Wave a white wand."

"Fat chance," Sheba says. "Daydreams. I just didn't forgive ya for thinkin' ya lived in outer space, that's all. For thinking you could keep your starched white petticoat clean. I *know*, see, the way the clean world and the dirty world mix. They mix every day on Brunswick Street and every night. It's the clean world that keeps the dirty world going. So it just makes me want to chuck up when clean people try so hard not to know about that."

"You should be happy about what Gabriel's doing then," Lucy contends. "Keeping a file on all those Mr. Cleans."

"There's ways and ways," Sheba says. "He's just gonna get himself killed."

But she drapes her warning around Lucy lightly as a streamer and moves along the bar and between the tables in the lounge, a ministering angel. Above her head, poised aloft on the wing of her graceful arm, circular trays laden with jugs of ale and glasses float across the top of the crowd. Sheba love, the men say, patting her generous behind. Watch where you put your fingers, mate, she says, smacking them. Or they'll get chopped off.

"Listen," she says to Lucy, returning through cigarette smoke and laughs, "I got a bloke over there can't keep his eyes off you. He's quite the gentleman, plum in 'is mouth, loads of dough. One of me sugar daddies, as a matter of fact, comes up from Sydney like clockwork, on business I suppose but how would I know? And he wants his naughty on the side, and back 'e goes. He's a dud fuck, bugger it, but aren't they all? That's why they come to me, innit?

"I'm fond of 'im," she says. "He's a gentle bloke with the usual blues, disappointed in love, he says. Well aren't they all?

"It's not fucking he wants from you, Lucy. He gets that from me," she says. "He wants to buy you a drink, that's all, he wants to talk. Well, that's all he does when he's *paying*, is talk the bloody leg off an iron pot.

"He's got the hots for you, Lucy. I told him you had this dirty secret life at the university, studying and that, and it really got his engine going." Sheba laughs. "I don't mean he wants to race you, he just wants to talk. You gonna go for it?"

"Sure," Lucy shrugs. "Why not?"

"That's him over there by the window. He's a bloody judge in Sydney, so mind your p's and q's. You can call him whatever you like, but I call him Sonny Blue."

There is no photograph, except in Lucy's mind, of the table at The Shamrock and the two glasses and the amber light that falls through the window onto Lucy and Sonny Blue. His Honor, Judge Sonny Blue.

They speak of this and that, of shoes and ships and sealing wax, of cabbages and kings, of the interesting ways in which the bonds of human kindness are both loosened and strengthened by a glass or two of Four-X beer, of the ways in which *communitas* becomes more elastic, more inclusive, more durable. They speak of the vibrancy of pubs as compared to the modes of community in law courts, say, or in universities.

Live and let live, they agree. At least, as a general principle. Though of course there are certain things which are over the top and below the belt and out of bounds. One did have to draw lines, or where would society be? One drew lines, and one turned a blind eye: this was an instinctive corrective measure in all so-cieties. Wonderfully complex, they agree, the social animal. Consider bees, Sonny Blue says. But neither of them knows enough about bees to pursue this analogy at length.

Consider the single-minded, Sonny Blue says. Consider the overly pure in heart. Consider the damage fanatic reformers have wrought: Cromwell, the French Revolution, the Puritan witch hunts in New England, the Stalinist purges, the Red Guards, Islamic fundamentalists, the thought police. Both the inability to turn a blind eye, and the inability to draw straight lines when they had to be drawn—these lacunae were always present in the recurring dark ages of civilization.

Yes, Lucy says. But how does one know when the lines must be drawn and *where* exactly . . .

It's a matter of instinct, he says.

Yes, she says. But are not the people with the power to im-pose their particular lines more inclined to draw them for their personal benefit? Can we, in fact, ever trust them? Doesn't the fact of power create an automatic conflict of interest?

Ah, he says sadly. I sense a streak of destructive bitterness. We *inherit* the lines, you see, they are sanctioned by time. We inherit the instinct for when it is appropriate to turn a blind eye. It is tradition, and respect for tradition, that makes the web of civilization. And it is the bitter zeal of those who want to redraw the lines which destroys.

I see, Lucy says.

Consider, he says sorrowfully, the zealous son of a colleague of mine. He's breaking his father's heart. His father asks me to keep an eye on him when I'm in Brisbane.

Why is he breaking his father's heart? Lucy asks.

He's trying to redraw the lines, Sonny Blue says. He doesn't know when to turn a blind eye.

Such sadness clouds Sonny Blue's eyes, such pain comes off the clenched knuckles on the beer glass, that Lucy impulsively leans across the table and puts her hand on his. She has a dis-turbing visionary flash: his eyes are not eyes, but deep black wells, they are cavernous scarred openings like quarry pits. She puts this vision down to the third beer.

(Even from this distance, I told Catherine, knowing what I

now know, I would maintain that his pain was intense, and it was real.

Yes, Catherine said. But the question is, what was the nature of the pain?)

Sonny Blue sighs. The young won't listen, he says sadly. I feel my colleague's pain as if it were my own. The young are so arrogant, he says. So unforgiving. Gabriel, for example, won't even speak to his father. It's breaking his father's heart.

Gabriel? Lucy asks, startled.

The son of my colleague, Sonny Blue says. You know him?

Lucy shrugs. Weird name, that's all. We meet too many blokes to remember who's who in here.

I suppose, Sonny Blue says. Yes, I suppose, with so many men. You should keep a lookout though. This is just the sort of place Gabriel hooks on to, and you're just the type he makes use of. Quite ruthless about it in his own zealous way. His father—my colleague, that is—is left picking up the legal pieces for him.

How exactly do you mean? Lucy asks.

Oh well, the judge says, gesturing with his hand in a manner that suggests *sub judice* taboos. Let's not . . . a long history, that's all. A certain kind of puritan zeal. A very *pure* sort of callousness, one might perhaps say, or a righteous ruthlessness. You know the sort of thing (Sonny Blue implies courteously, world wearily, that he and Lucy are all too familiar with . . .). You know, the old pattern of cozying up to barmaids and prostitutes, using them for information, until, well, you know, then dropping them like hot cakes, and then . . .

Sonny Blue brushes the legal pieces into a sorry little pile with his hand. And then . . . , he sighs.

And then *what?* Lucy asks.

Sonny Blue waves this aside in distress. He's so convincing, Sonny Blue says, as the earnest lover. Well, that sort of self-anointed charmer always is, isn't he? And barmaids are such suckers for that kind of thing, bless their little hearts of gold.

Apart from the debris, Sonny Blue says, and the legal fallout, it's the arrogance that bothers his father. There's a callous sort of self-righteousness to it.

Yes, Lucy says. In the glow of the Four-X signs, she holds herself very still. You can feel pain like an internal bleed. She can feel a bruise spreading forwards and backwards in time. *You would play upon me, you would seek to know my stops . . .*

Sucker! she tells herself furiously.

Sonny Blue picks up her hand and kisses the palm. If you ever come to Sydney, he says, I have a friend who owns several hotels, restaurants, pubs, that kind of thing. I'm sure he'd offer you a place.

The kind of place where you turn a blind eye? Lucy asks.

Exactly, he says.

Sheba, she says later, I've had it with Brisbane. I'm clearing out. I'm buggering off to Sydney in the morning.

What? Sheba says. Bit sudden, innit? I'm thinking of heading for the Big Smoke meself for a bit of a blast. But what about Gabriel?

Screw Gabriel, Lucy says. And you can tell him I said so.

THREE

Gabriel mapped the quarry with notations of his own. In back streets, in boarded-up buildings, in subway tunnels, in the sewers, he recorded intimate encounters between strangers. He filled notebooks. He used stealth, persistence, hunches, intuition, and his map-making was full of intimate detail. He prowled like a tomcat. His brooding eye monitored the night. He also chronicled the garish day and its artifacts: the hypodermics in gutters, the quick and furtive exchange of folded bills and other substances in doorways, the patterns of visitation to underground parking lots, the number plates of cars, the figures with upturned collars and downturned caps who cruised through the quarry's back passages.

He collected *faces*, he took Charlie with him to keep a record, he scribbled notes on the backs of Charlie's photographs, documenting and dating: the tired expressions at bus stops, the ravaged cheeks and great puppy-dog eyes of children in parks, the young girls in doorways, the glazed beatitude of those who dozed on the footpath outside pubs in the morning sun. Gabriel was following a trail. He was looking for clues. He was arrested by a certain kind of body, a facial type. (I was neither the first nor the last to catch his eye.) He was keeping records of the men whose eyes were caught by just such women, such types of women, of the men who returned and returned by night to certain underground haunts. There was something he needed to understand.

He was looking for the woman who rode one of the last Brisbane trams. He was looking for the men who stalked her, sniffing her scent.

He was driven by a riddle and by grief, but he also had a calm sense of inevitability. He knew that an answer lay waiting, he believed he was slowly reeling it in, that it lay beyond his patient unraveling of words spoken long ago. They were spoken by his father on an overhead bridge. *The law is like railway lines, Gabriel, straight and true. The law protects the truth. What the law decides is truth.*

Was the law the arbiter of truth?

His father's agitation on the bridge was part of the riddle and also part of the clue. That strange state of excitement had suggested to Gabriel, long before he could articulate it to himself, something lurking underneath his father's dogma: heresy, perhaps; a countertruth; a lie. He followed the riddle's thread.

Already in Brisbane—before my abrupt departure, before I fled from the calculated untruths of Sonny Blue, before I realized who Sonny Blue was—already Gabriel had a reputation as a maverick, a renegade law student, a troublemaker, an uncomfortably sharp observer and notekeeper of official behaviors, of the backroom-backstairs-off-the-record ways of the public keepers of public truth.

When you grow up with the habit—the *necessity*—of watching and listening closely, he said to me then (in those distant, tranquil, Shamrock and Cedar Creek days), you take note of every little inconsistency, every clue.

He couldn't mention his mother in Sydney, he said (it was an unwritten rule), but he studied her absence, he explored every nuance of its meaning, he became an expert, nothing escaped his eyes and ears. And when the Law, he said, in numerous dignified incarnations, was constantly in your childhood and in your home—at dinner parties, by the swimming pool, on the tennis court, on the harbor yachts, in discussions overheard, in partly listened-to phone conversations—well ... "You notice certain discrepancies," he said.

"Straight and true," he told me back in Brisbane before I fled, "is exactly what the law is not."

"Sheba says you're making some powerful people very nervous," I told him back then. And he only smiled in his calm, unruffled way, that *interior* way. "Sheba says you'll get yourself killed if you don't watch out," I had warned more sharply, distressed. "Sheba says that no one with any sense fools around with the Queensland police or the Queensland courts."

But I could never make any impact. Perhaps because of the way he refound his mother and her happiness, perhaps because of the way the woman on the tram led him to The Shamrock and to me, Gabriel trusted in the logic of the inevitable. And how could he worry if whatever was going to happen *would*?

Perhaps he was following me, perhaps he was following a different thread entirely when he came to Sydney. Perhaps the two threads intersected at Charlie's Place. Maybe everything, ultimately, leads to the Inferno and the quarry, who knows? Whatever. Gabriel was charting his way down through the labyrinth, looking for the nine-digit number at its core, keeping watch, taking notes, looking for the woman, looking. Gabriel led, and Charlie followed, keeping the photographic record so that both of them could see what they had seen.

"Charlie," I pleaded privately. "*Tell* him."

"I can't," he said. "*I can't.*"

"You could tell him *some* of it," I said. I couldn't stand it, there was something indecent about it. It was like watching a rat in a laboratory maze. So I told Gabriel what I could, which wasn't much. I told him what I could without violating a confidence.

"Charlie knew the woman on the tram," I said. "Charlie knows what she looks like. Her name is Cat."

"*Cat!*" Gabriel said, electrified, unearthing for a split second an argument, shouts, a white nightgown, his mother's cry. . . . But it was out-of-focus, staticky, getting fuzzier, gone. "So *that* was why . . .

"Cat," he said, exploring the name with his tongue. "Cat. Her name was Cat." He kept repeating it, *Cat, Cat,* but the shimmer had gone, the chink in time had closed over again.

And Gabriel couldn't get Charlie to talk, or not more than minimally. There was an accident when we were kids, Charlie said. Cat had been sent to reform school. Charlie missed her. He had lost track of her. That was all Charlie would say, except for this: "I'd like to find her again." The words gave him visible pain. "When I roam the quarry with you, that's who I'm looking for. The woman you saw on the tram."

"But what . . . ?" Gabriel pressed. *And when . . . ? And how . . . ? And when was the last . . . ?* But to no avail. Charlie would not, could not, speak of the past to the son of Robinson Gray.

"Catherine Reed knew her too," I told Gabriel.

He already knew Catherine Reed, who was part of his father's social scene; in a sense, part of it. In his last high school years, before he declared himself for his mother and Brisbane, pressured to put in an appearance at his father's parties, he'd met her from time to time, though she always came late and left early. She'd been overseas for many years, he'd heard. He thought his father was attracted to her, but edgy around her too, which interested him. He thought of her as gracious but aloof.

"Catherine Reed knew Cat," I told him. So he went to see her at the studios where she worked. He questioned her. He watched her non-answers in his attentive unnerving way.

He sifted through the meanings of her evasion, and of Charlie's too. He was an expert on gaps. The particular way in which Catherine and Charlie refused to talk was revealing to him. In their vagueness, he found illuminating clues.

There was an image that persisted in his mind like a street lamp in fog: the expression on the face of the woman on the tram. He wanted a translation. The word *cat* was surely part of the translation. He wanted to find Cat and make her translate. And what had her laughter meant? He had to know.

He knew he would find out in the end, he never doubted that, it was ordained, his journey was inexorable, there was no turning aside. And since Charlie and Catherine wouldn't talk, he decided he would have to ask his mother.

This was not something he had been able to do in our Cedar Creek days, so soon after he had found her again, too soon, when he'd been too afraid of loss and of distressing his mother in any way. But now he had to know. So he went back to Brisbane for a weekend, and I went with him.

They were alone together, sitting on the veranda of the farmhouse at Samford in the cool of evening. Half the sky was blood red with sunset, and the dark wall of the rainforest seemed to be advancing on them like an army of gigantic black horsemen. The young children of his mother's second family, of whom Gabriel was very fond, were already in bed. Against the dying light, they could see the silhouette of Gil Brennan out on the hillside, moving between the pineapple rows, checking the infant fruit in their spiky cribs, casting spells against flying foxes.

I was quite close, not far from them, invisible among the hibiscus bushes in the dark, breathing in the jasmine that hung from veranda posts. They had forgotten I was there.

"Remember," Gabriel said peacefully, "when you used to take me swimming in the pool by the falls?" Back in the golden time, he meant, the time of sugar doughnuts at McWhirter's, before things went awry.

His mother reached across to his deck chair and momentarily put her hand on his wrist.

"Were you happy then, Mum?"

She didn't answer for a long time, then she said: "Not as happy as I am now."

"Did you love Dad?"

"Yes, I did."

"Did he love you?"

Again she didn't answer for a long time. "I think so," she said. "In the beginning. In his own way." Though she had never been quite sure.

"Mum, the woman on the tram that day . . ." A look of such pain crossed his mother's face that he reached to touch her and she took his hand and held it, looking across the fields and the rainforest into the red sky. "I'm sorry," he said.

"No, it's all right."

Gabriel moistened his lips. "Why did you both laugh that day?"

Absentmindedly, his mother stroked his arm. Some time after he had given up expecting any answer, she said: "I suppose for her it meant that whatever had happened didn't matter anymore. It was irrelevant. She was free of it."

"What had happened?"

"I don't know," she said. "There was something terrible that happened when they were children. Your father would never talk about it, and nor would Catherine. I met your father at a twenty-first birthday party for Catherine Reed. You know, the one with the TV show."

"Yes," he said. "I know her. I see her in Sydney."

"Do you?" His mother was momentarily startled. "Yes, I suppose. We were at high school together, and she and your father lived next door to each other when they were kids. Has she ever . . . ?"

"I don't know her well enough for that," he said.

"Catherine's twenty-first," his mother said dreamily. She lapsed into reverie, smiling to herself. "Your father was like a skyrocket that night, I was absolutely dazzled. He got very drunk on champagne and drove me home and we sat in the car in a park and talked for hours and then we . . . Well"—she looked away, but he sensed from the way her body softened that she was smiling—"you were conceived that very night, I think. And the next day we announced our engagement."

She let go of Gabriel's hand and stood up and crossed to the edge of the veranda railing. She stood there, looking out at the bloody sky. "I'll never forget Catherine's reaction when I told her. About the engagement, I mean. It was shock at the suddenness, I suppose. No, perhaps more than that. She looked as though I'd told her I'd decided to shave my head or something. And then she said, 'Oh God, it's because of Cat. I feel responsible.'

"And I said, 'What do you mean?'

"And then she said, 'That was awfully rude of me, Constance. I'm sorry. It's just, you know, the boy next door, the past . . .' And then she said congratulations and all the conventional things and would never discuss it again."

Constance turned to face Gabriel. "The woman on the tram was at that party. . . . "

Here are the streamers and balloons again, and the Chinese lanterns strung across the lawn, and the hired band, and the dancers under the tent on Wilston Heights.

"She created quite a stir when she came. I mean, a twenty-first birthday party in those days . . . it was as formal as a wedding. And then suddenly, very late, a bit like Cinderella in reverse . . ."

Yes, let us add the trappings, for they are irresistible, and certain lives have a curious tendency to conform to ancient folk grooves. Is that what we have always done with such lives? Turned them into witches and wicked fairies and bad stepmothers and evil eyes? Do we wrap them up in fairy tales so that we can put them in the back of the toy cupboard with the bogeyman? Well then, very late, just before the stroke of midnight in fact, Cat appeared at the formal garden party and dance for Catherine's twenty-first.

"It was pretty startling. I mean, she was just there, like an apparition under one of the lamps at the edge of the tent, and she was dressed like a woman in one of those nightclub paintings by Toulouse-Lautrec. You might as well have put a whole box of firecrackers on the lawn and lit them."

She stands there, pale as Medea, pale as the ghost of Banquo at the feast of Macbeth and just as disturbing, except that everyone sees her and turns to stare. The musicians play on, unaware, for a bar or two and then trail into silence. Is this part of the entertainment? A skit? A joke? The joker in the party magician's deck of cards?

Or is this the uninvited guest, the thirteenth fairy, showing up to deliver her curse?

"I remember she wore a black strapless dress in a sort of cheap-looking satin, very shiny"—excessively shiny, let us make that, shiny as though slick and wet like the skin of a black seal—"and it was covered in sequins and it fitted her like a glove. Her hair was very short like a boy's and she wore these huge fake diamond earrings, they must have come from Woolworth's. She wasn't beautiful in the least—she was actually a bit scrawny, really. Sort of . . . sort of . . . she made me think of a possum, or an animal anyway—but there was something quite stunning about the way she stood there. She glittered. She seemed to give off some sort of heat."

The musicians are silent, the dancers are under a spell, you can hear a pin drop on the manicured lawn. Catherine moves. Someone else, a Chinese boy, a friend of Catherine's, someone Constance recalls seeing at Grammar formals, also steps like a heron across the grass blades of a trance.

There are missing frames, a jerky sequence, and then another frame with sound: three people hugging each other, laughing and sobbing, a little tableau of minor hysteria, joyful, distressing in some way, embarrassing, just a joke perhaps. Yes. Probably a joke. It is the instinct of a party to close over such incidents, for waves of talk to lap around them and blur their edges, for the music to start up and the dancers to move again.

"I'll never forget it," Gabriel's mother said, although it was the nature of such a memory that it never seemed quite real, that one began to wonder quite soon if one had imagined the event, or dreamed it even, or if rumor had expanded on something only momentarily glimpsed, or if memory had embroidered a comment.

"Anyway, then the music started up again, and I was dancing with your father and I already had stars in my eyes. He'd been on high voltage all evening and by then he was drinking champagne like water and practically flying and I can't even remember actually leaving the party. I can just remember getting all worked up in his car."

Gabriel's mother sat down in the chair again and took his hand, and he waited for her to surface from a fond electric time. "So on the tram," she said, "I suddenly made the connection, you know, between her appearance and the way your father . . . the way he was so wound up at that party and so reckless and so . . . magnetic. I was swept off my feet. But on the tram—it really was, well, an epiphany, it was like all those fuzzy years suddenly coming into focus, it was absolutely sharply clear; I suppose Catherine's reaction to my engagement had always buzzed away at the back of my mind, and now suddenly I had a translation, and in a strange way it was an enormous relief. I mean, he was giving off that same sort of . . . he was like a dynamo."

"Yes," Gabriel said. "I remember."

"And I recognized her, I remembered her, and it clicked. You see, I knew he'd been going off and seeing someone, sometimes he wouldn't come home till about four in the morning."

Gabriel flinched, seeing the men who came and went, upstairs at Charlie's Place, the way they averted their eyes from one another.

His mother smiled. "I suddenly admitted to myself it wasn't working with your father and me, it would never work, and it hadn't from the start, but that it wasn't because of something I'd done or not done. And now I just felt there wouldn't ever have been anything I could have done. And somehow I got swept up in her laughter and felt gloriously free.

"Once I realized it was her, you know, not someone else . . . I suppose that doesn't make much sense, but there was something about her, she had this ability . . . she somehow gave me this great rushing sense of freedom and power, I felt as though nothing could ever hurt me." She sighed. "But of course, that sort of euphoria never lasts long. Panic sets in. All that. Fear of loneliness, public embarrassment, that kind of thing."

"But that doesn't explain—" Gabriel began. Gil Brennan came out of the dark and into the soft light of the veranda lamp. Without speaking, he stood beside his wife's chair for a moment and put a hand on her shoulder and a sort of soft nonverbal murmur passed between them. Then he went inside and got a beer and returned and the three sat in companionable silence, listening to the shrill conversation of crickets. That doesn't explain the suddenness, Gabriel thought to himself. Perhaps it explained the fight he had overheard between his parents on the night of the tram ride, but it didn't begin to explain the suddenness of the departure for Sydney, or the absolute absence of his mother for so many years.

"Well," Gil said at last. "Reckon I'll be turning in."

"I'll join you in a few minutes, darling," she said.

Crickets and night birds and unspoken questions filled the air. "Mum," Gabriel said at last. "I don't understand why we left so suddenly."

In the light of the low-wattage veranda bulb, he saw her put her hands over her eyes, her fingertips pushing back, holding in, some kink of pain at the temples, but she said nothing.

"Why wouldn't he let me see you all those years? *Why?*"

"I don't know, Gabriel." She seemed to be negotiating something with herself. She got up and disappeared into the house and he waited, not sure if she had gone to bed or not. When she reappeared, she had something in her hand but had still not reached a decision. They sat there for half an hour, not speaking, then she gave him a matchbox. "I found it the next day, doing the washing. It was in his pocket," she said. "So he must have gone back to see her that night. Whatever happened between them has nothing to do with me, and it doesn't even concern me anymore, but I suppose it might concern you.

241

"For a long time," she said, "I thought I needed to know, but now I don't. I don't need to, and I don't want to." She closed her fingers around the box. "You'll be free when you don't need to know, Gabriel. And that's what I wish for you. That you won't need to know."

She went and stood behind his chair and put her arms around him and kissed the top of his head. "Good night," she said, and left him alone in the dark.

Inside he found a blue plastic butterfly brooch, the kind a child might buy in Woolworth's. He recognized it instantly. It was part of the bizarre costume of the woman on the tram.

When he took it out of the matchbox and held it in his hand, he touched that day again, the day of the tram ride, the day of the haunting laughter, the day of the unreadable look on the woman's face, the day of the loss of McWhirter's and sugar doughnuts, the last day of happiness.

It was one thousand kilometers back to Sydney, yet it seemed to me that Gabriel had traveled much further than that. He was on the way to his answer, I was watching him recede. I tried not to panic, I tried not to care. I'd always flown solo, after all.

Like knights on a quest for the Holy Grail, together now, daily, nightly, whenever they could leave Sheba and me in charge of the restaurant and bar, Charlie and Gabriel roamed the Quarry Perilous. They were both of them looking for Cat. They also wanted to catch the entire shoal of nine-digit numbers in their net. They believed that Cat and the nine-digit numbers were two sides of the same equation.

So did Catherine, who was making a documentary on people like me. "Voices from Underground," it was called. *A lost generation*, the voice-over said.

"I'm not lost," I told the eye of her camera. "I'm a tourist here. I'm wearing a costume. I can take it off whenever I want."

"Terrific," her cameraman said. "Terrific." He panned the room, he shot the view from my window, he caught the pimps and scouts on the pavement below. Her soundman swung his boom out the window to catch the raucous street cries and traffic din.

"*Can* you leave whenever you want?" came Catherine's off-camera voice.

"In my case," I said, "I reckon I can. But not everyone. For some, the only way out is down."

Afterward she said to me: "What on earth are you doing here? You don't belong."

"I do and I don't," I said. "Did Gabriel or Charlie set this up?"

"Neither," she said. "I was at a dinner party once, downstairs. You were a waitress and you interested me. Your watchfulness, your satirical eyes." She smiled. "I decided then I'd be back. But I think you should get out of here before it's too late."

"I've been driven to it anyway, by Gabriel."

"Gabriel," she sighed. "He's a very persistent young man." She said it as though she believed it would bring him to harm.

Oh, Gabriel was persistent all right. I have said that when we got back from his mother's, I felt him receding, moving away from me, and yet that is ridiculous in a sense. At his insistence, I was about to move in with him. I was about to move out of Charlie's Place and into Gabriel's flat. He'd worn me out. I'd wearied of him tapping on my door—very courteously—in the middle of things. He'd wrecked my business, he'd scared off all my clientele. He couldn't help it, he said. He couldn't stop himself. He simply couldn't bear the idea of those men . . .

"But you don't understand," I said. "They don't touch me. My body's just a costume, they can't reach behind it, they can't touch."

"It's intolerable," he said. He wasn't furious or jealous, it wasn't like that. He simply said patiently: "It's absolutely *intolerable*."

He had that quiet relentless kind of innocence, and I'd given in. I'd given in even as I sensed him slipping beyond my reach, entering the orbit of his riddle, moving into the answer's rare atmosphere where I sensed it might be difficult to breathe.

"I could do with someone who knows the city's underside,"

Catherine said. "I could do with a guide and a researcher. Does a job with me interest you?"

"All right," I said.

I moved into Catherine's profession and Gabriel's flat the same week. But in the evenings, I still helped out in the restaurant and its satellite pub. I still hung around Charlie's Place.

FOUR

 Gabriel saw a photograph of Charlie's called *Golden Boy*. For a long time he studied it. "Is this my father?" he asked at last.

"Yes," Charlie said.

Frowning, Gabriel murmured: "I can't tell if it's satire or tribute."

"No," Charlie said.

Gabriel nodded.

It sometimes seemed to him that if only he had never shown his father the newspaper photograph of their neighbors on the tram, nothing would ever have begun to go wrong. But then that was the way of things. Whatever was going to happen did.

Nevertheless, he wished he had a photograph of his mother tucking him into bed when he was five years old, his father leaning against the bedroom door watching them both. He remembered the look in his father's eyes as a weather of happiness in which he once lived. He wanted that weather back. Sometimes he could hardly breathe for the pain of that lost time. He was, he believed, on a long return journey to that weather. He would find it in time.

"What do you think of my father now?" he asked.

Ah, what?

This was Charlie's working position: that a chain of events set in motion long ago, at the railway cutting and afterwards in the long grass of Cat's front yard, had been costly, very costly, for Catherine and himself, and infinitely more so for Cat. They were all still in arrears, they were still paying heavily, they still dragged lead weights of silence and shame.

Yet these same events had cost Robinson Gray nothing at all, or they seemed to have cost him nothing, or *almost* nothing, and this imbalance of accounts disturbed. It lacerated. Charlie was waiting to see if unpaid bills ever fell due, or if, indeed, unknown to him, Robbie had been paying all along in some hidden coin.

Charlie looked at Gabriel looking at *Golden Boy*, an ambiguous photograph, and saw Gabriel's desire to be told that his father, though flawed like all of us, was a good and honorable man.

So are they all, all honorable men . . .

"When we were children," Charlie said, offering weighty evidence in Robinson Gray's favor, "Cat loved him."

Cat loved him, Gabriel thought with a surge of understanding, a surge of hope. My mother loved him. Do I?

Gabriel thought the answer was yes. Yes possibly. He thought that was surely the meaning of the fact that his father was almost never out of his mind. He thought *love* was at least as accurate a word for his thoughts as *anger*, though often neither seemed as accurate as *grief*. But there was some high, invisible, impenetrable wall between them. Perhaps he was as responsible for this wall as his father was; perhaps every uneasy perception, every doubt on Gabriel's part, had added a layer to the wall.

"Where did you take this one?" Gabriel asked, picking up another.

The photograph showed a swarm of backs, laden with sorrow, rising up a laddered wall. Each figure had his eyes on another's ankles, each hand was chained to its attaché case or its burden of dread. "On the law court steps," Charlie said.

Gabriel studied the backs with a magnifying glass and circled one figure in white ink.

He picked up another. "Which night was this?" he asked.

"Let me see." Charlie looked at one of his many shots of a Newtown pub. It was said that The Shaky Landing, in the quarry's first circle, was a true doorway to the underworld and that trapdoors existed in the tavern on the main floor, and in the back kitchens, and in the hallways and lavatories too. It was said that people had disappeared through these trapdoors. It was said that they were never seen again. "I can't remember," Charlie said. "We've been there so many times. It's probably last week's batch."

The entire photograph was actually of the mirrored wall behind the bar, but reflected in one corner of the mirror was a table at which sat three women of the night. (Such women, of course, always congregate in threes. That is the rule. There is nothing a recorder of events can do about this. *When shall we three meet again?* et cetera.) The reflection of one of the women was interrupted by the Toohey's sign painted across the mirror behind the bar. Charlie grabbed a magnifying glass and held it over the photograph. What was visible of the face and the almost shaved head stirred him to a sudden excitement. "My God!" he said. "This is where you heard her name the first time, remember?"

"Yes," Gabriel said. Then he frowned. "No, that wasn't the first time." He put a hand vaguely to his forehead because the chink in time had opened again and a flying pellet of the past hit him between the eyes. (He sees the white nightgown, hears the shouts, the door slams.) Gone again. And he wondered: was he remembering her name from those distant arguments? Or was he remembering the more recent discussion with his mother? Or were Charlie's memories growing over his?

I said to him sadly: "You're obsessed with your father, don't you see? You give him the power to go on hurting you, you *let* him. Your mother's settled for happiness, Gabriel. She doesn't need to know."

"His father is certainly obsessed with *him*," Sheba told me. "He hardly talks about anything else."

In the restaurant, I overheard Roslyn Gray who was having lunch with a woman friend. "Robbie's *obsessed*," Roslyn said. "Everything Gabriel does is designed to upset his father, and Robbie falls for it every time."

Invisible and deaf as waitresses are, I hovered and listened and wondered: was it true?

"The thing is, Lucy," Sheba warned, "he's a stirrer, he's a shit disturber. He's gettin' a lot of people very nervous again, you'd think he would've learned his lesson in Brisbane. There's a lotta talk going round, about the photographs. About all this note-taking stuff. Ya gotta get him to back off."

"Sheba says you're making certain important people very nervous," I warned.

"I hope so," Gabriel said.

"It isn't just my father," he explained. "It isn't just *personal*. It's the interconnections, it's the different forms of violence, it's violence itself, it's the importance of understanding why a society seems to *need* violence." Gabriel could not understand either the will or the ability to cause harm. He was baffled and disturbed by it. He probed the epidemiology of harm as a dedicated medical researcher might stalk a cancer cure or the black secret of AIDS.

"Come up the coast with me," I begged. "Let's get out of here. Let's go up to Collaroy or Avalon for a while, let's head for Byron Bay."

"There isn't time," Gabriel said. This world is burning, his eyes and his flushed skin said. This world is on fire and all things burn and there isn't time. Gabriel was burning, I could see. He was smoldering. He was slowly going up in smoke. "I'm sorry, Lucy," he said gently. "It never feels as though I have a choice." He stroked my cheek. "I'm sorry, Lucia." He held me against himself. Our kisses were so hungry, we might have been eating each other. "It'll be different," he promised, "once I *know*."

"Please, Gabriel." I had a vision of tunnels made of some dread elastic that stretched further and further into the quarry dark. Down the capillaries of all the nightmares of Sydney, I could sense Gabriel traveling beyond the vanishing point. "Please, Gabriel," I begged. "Please stop. Couldn't we go to Brisbane again? Stay awhile with your mother and Gil?"

"Soon," he promised. "Yes, I'd love to do that. That's what we'll do afterwards, Lucia, grow pineapples. We'll live in the rainforest. Maybe further north, maybe Cairns, maybe right up in the Daintree, somewhere as far away as possible from all this."

"Oh when?" I asked, mad with hope.

"Soon," he promised. "After, you know . . . I don't just mean about my father, I mean all the sordid interconnections, all the . . ."

I knew what he wanted. He wanted a miracle, he wanted *change*, he wanted to fix the whole bloody world.

"Gabriel," I said mournfully. "Why don't you lick the pus from other people's boils? Why don't you clean the quarry with your tongue?"

"I could ask you that, Lucia."

"Yeah, you did. But I've stopped, haven't I?" I said. "I was after *knowledge* and I've got it. And maybe in a hundred years I'll figure out how to use it to change a comma or two in the world, but we're no good to anyone dead, and I'd like to bail out."

"But you can't," he said. "That's my point. It's not so easy to bail out. Things are more tangled up than anyone knows. The quarry props up a lot of walled gardens," he said.

I had meant bail out of attachments, bail out of coming pain. I flew solo and I always had. I was unhurtable. I stayed clear of everyone's nets.

"I'm beginning to think it's no small accomplishment to build a walled garden," I said wistfully. I thought of Gabriel's mother and his stepfather walking between their spiked rows of fruit, the wall of the rainforest like a sheltering ring, the solar benedictions. "I thought we were going to grow pineapples and mangoes."

"We will," he said. "We *will*."

But this world was burning, the quarry had spread, there wasn't time.

Charlie took a photograph of us standing close together, talking, burnished with quiet intensities. He double-exposed it with a photograph of a fire so that we seemed to be walking untouched in flames. This photograph, I read in an art magazine last year (my heart turning somersaults), was on display at a recent Chang exhibition in Greenwich Village. The photograph is called *The Fire Sermon*.

I remember touching my own burning cheeks. It was attachment which caused all this pain, I thought. It was the savagery of love, the brutality of desire. These things were a match to skin and hair.

Charlie's body hummed with excitement. He was looking at another photograph of the bar in The Shaky Landing and the woman in the corner was there again. You could see her eyes and her short spiky hair in the mirror behind the bar, but the lower part of her face was obscured by painted words: TOOHEY'S, CARLTON, XXXX, SWAN LAGER.

"It's *her*," Charlie said. He could hardly speak for excitement. "It's Cat." He couldn't understand why he hadn't seen her when they were there, but she must have seen him first and slipped away, she must have hidden for reasons of her own. It was the only explanation, he believed.

But he had known she was close by, he knew she would send for him, he knew that sooner or later she would tap on his window and beckon him into the night. He had to let Catherine know. He had to show her the photograph. He saw her so rarely, except on TV. She never returned his calls.

He had to go to her.

"Ah!" Catherine said, startled, opening her office door at the SBS television studios. If she felt something more than surprise and ordinary courtesy, she managed not to show it.

"I've found Cat," he said.

Had she heard him? Was there some barrier around her that blocked out sensory invasion?

"I've found Cat," he said again.

He could see pain moving through her body like dye. She blinked and turned her head away from him. She buried her face in her hands. She went back to her desk and sat at it and rested her elbows on the desk. He could see the tips of her fingers through her hair. He could not see her face. She said nothing.

Charlie put the photograph on the desk in front of her, and she picked it up and pushed it back without looking. "Please Charlie," she said.

Amnesia, he knew, was hard work. It took all one's energies.

Charlie sat in the chair across from her and waited. He could feel the taste of Catherine on his tongue, he could smell her hair, he could feel himself returning to her body as naturally as seawater returns to hollows in the sand. He was at home there. My twin, he thought. *Myself.* He could even feel the rough texture of the office chair against the underside of her thighs and the abrasion of the wooden desk against her knees and the slight pressure where her ankles touched each other.

It seemed a very long time before she raised her head and looked at him. Her eyes were drugged. It was as though he had interrupted a long journey she had been making in her sleep. What do you want of me? her body asked.

He didn't say anything. He simply looked at her and wanted the missing parts of himself.

She nodded and came toward him as a sleepwalker comes.

And then they were back in his apartment. On the hushed side of the shoji screens, against the white sheets, above the raw gaudy life of King's Cross, they flowed back into each other as effortlessly as the whitewater braids of Cedar Creek meet in the pool. From the wall of his bedroom they were watched by photographs of Cat.

"The photograph you wouldn't look at," he said. "It's a cathouse in the quarry. Gabriel and I have been going there."

He could feel her whole body go tight in his arms. He trailed his fingers over her breasts and belly and rested his hand between her legs until she softened again. She said: "I feel responsible for Gabriel. For his *existence*, I mean."

"Why did you ask Robbie to your party?"

"You can't not ask the boy next door to your twenty-first."

"And Cat?"

"She must have seen my parents' announcement in the paper. They gave the *Courier-Mail* my graduation picture."

"You see, she watches. She sends signals. That's what she's doing now."

"Unless Robbie told her about the party," she said.

"Yes," he sighed. "Well." They did ignore each other excessively that night, he recalled.

Catherine ran an index finger around Charlie's lips and across his chin and the curve of his neck, and down the line of his sternum. She was remembering that moment at her party when the three of them, incredulous but euphoric, stood embracing each other in full view of fifty guests. She could smell Cat's musk again, that wave of cheap perfume (it was like entering pungent fog), she can smell it now, she can feel the stubble of Cat's hair against her cheek, she can feel the hum that always came off Cat's body, she can feel Charlie fitting like a matching puzzle-piece against her right side. She feels weak with desire. She begins to cry.

"What's in the photograph?" she asks.

But Charlie was still in the past. "Can you remember leaving the party?"

"No. Can you?"

"No. Who suggested it?"

"No one did. It just . . . My parents were furious the next day," she remembered. "Disappearing from my own party like that. But we were just there," she said.

They were simply there at Cedar Creek again, in the pool beside the two boulders, the moon shredded by the forest canopy, flakes of it white on the water, their naked limbs drifting like ghostly weed.

"We shouldn't have taken her back to The Black Pussycat," Catherine said. "I should've made her stay at my place."

"She wouldn't have. You know that."

"Yes. No. Do we know it? Do we know it for sure?"

Charlie thought of himself as a child beneath the mango tree, bloodied earrings in his hand, howling like a dingo for Cat. "I think," he said, "that she was terrified of pushing trust in us too far. If *that* went too . . . I think that's the explanation."

"But why did it happen, all that mayhem? That very night, *why*?"

He could smell them, he could feel their bodies, Cat's and Catherine's, how wet they were (they had no towels at Cedar Creek; wet and shining and reckless, they had pulled their ludicrous formal clothes back on, laughing, shivering a little, sopping wet), he could hear them squelching in their shoes, he could feel them dripping onto the car seat, sticking wetly to the leather, he can see them fogging up the glass. . . .

The three of them are damp and steaming in that car, Charlie driving, Cat in the middle. She never speaks, but her body gives off a high-intensity hum of happiness. So it seems to them. We were planning to go away, they tell her, Catherine to London and Charlie to New York, but now perhaps . . .

Cat is part of them. They are whole again. They speak of hopes and Cat listens. They can feel her hot damp body against theirs. Cat reaches toward Charlie's wet unbuttoned shirt and touches the gold chain and the earrings with her index finger.

The car bucks, Charlie brakes and swerves, but keeps going. He wants to laugh and cry and sing and never let either of them go. Without thinking about it, he drives to Chang's Grocers and Greengrocers on Newmarket Road.

But Cat will not get out of the car. She shakes her head.

"Will you come back to my place, Cat?" Catherine asks.

Cat shakes her head. Charlie and Catherine exchange looks. He starts the car.

Outside The Black Pussycat, Catherine says: "Cat, *why*? Why won't you come home with me? We've got a spare bed on the veranda."

Cat neither nods nor shakes her head. Perhaps she feels the undertow of something inexorable, the kind of thing that pulled the Sylkie back to the sea at dawn, the kind of thing that made Psyche's lover vanish when she looked at him. She reaches across Catherine and opens the car door. "Please, Cat," Catherine begs. "Can we see you more often? We *miss* you."

Cat walks into The Black Pussycat without looking back.

"There must have been a connection," Catherine said to Charlie over twenty-five years later. "Between us and the aftermath. But it doesn't make sense."

"Unless it had something to do with Robbie."

"Yes," Catherine said. "But it still doesn't make sense."

But then, Charlie thought, what *would* make sense in Cat's life? Does muteness tend toward explosion? Do all the unspoken words build up pressure and blow their container? Does love weaken the armor in devastating and near-fatal ways? Perhaps Cedar Creek washed the anaesthetic off and the pain was unbearable and Cat had to cut it away. Perhaps, in spite of everything, she missed Robbie at the pool. Perhaps she had to cut Robbie's absence away. Who knew?

In the debris of barroom brawl, broken beer bottles, slashings and stabbings, chaos, police sirens, arrests, who could trace a pattern that made sense? Some witnesses said she slashed at customers, others that she slashed herself. Certainly blood flowed on both sides, and nobody could remember how it began. Would a year in jail have been any more senseless to Cat than the years in reform school? Would it have made much difference to her one way or the other?

At least she'll be safe there, Charlie and Catherine, knowing nothing of the inside of prisons, told each other after seeing the papers the next day.

But she had already disappeared when they went back to The Black Pussycat. She had jumped bail, she was on the run, there were rumors that she was heading for Sydney, they would pick her up in time, never fear.

"I'm going to London," Catherine had said. "I want amnesia."

And Charlie said: "I'll come with you."

"No."

New York then. It didn't much matter where.

"She did serve that time, you know," Charlie murmured into the warm hollow between Catherine's breasts more than twenty-five years later. "She was caught in Sydney, and she did time. Then she worked out of one of those old hotels in New Farm, The Empire. She was still in Brisbane in '69. Gabriel saw her on a tram, well you know that, he gave you the third degree too. I've checked, via contacts, at The Empire. They said she just disappeared one day, per usual; right about the time Gabriel saw her on the tram. Took off to Sydney again, the rumor was. The quarry, they reckoned. So it fits."

"What fits?"

"The Shaky Landing, the photograph, it's her," Charlie said. "You can only see part of her face, but it's her. She just needs to *know*, that's what I think. That's why she came to your twenty-first. She just needed to know we still . . . And now she's sending out signals."

"I don't know," Catherine said.

"Look, I'll show you."

She studied the photograph for a long time.

"Well," he prompted. "It is, isn't it? Don't you think so?"

"I don't know," she sighed. "I *want* it to be her. But I know what lifespans in the quarry are, I've done too many documentaries. . . ."

"It's her," Charlie insisted. He had spent so much time with her, with both of them, they were both so hugely and constantly present inside his head.

Catherine hugged herself and shivered. "Sometimes in London I'd dream. We'd be swimming at the falls and she'd call me, and I'd wake and my heart would be hammering so much I could hardly breathe. She'd be caught in the whirlpool like someone going down a plughole in a sink, and I couldn't reach her in time, and she'd be struggling, she'd never give up. . . ."

"She'll never give up," Charlie said. "We can count on that."

And *the decayed willow may still produce flowers,* he thought.

So the *ta kwo* hexagram said.

"I want it to be her," Catherine sighed.

"It *is* her." Charlie unfastened the thin gold chain around his neck and dangled Cat's earrings before Catherine's eyes. He trailed them across her lips. She licked them with the tip of her tongue. "She's coming back for her earrings," Charlie promised. "She knows we're here."

Catherine sucked at the little gold hoops and felt the smooth nub of the glass beads with her tongue. The hoops had an empty metallic taste. She fastened them, wet with saliva, round Charlie's neck again. She wished she could believe him. She feared that grief and desire played terrible tricks with hope.

They sat at a corner table in The Shaky Landing: Charlie and Catherine and Gabriel, and I was there too. With Catherine was a soundman and a cameraman. No one could think, let alone talk. The music was like a heartbeat, it throbbed inside the skin, it filled the cranium the way pealing bells fill their tower, it deafened, it exhausted, it was meant to be taken with various white powdered substances. Catherine put her mouth against Charlie's ear and shouted: "I can't tolerate this for very long."

Lights in hot shredded purples and primary reds bounced across the skin like meteors. Auras buzzed about every head, migraines as large as dinosaurs flicked their languid tails and stirred their limbs and sent warning volleys of pain across eyeballs and temples and into the soft vulnerable cortices at the napes of necks. In the weird and constantly shifting light, bodies glowed green and magenta, they purred like leopards with lurid spots. They were distorted, elongated, flattened, turned fluid; they seemed to float as though the whole place were underwater.

A waiter dressed in black leather, whose hair resembled steel wool to which electric prods had been applied, brought a tray with jug and glasses to the table. In the light, the beer looked green.

Charlie showed the waiter a photograph and pointed to the woman partially visible in the mirror. Against the din, he mimed inquiry. The waiter fluttered eyelids shadowed with kohl and shrugged indifference.

Charlie shouted: "Could we talk to the manager, please?"

The waiter shrugged again and drifted into a shaft of purple light and purple noise and disappeared. We drank green beer and tried to think thoughts in whatever color thoughts would come, but it was difficult to think at all.

Catherine put her lips against Charlie's ear and shouted again: "I can't take this. I'll have to leave."

And as though her wish burgeoned into monstrous form, two bouncers in black leather pants and black muscle shirts, with biceps like the ropes on an ocean-going ship, appeared at the table with clear and unfriendly intention.

"Interesting," Gabriel shouted against my ear.

There was a knife. There was a scream. There were, it had long been rumored, two to three deaths a week at The Shaky Landing. In the quarry, the police had been saying, it was better to let civic infection run its course. *Triage*, various gentlemen of authority (political scientists, judges, members of the Order of Australia) murmured intermittently on TV. Those who live by the sword shall die by the sword, they said, and ditto for guns, knives, white powders, arson, dynamite, assault rifles, crack, and assorted sexual appetites.

Deaths in the quarry don't count, Gabriel told me (as though I didn't know). They only make the newspaper if they spill over into neat treed streets, he used to say.

Blood thumped in my ears, I could feel the hearts of Gabriel and Charlie and Catherine pounding inside my skin. Our departure from The Shaky Landing was sudden and undignified. There were trapdoors underfoot, knives in the corners of our eyes, dizzy craters, the dangerous shells of boarded-up shops on every side. Nevertheless we reached the lip of the quarry and escaped.

"The trouble is," Charlie said, "there's no way of knowing

if that meant anything much at all. It could have been just because we asked questions."

"Or it could be that our faces make certain people nervous," Gabriel said.

"It was probably because of the camera," Catherine claimed.

"I know she's around," Charlie insisted. "I'll go back. I'll wait there from two A.M. to dawn every night if that's what it takes."

"I want you to be right," Catherine sighed. "But I'm not going back. It's crazy. It's suicidal to go back."

"I agree," I said. "It's madness. It's asking for trouble."

But Gabriel said, "I'll go with you, Charlie."

Gabriel constructed flowchart sheets which he kept under lock and key. "The network is incredible," he said. "You can't afford to tip anyone off, you can't let anyone inadvertently give out clues, and you never know who's hooked in."

"He's writing the bloody book of secrets," Sheba said.

"I'm *reading* it," Gabriel contended.

"Look, mate," Sheba said, "I've been reading it for donkey's years. It's not exactly news to some of us, you know. You'll get yourself killed if you don't watch out, and a hell of a secret that's gonna be."

Gabriel paced our apartment like a tiger in a cage. (A tiger? Is that the right image? He was always so quiet, so calm, and yet I had the sense of tightly coiled intentions waiting to spring.) "Lucy?" he said.

"What?"

But the labyrinth sucked him down between the thought and its telling. He had traced tunnels all the way to Brisbane. "They come out in Brunswick Street," he said.

"Tell me something I didn't know," I said wearily. "Sheba could have told you that years ago. I could have told you that. Where d'you think I heard about Charlie's Place before Charlie did?"

"Where *did* you?" Gabriel asked with sharp interest. "And who exactly—?"

"Oh," I said hastily, slamming Sonny Blue back inside his box. "Some bloke in The Shamrock. Can't remember now. It isn't important."

"It might be," Gabriel said.

He was very solemn, I remember. He put his hands on my shoulders and made me look at him. "We've found someone who remembers Cat," he said. "We found someone who knew her at The Empire Hotel, an old hooker. She was working out of The Empire with Cat at the very time I saw her on the tram."

"God," I said quietly, awed in spite of myself.

"Cat disappeared right after that," he said. "But this woman thinks she knows what happened. She's got a longtime client who's an old Brisbane cop. We're meeting them both at The Shaky Landing, Charlie and me."

"Do they know where Cat is now?" I asked.

"They think so. I think we've located her. We have to go to Brisbane to check it out."

"Brisbane!" My heart leaped up. "We can stay with your mother and Gil."

"Not this time, Lucy," he said quietly. "I meant that Charlie and I—"

"Oh sure," I said, hurt. "When you bring her back," I said tartly, "we'll throw a bash."

"I'm not sure it'll be a party," he said. He seemed weighted down, absent, as though the answer he had hunted after for so long had now attached itself to him like a ball and chain. So now, I thought wearily, we enter a new phase, I suppose. I felt exasperated. Perhaps I was jealous of Cat with her hold on so many lives.

"So she's been in Brisbane all along?"

"Well, this old hooker thinks . . . But Charlie's sure she's in Sydney. A lot depends on what we hear tonight," he said. "Not that you can trust a Queensland cop, retired or not." At least we agreed on that, but I suppose I owed them something. I suppose he wouldn't have fled Brisbane and found me here if it weren't for the Queensland police. "We're leaving for Brisbane tomorrow anyway," he said. "We'll get away early and drive up in Charlie's car. It won't make sense for me to come back here tonight, I'll stay at Charlie's so we can leave at the crack of—"

"Sure," I shrugged. "See you again sometime."

"Lucia." He made me look at him, with my face between his hands. Minutes passed.

"What?" I demanded, not gently.

"After this, we'll grow pineapples," he promised. "We'll get as far way from here as we can. Innisfail, Cairns, I don't know. The Daintree, maybe."

But I wouldn't be won over, I wouldn't smile. I'll believe it when I see it, I thought.

"I love you, Lucia."

"Yeah, yeah," I said irritably, breaking free.

That was Monday night. Good riddance, I said lightly to myself as he left. Give The Shaky Landing my regards.

That was the Monday night.

FIVE

I would like to stop here. I would prefer not to go any further.

I once saw a woman flayed. You would not believe how it altered her appearance for the worse. The police have photographs of this, but I'm not going to speak of it.

I once saw a horse balk at a jump because it would not smash itself against the wall of its instincts. It would not. No amount of whipping or spurring could change its mind. It threw its rider. Later, the burrows of small animals were found beyond the jump.

I balk at having to look at the police photographs. I balk at mentioning the burglary. Well, the burglary. Burglary is nothing these days, is it? A free prize at the door to anyone who knows someone whose place hasn't been subjected to break and enter. Big deal. So I come home one day and the flat has been ransacked, and all Gabriel's notebooks have gone. So what? Also a small cache of Charlie's recent photographs, the ones Gabriel has been poring over late at night. I have no problem with mentioning that, but then I draw the line.

I will rummage only so far and no further in the rubble of the past. I am seduced by the desire to stay behind the bar in Charlie's pub, with the laughter and the jokes and the men averting their eyes as they go upstairs, with Gabriel distant and burning but nevertheless beside me in bed each night, with

Charlie and Catherine together again, at last, with Sheba rolling her eyes at us all and making a crude sign with her finger and tapping off draught, with Cat hovering about, flamboyant and indomitable, sending messages from just offstage, showing up in mirrors, beckoning and daring us, making claws with her hands, casting reflections.

End there.

Why not? Nothing's perfect, but that was close. Love had meaning, waiting had meaning, even anxiety had a meaning that was quite precise. Nothing was resolved, but what ever is? And as narratives go, that's reasonably acceptable these days, almost fashionable indeed, though most readers—and many critics—still declare without apology that they will have no truck with unsatisfactory endings or inconclusive final chords. Oh, and I agree. I cannot tell you how passionately I agree. I would like to go on record as being desperately eager to have no truck with unsatisfactory and inconclusive ends.

Here's Cat, I'd like to say. Yes, we coaxed her out of the mirror at The Shaky Landing and cleaned her up and got her a good therapist and she stopped slicing herself and exposing herself and selling herself, and Robinson Gray told her he'd never for a minute intended but was apologizing just the same because remorse and other transforming emotions were strangling him, and he paid for her to enter the University of Sydney as a mature student where she did extraordinarily well and where the fresh and original candor of her mind was a source of wonder and His Honor reserved a job for her in his law office and she bought a house and a car. She learned how to cook asparagus exactly right and she learned which wines to serve with fish and which with fowl, and she so captivated Robinson Gray with her dinner parties that he, having tired of his tedious third wife, at last married the Cinderella of his childhood for she had long ago stirred him sexually as no other woman ever had. And then Robinson Gray, rinsed pure and transfigured, had all the nine-digit numbers rounded up and put on trial and put away and he ensured that the quarry was turned into Luna Park (with jobs and social security for all former residents and hot dog stands on the corners) and he had it planted with banksias and paperbarks and wattles and the soft pink flowers of Geraldton wax and he looked upon his work and it was good. It was so good, so meet and right, so worthily done, that it touched the heart of dearest him who had gone away. Gabriel and his father embraced, there were reconciliations on all sides, bells pealed, a new golden age was ushered in. And Charlie took Catherine for his wife, and Gabriel and myself got married too . . . no, of course we didn't get married, this isn't Shakespearean comedy, this is modest late-twentieth-century social realism, but Charlie and Catherine, and also Gabriel and myself, did cohabit joyfully in two nice little side-by-side terrace houses in Paddington, with season subscriptions to the Opera, and correct opinions on Aboriginal Rights and the Gulf War and the *Australian* and Mr. Murdoch, and we read Chekhov and Proust and a few sanctioned Australian writers appropriate to these times, and we gave dinner parties where the discussions were exceedingly literate and high-minded and where the utmost care with asparagus and hollandaise was always taken, and we lived happily ever after, amen.

No, no, the fashionable critic says: That is not what I meant. That is not it at all.

There is no warrant for crude mockery or slapstick, that is not what was meant, not at all. The true satisfactory ending is shot through with tender angst and subtle shadows the way shot silk is dappled with light, it is indeterminate in a suggestively closed sort of way.

. . . and twisting away from the table, he bent to pick up the napkin ring.

"The oddest thing," Andrew said. "Wouldn't you say, Rob? Of all the cases we've had referred since I've been on the Premier's Board of State Police, this has to be the most bizarre."

Catherine, taking the napkin ring from Robinson Gray, paused momentarily then placed the ring neatly beside her glass.

"We're not even clear who the principals are," Andrew said, "though that woman would probably have to be counted as one of them. How she fits into the picture, though, is anyone's guess."

"*Habeas corpus,*" someone joked.

"Exactly."

"They say she was practically tattooed with scars," Andrew's wife said. "Most of them from her own hand."

"I think perhaps I should have poached the salmon a minute or two more," Roslyn said. Against parsley, the silver and pearl-handled servers gleamed modestly. Roslyn Gray, expertly sliding silver blade between pink flesh and bone, bisected the fish. Tenderly she peeled the backbone away and displayed it in the candlelight. Ahhh, they murmured. It was like an exotic translucent comb.

"It's like an arsenal of tiny pearl daggers," Andrew's wife offered.

"Speaking of daggers. According to the coroner's report, there were thirty-six stab wounds," Andrew said. "Incredible ferocity. Rob actually knew her once, didn't you, Rob?"

His Honor mused a little space. He thought wistfully: she had a memorable face.

"Not really," he said. "Only very slightly. Years ago, when we were children."

Roslyn marked out the indentations of the ichthyoid spine with lemon segments, and passed the platter and the drawn butter sauce down the table. "Didn't you go to school with her, Catherine?"

"Yes," Catherine said. She balanced a slice of fish between the servers and set it, fragrant with parsleyed butter, beside the grilled sweet peppers on her plate. She pressed a lemon wedge against her fork. Using the linen napkin as grip, she took the serving dish with both hands (it was quite heavy) and passed it on to her host. "It's odd, isn't it," she asked mildly, "the way memory pivots around food? We had salmon at my twenty-first, I remember. Isn't that an eccentric association?"

Sliding wetly on slick glass, the salmon made a small sucking noise. Four hands, like duelists waiting, held the platter, the fingers of one pair quaintly fat and flattened through dimpled glass, the fingers of the other wrapped in white.

"It's strange," Catherine said, "the way it keeps coming back to me lately. Because Gabriel had so many questions, I suppose."

Roslyn nestled a crescent moon of lemon in the palm of her hand and slowly crushed it. "The cross we had to bear," she said mournfully. She was absorbed in the task of extracting every last drop of juice. "It was a duel to the bitter end."

"Look at those two," Andrew's wife teased, indicating Catherine and their host by the delicate tilt of her fork. "Are you casting spells over the fish, or what?"

"I wonder if you'd excuse me for a moment?" His Honor said. He set the platter on the tablecloth with the care of a man stacking eggs and left the room.

Roslyn pressed her lips together and studied her plate. "He's doing remarkably well actually," she said. "Considering everything."

End there.

That would be bearable.

And yet, though this narrative is private, though it has a reading audience of one, the traditional expectations still intrude because the very reason for telling stories (even to oneself) is to insist there is shape and meaning and direction in the messy flood that we find ourselves floundering in, the one that sweeps us up at birth and hurls us along, lumping us in with flotsam and random event, making a pattern as it goes. Yes, it must make a pattern. We want to insist on that.

Humankind cannot bear very much lack of meaning. If we have to experience horror, there has to be a point. There has to be. In fact, it is not the horror itself that torments us so much as the need to understand. We have to get to the heart of the labyrinth where the minotaur lurks. We want to know that the labyrinth is mappable, that there *is* a minotaur, that there is at least *something* at the core of things which is responsible for all this dread, and we want to reassure ourselves that if we trail Ariadne's thread behind us we can find a way out again.

Still, there are terrible risks. How close to the minotaur can we get and still survive? We only want a glimpse. As a matter of fact, the beast as *metaphor* will suffice. A lot of bull, we can then say flippantly. Or, in angrier, more distraught moments, we can say: I've had a run-in with one hell of a beast. But we can do without close-ups of the corded throat and slavering mouth, and we can certainly skip the actual goring and devouring and the tearing limb from limb and all that.

Of course terrible things do happen. Of course the newspapers report atrocities every day, we acknowledge this readily and sagely enough in the literary salons over sherry, but those who need direct private explanations should pursue them in the decent privacy of their minds. A work of fiction has nothing to do with this. It may have had for Sophocles and Euripides, but not for us. Modesty and the intimate domestic scale are the appropriate postures for our time. Also: good taste is better than bad taste, this is an axiom. And we are all in agreement, are we not, on what constitutes the boundaries of good taste?

In a drawing room somewhere, perhaps, a critic of exceptionally good taste and modesty smooths the brocaded arm of her chair with delicate fingers. Reference to the *literal* violence of the minotaur, she says, is a bid for cheap glamor, I'm afraid. (The critic always does speak in this *ex cathedra* way.) The intention, she says, sipping her sherry and noting *en passant* the exquisite oysters, the intention, I'm afraid, is transparent: titillation of the reader, plus the comfort of horror happening to someone else.

Quite so.

Consider Cat.

There she stands, tarted up in black with Woolworth's glass in her ears and self-inflicted scars like jewels on her shoulders and arms. Pure transparent provocation on her part; and thank God she isn't us. She is an exhibitionist to the core, a slut in fact, as a number of schoolteachers and judges and owners of bars and cathouses pointed out to her over the years. (But Cat is a slow learner, and willfully so no doubt. We wash our hands.)

Moreover Cat slashes herself. She sculpts her own body into an artifact of abuse, she makes a monument of her own pain. This is not only ideologically unsound, it is distressingly un-Aristotelian.

The critic spears her asparagus through hollandaise. "Ahhh," she says, closing her eyes. "Perfection." She tests the hollandaise with the tip of her tongue. "A soupçon more lemon, perhaps," she says. "Violence in fiction," she says, "should illuminate. It should not simply horrify." She sips her wine.

"If it is boiled just seconds too long," she sighs, "asparagus is ruined."

If the text simmers more than glancingly in horror—in murder, or the dismemberment of a body, or violent rape, let us say—the flavor is spoiled. The deft touch is what is required, the sleight-of-hand, for example the quick decoy of Leda's swan, *the great wings beating still . . . her thighs caressed by the dark webs . . . the feathered glory . . .*

Ah, the sensual transcendence of brutal assault, the soft way the light falls on rape.

And did Leda *put on his knowledge with his power?*

Have her *terrified vague fingers* found illumination yet? Or are they still scrabbling, gnarled and untransformed and unenlightened, in mud and in their own shit?

Howl, howl, howl, howl, as Lear said, and as Charlie screamed at the mango tree.

End there.

I would like to end there.

I don't want to look at the police photographs.

It is quite amazing, actually, how many photographs they have of Cat. More than Charlie does, I would say. Reform school files, court record files, surveillance photographs from various places of employment that were considered volatile elements in the tapestry of urban life, medical files from reform school and prison archives (each self-inflicted slash dated and numbered and thoughtfully commented on). *I once saw a woman flayed . . .* You would not believe how she altered her own appearance for the worse. It is amazing, really, how many expert and professional words have accumulated on the incorrigibility and incomprehensibility of the propensity to self-destruct. One could almost see the endless reports and treatises, *words, words, words,* as in inverse ratio to Cat's silence.

Of course, both the propensities and the stupefied responses have an honorable tradition in our national history. Perhaps Cat received certain hereditary tendencies in her genes.

Consider, for example, the 1827 report on Ann Bruin by the superintendent of the Hobart Female Factory for convict women. For absenting herself overnight from her master's house, Ann Bruin's head was to be put to the razor and shorn. Considering alternatives, the superintendent thought, hardly a severe or brutal punishment, right? And yet, he wrote . . .

She screamed most violently, and swore that no one should cut off her hair. . . . She then entered my Sitting Room screaming, swearing, and jumping about the Room as if bereft of her senses. She had a pair of

Scissors in her hand and commenced cutting off her own hair. . . . Coming before the window of My Sitting Room [she] thrust her clenched fist through three panes of glass in succession. . . .

Proof enough, as the superintendent pointed out, of dementia.

Proof enough, said the Brisbane police and the Brisbane courts and the guardians of the Holy Family School for Little Wanderers. Proof enough, they said, when Cat, caged and shorn, carved herself with broken glass. Perhaps she was simply following a recipe handed on by Ann Bruin, a pattern that came down in the blood.

Or consider the account of convict Françoise-Maurice Lepailleur, French-Canadian political prisoner transported to Botany Bay in 1840, fresh from ructions in Lower Canada:

During the afternoon a drunken woman, just come from the factory [for convict women] at Parramatta, began to abuse the woman who lives in the small cabin in front of the gate. After she had sworn a lot, cursed and blasphemed . . . [she] turned her back to us, lifted up all her clothes and showed us her bum, saying that she had a "Black Hole" there and slapping her belly like the wretch she was. Nothing more vile than that tribe, animals are more decent than they. I would say much more but it would dirty my little journal to go on.

Quite so.

The woman who shaved her own head in Hobart and the woman from the female factory in Parramatta kept no journals, unfortunately. Neither did the woman in Brisbane, the one on Brunswick Street station, the one who pointed to her own black hole and shunted my life onto different tracks.

Neither, alas, did Cat.

But the police did keep photographs.

What is the reason for your interest in this woman? they wanted to know. And when did you first notice the disappearance of Gabriel Gray, son of the eminent judge? When did you first notice the disappearance of the Chinese proprietor of the restaurant known as Charlie's Inferno? What was the nature of your relationship to these men? Anything you say, they cautioned, may be used as evidence against you. Anything you say is bound to lead you into our web. Let us go back to the beginning, they said. Let the inquisition begin.

❖ ❖ ❖

When did you first become aware of the disappearance of Gabriel Gray?

When did I first become aware of a growing inner emptiness that was the future absence of Gabriel? Oh, long ago. He was still Gabriel Brennan to me then, and I was a barmaid at The Shamrock in Brisbane. I should have trusted my instincts then. I could have escaped relatively unscathed. How stupidly, haplessly, we head for grief the way moths head for the flame.

"I didn't know he had disappeared," I said faintly. "Actually, he hasn't disappeared. He's gone to Brisbane."

When did you last see him? (The voices of policemen always seem disembodied, reverberating, magnified by the echo chamber of official power.)

"Let me see. If this is Friday . . . is this Friday?" (The voices of those who answer the police seem small, like the whispers of guilty mice.) "Yes, Friday. Well, let me think . . . Sunday, last Sunday, we both worked in the restaurant." (Behind a smoke-screen of words, I was stalling, watching for clues.) "And then after, when the restaurant closed at two A.M., Gabriel and Charlie went off to The Shaky Landing, they'd been doing it every night for several weeks."

The policemen exchanged a look. This was damaging information, the look implied.

"And then Monday," I said, reading their look, thumbing through meanings and translations—almost anything you say, the translation read, will be used against you and is evidence of guilt—"let me think. Monday? Umm, Monday night Gabriel was here. Yes. And they were planning to leave for Brisbane the next morning."

Is that so? (You can smell entrapment on a policeman's breath, you can smell their watchful spider sweat, you can taste your own haplessness.) *And Tuesday?*

"Tuesday," I said carefully. "Tuesday. That was the burglary. I went to work as usual—at the SBS studios—and when I got home . . . I *did* report it. I reported it immediately but the police never came. I suppose these days, with break and enter so terribly common—"

At what time on Tuesday did you last see Gabriel Gray?

"At what time on Tuesday?" I parroted stupidly. There was a vague unlocatable pain; my lungs perhaps? I could feel myself going under the question, sinking, beginning to gulp panic, but I managed to surface again with words. "I didn't see him on Tuesday. They got away early, they left for Brisbane at the crack of dawn."

Is that so? (There were two of them of course, two cops. There always are. And one is always nicer than the other.) *A very interesting claim,* they said, *since they were both seen in Sydney on Tuesday night.*

Then the nice cop asked gruffly: "Are you all right, Miss?"

"Yeah," I said. "Just give me a minute." (But I was winded, I'd plummeted right through four days, I'd freefallen straight back to Monday when I'd thought *Good riddance* and then lain awake all night. I'd pictured them at the crack of dawn, I'd watched them getting into Charlie's car, I'd followed them getting out of the city before the traffic, heading up the coast road, maybe taking the Brisbane hooker and the Brisbane cop, two old bawds hitching a free ride and necking in the backseat of Charlie's car, oh yeah, I'd pictured that, I'd been seeing them all week burling along past Newcastle, Taree, Port Macquarie, Coffs Harbour, Grafton, Byron Bay, Tweed Heads, watch out Queensland, here we come, maybe reaching the border Tuesday night, depending on stops. Wednesday, Thursday, and now all day Friday in Brisbane, what did I care that Gabriel hadn't even phoned? What did I care? Cat's got their tongue and she can bloody well keep it, was what I thought.)

What exactly was the nature of your relationship with these two men?

(Oh, *there* was a question, and the answer hit me as vertigo.) "They are part of me," I said, though I hadn't meant to say it aloud.

The policemen exchanged another look. *You had sexual relations with both men?* (What they didn't say, what I could see in their eyes: *And a couple of hundred other men besides. Upstairs at The Inferno. We know all about you.*)

"No," I said, dignified. "Not with both men."

You had sexual relations with Gabriel Gray.

"Yes."

On the night of his disappearance?

"Not on Monday night," I said wretchedly. "No." (Oh, if

only we were given advance notice of which words could become our famous last.)

The night of his disappearance was Tuesday night. Did you have sexual relations Tuesday night?

"No."

You didn't see him the night he disappeared?

"He hasn't disappeared, he's gone to Brisbane."

You didn't see him Tuesday night?

"No."

You haven't seen him since Monday night?

"That is correct."

This is Friday, and you haven't seen him since. You weren't alarmed?

"I would be if he hadn't gone to Brisbane."

These all-night junkets in the quarry, you didn't find them alarming?

(How much can you explain to the police? What can you say about the kind of dread that seeps into dreams?) "Yes," I said. "They worried me. It's not the safest place in the world, is it? But they always did come back."

The police produced photographs of the bar at The Shaky Landing. *This is where Chang and Gray were on Tuesday night. The camera doesn't lie.*

I looked at the photographs. "I don't see them," I said. "I don't see Gray or Chang."

We have black-and-whites at the station, surveillance stills, a number of frames, we didn't happen to bring them along. (Oh, right. They just forgot to bring those particular shots.) *And we have evidence on videotape. You can take our word for it.*

(I didn't. Though if Charlie and Gabriel *were* there, it meant they had needed to see the Brisbane hooker or the Brisbane cop again. Perhaps the hooker or the cop had contacted *them.* We've got more information, they might have said. Or perhaps they said: We've arranged a meeting with Cat. She's not in Brisbane, she's here, Mr. Chang was right, we just wanted free transport up the coast, but we do know where she is, and we'll take you to her in the quarry for a fee. Or else: She *is* in Brisbane, but we've had a spot of difficulty, we've had to do some fancy footwork, it's been nip and tuck, but now we've set up the place and time. And all Tuesday Gabriel would have been obsessed, he would have been much too obsessed to phone, or he could have been still hurt because I'd pulled away from him Monday night, and then by Tuesday night they wouldn't have wanted to wait, they would have left the minute they had definite word, and then in Brisbane they may have had their hands full with Cat herself. . . .)

Do you recognize this place? The police fingers jabbed at the black-and-white Shaky Landing stills.

"Yes."

Have you ever at any time visited this place?

"Once. I was there a couple of weeks ago. We all were."

We all?

"Gabriel and Charlie and Catherine Reed and myself."

Catherine Reed? The one with the interview show on TV?

"Yes."

And what was the nature of the business that would take you all to a place such as this?

"We were looking for someone," I said. (What was safe to tell or not tell? Answer: it makes no difference; everything is evidence or guilt.) "There was a woman we thought might be there, a friend of Charlie's, that's all. We had some photographs."

Are these the photographs? And there were the prints that had so recently disappeared from our burgled flat.

"Jeez!" I said. "Whew." This changed things. I thought I knew how to handle this, I could pull those policemen out of their echo chamber now, I could turn their amplifiers off. They were just ordinary human cops again, cruising, off-duty, out for a little provocation and harassment on the side, you scratch my corruption, I'll scratch yours. Hey, I was an expert. "You blokes take what you want pretty fast, don't you?" I laughed. I used my teasing *let's make a deal, guys* voice. I get on with moonlighting cops very comfortably and always have. The barmaid instinct, the hooker's stock-in-trade, a skill I picked up from Sheba, I suppose. "You got a warrant to raid his things?" I demanded.

They grinned at me. "Stroppy little tart, aren't you? We *have* got a warrant, as a matter of fact. Whenever there's evidence of foul play."

I blinked then. My heart skipped a few dozen beats. "What evidence of foul play?"

"A violent brawl at The Shaky Landing late Tuesday night. Around three A.M."

"But there's a violent brawl there every night."

"Mayhem this time," the cops said. "Bodies all over the place. Some of them so badly hacked they haven't been identified yet. Your boyfriend could be one of them. And so could the Chinaman."

"Charlie's Australian," I said. One is curiously precise about details when one is in shock.

"Whatever," they said. They flashed some very gruesome photographs. "Any identifying marks or signs?"

"No," I said, turning away, my hand over my mouth. "I feel sick," I said.

"Yeah. Sorry."

"Do you mind if I . . . ?"

I had to lock myself into the bathroom for a while. But I knew Gabriel's body intimately, and it was not in the photographs. Nor was Charlie's. I took some deep breaths and began to feel better. Then I went back.

"Okay," I said. "I'll be okay."

"The thing is," they said. "There were bodies that disappeared before we got there, according to witnesses. Whisked away for reasons interesting to speculate on. Any ideas?"

"No," I said faintly, feeling sick again.

"We'd like you to look at some photographs," they said. "Know anyone in this one?"

I stared at it. I felt very calm now, I felt no anxiety at all, I felt as though I'd dreamed the police up, I felt as though this wasn't really happening at all, which is one of the minor blessings of shock. "Yes," I said indifferently. I could see Charlie and Gabriel at a table with a woman. The woman had her back to the camera. "There," I said. "Those two. Gabriel and Charlie."

"You're positive?"

"Positive."

"That was Tuesday night," they said. "Just before the fight broke out. We can assume they were there for the big bang."

"Oh," I said in a faint voice, and I felt something like needles reaching me through the buffering pillows of shock, but they went away again and nothing seemed real. It is curious, however, the way a detached analytical part of the mind keeps watching, keeps making comments. In fact, stripped of all emotional reaction, details actually seem to take on a shaper edge. "You said you didn't have this evidence with you."

"Interrogation technique," the nice one shrugged, grinning. "Have to catch you off guard, don't we, love?"

And since they had me off guard, they produced the documentation on Cat, the files, the photographs. It is astonishing, the details of a life on film and microchip. I sifted through the folder and they watched me, but it must have been disappointing for them because my gaze was blank, I felt nothing, I had no reactions at all. No doubt the information logged itself somewhere in my brain, willy-nilly, as I've read that it does, but it didn't get through to *me*.

They produced a folder with photographs of bones. These were close-ups, showing scars and indentations on the bone. I remember thinking what a sense of drama the body had, how extraordinary its shapes, how I'd never realized before the stunning beauty of bones. "Brutally and viciously stabbed," they said. "Thirty-six times, to be precise." They pointed to the nicks and chips in the bone. "Incredible ferocity," they said.

"Yes," I agreed. I could see their logic, the way it coiled itself around femurs and ribs.

"Suppose we told you," they said, "that we were very curious indeed about Chang and Gray's interest in the woman called Cat. *Obsessive* interest, I think we could say. What would you say to that?"

The only thing that came into my mind to say was a little bubble of nonsense. Curiosity killed the cat, I thought, and swallowed the thought in time, and said nothing at all. I could taste the edge of hysteria in the words I had swallowed, I was afraid I would burst into something unstoppable, laughter or sobbing, I wasn't sure which.

"Suppose we told you," they said, "that these are the bones of the woman called Cat."

Oh God. *That* shook the cobwebs in my brain. Was that what Gabriel and Charlie had found out? And was the news unbearable, was that why they hadn't even phoned? Had they simply fled? People run away from pain, I know that. I bolted from Brisbane once. Catherine fled to London, Charlie to New York.

Unsolved mystery, the police said. One of her lovers, we think. They went on and on, but all I could hear was the door closing behind Gabriel on Monday night. Obsessive interest on the part of Chang and Gray, I heard, and I struggled to concentrate again. Maybe dead in a tavern brawl, and maybe not, they said. Maybe arrangers of their own "deaths," wouldn't be a first for that trick, eh? They watched me for a reaction, but I didn't have one. Or maybe got out of the way by someone else, they said. But why? That was the interesting question. All very curious, they said.

Wait a minute, I thought dizzily. Wait a minute, what's going on here? (*Interrogation techniques. We need to catch you off guard, don't we, love?*)

Suppose we told you that these are the bones . . . Suppose they told me the moon was made of green cheese? What proof did I have that the woman was Cat?

(*You can't afford to tip anyone off*, Gabriel had warned about notes that he kept under lock and key; notes that had disappeared in a burglary. The network is incredible . . . *you never know who's hooked in.*)

(That is Cat in the mirror, Charlie had said of a photograph that was stolen from my place and then shown to me again by the police.)

What proof did I have that the woman in any of the police photographs was Cat? What proof did I have that the photograph of Charlie and Gabriel was taken just before the fight broke out? What proof did I have that it was even taken on Tuesday night? Just what kind of information were the police fishing for?

I felt a huge swooping upcurrent of relief, and I glided on it straight into happiness. They were on their way up to Brisbane, just as they said. Maybe they'd found Cat, maybe they even had her with them. It wouldn't be the first time Cat had fled from the police, goaded the law, driven them all to a feral possessive frenzy. What did all this sudden official interest in her mean, anyway? *Obsessive* interest, I think we could safely say. Oh yes. In my mind's eye I could see the three of them in a car on the Pacific Highway, heading north. I could see them in Brisbane. I could see them at Cedar Creek.

"I'm afraid I can't tell you anything," I said.

"We'll get back to you," the police promised.

Naturally I thought it was Gabriel. In my dream, the knocking figured as hail on an iron roof. I was back in Queensland, childhood, a tropical thunderstorm. In the dream I was walking down a long dark corridor that branched off on every side. I didn't know where I was going. The rain and the hail were hammering down and I ran into total darkness and opened a door. . . .

It was Gabriel's father.

"Wha . . . ?" I blinked. "What time is it?"

He came inside and closed the door behind him. I blinked at my watch. Five A.M.

"Oh God, what's happened?" I said.

"Where is he?" Robinson Gray demanded. He walked down our hallway and into the bedroom. He looked under the bed. He roamed around our apartment as though he owned it. He picked up books of Gabriel's, he picked up a shirt, he picked up a framed family photograph and put it down. His movements were jerky. "Do you know where he is?"

I suppose his anxiety brought the smell of harm into the house like fog. It smelled of uncollected garbage, of vinegar, of public toilets long uncleaned. I could feel my heart thumping like a piston, then skipping and doing little butterfly beats. I had to lean against the wall before I could speak. "He's gone to Brisbane," I said.

I don't think he even heard me. He was like someone going through a house frantically to shut off a burglar alarm he couldn't find.

I made myself count to twenty. "I'll put coffee on," I said. "Would you like some?"

He didn't answer but he followed me into the kitchen and sat at the kitchen table and put his head in his hands. "Do you think he's alive?" he asked.

I spilled ground coffee all over the counter and had to wipe it down. I couldn't answer. I turned to look at him, but he wasn't listening for answers anyway. He had his hands on the side of his head in a curious way, like claws, his thumbs against his cheekbones, his fingers like cages over his eyes, the fingertips on the temples.

"It's full of borers," he said. "I can feel them tunneling and boring and blasting inside my head. They never stop. They never stop. I know what they're after, they're digging me out."

I watched him nervously.

"I keep having this nightmare," he said.

They wait just beyond the borders of sleep and every night he walks the streets to stave them off. He prowls through back alleys, he watches the figures in doorways, he goes into phone boxes and dials a number and listens when a voice answers. He says nothing, he inserts no coin, he pushes no button, he listens, he waits.

Sometimes he keeps sleep at bay for several nights in succession, but they always get him in the end.

They start in his head, chip chipping away at his skull, but they are everywhere, they have taken over his arteries, his veins, his capillaries, he has been invaded, he has been quarried, the Mole People have set up camp in his intestines, they are photographing him from the inside out, making flowcharts, keeping notes. He is mapped and drawn and quartered. He is known. He has become the quarry.

He writes and beats off their maggoty advance and wakes.

(I have seen this nightmare on Charlie's wall. Has *he*? Which came first, Charlie's photograph or Robinson Gray's black dream?)

Robinson Gray shook himself as though he were sloughing off the effects of a drug. He looked at me and asked me quite lucidly, "Do you think he's alive?"

I swallowed. "Of course he is," I said. Once I had spoken, I felt calmer. "They've gone to Brisbane. They were looking for someone, *something*"—I corrected myself quickly, delicately— "and they had to check something out."

"Check what out?" he asked sharply. "What did he tell you?"

"Oh, nothing," I said. "Not really. He just said they had to check something out."

I poured the water into the top of the coffee maker.

"Poor Gabriel," he said at last. "Poor Gabriel. He couldn't finish anything. Maybe it was my fault, I don't know. There just seemed to be some sort of fatal flaw. He couldn't stick at jobs, he couldn't stay settled, he couldn't finish his degree, he couldn't stay still. *Bartending*, for God's sake," he said bitterly. "Pub crawling! The only thing he could stick at was trying to upset me. He hated me."

He put his head down on his hands, against the table.

"No, he didn't hate you. He *doesn't*." The past tense bothered me. "He doesn't hate you."

"I *loved* them," he said, jumping up again, pacing, his face twisted with baffled pain. "I *loved* them, and they turned on me."

Them. Cat and Gabriel, I thought. Such a force field of grief and pain came off him, that I went to him and put my hand on his. Then: shock. Something happened as it happened once before, in The Shamrock in Brisbane. When I looked into his eyes, I had the sense of looking into black and bottomless wells. I don't mean that as a simple metaphor. I don't quite know what I mean, but it was more than metaphor. I wouldn't know what to call it, I wouldn't know if that is what a vision is, or a premonition, or what the psychological explanation would be. All I know is that I had a dizzy sensation, that I felt as though I were standing on the lip of a pit looking down twin craters that opened out vertiginously into nothingness. *Howl, howl, howl, howl,* I thought. Something has happened to Gabriel, I thought, and in some fearful prescient way our bodies know it. Something has happened to Gabriel and Charlie and Cat.

I felt such anxiety that I recoiled. And when he registered my recoiling, I felt such pity that I simply held him, and we stood there (I have no idea for how long, it could have been fifteen minutes, it could have been one) and then without saying a word, he left.

Catherine sat in her office in the television studios and stared at nothing.

"Catherine," I said. "There's every reason to believe they'll turn up, and they'll have Cat with them. It's tracking her down that's taking so long, they won't give up. Would they stay on her trail this long if it didn't go anywhere? If they didn't think it was worthwhile? You *know* they wouldn't. Four weeks, that's nothing really."

I *believed* that. I insisted on believing that.

"The police have a file on Cat," Catherine said.

"I know."

"I should never have come back," she said. "I should never have come back."

"Catherine, what proof do we have that those bones are Cat's? You can't trust the police anymore."

"Lucy, I've arranged with London." She sounded very brisk and businesslike. "I'm going next week."

Panic was what I felt, domino losses, a gaping row of absences. I had to grab hold of her desk to steady myself. Already, I danced like a fish on a line for every footstep behind me, my heart turned somersaults at every knock on the door, every ring of the phone. Adrenaline sloshed around inside me like a choppy sea. It was exhausting. It was like having vertigo all the time.

"If you want to come," she said, "there's a job."

"Yes," I said, grabbing at the life belt she threw. "Yes, I'll go with you."

"I want amnesia," she said.

Book

Four

The Last Magician

Newton was not the first of the age of reason.
He was the last of the magicians.
                                    John Maynard Keynes

ONE

In the middle of the journey, I came to myself in a dark wood where the straight way was wholly lost and gone. A spotted leopard snarled fitfully in my dreams all the way from London to Singapore, and after Singapore there was a gray wolf and a winged cat and black holes.

I fell through a black hole.

I found myself back in a pub in Sydney where everything had changed and nothing had changed.

This puzzles me.

I understand neither time nor memory though I thrash about between them constantly, and I resent being caught again in Charlie's net. In the beginning all this had nothing to do with me, and then it did, and then I escaped again. I resent being caught unawares, I resent coming face to face with myself on a screen, I resent finding myself back here reliving the past.

Everything has changed and nothing has changed.

I watch two men at a table in the corner of Charlie's Place (of course it's someone else's place now, I don't know whose), I watch these two men, a jug of beer between them, a litter of empty glasses at their elbows. I cannot quite hear their conversation, but one appears to be telling the other a joke. They are big loose-limbed men and they throw back their heads and fill the room with a deep joyful laughter that sounds like a convocation of tippling frogs. And it's infectious. People half turn in their direction and little smiles wing their way from face to face. I can even feel my own cheek muscles relax as though a butterfly of a smile briefly settled there. And yet, simultaneously, I feel a weight of desolation so heavy it is as though I have been given lead shot intravenously. How is it possible for a roomful of people to laugh when grief, and matters far more disturbing than grief, silently prowl around this very building on their clawed padded feet?

"Lucy," Sheba says, "you gotta snap out of this. It doesn't do a bloody bit of good, moping round, it doesn't bring anyone back."

"I know." And yet I understand the handling of relics now, I understand the veneration of totemic objects. When I sift through the boxes and boxes of photographs that Sheba keeps stashed under her bed, I feel something approaching tranquillity. It's as though Charlie's photographs retain the lost essence of their maker and their subjects and the essence comes off on my hands. It's like ointment. Of course I know that's ludicrous, even pathetic. It's not the sort of thing I would want to confess in public. But that's how it feels. I spend hours every day just sitting on the floor in Sheba's room, fondling the past.

"I don't know what you're trying to make Charlie tell you," Sheba says, exasperated. "We already know what's what."

I stare at her. "I don't know anything," I said. "I don't feel that there's one single thing I know for certain."

"We know and we don't know," she shrugs. "And you don't want to know, Lucy."

There's some truth to this, I suppose. In London, Catherine and I lead busy lives and never speak of the past except perhaps late at night, after too many drinks. At such times, we have worked things out to our own satisfaction. Charlie, we agree, is in New York. He didn't find Cat, or else he found out that she was indeed dead, and either way he couldn't bear the disappointment so he fled (or else he did find her and took her with him, he had to keep her out of prison, he had to get her away from the police). He wanted amnesia (or else he wanted amnesia for Cat; he wanted a fresh start for her, no baggage). We understand this instinct completely. We subscribe to it. The occasional appearance of Charlie's photographs in small galleries and of his films in small cinemas bears this theory out. Let sleeping dogs lie, we say. One day one of us will bump into him in a bar in Greenwich Village (we both go back and forth a lot between London and New York). I've been meaning to get in touch, he'll say. But you know how it is.

Yes, we'll say. We know how it is.

And we'll all get blind drunk and we'll swim in hilarity and we'll go skinny-dipping in the East River or the Thames or somewhere, well, maybe not the East River or the Thames, maybe we'll just hop on a plane and head for Cedar Creek.

Gabriel, we agree, is in Queensland, possibly Brisbane, but more probably further north: Heron Island, Dunk Island, Green Island, somewhere with rainforest and coral cays, very likely the Daintree or Cape Tribulation. I have no trouble at all seeing Gabriel moving between rows of pineapples, or between tea bushes perhaps, in a clearing in the Daintree forest. He has found the same peace his mother found. He doesn't need to know anymore.

It's typical of them, we feel, to bugger off, and it certainly doesn't bother us. We don't miss them (well, sometimes we do, if a pause in work creeps up on us, or if we've had too many drinks, but we've come to terms with this, we've adjusted to it). Anyway, we know they're stuck with us, just as we are with them, and they'll never quite get us out from under their skin. We don't have a shadow of a doubt about that. They're solitary types, like us, with crowded heads.

We're like war vets, Catherine says. We can't talk to anyone else.

We never do talk much, not even to each other, though the long silences we share are noisy with thought and sometimes the tip of a memory will show and will splash into words. There was that photograph Charlie did, I might say broodingly, without noticing I'm thinking aloud. *Hot News of Gabriel.* It was very early on, that's what's so puzzling, a newspaper on fire, Gabriel going up in smoke.

Yes, Catherine will say in a drugged sort of voice. Well, that was Charlie. There was a very disconcerting edge to his wit.

Yes, I'll sigh. And then we'll lapse into silence again.

We hardly speak at all on our TV shows, we let the interviewees do the talking. We tend to do a certain kind of documentary. We like to listen to the people no one listens to. I suppose we have this fantasy of catching Ann Bruin on tape, Ann Bruin who went berserk and sheared off her own hair and smashed her own hand through glass in Hobart in 1827.

I suppose we're waiting for Cat's voice to bubble up through someone else's throat.

And Cat could be anywhere. She could be with Charlie in New York, or she could be back in Brisbane, or she could be dead and buried, or holed up in a burrow in the quarry. I picture her, black and lithe in the moonlight, moving across the rooftops of proper Sydney on her silent padded feet, letting herself in through windows and chimneys and terrace-house balconies, quiet and quick-fingered, gathering up the loose silverware and cash. When she leaves she lifts her hands to the sides of her face like claws and hisses softly. Fuck you, she says. Fuck all of you.

She says it over and over again from Charlie's photographs.

Photographs seduce.

The longer you look at them, the more you see.

Take *Giacometti's Foot*, the black-and-white photograph of a pierced earlobe sporting a small gold hoop on which is strung a single bead that I know to be blue. When I saw that photograph for the first time last week, it hit me like a medicine ball thrown hard at the gut. It had the same dizzying impact that the sight of myself on a screen in London had. I doubled up. I felt like a geiger counter. I would imagine that the rind of air encasing my body was visible as blue fire.

But why? I thought. Why? What is it about Cat's earring that affects me this way?

I tried to be analytical about it. Okay, I thought, *one*: seeing the earring in the photograph brings back the initial and over-whelming shock of seeing it in my hand in Charlie's film.

But why did the film barrel into me so violently in the first place? *One*: mainly the sheer shock of seeing myself at all when I wasn't expecting it. And *two*: seeing myself in that particular place, a place that thumped into me with a tidal wave of erotic memories (my own, and Charlie's, and Catherine's too). And *three*: the mind being a swift and powerful retrieval system, I was affected by Charlie's story of Cat ripping the hoops from her ears, I was affected by his intensity as he told me about that night. And *four*: the shock of seeing the thin gold chain and its pendant earrings in *my* hand.

But what was the nature of that particular shock? It was mainly a sense of sacrilege, I think. Charlie had shown me the chain and the earrings once, but I'd never held them. I'd never touched them. I knew what they meant to him who wore them always against his skin, his own little reliquary to ward off harm. So I was shocked, as though I had been taken in blasphemy, to see them idly dangling from my hand.

And I was mystified too, and quite profoundly disturbed, because the conjunction of things that don't belong with each other affects the sense of balance in primal ways. I remember something I saw at a fair in Brisbane as a child: a cow with five legs. The fifth leg dangled uselessly from the cow's breast, between the two front legs, and didn't touch the ground. It wasn't a trick, it was a genuine freak, a birth abnormality. I sobbed and sobbed and then I vomited.

That was roughly the way I felt when I saw Cat's earrings dangling on a chain from my index finger.

They're an arrogant and dangerous lot, the photographers, the filmmakers, the storytellers and spinners of images and words, the black magicians. They make hay with a lot of memories and lives, they tamper with things, they hold nightmares up to the light and they don't consider the consequences carefully enough.

I think now about the photographer's technical sleight-of-hand, the nature of celluloid magic. Of course, it had simply been an illusion that it was *my* hand holding the chain. It was like the switching to doubles in movies for nude love scenes and dangerous stunts.

I can piece it together now. Gabriel had a photograph of me on the rocks at Cedar Creek. I'd been talking away, gesturing with my hands as I always do, fingers extended, the index finger making a point. Charlie had seen the photograph and used it. He'd added a close-up of a different hand, a woman's hand, holding the chain. He'd spliced the two together in that seamless way that constitutes film-making magic. Hey presto, the rabbit pulled out of the hat, the coin from behind the ear, Cat at my fingertips.

Whose hand did he use, I wonder?

Catherine's, I would think. I can't imagine who else would be holding the relic. Who else would be permitted to?

And it must be Catherine's earlobe in *Giacometti's Foot* when I think about it, because Charlie certainly wasn't taking photographs in those distant days when Cat yanked her earrings off under the mango tree.

Is it this realization of Catherine's presence in the photographs, then, which for some reason continues to register on my personal Richter scale?

I don't know.

If only we could know what we know, as Charlie used to say. If we could see what we've seen. Because whatever Sheba may say, I don't know what's what. I don't.

Of course, I can easily find out if it's Catherine's earlobe and Catherine's hand by phoning her, which I will certainly do in a day or two, a week or two. I know she's still there in London, of course I know, of course she is, Sheba saw her on TV last week. It's just that every time I contemplate putting the call through, every time I start dialing, I decide to wait a little longer just in case she's not there, though she may very well be panicking about me by now. We know we overreact on this issue and we make allowances for each other. We have a terrible fear of sudden disappearances. But in any case, what will it prove if it's Catherine's earlobe and Catherine's hand?

Nothing.

I don't think it will shut the geiger counter down.

"I notice you haven't even opened the box full of *me*," Sheba says, faking offense.

"I don't need to look at photos of you, do I? You're still around. It's the ones Charlie took—"

"A lot of these *are* Charlie's." She crawls under the bed and pulls a shoe box out from the wall. "And a lot are by other blokes. It's a hell of a turn-on for some of them, taking pics."

"Okay, Sheba," I say fondly, "I'll look." The persistence of someone in my life is a miracle to me, I feel weak with affection, I feel maudlin with gratitude to Sheba. "I can't tell you how much it means to me, Sheba, that you're still here."

"Oh, cut the crap, Lucy. Why wouldn't I be? Shut up and tell me what you think of this set."

"Okay," I say, rallying, working up to flippancy. "I know what you're after. I know you just want to be admired."

"Fuck off!" she laughs. "I *charge* for that. Now you gotta

make allowances, remember. Blokes are into costumes and props."

"Yeah. I remember." I idly flip through a sheaf of Sheba dressed as an army sergeant with shirt unbuttoned, Sheba in nothing but black stocking and nun's veil, Sheba in pink feathers, Sheba painted blue, Sheba as the Tattooed Lady ("That's an old bloke, an electrician," she says. "Can't get it up till he's drawn all over me with Magic Markers"), Sheba in a tiger-striped bodysuit with strategic peek-a-boo holes.

"Sheba," I ask with sudden interest. "If *you* were looking at you, how would you photograph yourself?"

"Jeez, Lucy," she laughs, shaking her head. "Reckon the minute I first laid eyes on you on Brunswick Street station I knew you'd drive me nuts till kingdom come. Here's someone with a bloody tiptruck full of dumb questions, I says to meself. Here's someone to give me laughs on a rainy day."

"Yes, but tell me. How *would* you photograph yourself?"

"I wouldn't, would I? I don't look at meself at all."

"But you keep these photographs," I point out. "And you look at them. And you want *me* to look at them."

She taps her forehead with one finger to indicate I am not very bright. "We're not looking at *me*, you drip. We're looking at the blokes who took the pics. This one now." She picks up the tiger-bodied one. "He's got leather boots on and a whip in his hand, a poor weedy little bloke, shy as a possum. He's a postman, he rides his bicycle around and puts messages in other people's boxes, and he lives by himself. Pretty sad, huh?"

"Yeah. But Sheba . . ." I am immensely curious. "You must have some image of yourself."

"Well, sure," she says. "I'm me. Sheba. I think the world stinks but I don't take crap from anyone and I know how to have a good time."

"You're a feminist's nightmare, Sheba," I laugh.

"Feminists," she says witheringly. "Don't give me feminists. I'll tell you how I know a feminist: they treat me like dirt. They treat me worse than any of the blokes do."

"Oh, ouch. But the ones who treat you like dirt don't have a monopoly on the definition, Sheba."

"Yeah?" she says. "Who cares?"

I care, in fact, but Sheba would be supremely uninterested in my theories, so I turn to the photographs. "Ah. Here's one that Charlie took," I say with a connoisseur's eye. It's just a Polaroid snapshot, three and one-half inches square, but it's unmistakably stamped with Charlie's mark. Sheba is wearing black mesh stockings and black bodysuit and sits astride a chair with an open curved back, her stockinged calves hooked around the chair's hind legs, her hands at the sides of her face like claws. "That's one of Charlie's, all right."

"Wrong, smartypants!" she says gleefully. "That's Sonny Blue."

I feel a buzz of excitement. Well of course, I think. Of course. They were both obsessed with Cat. I feel as though the photograph will yield something if I look at it long enough. "Can I borrow this for a while? Can I take it back to my hotel?"

"Got the hots for me, eh?" she grins. "Sure. Why not?"

"Can I keep the boxes of Charlie's photographs?"

"That's why I saved them," she says. "I thought you'd want them."

"How come the men give you the pictures they take? Don't they want to keep them for . . . you know . . . ?"

"Jerking off. Yeah, they do. But I always ask for a copy. It's my scrapbook of *them*. I look at a pic, I can always remember the bloke, and that one is definitely Sonny Blue."

"Does Sonny Blue ever talk about . . . ?" But I seem to have developed a superstitious aversion to saying certain names out loud. It is as though only silence can keep them safe.

"Gabriel?" she prompts.

"Yes."

"All the time. He always did. He's obsessed. That's why Lady Muck left him in the end."

"Roslyn?"

"Yeah. He's married to his son, she says. So now there's a Number Four who's very young."

"But he still comes to see you?"

"Oh yeah." She puts her hands up to her face like claws and hisses. "Pussy on the side," she says.

"Sheba . . ." I swallow, but there are a couple of questions I have to ask. "When you say you know what happened . . . what do you mean?"

She gives me a hard look. "You sure you want me to say this?"

I nod.

"I mean that Charlie and Gabriel were killed in a barroom brawl, Lucy. There's no point kidding yourself."

I don't bother to argue, but in fact I do think (and Catherine and I, who know the principals more intimately than Sheba ever did, have thrashed this out endlessly), I truly do think there is every reason to believe they are off in the wide world somewhere being their celibate selves.

"And Lucy, I have to tell you I'm angry with them," Sheba says. "I'm angry as hell with them. You have to admit they were looking for it. Jeez, anyone who goes night after night to a bar where deals get done and takes photographs, what the hell does he expect, a Sunday school prize?"

"But their bodies weren't there," I remind her.

"Panic, I reckon. Cops call a few bigwigs in the middle of the night—maybe they even call Sonny Blue himself—and they all agree shit like this won't help, judge's son, quarry hysteria, et cetera et cetera, and pouf! Two bodies disappear, abracadabra. That's what I mean."

"No," I say. "I don't think so. Who would have done it?"

"The killing? Person who did it probably doesn't even know who did it. Jeez, haven't you ever seen a drug fight in a bar? And the cover-up? Could have been anyone from Sonny Blue down."

"Sonny Blue? You're not serious."

"Fair chance, I reckon, but also a fair chance not. Wouldn't be the first time a few cops panic, a few cops make their own decisions. Cops do that all the time, CYOA, cover your own arse, that's their motto. That's their very first rule."

"But you said Sonny Blue talks about Gabriel all the time."

"So what? Jeez, Lucy. I get blokes talk to wives who've been dead twenty years. I get blokes tell me they gotta go, Barbara's waiting at home with the kids, she'll be mad with them, and I know damn well Barbara buggered off and left them half a lifetime ago."

"Sheba," I say, "you've got an even wilder imagination than Charlie has."

Two

On the way, perhaps with a kind of perverse black nostalgia, perhaps with my documentary eye for rank incongruencies, I get the taxi to make a long detour through the quarry (that is, through its upper and outer edges) before heading to Point Piper, enclave of urban delights. Needless to say, the taxi driver is not at all keen and has to be financially cajoled. He has to be cajoled in spades; and also in bills of large denomination.

"Jeez," he mutters, threading the dead-ended streets in Newtown and Redfern (his car door locked, the windows tightly closed), "now I seen everything. Gotta be outa your mind, lady. You a danger freak, or what?"

"I make documentaries for television," I tell him.

"Yeah? Well put this in yer dockermentry," he says. "Here's what Joe Blake, taxi driver, thinks. They should drop a bomb on it, blow the whole quarry to kingdom come. It's a sewer, that's what, it's crawling with cockroaches and criminals and druggies and wogs and whores and it's spreading like a fucking cancer. There's tunnels comin' up through the sand at Bondi now, they reckon, and all the way out to Parramatta. They should blow the whole thing up before it's too late."

"What about the kids?" I ask. "I believe there are nine- and ten-year-old kids in the quarry, in fact I believe there's a heavy market in—"

"Blow them up too," he says. "Just gonna grow into full-size criminals, aren't they?"

"Unless we do something," I say as the taxi swings into another world, the grotto of laurels, the wisteria-thick homes against the harbor so brilliantly blue, with a flock of white sails bucking in the wind off the heads.

"Right," he says, depositing me at the gates. "Unless we do something. And what we gotta do is drop a bomb. Mention me name on yer dockermentry, okay? It's Joe Blake."

The gates are locked, but when I push the buzzer a voice asks me to identify myself, and then the delicate scrolls of wrought iron part soundlessly. I move beneath wisteria and jasmine, manicured, toward the soft clink of glasses and talk. Mostly TV and film people, I've been told; and some painters and actors and one opera singer, and the inevitable clutch of graziers and wives who've flown in for a few days from sheep or cattle stations at Wagga Wagga or Forbes or back of Bourke. Beyond voluminous quantities of floral silk and black bow ties, the harbor shimmers like cut glass, blue as sapphires. It is late afternoon. Another hour and the sun will slash itself into blood-reds and purples, sluicing primary color over the bridge and the graceful white wings of the Opera House. Then the quick summer dark will gulp everything down.

I'm nervous, I'm not exactly sure of what.

I'm not exactly sure who my hosts are either, only that I'm considered a minor luminary because of an urban documentary or two that has shown up here on SBS. This has put me in the margins of someone's list for cultural do's, and I do mean the margins, for God knows, to have been born here and gone away is about as good as having been born here of Chinese stock. No known category. Please check "Other" on all forms and beware the jabberwock, my son, for the jabberwock was not true blue.

I wish Catherine were here. We would head for the bar and then for that dark little nook under the galloping avocado where we could stare at the harbor and the bridge and the Fabergé eggshells of the Opera House and toss thought back and forth without speaking.

Or Catherine might say: When it gets a bit darker, the view of the harbor from here reminds me of Cedar Creek Falls.

Except for the bridge, I'd say dryly. Except for this congestion of seven-figure real estate. Except for that smog of noise on the skyline, that haze coming off the quarry from the other side of Bennelong Point.

You're not mellow yet, Lucy, she'd say. You've still got that sardonic edge to you, you need smoothing out, you need softening, you need to have another beer or two.

Luckily, no matter where in the world I bump into them, I do feel at home with the people who tap off beer and dole out ice cubes for the cocktail crowd, so I set sail for the bar. I can sit down in comfort in the easy jaundiced-eye view from behind the kegs and swap jokes in whatever idiom is required.

"Got any Four-X?" I ask this redheaded bloke with freckles from collar to scalp.

"Christ," he says. "Not a Queenslander in the Holy of Holies. Who brung you?"

"The cat brung me," I say. "By accident. So who's the Boss Cocky here, could you point him out for me? Discreetly of course."

"Gonna have to ask someone else, luv. I'm the caterer's bartender's bartender. I get paid by the hour for smiling and pouring grog and sweating like a pig in this bloody rented tux. Knowing who's who is right outside my field."

I gulp the Four-X down as though it were water because I can't take this kind of occasion straight. I lean over the padded vinyl of the outdoor bar and confide to the bartender's bartender. "I have no idea why I accept invitations to this kind of do. I must be a masochist at heart. Can I use your phone?"

He grins at me. "And you're not even being paid to be here," he says. He pushes one of these white cordless things across the vinyl counter, which is trying unsuccessfully to look like grained wood. "You gotta pull the aerial out," he explains.

I pull the aerial out to its full chrome length and call Sheba.

"What the hell's the matter with you, Lucy?" she says. "You only left here an hour ago."

"Yeah," I say. "Sorry. Panic attack. I'm feeling maudlin all of a sudden. I'm feeling godawful lonely."

Sheba's annoyed with me. "Lucy," she says, "you think you're the only person in the world who's lost someone? You think you're the only person who's had someone go and die on them? Join the fucking Lonely Hearts Club and pull your fucking self together, for God's sake!" She slams down the phone.

She's getting angry with me the way she got mad at Gabriel and Charlie. Sheba has precious little patience with anxiety attacks. Of course I know only too well she's right. I know there's nothing more tedious than someone else's grief or state of shock.

"I'm pulling myself together," I tell the bloke with the freckles and red hair. "I can't remember why the hell I came, and I want to get out already, only I can't remember how. I need a drink to help me think about how to leave, and then I need one for the road."

"Another one coming up," he grins. "But I gotta tell ya, this lot'd drive anyone to drink. Go and tell 'em from me they'd make a possum piss."

And I do. Schooner in fist, I move swimmingly across the lawn and join the outskirts of a group which is tossing confetti talk around.

"What I think," this woman is saying (she sounds like Roslyn Gray, but she's not), "what I think is that the quarry is a figment of the morbid imagination, and of certain elements in the press and the cultural sector. I mean, look around you. . . ." And she sweeps her arm toward the sunset over the bridge and the indigo waters. "I mean, *look!*" she says. "If this is urban blight, I'm all for it."

"Hear, hear!" I say, and everyone turns to look at me.

"But according to the latest demographic studies," a gentleman says. . . .

". . . only you can't compare North American cities with ours, apples and oranges, it just doesn't . . ."

"Asia in many respects is a truer model, Singapore, for instance, or Bombay. . . ."

". . . look, mate, it's the same old cringe rearing its head in new shapes, we don't need to cite models, we've got Third World in our own back pockets, we've got *bona fide* Third World. . . ."

"Frankly, all this Third World bunkum drives me right up the wall, all this drivel from daggy artists who don't know their own arse from a—"

"Better watch yourself, mate, or you'll find your face sticking up your bum. . . ."

And then friends are restraining friends and I have to go somewhere urgently to laugh. Jesus, I think. Could this party be happening anywhere else than Australia? Where else is the membrane between manicured lawn and quarry so wafer thin?

". . . quarry's like the Loch Ness monster," I hear at the edge of another group. "Everyone's heard the rumor but no one's ever seen it and no one can prove it exists."

"It doesn't," someone says, and I move away to an arc of deck chairs beside flowering grevillea where someone is holding forth on the importance of triage, not my cup of tea, and I keep moving on. I veer toward the goldfish pond though fragments of triage theory reach me. There comes a time, a gentleman is saying, radiation therapy and cancer cells, the amputation of a limb to save the whole, the necessary pruning of the rhubarb plant, blah blah, and urban blight, and *jug jug* to quarry ears.

"What I might even call the judicial poetry of urban grief," says a voice that makes me turn my head. Well, well, well. Sonny Blue. "The courts, in this sense, are the prophets crying in the wilderness," says Sonny Blue. "The voice of the turtledove in the land, the memory of order in chaos, the wish to survive."

I would like to vanish now, I would like to move quietly through the crowd and disappear, but I can't seem to move.

"But do you think, Robinson," someone challenges, "that our judicial history is such that we can draw any confidence at all. . . . I mean, consider the early governors, not Phillip, but the next lot, and their record of penal justice, talk about *triage*, talk about scapegoating an entire segment of—"

"And yet from those very seeds has come the most egalitarian justice system in the—"

"Oh *please*, Robbie. Next you'll tell me Australia's a classless society. Pull the other one, mate."

"There's no real logic to the history of justice," the sonorous voice ripostes. "Case by case, I'd be the first to admit it's riddled with . . ."

"Exactly. Any reforms have been more by good luck than good magistrates. I say that until the judiciary admits its history of expedience and impotence and outright error . . ."

"But you could say that for the progress of most ideas," His Honor replies. "And for the seminal changes in western consciousness, for that matter. Lucky accidents. Take Newton, for instance. He revolutionized scientific thought in the seventeenth century, and yet he was mentally unbalanced, we have plenty of evidence."

His Honor seems to suck admiration from the circle around him, he draws himself up a little, he radiates charm, he ascends a pulpit of hot air.

"Newton was an alchemist," he says. "His genius was as much hocus-pocus as anything else, his *Principia* and his *Opticks* and the laws of gravity were almost accidents, the voodoo man's sideline. His main interest was deciphering the secret codes of the universe, and he computed the year that Jason found the Golden Fleece. Can you believe it? He may have got the guernsey for the laws of motion and gravity, but that's sheer fluke. According to Maynard Keynes, and I agree, Newton wasn't the first note of the enlightenment, he was the final trumpet blast of the wizards and seers, he was the last of the magicians, in fact. And the law's a bit like that, I think. A bit hit-and-miss, but the bearer of our highest aspirations just the same."

Perhaps the needling spirit of Catherine enters me. Perhaps my mind, an impetuous retrieval system, merely connects two occurrences of a phrase before I have time to think. I know there are words bobbing around in the air and apparently they fell out of my mouth.

"I used to know a photographer named Charlie Chang," I say. "The New York police once called him the last magician."

There is one of those awkward silences and people swivel in my direction, a bit bemused, waiting for an anecdote or a joke but my voice and my mind have come to a dead halt.

So has His Honor, Mr. Justice Gray, member of the Order of Australia.

It is as though the last magician dropped a spell of slow motion from the sky. Robinson Gray turns (it seems to take an infinitely long time) and I don't know who is less publicly prepared, he or I, but I do know I seem to come as Banquo to his feast and that most people have their eyes on him, not on me.

"Are you okay, Robbie?" his consort asks.

His face is white, but then again, so is mine, I would think. It's natural, given that the last time we saw each other we had police news from underground, none of it propitious. Also, I trail ghosts like balloons, I evoke the inscrutable Charlie, I give off the faint desired scent of the lost child, the son and heir. Robinson Gray and I bring each other, as it were, hot news of Gabriel. I'm sure I would have turned and left first if I could have thought how it was done, but he beat me to it.

To me, it seemed that he moved with the slowness of a drifter in a dream, but according to the bartender, he left as abruptly as he once must have left Chang's Grocers and Greengrocers on Newmarket Road, on the day that Cat appeared in the rear doorway to the shop.

"That tells you something," Catherine will say.

"Yes, but what?" I will ask.

Evidently I found my way back to the bar and the bartender and the cellular phone and called a cab. Instinct would have taken me back to Charlie's Place, but I suppose I also knew instinctively that I wasn't equal to one of Sheba's "pull yourself together" talks. I wanted to brood disgracefully, I wanted to sit in my hotel room and feel Charlie's photographs in my hands.

So here I am.

I fondle my relics, and that mysterious peacefulness comes off them again.

I tuck the edge of *Gabriel Comes with Clouds Descending* under the frame of the dressing-table mirror and it seems to light the whole room. It shows Gabriel stepping into the storage cellar of Charlie's pub, the sun behind him. A nimbus comes off it, and foggy rings of gold slip themselves over me like magic quoits. I feel folded into great soft wings. I can smell the faint scent of Gabrielness, I can feel the imprint of chest hairs against my cheek, I can taste his sweat.

The relationship between a photograph and its viewer, Charlie said, is an act of seduction. A photograph beckons you.

I am beckoned, I yield, I enter a cessation of pain.

Where are you? I ask the light.

All you have to do is wait, Charlie says. Remember: a butterfly moving its wings on a rock near Perth may cause flooding in Queensland. Something was set in motion long ago. If you wait, it will play itself out.

I place side by side Charlie's photograph of me as *Wildcat* and

Sonny Blue's photograph of Sheba. They beckon me. Unravel our secrets, they tease.

It is odd, but the girl in *Wildcat* seems a total stranger. I know I knew her once but she is blurred, she is inadvertently stepping into Charlie's obsessions, she is unwittingly mimicking an instinctive childhood gesture of Cat's, and is thus caught at the very moment of stepping into a labyrinth she will never escape. The expression on her face is bewilderment and a touch of panic. She is in motion, blurred, on the cusp of entrapment and flight.

Sheba, however, is as familiar and prickly as today. Comfortably back to front on her chair, half her bosom visible above the chair's curved back, she smirks knowingly. Hiss, hiss, she says from behind her clawed hands. I am a mirror. When you look at me, you see the man who holds the camera.

The man who holds the camera wants her to look like a waif or a little girl or a very young tart. Sheba's long hair has been pulled back to look like a boy's, and she wears a child's plastic hair clip above one ear. She wears a child's locket around her neck. She wears black mesh stockings and a black bodysuit. It is, I suppose, the child's gesture of the hissing cat which most suggests innocence.

I put Sheba up against the mirror, alongside Gabriel coming with clouds descending, the top edge of the photograph tucked under the dresser frame. I sit cross-legged on the floor and stare at the photographs.

Then I hunt through one of Charlie's boxes, looking for a picture of Cedar Creek. What I find, with a little inner click of excitement, is the one he must have begged or borrowed from Gabriel and used in his film. I am sitting on the rocks, leaning forward, talking to unseen Gabriel, gesturing, my index finger (with no chain or earrings attached) extended. So fragrant with our presence at the falls is this photograph that I close my eyes and hold it against myself and dream.

Then I tuck it under the dresser frame to the left of Gabriel and stare at the three images until a kettledrum of knocking at my door interrupts. It is Gabriel's father. I realize I am not surprised.

"Can I come in?" he says, though he walks past me without waiting for an answer. He sits in one of the armchairs and stares at me, and I sit in the other and stare back. Sadness envelops him, though I have the sense that his being with me brings him the same kind of abeyance of loss that handling Charlie's photographs brings me.

"Do you know anything?" he asks at last, with equal measures of hope and anxiety, it seems to me. "Have you found him?"

"No," I say.

"Why did you come back?"

"I don't know really. Well, because of a film. Because of a photograph."

He frowns a little and looks around the room and sees the three photographs tucked under the upper edge of the dresser mirror. I see his fingers tighten against the arm of the chair. He gets up and stands in front of the mirror and studies the photographs. I stand behind him and just a little to one side, so I can see his face in the mirror and he can see mine.

No one moves, no one speaks.

"So you know," he says at last to my reflection.

Does he mean I know about him and Sheba? Since way back at The Shamrock, I could tell him. Does he refer to Gabriel transfigured? But neither of us is willing to accept a verdict on that.

Does he mean I know of his obsession with Cat?

That is most likely what he means, I think, so I say yes.

"I *loved* them," he says.

"I know."

I put my hand on his arm but he backs away as though I have scorched him. "So you know," he says again, and turns and leaves.

Then I look at the photographs again. I know the one of Sheba has something to tell me—something about her hands and her eyes—but I cannot translate. The picture of myself at Cedar Creek beckons me. You have to come back, it says.

THREE

Everything has changed and nothing has changed.

Gil Brennan moves between his rows of pineapples in the morning light, Constance and I sit in deck chairs on the veranda and look across the paddocks to the dark green rainforest wall. Constance rests her right hand on the back of my left.

"I hoped you'd come one day, Lucy," she says. She squeezes my hand tightly and smiles. Her eyes are very bright. "And now you have."

I think of all the questions I'm afraid to ask, all the answers I might not want to know.

"It makes other things seem more possible," Constance says.

I know what she means. I know she means that if I step out of absence suddenly, why not Gabriel?

"Catherine and I think he might have gone to North Queensland," I say. "The Daintree maybe. You know he has that solitary celibate streak, and he had a dream of living like you and Gil one day. Growing pineapples somewhere."

"Yes," she says. "He did, didn't he?"

We sit there silently, her hand resting on mine, for the longest time. Then she asks, not looking at me: "He's never contacted you, then?"

"No," I say.

But there are so many reasons why people refrain from making contact with those they love. So many reasons. Think of all the years—twenty-five years—that Catherine never answered Charlie's letters. I've never wanted to ask Gabriel's mother if he ever reached Brisbane that week, and I don't want to now.

She says quietly: "A very strange thing happened about six months after he disappeared. A very lovely thing, Lucy."

Hearing the tone of her voice, I can hardly breathe. She begins to play with my fingers as she must have played with Gabriel's when he was a child. She smiles fondly. "A delivery boy, just one of the local Samford boys from the grocer's, came riding in on his bicycle. 'Here's yer pastry delivery, Mrs. Brennan,' he said. And I said, 'But I didn't order anything.' And he dug a notebook out of his pocket and checked it and he said, 'Well, that's what I got on me list.' It wasn't their own pastry, he said. It was a special order, it had been sent out from the city. 'Must be yer lucky day, Mrs. Brennan,' he said. 'Must be a present.' And he hopped on his bicycle and off he went. Lucy, do you know what it was?"

I just wait.

"One dozen sugar doughnuts," she says.

We stare at each other. I try to say something but can't. My eyes ask instead: any message?

She shakes her head. "No card. And no name on the box. Nothing. Of course, McWhirter's isn't a shop anymore. And then the next day, the Samford grocers called and said they were terribly sorry, there'd been a mistake."

"A mistake," I repeat.

"Yes," she sighs. "A mix-up with the deliveries."

"Still," I say.

"Yes. That's what I thought too."

"Sugar doughnuts. It's such a strange coincidence."

"Yes," she says. "A lovely thing."

We smile a little, watching Gil Brennan against the rainforest wall.

"Since then," I say after a while, "he hasn't . . . ?"

She doesn't answer. But there are so many reasons why people don't. So many convoluted reasons.

"I thought I'd go and sit on the rocks at the falls," I say, and suddenly she shivers a little. "Will you come?"

She shakes her head. "I don't go there now."

"I've got a photograph Gabriel took." I can say his name now that she's told me about the sugar doughnuts. I take the photographs out to show her but she can't even look at the one of me at the falls. She averts her eyes as though I'd shown her something grotesque. "Sorry," I say hesitantly, and she brushes this aside with her hand, embarrassed.

"It's just . . . It's nothing. It's the falls, that's all. I don't—"

So I show her *Gabriel Comes with Clouds Descending* instead, and now her face softens and she holds it and gazes and smiles and her eyes are so bright she has to blink.

"It's the light in the photograph," I say.

"Yes," she says. "Extraordinary."

Then I show her the one of Sheba as Cat, I'm not sure why. She stares blankly for a moment and then she tenses as though heartburn is suddenly behind her ribs.

"What is it?"

"Who took this?" Her face is white, the color has gone from her lips.

I feel the buzz of anxiety again, the sense of a coming translation I do not want to have. (*It's not a picture of me, you drip. It's of the bloke who took the photograph.*)

"Who took this?" she asks again.

"Gabriel's father," I say. I moisten my lips. "Why?"

"It's the clip," she says, and points to the plastic trinket in Sheba's hair. I look at the photograph again. It's Sheba's eyes and hands that have been distracting me. I haven't paid any attention to the clip in her hair, but now I make out the butterfly shape and instantly I see the bizarre woman on the tram through Gabriel's six-year-old eyes, I see her bobby socks and her short shaved hair and the blue butterfly brooch on her dress.

Constance is pale. "I gave it to Gabriel," she says.

I remember, I remember, though he never showed it to me. Across an immense distance, I can see him holding it. He is on the far side of the gaping space between seeing and interpreting.

Constance breathes slowly. She looks stricken. "Where . . . ?" she says. "How . . . ?"

"What does it mean?" I whisper.

Constance looks at me, startled. She shakes herself as though she is waking from a trance. She looks at me as though a suggestion has been proffered that is quite beyond the pale and is not to be countenanced. I have the weird feeling that she thinks this suggestion has come from *me* and must be rebutted. "Well, I don't suppose it means anything. You can buy blue plastic butterflies in Woolworth's," she says. She is silent, breathing raggedly, searching within herself for an explanation for her distress. "For me, it brings back that day. That night."

Memories of cosmic laughter on a tram, of panic, of chaos, wisp around her. "I used to feel I had to know what happened," she says. "But then gradually, it didn't matter anymore."

She hugs herself in the damp night air. "I've never told a living soul, Lucy, not even Gil." She is speaking with difficulty, gasping a little. "Sometimes such terrible thoughts have crossed my mind. I've always been afraid that if I put them into words . . ."

She shrugs and gives me a small self-deprecating smile. "When your life is falling apart, very black thoughts come to you. But you can't trust them, and after a while they go away."

Crickets call from the hibiscus bushes beyond the railing and there is the soft thud of ripe fruit falling somewhere beyond the line of the veranda light.

"We both laughed," she says, musing. She is not so much talking to me as thinking aloud. "It's strange, Gabriel remembering that all those years. I felt *freed* that day." Her body relaxes slightly as the memory of that fleeting freedom visits it. "But then . . ."

The silence goes on and on and I dare not break it.

"But then," she says at last, "he must have gone back to her hotel to find her. That's what I assumed. It must have been later than three in the morning when I finally heard him come in, but then such a long time went by that I wondered if he'd hurt himself or something, or was drinking, or . . . I didn't know what. I was groping for my robe—I only had my nightgown on—but I couldn't find it, and I went out to the kitchen. . . . I didn't mean to surprise him, that wasn't my intention at all, but he flew into a terrible rage. . . ." She licks her dry lips. She looks so ghastly and ill that I go into the kitchen and get a glass of water and bring it to her.

"He was like a caricature of himself," she whispers. "It was someone else in his body, it wasn't him, it was horrible. And he was spattered in . . . he seemed to be spattered in . . ." She shakes her head hopelessly. "He'd been in a fight at the pub, I think, and put his fist through glass, but I don't trust any of my perceptions or my memory of that night.

"In the morning, I wanted to believe it was a nightmare, that nothing had happened, and in a way he acted as though nothing had happened, except he was very brisk and efficient and cold, and he was packing. He said he'd move into a hotel for a few days, and then he was taking Gabriel away. He said I was hysterical, and he thought I might be deranged."

She turns to me. "And I was frightened of that too, Lucy. I was frightened I was mad, maybe I wanted to believe that. In a way, it was a less disturbing explanation." She falls silent again and breathes slowly and heavily. "After a time it didn't matter. You just stop gnawing away at puzzles that don't make sense. You want amnesia."

We can hear the shriek of a flying fox in the mangoes. Night birds call. A weary heavy breeze moves the hibiscus against the damp veranda rails.

"You should never remember someone in rage or panic," she says. "It isn't fair to them, they're not themselves. The way I remember Robbie is sitting on the end of Gabriel's bed telling him stories. Gabriel was the sun and the moon and the stars to him. It's sad he didn't have more children. There's too much strain, too much expectation on both sides when there's only one."

There is the soft thump thump of a frog on the veranda steps. When it senses our presence, it stops and watches us unblinking from its black bulbous eyes. It wears its heart on the bleating balloon of its chest.

"You don't see the green ones much anymore," Constance says. "The cane toads have just about killed them off."

The frog makes a faint hiccupping sound, a little pre-croak.

"Years and years later," she says, "when they found a body at the falls, I had such terrible thoughts, such awful dreams." She puts her head in her hands and begins to shake.

"At the falls? They found a body at the falls?"

"Some children found it, pushed down between those two big boulders, weighted down in the mud with rocks. It was a skeleton, a woman's skeleton, they said, and it could have been there fifty years, how would we know? Anyway, nothing came of it. Nothing happened." She looks at the photograph of Sheba again and looks away. "You can't trust anything you think in black times," she says. "It's your own blackness. It breeds black ideas."

I can feel horror seeping into me, I feel the suck of dread, I feel lost in a vast dark wood with no way on and no way out.

"Lucy," Constance says at last. "I had to tell someone, it's been strangling me."

The passing on of secrets, I think, is like the passing of time in the rainforest, strangler figs on dead hosts putting forth their new shoots, the smell of decay and the smell of yeast always there.

"But black times go away," she says. "And you know bad dreams don't mean anything except your own worst fears, that's all."

We can see Gil coming in from the hillside like the coming of warmth, a red sunset behind him.

"Lucy," she says. "You won't go to the falls, will you? Please don't go to the falls."

"No," I say. "I won't go there."

I walk along the Samford road for miles and miles in the dark and then I walk back. I don't think anything, I don't feel anything, I just walk. Something black and suffocating moves with me, a cloud of dread. I will have to get used to it, I think.

I am seeing the documentation on Cat in those police reports. The skeleton found (the file didn't say *where*: in a rural area on the outskirts of Brisbane, was all it said), the forensic reports, the chips in the bone denoting ferocity of the multiple stab wounds. Unsolved mystery, the police said. Trail long gone cold, one of her lovers no doubt.

(*An act of violence is an intimate act,* the police say. *The greater the violence the greater the intimacy.*

Strangers kill quick and clean, but family is vicious, they say.

When it's savage, we know. Only love does that.)

Old bones, the police said. One of her lovers no doubt.

So you know, Sonny Blue said.

But the truth is, we don't know anything, and even less do we want to know.

We don't know anything.

When I come back, Gil and Constance have gone to bed and I sit on the veranda, indifferent to mosquitoes and moths, and watch the night till the sun comes up. By dawn light, I look at the photographs again. The photograph of Sheba is so small, just a Polaroid snapshot, that you'd never notice the clip was a butterfly clip unless it was pointed out to you. I reach for Constance's reading glasses left beside her chair, and look at the clip again through them. The magnification makes me feel giddy, the photograph seems to undulate like a wave. And then I notice that the locket around Sheba's neck is not a locket at all. It is a thin gold chain threaded with two tiny rings, each with its own glass bead, and the earrings hang between Sheba's breasts.

No worst, there is none, I think.

Pitched past pitch of grief, I feel the suck of all the whirlpools, all the nightmares, all the black bat fears. . . .

I stumble off the veranda and run drunkenly across the paddocks, howling and sobbing like a wild child who has been brought up by dingoes. I run until I am safe in the arms of exhaustion. I collapse between the pineapple rows.

And then, like a drowning woman grasping at a straw, I think with a sudden delirium of relief: sexual obsession is not a crime. Anyone can buy cheap earrings and a butterfly clip at Woolworth's to deck out a fantasy. It doesn't mean anything.

It doesn't mean anything.

So you know, he said.

But what do we know?

There is not one single thing we know for sure, except perhaps the fact of Cat's skeleton. And perhaps also the fact of love.

(I *loved* them, I *loved* them, he said.)

(Only love does that.)

(So you know.)

There are things we know. And there are things we don't realize we know. And there are times when we decide it is better not to find out what perhaps we unconsciously know.

If I know anything at all, I know that Gabriel's father twists and turns and writhes in private torment. If I feel anything, I feel pity.

But I don't know anything. Nothing can ever be known for sure.

Unanswerable questions are the ones that engage us, Charlie said.

There are only these three facts: the fact of Cat's skeleton, the fact of love, and the fact of absences.

I feel a need to talk to Catherine so intense that I can scarcely breathe. The house is quiet and still awash in the gray light between night and day. I pad barefoot into the kitchen to the phone and my fingers tremble violently as I dial a number in Harrow, county of Middlesex, London.

Three rings, four, my throat is dry.

She answers on the fifth ring.

"Catherine," I whisper. "Oh, Catherine, thank God you're there. It's Lucy."

"Hello?" Catherine says. "Hello? I'm afraid I can't hear you."

Catherine, I try to say, but I can't make a sound.

A tentativeness comes into Catherine's voice. "Lucy?" she ventures. "Lucy, is that you?"

I nod furiously, awash in salt water, but I can't seem to speak.

"Lucy," she says, "if it's you, please say something."

"It's me. It's me, Catherine."

"Oh God, I can hardly hear you. God, Lucy, how could you do this to me, where are you?"

"I'm sorry," I say. "It was panic. I'm in Brisbane. I'm in Samford, at Constance and Gil Brennan's place. I saw one of Charlie's films and I just freaked out."

"Yeah," she says. "I know. I saw it too. But Lucy, listen. Listen to this." And now I hear the burr of excitement in her voice. "This has been the strangest week. Last weekend I saw Charlie's film, and today you call, and yesterday I got a call from New York. It was the strangest thing. This operator says, 'I have a call for you from New York. Go ahead, please.' And I wait and wait, and no one comes on the line, and I'm saying 'Hello, hello,' and I'm about to hang up in disgust, when suddenly I begin to have this certainty, this *certainty*, Lucy, that Charlie is on the other end of the line. And I just stood there holding the receiver and I felt as though . . . I felt as though . . . and then I remembered something Charlie used to say about Lao Tzu. 'Lao Tzu says that speaking in words is like trying to sound the middle of the ocean with a six-foot pole.'"

I can hear her breathing coming in the ragged little spurts of hope, and she begins to laugh in a high brittle way and I think:

hope and love are all we have and they are very potent baggage for people who travel light.

"Lucy?" she says.

"Yeah. I'm here."

"I'm not going crazy," she says. "I don't want you to think that I literally mean . . . but just the same . . . I mean, it *could* be."

"Yeah, I know. God, Catherine, I can't tell you how glad I am to hear your voice."

"Yeah, me too," she says. "We're like bloody war vets, Lucy."

"Yeah." No point in telling her anything yet, I think. Maybe never. Or maybe one of these nights in the wee small hours when we've drunk too much.

"Lucy," she says, "I didn't think I would ever want to go back, I didn't think I could be that stupid again, but I don't know. What's the air smell like?"

"I can smell the rainforest," I say. "I can hear scrub turkeys on the veranda."

"Oh God," she says. "They've been asking me to do something on Aboriginal land rights in northern Queensland, but I don't know."

"You want to meet me there?" I say.

I can hear the mix of desire and panic in her voice. "Oh God," she says. "I have to think about it."

The body, I think, seeks to return to the sites of joy and pain. Something pulls us, something simple and primitive and as old as the soft broken trees on the rainforest floor.

"I dreamed about Cat again this week," she says. "After I saw the film. We were in the pool at the falls—"

"Don't," I say.

We send each other silence, and I think that today I will begin to travel north. I'll hug the coast and go out to the coral cays and I'll work my way up to the Daintree, because who can say what I'll find up there, who can say for certain where Gabriel is? And if anyone should presume to mock this hope, let him remember it comes with a long pedigree. Let him remember how Dante found his way out of the wood when the path was wholly lost and gone. Let him not cast stones. And if he thinks he knows better than we do how Catherine and I should respond to absence and loss, let him consider Charlie's story of Chuang Tzu and the fish in the River Hao.

Chuang Tzu and a friend leaned on a bridge and looked into the River Hao. "Look at the way the fish play," Chuang Tzu said. "They ignore the fisherman's hook, they refuse to think about it, they give themselves over to delight."

And his friend said: "Chuang Tzu, you are not a fish. How do you know what they feel?"

And Chuang Tzu said: "My friend, you are not I. How do you know I don't know how the fish feel?"

I begin to laugh. "Catherine," I say, "do you remember Charlie's story about the fish in the River Hao?"

"Speaking of fish," she says, "what about that story Charlie used to claim he'd heard in his pub, the one about King Bluey Kuttorze and Madame de Sévigné and the cook who ran himself through and all the crates and crates of seafood coming in—"

"That wasn't funny," I say, spluttering with mirth. "That was awful, that was a dreadful story, that was sad—"

We are weeping with laughter.

"What about Giacometti's Foot?" she says.

What about Hot News of Gabriel, I think, and the thought scalds me, it winds me, but oh how potent these absences are, how they fill the air with the beating of their radiant wings.

"Catherine," I say. "I'll wait for you in Cairns, okay?"

"Okay," she says.

"Catherine. You know, we should do a documentary on the quarry. We owe it to Gabriel."

"Yeah," she says. "I know. It's something I owe Cat and Charlie. When I can handle it."

I think of the camera moving along the back alleys and tunnels, falling on Old Fury's face, on Danny's, on Julie's, giving Old Fury's voices a window on the world. . . .

But first the rainforest. Today I'll start traveling north, partly because who knows where Gabriel might be, but mostly because I've never really lived anywhere but Queensland and it's time to come home.

"Lucy?"

"Yeah. I'm here."

"We're like bloody war vets," she says.

And we hang on to the lifeline of the silence that connects us, the great beating wings of our absent ones deafening us and filling the air with light.